A PLACE CALLED
ARMAGEDDON

Constantinople 1453

C.C. HUMPHREYS

D0170166

An Orion paperback

First published in Great Britain in 2011
by Orion
This paperback edition published in 2012
by Orion Books Ltd,
Orion House, 5 Upper St Martin's Lane,
London WC2H 9EA

An Hachette UK company

1 3 5 7 9 10 8 6 4 2

A CIP catalogue record for this book
is available from the British Library.

ISBN 978-1-4091-2026-1

Typeset at The Spartan Press Ltd,
Lymington, Hants

Printed and bound in Great Britain by
Clays Ltd, St Ives plc

The Orion Publishing Group's policy is to use papers
that are natural, renewable and recyclable products and
made from wood grown in sustainable forests. The logging
and manufacturing processes are expected to conform to
the environmental regulations of the country of origin.

www.orionbooks.co.uk

C.C. Humphreys was born in Toronto and grew up in Los Angeles and London. A third generation actor and writer on both sides of his family, he is married and lives with his wife and son on Salt Spring Island, Canada.

To Allan Eastman

And he gathered them together into a place called,
in the Hebrew tongue, Armageddon.

Revelation 16:16

CONTENTS

DRAMATIS PERSONAE

The Greeks

Gregoras Lascaris (also known as 'Zoran the Ragusan' and
    'Rhinometus')
Theon Lascaris
Sofia Lascaris
Thakos Lascaris
Minerva Lascaris
Constantine Palaiologos, emperor
Theophilus Palaiologos, cousin to Constantine
George Sphrantzes, historian
Theodore of Karystenos, imperial archer
Flatenelas, naval captain
Loukas Notaras, *megas doux*
Athene, maid

The Turks

Leilah, sorceress
Mehmet 'Fatih', sultan of the Turks
Hamza Bey, adviser
Achmed, farmer
Abal, Achmed's daughter
Zaganos Pasha
Candarli Halil, grand vizier
Baltaoglu Bey, admiral
Raschid, *bashibazouk*
Farouk, *bolukbasi*
Aksemseddin, imam
Ishak Pasha
Karaca Pasha

The Genoans

Giovanni (or Gian) Giustiniani Longo, 'the Commander',
   leader of defence
Enzo the Sicilian
Amir the Syrian
Bastoni, naval captain
Bartolomeo

The Venetians

Girolamo Minotto, *baillie* (leader) of Venetians in city
Coco, naval commander
Bocciardi brothers
Trevisiano, naval commander

Others

John Grant (also known as Johannes), engineer
Farat, Achmed's wife
Mounir and Mustaq, Achmed's children
Isaac the Alchemist
Urban, Transylvanian cannon maker
Abdul-Matin, bodyguard
Stanko, Omis pirate
Don Francisco de Toledo, Castilian soldier
John of Dalmata, imperial councillor
Archbishop Leonard
Cardinal Isidore
Radu Dracula
The Man with Long Sight
Ulvikul, cat

To the Reader . . .

A city's fall is rarely as sudden as Pompeii's. Like an old man tottering on a precipice, it is a long decline that has brought him to the edge.

In 1453, such a city is Constantinople.

Blessed by geography, straddling the continents of Europe and Asia and the most important trade routes on earth, Constantinople and its Byzantine Empire had thrived, at one time controlling two-thirds of the civilised world.

Yet a thousand years of wars – foreign, civil, religious – has sapped its strength. Other Christians plundered it. The great powers of Venice and Genoa colonised it. By the mid-fifteenth century, the empire consists of little more than the impoverished city itself. Now, with doom approaching, those fellow Christians will only send help for an unthinkable price – the city has to give up its Orthodox Christianity and unite as Catholics under the Pope.

While the people riot, the emperor has no choice but to agree. Because he accepts what they do not.

The Turks are coming.

The Prophet foretold Constantinople's fall to jihad. Yet for eight centuries, the armies of Allah have broken themselves on the city's unbreachable walls. Even Eyoub, Muhammad's own standard-bearer, died before them.

Then a young man picks up the banner. Determined to be the new Alexander, the new Caesar, Mehmet, sultan of all the Turks, is just twenty-one years old.

The old man totters on the precipice . . . and prays that he has not given up his faith in vain. Prays for a miracle.

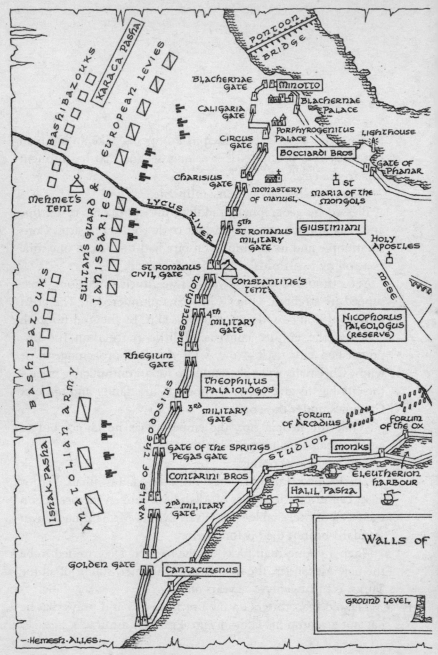

Map based on a drawing by Allan Eastman

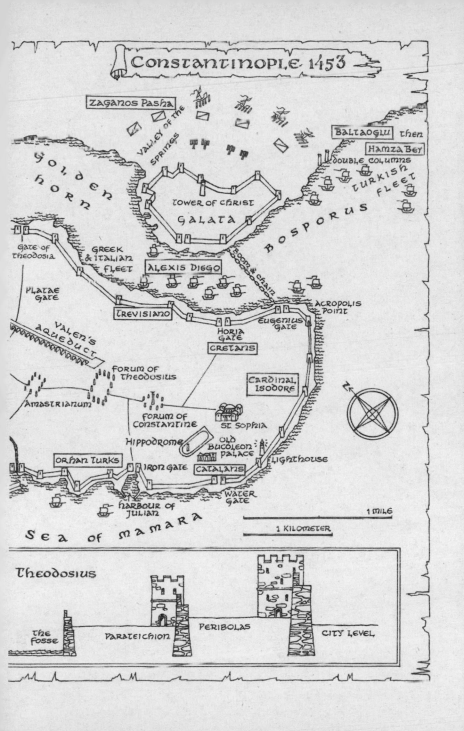

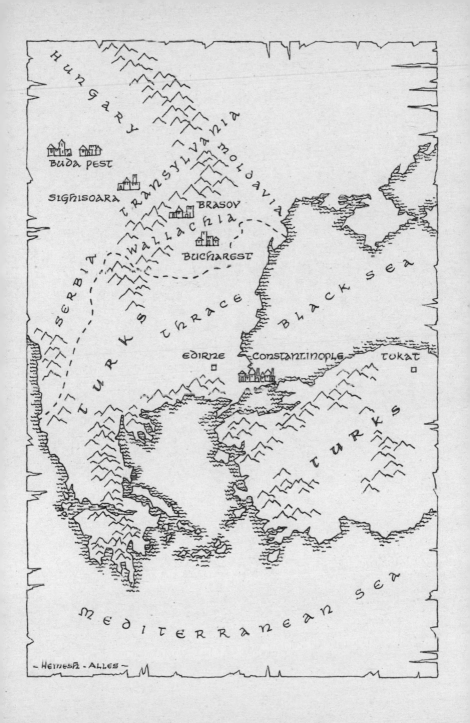

PROLOGUS

6 April 1453

We are coming, Greek.

Climb your highest tower, along those magnificent walls. They have kept you safe for a thousand years. Resisted every one of our attacks. Before them, where your fields and vineyards once stood, are trenches and emplacements. Empty, for now. Do you expect them to be filled with another doomed army of Islam, like all the martyrs that came and failed here before?

No. For we are different this time. There are more of us, yes. But there is something else. We have brought something else.

Close your eyes. You will hear us before you see us. We always arrive with a fanfare. We are people who like a noise. And that deep thumping, the one that starts from beyond the ridge and runs over our trenches, through the ghosts of your vineyards, rising through stone to tickle your feet? That is a drum, a *kos* drum, a giant belly to the giant man who beats it. There is another . . . no, not just one. Not fifty. More. These come with the shriek of the pipe, the seven-note *sevre*, seven to each drum.

The *mehter* bands come marching over the ridge line, sunlight sparkling on instruments inlaid with silver, off swaying brocade tassels. You blink, and then you wonder: there are thousands of them. Thousands. And these do not even carry weapons.

Those with weapons come next.

First the Rumelian division. Years ago, when you were already too weak to stop us, we bypassed your walls, conquered the lands beyond them to the north. Their peoples are our soldiers now – Vlachs, Serbs, Bulgars, Albanians. You squint against the light, wishing you did not see, hoping the blur does not conceal – but it does! – the thousands that are there, the men on horseback followed by many more on foot. Many, many more.

The men of Rumelia pass over the ridge and swing north towards the Golden Horn. When the first of them reach its waters, they halt, turn, settle. Rank on rank on the ridgeline, numberless as ants. Their *mehter* bands sound a last peal of notes, a last volley of drumbeats. Then all is silent.

Only for a moment. Drums again, louder if that were possible, even more trumpets. Because the Anatolian division is larger. Can you believe it? That as many men pass over the hilltop again and then just keep coming? They head to the other sea, south towards Marmara, warriors from the heartland of Turkey. The *sipahi*, knights mailed from neck to knee, with metal turban helms, commanding their mounts with a squeeze of thigh and a grunt, leaving hands free to hoist their war lances high, lift their great curving bows. Eventually they pass, and then behind them march the *yayas*, the peasant soldiers, armoured by the lords they follow, trained by them, hefting their spears, their great shields.

When at last the vast body reaches the water, they turn to face you, double-ranked. Music ceases. A breeze snaps the pennants. Horses toss their heads and snort. No man speaks. Yet there is still a space between the vast divisions of Rumelia and Anatolia. The gap concerns you – for you know it is to be filled.

It is – by a horde, as many as each of those who came before. These do not come with music. But they come screaming. They pour down, and run each way along the armoured fronts of Anatolia and Rumelia. They do not march. They have never been shown how. For these are *bashibazouks*, irregulars recruited from the fields of empire and the slums of cities. They are not armoured, though many have shields and each warrior a blade. Some come for God – but all for gold. Your gold, Greek. They have been told that your city is cobbled with it, and these tens of thousands will hurl themselves again and again against your walls to get it. When they die by the score – as they will – a score replaces them. Another. Each score will kill a few of you. Until it is time for the trained and armoured men to use their sacrificed bodies as bridges and kill the few of you who remain.

The horde runs, yelling, along the ordered ranks, on and on. When at last it halts, even these men fall quiet. Stay so for what seems an age. And that gap is still there, and now you almost yearn for it to be filled. Yearn too for the hush, more dreadful than all those screams, to end. So that this all ends.

And then they come. No drums. No pipes. As silent as the tread of so many can be.

You have heard of them, these warriors. Taken as Christian boys, trained from childhood in arms and in Allah, praise Him. Devoted to their corps, their comrades, their sultan. They march in their *ortas*, a hundred men to each one.

The janissaries have arrived.

You know their stories, these elite of the elite that have shattered Christendom's armies again and again. In recent memory alone, at Kossovo Pol, and at Varna. As they swagger down the hill, beneath their tall white felt hats, their bronzed shields, their drawn scimitars, their breastplates dazzle with reflected sunlight.

They turn to face you, joining the whole of our army in an unbroken line from sea to sparkling sea. Again a silence comes. But not for long this time. They are waiting, as you are. Waiting for him.

He comes. Even among so many he is hard to miss, the tall young man on the huge white horse. Yet if you did not recognise him, you will by what follows him. Two poles. What hangs from one is so old, its green has turned black

3

with the years. It looks to you what it is – a tattered piece of cloth.

It is the banner that was carried before the Prophet himself, peace be unto him. You know this, because when it is driven into the ground, a moan goes through the army. And then the second pole is placed and the moan blends with the chime of a thousand tiny bells. The breeze also lifts the horsetails that dangle from its height.

Nine horsetails. As befits a sultan's tug.

Mehmet. Lord of lords of this world. King of believers and unbelievers. Emperor of East and West. Sultan of Rum. He has many titles more yet he craves only one. He would be 'Fatih'.

The Conqueror.

He turns and regards all those he has gathered to this spot to do his and Allah's will. Then his eyes turn to you. To the tower where you stand. He raises a hand, lets it fall. The janissaries part and reveal what you'd almost forgotten – that square of dug earth right opposite you, a medium bowshot away. It was empty when last you looked. But you were distracted by innumerable men. Now it is full.

Remember I told you we were bringing something different? Not only this vast army. Something new? Here it is.

A cannon. No, not a cannon. That is like calling paradise 'a place'. This cannon is monstrous. And as befits it, it has a monster's name. The Basilisk. It is the biggest gun that has ever been made. Five tall janissaries could lie along its length. The largest of them could not circle its bronze mouth in his arms.

Breathe, Greek! You have time. It will be days before the monster is ready to fire its ball bigger than a wine barrel. Yet once it begins, it will keep firing until . . . until that tower you stand on is rubble.

When it is, I will come.

For I am the Turk. I come on the bare feet of the farmer, the armoured boot of the Anatolian. In the mad dash of the *serdengecti* who craves death and in the measured tread of the janissary who knows a hundred ways to deal it. I clutch

4

scimitar, scythe and spear, my fingers pull back bowstring and trigger, I have a glowing match to lower into a monster's belly and make it spit out hell.

I am the Turk. There are a hundred thousand of me. And I am here to take your city.

— PART ONE —
Alpha

ONE

Prophecy

Edirne, capital of the Ottoman Empire
April 1452: one year earlier

The house looked little different from any other that faced the river. A merchant's dwelling, its front wall was punctured by two large square openings either side of an oaken door. These had grilles to keep out intruders, while admitting the water-cooled breezes that would temper the summer heat.

Yet this was early April, the openings were shuttered and Hamza shivered. Though it was not truly the chill that caused his skin to stand up in bumps. It was the midnight hour. It was their reason for standing there. It was this house, especially.

'Is this the place, lo—' He cut himself off. Even though the two men were obviously quite alone, they were not to speak their titles aloud. 'Erol' his younger companion wished to be called, a name that told of courage and strength. Hamza had submitted to 'Margrub'. He knew it meant 'desirable'. The young man had insisted on it with a smile because he did not find Hamza desirable in the least.

Undesired but useful. It was why he had insisted that only Hamza accompany him to the notorious docks of Edirne, where merchants built their houses into forts and men of sense travelled in large, well-armed groups. He hadn't been brought for his bodyguard skills, though he was as adept as most with the blade he concealed beneath his robes. It was his mind the younger man needed.

'Come,' he'd said. 'Allah is our bodyguard. *Inshallah.*'

Now, at their destination, the reply to Hamza's query was a

gesture. He lifted the lamp he carried, opened the gate on it, held it high. His companion peered up beside the door. 'Yes, this is the one. See!'

Hamza looked. There, nailed to the frame beside the door, was a wooden tube, smaller than his little finger. He knew what it was, what it contained. He lowered the lamp, closed the gate, returning them to near darkness and river mist. 'You did not tell me she was a Jewess.'

He could not see it but he could hear the smile in the reply. 'All the best ones are. Knock!'

His knuckle had barely struck a second time before a small gate in the doorway was opened. They were studied, the small door closed, the larger one unbolted. They were admitted by someone who remained hidden in the darkness behind the door. 'Straight ahead . . . friends,' ordered a soft male voice, and they obeyed, moved into the roofless courtyard beyond, blinking against its sudden light, for reed torches burned in brackets, flame-light spilling onto a garden, four beds of earth around a central fountain.

The younger man gave a little sigh, halting. Hamza knew that one of the greatest of his companion's passions was the growing of plants and flowers; that the trade he practised against the Day of Disaster, as all must practise one, was gardening. 'See the wonder I told you of . . . Margrub,' he murmured. 'When I came here in the summer, she told me this was her work – and see! She has contrived to keep herbs alive through our winter that should not survive here. Do you savour them?' He bent, inhaled deeply. 'I would question the Jewess on this.'

Hamza knew he wouldn't. The young man was there with questions, certainly. They did not concern the cultivation of plants.

The man who'd admitted them had vanished. Now an inner door opened, a rectangle of reddened light spilling out. They crossed to it, entered, just as another door beyond shut softly. The room was lit by a single lamp, flame moving behind red glass. Dividing the room in half was a near-ceiling-high screen made of dark reeds, the weave large enough to allow gaps the width of a fingertip. From beyond it came the sounds of wood crackling in a clay stove. This accounted for the warmth of the room . . and perhaps also for some of the scents within it. Some were pleasant, and Hamza detected sandalwood and myrrh. Some were not. One was sweet and sickly at the same time, and it made the top of his neck ache. Another was sulphurous, a savour of rot that the incense was failing to disguise, accentuating it rather. Hamza had smelled such things before, at the houses of friends who experimented with metals and certain volatile spirits. It made him frown. Sorcery was usually a very different science to alchemy.

Removing their shoes, they sat, cross-legged. The cushions, and the Izmiri kilims that lay between them, were of the finest, the patterns intricate. The merchant who owned the house – and alchemist too, perhaps? – was not poor.

They waited in silence; but his companion could never stay silent for long. There was too much to plan, too many details to be refined, if he was to achieve his destiny – this destiny, he hoped, to be confirmed there that night.

They talked of various things, as ever. But one subject had been his obsession of the day and he returned to it now. 'What do your spies tell you?' he asked, his voice low but excited. 'Have my enemies rediscovered their "Greek Fire" or no?'

It was usually better to reassure the younger man. Yet reassurance now was no substitute for a serious disappointment later. 'I am told that they have not. They experiment – but they seem to have lost the recipe.'

'A secret recipe. Whispered in the ear of the founder of their city, was it not?'

'That is the story.'

'Then we are safe, are we not?' He shuddered. 'Too many of my ancestors died in flames before those accursed walls.'

'I hope we are, ma — Erol. Yet I fear.'

'What?'

Hamza shifted. 'Only today, a spy reported rumours. Of a man of science who has also heard that whisper. The Greeks hunt everywhere for him. A German, it is said. Johannes Grant.'

'Johannes Grant.' The vowels sounded strangely in their tongue, Osmanlica. 'We hunt too, I trust?'

'We do.'

'Good.' The younger man stretched out his legs . 'Find him.'

'He is found. The pirates of Omis hold him.'

'Omis? Those sea rats? I thought Venice had burned their nest and scattered them.'

'They did. But they still steal when they can. Kidnap. A gang holds this German on some island in the Adriatic. Korcula, I think.'

'What if we used their own fire against them?' A whistle came. 'Buy him, as we have bought the others like . . . that gunner, the Hungarian, what is his name? The one who is building the great gun for us?'

'Urban, lord.' Hamza bit back the title, but the other man didn't flinch. 'But I believe your last order was to offer steel and not gold to any who would aid the Greeks.'

'Was it? I was perhaps in my rash humour when I ordered so. And yet . . .' The man scratched at his red beard. 'Well, perhaps it is for the best. Dead, I am certain of him. Alive, he will always be a threat.'

Hamza knew that the younger man's logic usually led him to that conclusion. When his father had died the year before, he had concluded the same – and concluded his baby half-brother's life, having him drowned in a bath while he distracted the boy's mother with sherbets in his *saray*. He had denied any order later, executed the assassin, cried genuine tears for days. But he had slept easier at night.

Hamza shivered, certainly not from the cold now. He had been this man's father's cupbearer. Sometimes his lover – though not in recent years, when Murad had been more enamoured of the contents of the cup than the one who bore it. Still, Hamza was associated with the old regime. And to get

12

ahead in the new, to maintain the favour he seemed to have attained, he knew he would have to obey – and shiver away any doubts.

He was about to speak, to reassure . . . when he heard the inner door open and close again. Someone had come through. They heard that person settle on cushions the other side of the screen.

'Are you come?' the young man whispered, leaning forward.

She'd been there the whole time. It was useful to be unobserved and hear those who thought themselves unheard. Though Leilah was confident in her powers, it was hard to sift through all her visions. To know a subject's desires and fears allowed her to focus on them. To caution. To entice. To . . . prophesy. She was paid for results. She would not have the reputation she did, nor be visited by such men as those before her now, if she did not satisfy. If she had inherited from her mother the ability to see what others could not, it was her father who had grounded her in the visible. In knowledge. 'Know the man,' he'd said.

She had known many. She had even loved a few, loved them passionately, even after she'd seen their death written upon their faces as clearly as words in the books she treasured. Loved them and watched them die, sent them to their inevitable fate, content in knowing that she and they could do no other.

She had never known a man like the one before her now. When he'd come the previous summer, she had been almost overwhelmed by his force – for he had brought nothing less than destiny with him. All he had sought then was how to establish himself, how to secure what was fragile. She'd helped. She'd foreseen . . . consolidation based on a little blood, a lot of smiling. Now he was back and it was clear that the time for consolidation was past. It was time for adventure. His whole being surged with it. His only desire was to remake the world.

She would help him with that. It was what she did.

When she'd heard enough, she'd risen on bare feet, moved

13

silently to the door, opened it, closed it, and returned less quietly to her place. 'Yes,' she replied to his question, 'Leilah is here. And honoured by your return.'

Hamza was surprised at the voice. It was youthful, deep, while all the soothsayers he'd attended in his own youth had been shrill-toned old harpies who he'd been happy to pay swiftly for a love philtre or a horoscope and escape from. But more than its tone, the accent perplexed him. It wasn't like any Jew's he'd ever heard. More like . . . a gypsy.

Most seers are, he thought, and shrugged. He could do without them all. Now he was near thirty, he sought wisdom only in the Qur'an and his own intellect. Others, like the man beside him, were as devout yet saw no gap between what the Prophet had spoken, what their instincts taught them – and what such women vouchsafed. 'Erol' would act on his judgement. But he liked it to be confirmed, even preceded, by a starred intimation of success.

The younger man pushed his face close to the screen. 'And what can you tell me, Leilah? What have you seen?'

A silence, and then her breath came on a whisper. 'I have seen your sandals raise the dust in the palace of the Caesars. If . . . if . . .' Her voice trailed off.

'If what?' he asked, also in a whisper.

She replied, more firmly, 'There. Beside you. Open it.'

The young man reached eagerly into a cedarwood box. He pulled out a scroll, tied with a scrap of silk. Slipping that off, he unrolled the paper, and Hamza saw the lines and symbols of a horoscope. 'What do you see here?' he breathed.

The voice came softer, causing both men to lean forward. 'You were born under the Ram, and Mars, Ruler of War, is your planet. He sits too in your ninth house, the place of journeys. It is the chart of a warrior, for you will ever be at war.'

Hamza grunted. The youth's expression showed he would brook no doubting. But what the woman had said about his ambitious companion, he could have heard on any street corner in Edirne.

Leilah heard the grunt, the doubt in it. This other who accompanied the seeker, he was a little older, less excitable, a thinker. Another time she would have liked to engage him in debate, to probe the extent of his knowledge and his beliefs. Before, after or during, she'd also have liked to take him to her bed. Knowledge of men could be gained in all sorts of ways. And maybe she would consider him, since she was shortly to be losing her current protector.

No, she thought, sighing out. For if the younger man achieves the destiny foreseen, he will achieve mine as well. He will open the door to unimaginable riches. And with those, I will never need a man to protect me again.

She began to pant. Great heaves of breath, sucking in air, expelling it on a moan. And her voice when it came was even deeper. It sounded like a man's, and both the men drew back from the screen and sought the comfort of a dagger against their palms. 'Know this, Chosen One. If you would do what you must do, you must do it within the year, or the heavens will turn against you. On this very day, but one year from now, at the eleventh hour of the day, let the dragon breathe fire, let the archer shoot true with his first shot. It will take time, and Allah will hold the scales and weigh your actions. Then, when the moon hides half her face, call me and I will come – to see for you again.'

The young man's face had blanched when the voice changed. Now, on the words, red flooded back, deeper even than the red of beard and brow. 'I will,' he whispered.

Leilah sat back. It was time to act for herself. When she was younger, scarce fourteen, and had lived with a janissary, Abdulkarim had brought her into the mysteries of the Bektashi school of Islam, taught her some of the mysticism of the Sufi. Yet since Bektashi drank wine guiltlessly, and soldiers when drunk talked of little but martial glory, she had learned something about siegecraft. Gossip in the barracks she still visited had developed her knowledge. All the talk now was of the city known as the Red Apple. It had dangled above Muslim heads for a thousand years. Barracks wisdom had it that the first step to bringing it down would be to cut it off. To cut its throat. It would be wisdom in the palace too. And she had learned that wisdom, supported by prophecy, led not only to confirmation of her skills, but to action.

'Mark,' she intoned softly. 'I see a knife, like the one you now grasp, reaching up to a stem. Cut it. Slit it like you'd slit a throat.'

Even Hamza gasped at that. It had been the secret talk for months now. If the Red Apple was to fall, the first step would be to starve it. Cut it off from its supplies. Plans had been discussed. This prophecy spoke to them.

'Yes!' His companion had been hard at work, developing those very plans.

Now she was ready. There was something other than gold that this man of destiny must give her this night. Deliverance. 'But beware! Return to your *saray* but do not speak to any except your companion. If any recognise you, greet you by name, your plans will shrivel, like dates in a sandstorm. Unless . . . unless you slit the throat of the one who sees you.'

'What . . . what do you mean?'

Her voice dropped low again. 'This is all you need know, for now. This is enough – until we meet again.'

She rose. Though they could not see her, they rose too as if they sensed it. But legs that had been cramped too long wobbled. Hamza lurched – and the man beside him stumbled, tried to catch himself on the screen . . . which fell inwards.

Leilah leapt back, just avoiding the crashing wicker. Righting himself, the young man stood straight and stared.

As before he could not help the grunt, now Hamza could not contain the whistle. His youthful dealings with withered crones had led him to expect another, despite the voice. But this woman was young. Her body was beautiful – and revealed, for she was scarcely dressed in a few silks – at face, at breast, at hip – while her black hair was unbound, in the way of some Bektashi women he had known.

16

His companion began stuttering apologies, bending to right the screen . . . then freezing when he beheld what it had hidden. His voice, when it came, was huskier too. 'I am sorry. And yet not so. For I never cease to admire beauty. And you are . . . beautiful.'

She said nothing, just stared back above her mask from eyes that seemed to Hamza to be huge caverns of darkness. 'Leilah', he remembered now, meant 'rapture'. The woman had been well named.

His companion stepped forward. 'And now I have seen you, and you have seen me, why should we be parted again?' He raised a hand towards her. 'If you were to join me in my *saray* . . . you would have a place of honour there. I could visit you . . . often. And I would not have to come to the Edirne docks for my prophecies.'

Leilah smiled. To be the lover of such a man meant power . . . for a time. Until another caught his fancy – woman, boy, man, it was rumoured his tastes ran to all. Then she would be trapped, as she had been once before, a slave to the man who had caused her parents to be killed, subject to his . . . every whim, from the age of ten till his sudden death two years later, after eating some figs she had specially prepared.

She would never be a slave again. In a *saray*, she would be. Outside it, her prophecies gave her power. Unlike nearly every woman in Edirne, in the world, they also gave her a choice. And if her prophecies came true for this man, he was just another she would not need.

She stepped closer, moving in the way she knew men liked her to move. Into red lamp-spill, directly above her now, that revealed the darkness at her large nipples, at her groin, beneath the silks. 'Master,' she breathed, 'you honour me with your desire. And were I to choose to give up my treasure, there is no one alive whom I would rather . . . took it.' She emphasised the taking, saw him shudder, dropped her voice to a whisper. 'But there are many others who can offer you that. While

17

few can offer you the gift I have. A gift I will lose, should you *take . . .*' again, the slightest of inflections, 'what I yearn to give you.' She stepped away. 'So which would you have, master? Me, or my prophecies?'

Hamza watched, fascinated. His companion was young and was used to having anything – anyone – he wanted. .

Yet there was something he wanted that was beyond such desire. The young man knew it, and looked away. 'I need your . . .' he sighed, 'prophecies.' He looked back, his voice hardening. 'But when they are fulfilled, come to me and I will give you anything you want.'

She smiled. 'Then I will come to you, on the eve of destiny. I will ask a boon of you. I will give you something in return.' She gestured towards the door. 'Now leave, master, remembering this – if anyone recognises you tonight, your dreams will crumble. Unless he does not live to tell of it.'

Hamza was puzzled. It was the second time she'd mentioned that. But he had no time to think. His companion gestured the pouch of gold coin from his belt and Hamza dropped it onto the floor. Then his arm was taken and they moved together through the courtyard and out the house's door, opened for them by a shadow within a shadow, barred silently behind them.

In the room, Leilah bent and threw a cushion over the gold, then stood silently till she heard the outer door close. Only then did she call out, 'Come.'

The inner door to the house opened. Isaac bustled in. 'Well,' he demanded, roughly seizing her, 'did you do it? Did you ask him?'

'Yes,' she replied, almost relishing the pain in her right arm since she knew it was the last time this man would hurt her. 'I did as you commanded. Refused his gold, exchanged it for his promise – that when the city fell, I would have free access to the library you spoke of.'

'You?' he barked, shaking her. 'It is I who need Geber's book, not you, you stupid whore.'

18

He raised a hand above her and she cowered back, as he liked her to do. 'I did name you. Blessed you as my guardian. Perhaps . . .' she chewed at her lower lip, 'perhaps if you were to approach him, tell him what I failed to, even now . . .' She trailed off.

He looked out to the courtyard. 'You named me? He would know me then, favourably, if I spoke to him?'

She nodded. 'Oh yes. But he is . . . occupied with many things. Perhaps he will forget even me.' She looked up. 'Go after him. Speak.'

The man moved to the door. 'He can't have gone far. I will catch him.'

He was halfway across the courtyard when she called, 'Remember, Isaac. Greet him with all his honours. Name him as he is.'

'Of course I will,' he replied, not looking back. 'Do you think I am a fool?'

She watched him fumbling at the bar. 'I do,' she whispered, and smiled. The Jew had been good for a while, easily satisfied in their bed, teaching her many things beyond it. Of the Kabbalah; and especially secrets of the alchemical art. She had become adept in the basics of both. But it was his greatest desire, confessed in cooling sweat after lovemaking, that had suddenly revealed her destiny.

'It is the original text,' he'd sighed. 'Annotated in Geber's own hand. Centuries old, yet with forgotten knowledge that, remembered now, would make me the greatest alchemist in the world.'

He'd sighed again, with greater lust than she'd ever brought forth, and she'd thought immediately, clearly: how valuable must this document be? This ancient scroll, collecting dust in a monastery in the city they call the Red Apple.

From that first mention of it, she was distracted. Less attentive to his needs. Plotting the way ahead. He had begun to strike her. The first time he did, he wrote his fate. Yet figs were not in season.

The door opened. He was gone.

She began to dress swiftly, in men's clothes. While she did, she wondered, where next? She had a year and a day at least. Or perhaps the question was, who next? She knew he was out there, waiting in the shadows. She had seen him too, in the stars. In dreams. Two men of destiny stalked them. The young man who'd just left, armed with her prophecy, was one. But who was this other?

Something her visitors had discussed came to mind. A man, a German, who understood Greek Fire. He was a danger to their cause. 'Johannes Grant,' she muttered, stumbling over the hard sounds as the man known as Erol had. Then she smiled. She would find this German. Kill this German. For as much as the man who'd just left wanted the Red Apple to fall, so did she. Besides, the German's death would bring a great deal of gold. She'd need that, now she was losing her protector.

She heard the first cry, her ex-lover's. Isaac was hailing the recent guest in his house. 'Farewell,' she said, and stooped for her bag.

They had stood before the door for a few moments, clearing the sulphur from their lungs with river mist, so had only taken a few steps when the door behind them opened again and a voice called. They turned to see a man striding swiftly towards them. 'Lord of lords of this world,' called the man – a Jew by his garb. 'Greetings, oh balm of the world. Oh bringer of light.' He knelt before them, arms spread wide. 'Oh most noble Sultan of Rum,' he cried.

Hamza felt almost sorry for the Jew. His master never liked to be recognised on his midnight outings. His anger could be swift and violent. Tonight, freighted with frustrated lust, and with prophecy, it wasn't an importuning subject on the ground before him. It was a threat to his very destiny.

'Cur!' screamed his companion, stepping forward, back-handing the man across the face, knocking him into the dust. 'Hold him, Hamza.'

There was no choice, and little conscience. The word of the man he served was final. He had learned that from the old sultan. And if it had been true of the even-tempered Murad, it was even more so of his fiery son, Mehmet.

As Hamza took his arms, Mehmet reached forward and pulled the man's head up by the hair. 'What is your name?' he shouted.

'I . . . I . . . Isaac, master.'

Mehmet laughed. 'Isaac?' He looked at Hamza. 'Son of Abraham, as we all are. But I see no ram in a bush nearby. So there is no need to seek elsewhere for a sacrifice.'

One of Mehmet's titles, that the Jew had left out, was 'possessor of men's necks'. And he made the slitting of this one look almost easy, though it never was. Hamza held the twitching body at arm's length, trying to keep the spraying blood off both his master and himself, only partly succeeding. Yet what he thought about as life left was how the sorceress's first prophecy had already come true. Then, as he lowered the body to the ground, he realised that was wrong.

She hadn't seen this. She'd ordered it.

I will watch out for this sorceress, he thought.

The other man leaned down, and wiped his blade on the dead man's cloak. 'A throat cut. A sacrifice made,' Mehmet said, smiling. 'Now, Hamza, let us go and cut the throat of a city. Let us go to Constantinople.'

— TWO —

Prayers

Genoa, Italy
2 November 1452

It was hard to find God in Genoa.

At least, it had become hard for her. Sofia was sure the Genoese managed it. It had to be her fault. Her weakness.

The master who had painted the ikons in her wooden altar was not weak. His belief shone in his dazzling brushstrokes, in those depicted – Madonna and the Infant Christ. Saints either side venerated the holy pair. The paintings had always inspired her, centred her, joined her to the Divine. Yet now she knelt before them mouthing words, inhaling incense, seeking union, feeling . . . nothing. Because she kept hearing her son's laugh, her daughter's cry. She'd turn away from God to the door – and remember that they weren't there. Half a year since her husband had taken her away from Constantinople. Half a year, and they were growing and changing beyond her sight.

Her husband. Sofia heard him moving around the other room, awake at last. He had come in after dawn, and had collapsed, wine-heavy, onto the bed beside her. She'd thought to leave him, try and pray, but he had pulled her back and taken her, which he had not done in months. Taken her swiftly, caring nothing for her. After he'd collapsed immediately into sleep, she'd managed to slide from beneath him, gone to her house altar, knelt, sought God. She had not found Him.

Yet. Perhaps it was a demon that afflicted her? There was one, the Demon of Midday, who brought this sluggish despair.

Reaching beneath into her robes, she pulled out her *enkolpia*. It was an amulet her mother had given her, a picture of St Demetrios worked in lapis lazuli. Lifting it to her forehead, she closed her eyes and tried to pray.

'Do you beseech God for our coupling to give us another child?'

Theon's voice startled her. She hadn't heard the door open. He was standing in the doorway, already half dressed in his under robe and socks. She rose, letting the amulet fall against her breast. 'I will fetch you food,' she said, moving to the shelves where provisions were kept.

'I want nothing. Maybe some water. I must go out.'

'Then I will bring you water,' she said. It was on the balcony off the bedroom. At home, a snap of fingers would have summoned three servants to do her bidding. Here, one sullen girl came by later in the day, to cook and clean. Sofia tried to go past him in the doorway as she spoke, but he took her arm, preventing her. 'You did not answer me,' he said.

What was his question? The Demon of Midday still held her in its thrall. Oh, something about another child. 'If it is God's will,' she said, and tried again to move past him.

He did not let her. 'Hasn't man something to do with it?' he asked, his grip tightening. 'Shall we plant more seeds and see?' She was never good at hiding her feelings. He must have noted her revulsion, because he smiled, released her.

She dipped the ladle into the amphora and took her time filling a water jug. She needed to think. What was this talk of children? He hardly ever touched her. She knew he had other women. She did not care. What did he need her for?

She replaced the ladle on its hook. He could hire a whore to fetch his water, cater to all his needs. She had served the small purpose he had brought her to Genoa for in the first week, so perhaps . . . perhaps he would let her go home. Where her city, her children and, she hoped, God awaited her.

He was standing by their scrap of mirror, tidying his beard with a blade. She put the jug beside him, went to the wardrobe to fetch his tunic and cloak. Laying them carefully across the arms of a chair, she straightened and looked at him. 'Theon . . . Husband.'

His reflected eyes flicked to her. 'Sofia. Wife,' he replied, a slight smile for the formality.

Her hands clasped and unclasped before her. 'I wish to know . . . I wish to ask . . .'

'What?'

'I wish to ask if I may go home before you.'

His blade paused at his throat. 'Go home? When my mission here is not complete?'

She swallowed. 'I do not see . . . I am not sure what use I am. You do not seem to need me here.'

'Need? Does a man not always need his loving wife beside him?' His voice was uninflected, all the more mocking for that.

She breathed, spoke softly. 'You said that my presence would aid the cause you plead. That I would make the Genoese think on chivalry, when they considered the fate of the women of Constantinople if they do not act.'

He resumed shaving. 'I think your appearance at the welcoming feast did that. For about a minute. After which these Italians briefly focused on your voluptuousness and envied the Turks their possible fortune.' He laughed. 'Then once chivalry and lust were dealt with, they reverted to the only thing truly important to them. Profit.'

She was no longer shocked by his levity – even when he was discussing the possible rape of his wife by infidels. But she had hoped for better from the men of Genoa. 'Are they not concerned about God?'

'God?' Theon laughed. 'I think he ranks somewhere down their list of priorities.'

Maybe it was her own self-doubt before the altar. Or maybe her noble parents stirred in her. For she felt her first flush of anger in a long while. 'And yet you spend much of *your* time in discussing how we can sell our vision of God for Roman gold, do you not, husband?'

24

He turned to look at her. 'Well, well,' he said softly, 'I think that is the first passion I have seen from you in an age. I certainly saw none this morning.' He waved his razor at the other room, turned again to the mirror and his toilet. 'So are you come to the belief of your cousin Loukas Notaras? Would you rather see a turban in the Hagia Sophia than a Roman mitre?'

As quickly as her anger came, it went. Though she had been educated like any noblewoman – she could read and write well – her husband had been trained almost from birth. Years of schooling under rigorous tutors, university and a dozen diplomatic missions had honed his mind far sharper than the razor he wielded. There was no point in arguing with him. Besides, she didn't believe, like so many did, that to give up aspects of the Orthodox faith and reunite the Churches of East and West was a sin. She still trusted in God to save her city. But unlike many there, she knew that God needed men's help. Men in armour, with cannon and crossbow.

'You know I do not. All . . .' she hurried over his interruption, because she knew if she gave him a chance he would use her like a whetstone for the wit he would deploy in the confrontations of the day, 'all I now ask is that you consider letting me return. Our children need me. And I believe I can be more use to our city there than here. As you have said, I have already fulfilled my . . . meagre purpose.' She lowered her eyes.

'Well.' He considered, looking above her. 'I do need to send messages back to the Council. My talks here are almost concluded and then I must go briefly on to Rome and rejoin the main embassy.' He studied her for a moment, then returned to the mirror. 'I will think on it.'

She turned to the bedroom, unwilling to show him hope on the open book of her face. His voice halted her. 'But you can do something for me.'

She did not turn. 'Of course. What?'

'That *enkolpia* you wear. Give it to me.'

She looked down. Fool that she was, she had not tucked her

amulet away within her tunic. 'It is my protection and . . . and my mother gave it to me.'

'God is our protection – or so you always tell me, wife. Your mother, bless her memory, is dead. And the funds the embassy left with me have nearly run out. I need the means to bribe one more minor official here. You have them round your neck, in gold and lapis.' In the mirror he returned the gaze she gave him. 'And what's left might buy your passage home.'

She knew he could have just taken it. She could not have denied him, as she could not have denied him that morning. But she also knew he was using her as his whetstone still. He would spend his day trying to win arguments. He might as well begin with her.

She lifted the gold chain from round her neck, kissed the amulet once, and laid it on the table. Then she continued to the bedroom, closing the door on his soft laughter.

Theon stepped through the iron grille onto the street. His bodyguards rose from beside the entrance but he did not acknowledge them. They would follow. They would defend him, if the odds were not too great. They did not exist beyond their function. And he wanted to remain for a moment in the rooms he'd left, even as he walked away from them.

He observed his sense of triumph and wondered at it. Such minor victories, scarcely worth the fight, against an opponent who barely fought back. He had given her what she asked for, when he'd been planning to send her back anyway. In return he'd taken something she loved, for which he had a slight use. He had taken her, though it probably gave him as little pleasure as she. But that was not about pleasure, he reminded himself. That he got elsewhere, and the sending away was part of it, so he could indulge himself without even the slight restraint that Sofia provided. It was not about the hope for more children – the two he barely knew back in Constantinople were proof enough to the world of his potency.

What was it, he wondered, that he had once gone to such

lengths to obtain? Her beauty? He had not been immune to it, but it had not driven him. The fact that she seemed to possess a secret? Well, all people were locks and his delight was in seeking their key. He'd been disappointed to discover that hers was little more than a deep capacity for love for God, for her city, for her children . . . even for him, if he'd chosen to accept it. He had not. Love blunted, it did not sharpen. He observed it, as he did everything else.

As he turned into the Piazza de Ferrari, his larger bodyguard opening a passage in the noonday crowd, he realised what the small triumph was. Heard it like the faintest echo of a greater triumph.

He hadn't conquered Sofia. He'd conquered his brother. He'd conquered their love – observed it, taken it, severed it. It was his first real triumph in a battle that had begun in the cradle. In the womb, no doubt. He had preceded his brother by a breath and it had been the only time he had beaten him to anything. Gregoras had always been faster, stronger, near as skilled in rhetoric, far more skilled in arms. Yet who had ultimately won? Who had taken for wife the girl they'd grown up with? And where was Gregoras now? Dead, probably. Disfigured, certainly, the beauty that had come from their mother, and manifested only in the one twin, marred. Wit had triumphed over beauty. Brother over brother.

Theon chuckled, surprised that this old victory still gave him such pleasure. Far, far more than the fruits of it had given him that morning.

They'd reached the entrance to the Doge's palace. Piero was announcing him to the gate guard. Over the hubbub of solicitors demanding entrance, Theon heard his other servant, Cassin, arguing. He turned – and saw that his man had his hand on the chest of a large Turk, whose outstretched arms spread his robes wide to show he was unarmed, whose dark brown eyes sought Theon's.

'Let him come,' Theon called, and Cassin stepped back, allowing the Turk closer, but not near.

'Peace be with you,' the Turk said.

'And with you and all your family, friend,' Theon replied, the Osmanlica coming as easily as the second tongue it was for him. 'What is your desire?'

'Only this, most esteemed. To inform you that my master, Hamza Bey, seeks conference with you this night.'

Theon had heard of Hamza, a rising man at the new sultan's court. He was surprised to hear he was in Genoa but kept that surprise from his face. 'When and where?'

'At the ninth hour of the evening, excellence. My master has taken a room for the purpose above the tavern of the Blue Boar.'

'I know it. Tell your master I shall be honoured to meet him there.'

The messenger nodded, bowed, and was gone.

A Turk wants to meet me in a tavern, Theon thought. Perhaps the bishop I am about to bribe will take me to a brothel?

He allowed himself another chuckle. After several weeks, he now knew, almost to the ducat, what concessions the Genoese would demand for their aid. It would be very interesting to hear later what the Turk had to offer.

THREE

Rhinometus

Genoa
The same day

Gregoras ignored the mockery, the disparagement of parent-age, the comparisons of his marred beauty with a donkey's puckered arse. Another time he would have given as good as he received, traded verbal blows; triumphed too, for his years of schooling had given him thrusts that most of the illiterate mercenaries lying around the courtyard of the Black Cock tavern could not parry. But their rough jests were not ill-meant; it was their way of expressing pleasure at his return. He had fought with them in a dozen campaigns, and they appreciated his skills of war even as they winced at his wit.

Later, perhaps, he thought. Later to sit down with Half-Ear Mario or Giovanni One Thumb and compare mislaid body parts, losing himself in camaraderie and flagons of wine. First, though, he needed money, and plenty of it. For that he had to see one man.

'Rhinometus!' came the bellow as soon as he stepped into the room. 'Now I know we are doomed, boys, when this beak-less raven appears!'

'Eminence.' Gregoras bowed, sweeping off his hat with a flourish, holding the courtesy.

'Eminent arseholes, Zoran. Where have you been? I have had messengers out for you for months now. I thought we were going to have to set forth without our talisman of ill-fortune. Rather have it beside me than levelling his crossbow at me, eh?'

Gregoras rose from his bow. Giovanni Giustiniani Longo had changed little in the year since they'd last fought together. A little greyer, a little stouter perhaps, but still the tall and vigorous figure he had followed over ship's gunwales and through breaches, dressed as ever in his blue-black armour, the large medallion of San Pietro ever at his throat. Like most killing men, the great mercenary leader was deeply religious. Superstitious, too. Years before, in a galley fight off Crete, Gregoras had deflected a crossbow bolt that would have ripped out the Commander's throat. The Genoan had considered him his lucky star ever since.

Gregoras extended his bow to Enzo the Sicilian and Amir the Renegade, Giustiniani's most trusted lieutenants. The latter brought him a goblet of wine from around the table they all stood behind, muster rolls and maps scattered among the daggers and bow strings. 'Welcome back. Allah's blessing on you,' he murmured.

'And Christ's on you,' Gregoras replied in Arabic. He and Amir had a history of wine-fuelled religious debate all the more furious because neither of them cared much for the faiths they'd been raised in. It made him feel immediately at home, the only home he'd known since his exiling. Though if the money was good enough, perhaps that was about to change.

'So where *have* you been, Zoran?' Giustiniani repeated. 'We wondered if you'd settled down with a whore, or been knifed in some Ragusan tavern by now.' The lined brow contracted. 'Or worse – that you'd taken a contract with those sodomite donkeys the Venetians.'

It had suited Gregoras to claim a name and a city that were not his. It was not entirely untrue either, for he had a home of sorts in the city some called Ragusa and others Dubrovnik and he was known as Zoran there. It made for fewer questions. For if they knew his real name, his birthplace . . .

A home, he thought. It was why he was there. Why he'd picked up his sword and his crossbow again and made the arduous journey to Genoa. His home was a hovel. But it had the best view in Ragusa, out over the Adriatic Sea. It was like the view from his childhood home, when his parents had been wealthy. He wanted to build a home just like it. But Istrian stone was expensive, as were its crafters. He needed one last campaign, for the wages and especially the booty it offered. Then he would hang his crossbow on the wall of his new home and stare at the view for ever, unmasked, unaccompanied, with no one there to pity him.

'Venetians? Never. I care too much for my reputation – and my arse.' The three men laughed, and he continued, 'No, my lord, if I am going to get fucked, it may as well be by people I love. So I came to seek you out.'

'Love? The Pope's testicles, Zoran.' Enzo smiled. 'You heard we were paying double wages.'

'Good.' He hadn't. Had heard nothing, because he'd stepped off a boat and come straight to the company's tavern from the docks of Genoa; but it was excellent news. 'Even though, as you know, I'd work for less than nothing for the pleasure of your honoured company.' He rode over their guffaws. 'So who do you want me to kill?'

All three replied. 'Turks.'

'Better. Storing up treasure in heaven with the slitting of infidel throats.' He crossed himself, careful to do it the Roman way and not the Orthodox he'd been raised in, two fingers not three, right-left not left-right. Two of the men imitated him, one did not, and he looked at him. 'No insult meant, Amir.'

'None taken, uncircumcised dog.'

'And when does this well-paid crusade begin?'

'We sail within the week.'

Gregoras smiled. 'Best,' he said. 'Then I will go fetch my gear from the whore I've been living with.' It was not true, but it was what they wanted to hear. 'I'll sign the articles straight-away so you can pay for my wine. Till later, comrades.' He turned to the door, then turned back. 'Not that it matters much, your eminence, but where do we fight this time?'

31

'Oh, some backwater.' Giustiniani spun a map round. 'See?'

There was a restrained excitement in the Commander's eyes, in his tone, that made Gregoras, who truly did not care where he was going, who he was to kill, turn back, look down . . . and have his breath taken. Though he had tried to erase every aspect of the place from his mind and memory, the hound's head of land thrusting into water was unmistakable. And it was as if a dog had come and snatched his last bite of food, for all his hopes were gone.

'It's always hard to tell beneath that mask,' Giustiniani was saying. 'And if it is true, it is as rare as a nun's virginity. But do you know, my boys, I think we have finally shocked the Ragusan.'

Gregoras sought a quip, failed. He could not summon breath, let alone words. The home he had envisaged crumbled in his mind. The journey that had exhausted the last of his funds had been wasted.

The silence lengthened. 'It's Constantinople,' Enzo said, helpfully.

'I know what it is.'

'And you know the Muhammadan is planning to take it.'

'As he has for eight hundred years,' Gregoras murmured.

'But this time he means it.' The Commander rested his knuckles on the table. 'Their new sultan, Mehmet? A kid, full of piss and wind. But he fancies himself the next Alexander. Another Caesar. It's said he's assembling the biggest army the Turks have ever raised. And he's already begun to take the city. Did you hear that he built a fortress here?' Giustiniani jabbed his finger down on the map and, reluctantly, Gregoras looked. 'See? It's right on the water, opposite their older fort. He calls the new one "the Throat Cutter". You can see why.'

Gregoras could. As a young man, he had often ridden on that stretch of cliff, standing in Europe and staring at Asia across the narrow sea channel the Turks called Bogaz, 'the Throat', and the rest of the world knew as the Bosphorus. If the Turk now had a fortress either side, he commanded one of the busiest shipping lanes in the world. He could sink any ship trying to bring grain from the Black Sea into the city. He hadn't so much cut Constantinople's throat as closed it, preventing it from feeding.

Giustiniani spoke as if to his thoughts. 'A Venetian captain, name of Rizzi, tried to run the gauntlet. Wouldn't heave to when ordered. The Turks sank him with one fat ball, fished him from the waters – then shoved a stake up his arse.' He winced. 'Still, being Venetian, it probably wasn't much of a hardship.'

The three men laughed. Gregoras didn't. Looking at the place of his birth, the source of his disgrace, hearing tales of it, his mind was numbed as it never was under cannon fire or swung swords. One thing came through, and he voiced it. 'Why . . . why would you go and fight for them? Who would pay you? They have no money.'

'This very city, son,' Giustiniani said, straightening. 'It has been decided in the last few days.'

Gregoras raised a hand to scratch a sudden itch on his nose, dropped it fast, when he remembered there was no nose to scratch. 'But why? Does not Genoa still have a treaty with the Turks?'

'Aye. And we will not break it either. Even though I am a nobleman from one of the foremost families of this city, yet I will go as a leader of a rabble of Genoese mercenaries – and the odd renegade Musselman.' He threw a punch at Amir, connected with his shoulder, the Syrian trying to smile away a painful blow.

'The sultan will not believe that . . .'

'The sultan will turn a blind eye, because it suits him to do so. If he takes Constantinople, he will still want to trade with us afterwards. If he does not – he will still want to trade with us afterwards!' Giustiniani stabbed the map again, on the point of land opposite the city. 'And remember, we fight for our land there too, our colony of Galata. If the Greek city falls, Galata will too.' He grinned. 'No, on balance, we'd rather have those

33

cheating sodomite Greeks in Constantinople. As you've said, they have no money any more, no power. Less serious rivals for our trade, eh? The Turks drive too hard a bargain. Bad as Jews!' He grinned. 'And the Pope is now calling it a crusade, since those blaspheming Greeks have agreed to full union of their Orthodox and our true Roman Church again.' He crossed himself once more. 'So we serve God and our city both. Profit on earth and in heaven.'

This was news to Gregoras – and there was a time when it would have mattered, deeply, this abject surrender of his people's ancient faith in exchange for begrudged aid in the fight all knew was coming.

It did not matter to him now. Nothing to do with that cursed city had, since the moment the knife had cut down and Constantinople had taken his everything: his love, for Sofia was lost to him; his name, for he was Gregoras Lascaris no more. And the final loss, the one that marked him as exile, as traitor, gave him the new title he would for ever be known by there: Rhinometus – the Noseless One.

He looked up, seeing the face before him as if through a mist. The Genoan was raising his goblet. 'So what do you say, lad? Will you toast with me to Byzantine gold, Christ's glory and Musselman blood on the stones?'

Gregoras shook his head. 'I will not. I will not fight for that . . . place. *In* that place.'

The goblet paused before the mouth. 'Eh?' Giustiniani managed, his eyes widening.

'I will not fight there.' He forestalled the question. 'And I have no need to tell you why.' He shrugged. 'Have you not some other deal?'

'Deal! You . . . dare . . . dare . . .' The Commander's fury was ever instant, all-consuming. Gregoras had often seen it, directed at enemies and any failings in his own men. Never at him – until now. 'Do you think I am some fucking . . . broker?' he roared. 'I am a prince of Genoa and commander of its armies and I do not . . . deal!' He smashed the goblet down

34

on the table, slopping out wine, which flowed, like a bloodied crimson river, over the dog's-head outline of Constantinople. 'So you will follow me into whatever hellish hole I order you, kill whomever I command you to kill – or you will return like the noseless cur you are back to the shithole you've just slithered from.'

Gregoras would take mockery about his maiming. Insult was another thing. Enzo and Amir had both seen what happened when one came, and both stepped slightly closer to their raging, oblivious leader, hands clasping hilts.

The eyes above the mask narrowed. Then they closed and Gregoras breathed deeply. Breath gave him pause . . . and memory. In a strange way, he loved the man before him, and would do him no harm, even if he was able – no means certain with hard men like these at his side. So instead he stepped forward, placed his half-filled cup on the table. 'Good fortune attend you all,' he said softly, as he turned to the door.

'Wait!' It was Amir who spoke, and turning back, Gregoras saw him stand on his toes – for Giustiniani was huge – and whisper in his ear. The Genoan's eyes had narrowed in his storm, and for a while they darted about as if seeking a target for his rage. Then, suddenly, Gregoras saw the storm pass and light return. Instantly, as ever with him.

'Well,' Giustiniani said, chuckling, 'wouldn't that just serve him right?' He turned to Gregoras. 'Listen, you insubordinate dog. I do have an offer to make you, and it's one that is quite likely to end with your throat being cut, which would be only right after your insolence. If you refuse it, you will live for ever in the shadow of my displeasure and I shall seek no more delight than stringing you up by your balls. Is that understood?'

The words were harsh, the tone less so and belied by the obvious amusement in his commander's eyes. Gregoras breathed a little easier, then nodded. 'You know I obey your every command, eminence.'

Giustiniani nodded, ignoring the obvious. 'Then obey this,

Zoran. There is a man who is said to have recovered the secret of a weapon thought lost. It is one dear to Greek hearts and it bears their name: Greek Fire.'

Gregoras frowned. Greek Fire had saved Constantinople from its enemies many times. Eight hundred years before, this fire sprayed from brass siphons had destroyed a besieging Arab fleet. But the exact formula was a mystery and few if any had been able to replicate it for a hundred years or more.

The big Genoan continued. 'The man in question is said to be a German. Name of Johannes Grant, which seems an odd sort of name even for that nation of shit-wallowers. We would like him on our side. The trouble is, the Turks would like him too. Preferably in hell.'

'Good,' said Gregoras. 'And you would like me to find him for you?'

'Oh, we know where he is.' A smile was coming to the Italian's thick lips, one that Gregoras did not like. 'He's in Korcula.'

Better. Korcula was an island in the Adriatic Sea, not far from his hovel in Ragusa. He could fetch the fellow and visit his home at the same time. With an advance of Genoese gold – for special contracts like this paid special wages – he could even get the builders to break ground. 'Then I will collect him for you. A German in Korcula should be easy to find.' A frown came. 'But where do you want him? More importantly, where will I be paid? I will not bring him to . . .' He gestured at the wine-stained map.

'You will not have to.' Giustiniani was smiling broadly now. He shuffled through some papers, brought out a different map. 'I have men to collect in Chios. Given good winds, I will be there sometime late December. You can meet us there.'

He would need the same good winds. But he would not be travelling with an army, so it was possible. Tight, but possible. 'Good. Then that's where I will meet you. We will celebrate our Lord's birth together there.'

'Oh, that will be pleasant.' Giustiniani's eyes were almost

afire now, so brightly did they shine. 'Enzo here will give you some gold. Shall we say, a quarter in advance?'

'I'd prefer a third.'

'I am sure you would. But even a quarter might be enough to turn your head.' He nodded, and Enzo went to a large chest in the corner of the room and pulled out a bag that clinked. 'Count him out one hundred ducats.'

One hundred. Three hundred more on delivery. He could build a small castle in Ragusa for that, let alone a house. Gregoras kept his whistle within his mask and watched carefully as the coins were being counted. He could not count them again without insult. 'Is he worth so much?' he murmured.

'The Turks would pay you double to kill him.' Giustiniani nodded. 'But I know you, Rhinometus. You never like to change sides in the midst of a fight. Most un-mercenary-like.' He smiled. 'A deal is a deal with you, is it not?'

'It is.' Gregoras's tally matched Enzo's. He watched until the coins were safely in a leather purse, took it, cinched it, tucked it under his cloak. 'Then with God's good winds in all our sails, I will see you in Chios.'

He bowed, as did they. As he rose, he saw the amusement yet lingering in the man's eyes. 'There's something else, isn't there, my general?'

'There is.' The Genoan glanced at the men either side of him. Enzo shared his amusement. Amir less so. 'The German,' he continued, 'is not in Korcula willingly. He is a prisoner.'

'Of whom?'

'The pirates of Omis.' Giustiniani's smile grew as he saw the expression in Gregoras's eyes. 'So you better make your peace with God, Zoran, however you worship him. Because you are going to need all the help you can get.'

— FOUR —

Beloved of Muhammad

It was the drunken gang swaggering past – praising Christ, cursing Allah, lauding the Doge – that changed Hamza's mind. The man he'd come to see had brokered the deal they celebrated. Though the soldiers to be sent were few enough indeed, they would bring hope with them to Constantinople in a few months' time – and profit to Genoa's taverns tonight. It was never a good tactic to deride a man's most recent accomplishment. Churlish, at the least; while the plan to emphasise the disparity between attacker and defender was always going to be a blunt club. Both men knew it already. Knew too that in the end, the choice to fight or not to fight would not come down to the odds.

Hamza shrugged. He possessed subtler weapons. Full of hope, not despair – why back a man into a corner when you can bring him into the light? – while the subtlest was personal to the man he was about to coerce.

Lascaris. There had been emperors of Constantinople of that name, centuries before. No doubt this one could trace his family further back, perhaps to the city's very founding. Hamza smiled. He could trace his family back to his grandfather, the goatherd.

Lascaris. Also the name of a traitor. This man's brother. Does more than noble blood run in this family? Hamza wondered, as the danger passed in shouts down the street and he tapped his bodyguard on the shoulder.

They stepped from the doorway they'd sheltered in, lifting their cloaks over the muck that flowed down the lane's centre.

Abdul-Matin struck the door opposite three times with the butt end of his dagger. They waited. He rapped again. Then, as he raised his hand a third time, shutters above were pushed out a crack.

'Who's there?' a man's voice called in accented Italian.

Hamza recognised the accent. 'A friend,' he replied softly, in his own tongue, 'seeking shelter.'

Theon stiffened. This had to be the man he'd been about to go and meet. The plan had changed – or the Turk sought some advantage in this surprise, for Turks were cunning as snakes. He sucked at his lip, considered – but there was little he could do. The man could not be left on the street. 'A moment,' he called, before turning back and hissing, 'Sofia! Tidy this room. Swiftly.'

As his wife poured the dregs of tripe stew into one bowl, adding the date pits and crusts of bread, Theon slipped his embroidered surplice over his tunic, then opened the chest and put away the copy of the agreement he had signed with the Genoese, his notes in the margins. He wasn't sure why he bothered. He suspected his visitor would know most of the details already.

The little they had was soon tidied away. The room looked like what it was: cheap accommodation for an envoy whose country could afford nothing more. It was why he had been happy that they were meeting at the inn. Yet at least his clothes, under Sofia's care, were immaculate. 'Go,' he said, and Sofia went into the bedroom, pushing the door closed behind her. Taking a breath, Theon descended the stairs.

Bolts were shot, the door opened. 'Peace be with you, friend,' Hamza said, making the obeisance of forehead, mouth and heart.

'And with you, friend. You honour my house with your visit. Will you enter and rest?'

'I will, and I thank you.' Bowing, Hamza stepped over the threshold. Abdul-Matin immediately squatted in the doorway, pulling his cloak around him.

As he followed his host up the stairs, Hamza was pleased. On the neutral ground of a tavern they might have wrestled for tongue. Here, as host, Theon was obliged to speak that of his guest.

At the entrance of the room was a woven mat. 'There are slippers for your use.' Theon gestured.

'Thank you. I have my own.' Hamza reached into his satchel, pulled out a pair lined in sheepskin, struggled out of his heavy boots. 'I can never get used to these,' he said, placing them by the door. 'Italians do not understand the necessity of good footwear. Unlike us.'

'Us?'

'We of the East.'

Theon considered. The sought kinship was a small enough point to concede. 'They do not. But they need thick boots to kick their wives and walk down the sewers they call their streets.'

Hamza laughed. 'Do they not?' He stepped into the room, glanced around, his face revealing nothing. 'I am sorry for the surprise of my visit. But those filthy streets are filled with young men seeking mischief this night. And they begin their search in taverns. One of my hue . . .' he gestured to his face, 'is a provocation to them.' He turned back to Theon, still at the door. 'You have heard why they celebrate?'

'Some saint's birthday? Or two? They have more saints than days here.'

Hamza tipped his head. 'Ah, my friend, I think you know. Because I think you are, how shall we say, the host of the celebration?'

'Host?'

'Its cause. The accord you have concluded with the Doge and the Council.' Theon's face did not change, so Hamza continued, 'The force that will go to defend your city?'

'Ah. Is that what they celebrate?'

'Indeed. A new . . . crusade against the Turk.' Hamza laid his open palm against his chest.

'Hardly a crusade. I heard that Genoa itself does nothing. But it will not stop certain . . . concerned citizens going to Christendom's aid. A few thousand men perhaps.'

'Ah, there our reports vary. I heard a few hundred. And though perhaps they will not trumpet this, all paid for by Genoese gold.' Hamza nodded. 'Still, you have succeeded in your embassy, have you not? Even so few men. When I was here, trying to persuade the Doge to send none.'

He sighed . . . and Theon suppressed a smile. Hamza had not truly entered the room and their duel was already in its third pass. 'Please,' he said, gesturing to two chairs before the fireplace where wood burned, 'warm yourself,' adding, as the Turk crossed the room, 'Despite the danger, at least at a tavern I could offer you wine.'

Hamza stretched hands towards the flames. 'I do not drink wine.'

'A true believer?' Theon stepped closer. 'And yet not all of your faith are so . . . true. Did not your recent sultan, peace be with him, love the distillation of the grape?'

Hamza stared. If he knew something of the Greek, what was known in return? For the late sultan was Murad, the Great. Supreme warrior, diplomat, administrator, poet. Hamza had been his cupbearer, his confidant . . . his lover. It was Murad who had taken the handsome tanner's son from Laz, educated him, trained him, loved him. Created him. Hamza had loved him in return, even for the weakness that had killed him. It was not only true belief that kept Hamza from wine. 'He did. May Allah, most merciful, give him rest,' he said.

'And his son? Your new ruler? Does he share his father's . . . tastes?'

Hamza looked at the Greek. There was an emphasis on 'tastes' he didn't like. 'Mehmet is a true believer too. But his passions lie elsewhere.'

'In what?'

Hamza spoke the words softly. 'In conquest.'

Interesting, thought Theon. Some weakness there, something

to probe later, perhaps. The man turned away, shifted closer to the fire, and he was able to study his face for the first time. It was not as dark as he had claimed. Sun rather than race had given him his 'hue'. The beard was almost fair. The eyes a pale blue. 'Well,' he said. 'Perhaps we should talk more of that. But first . . .' he forestalled the Turk's reply, 'can I offer you anything else? Some dates and cheese perhaps? Some water? The water seller in this street is surprisingly clean-fingered.'

'Some water, thank you.'

Theon took a step towards the bedroom to collect it, but stopped. He had opened up something in the Turk. It would be interesting to probe it further. 'Sofia,' he called, 'come and meet our guest. And bring some water.'

Hamza was surprised, though he did not let it show. He did not know that Theon kept a woman there. It would be odd to parade his whore before such a visitor. But Greeks were odd. And slippery as the eels I fished for in the canals of Laz, he reminded himself. He had proved that in his first sentences.

Then Sofia came into the room – and Hamza's breath caught. She was no whore. Neither was she a woman of Genoa. She had a different sort of darkness, and a bearing, a way of standing, that showed nothing less than nobility. Tall, graceful, with a face whose features hinted at the East, and a body that showed even through the enveloping gown.

'This is my wife, Sofia.' Theon waved her in.

'Peace be with you, lady,' Hamza said, switching to Greek, sweeping into a bow.

'And with you, sir,' she answered, coming forward. She went to the table and poured water into two goblets there. Putting the pitcher down, she carried them to the men. 'Welcome to our house.'

More interesting, Theon thought. He had not looked at his wife as she came in, but kept his gaze fixed on his visitor. The Turk's eyes betrayed him, just a little, just enough. Theon believed that, like many of his kind, Hamza would love both men and women. But the narrowing in the Turk's eyes showed he would probably prefer the latter.

Theon shook his head imperceptibly. It surprised him when his wife provoked such reactions. He saw ice where other men saw fire. But they did not know her as he did. And there had been a time when he had wondered what the Turk was probably wondering now: what would it be like to lie with her naked?

Sofia kept her eyes lowered as she gave the goblets over. But they came up for a moment when Hamza murmured his thank you . . . and he was startled again. Not so much for the colour and swirl of them, that he'd only seen once before in jade from Samarkand. For the darkness within them.

He didn't think he'd ever seen such melancholy in his whole life.

She turned – and tripped! Hamza was to her in a moment, reaching an arm to her elbow. It was a moment of contact, a moment when those eyes turned to him again – and then she freed her arm to receive what she'd tripped over, what leapt up now.

'Ragazzo!' she cried, scolding.

The cat twisted its neck up, purring loudly. Hamza, who had not moved away, saw the melancholy swept away and be replaced with such joy that he felt an actual, contrasting sadness. He reached out a hand to the cat, and ran a finger between his eyes.

'You like cats, sir?' she asked.

'I do. Especially a handsome fellow like this.' He scratched. 'May I?'

Sofia released Ragazzo into his arms. The cat was completely comfortable there, even when Hamza turned him over on his back and rubbed his exposed belly. 'Did you know, lady, that our prophet Muhammad, praise be to him always, was a lover of cats?'

'I . . . I did not.'

'Especially of this kind. The stripe on his back, the markings as if some calligrapher has dipped his hands in black ink and drawn thick rings around this grey body. But look here,' he said, righting the cat and scritching him under the chin to lift his head. 'Do you see what is above these stunning green eyes? This proves he is beloved of Muhammad. For has not the Prophet, praise him, blessed the animal with his own initial?'

Sofia looked – and laughed. 'It is true,' she said, clapping her hands together in delight. 'Look, Theon. Above the eyes. The letter "M" clear as day. I never saw it till this moment.'

She laughed again and Hamza with her. Theon frowned. When had he last heard her laugh? He didn't truly care if men lusted after his wife. But this . . . complicity between them? It annoyed him. 'And do you think that "M" is a letter used by Arabs or Turks?' he snapped. 'Take it away, Sofia. You know how I hate the beast.'

They both looked up at him. Hamza's gaze was keen and Theon was angry again that he'd revealed any sort of emotion. He changed his tone. 'It makes me sneeze,' he explained.

'Ah, and I wager that he loves you best of all. It is always the way. They desire those who shun them. Perhaps like Muhammad, most exalted, whose mark they bear, they seek to bring you to the one true faith – the worship of cats!' Reluctantly he handed the animal into Sofia's arms.

She scratched the cat between the eyes. ' "Beloved of Muhammad." What is that in your tongue, sir?'

Hamza considered, reaching out to stroke. 'I would say "Ulvikul",' he replied.

'Ulvikul,' she repeated. 'Would it be a sin against your faith to name him thus? Ragazzo is just what our maid yells at him when he steals food.'

'Lady, from you, it could be no sin.'

There was a silence. More complicity, Theon thought, and broke it. 'Leave us, wife,' he said tonelessly. 'And keep the cat with you.'

It is like a veil, Hamza thought, as Sofia's eyes changed and she turned away. I am privileged to have glimpsed beneath it.

44

The two men watched her leave, and the door close behind her. 'You are blessed in her,' Hamza said.

'In ways you cannot imagine,' Theon replied briskly, sitting down. 'Do you have a wife?'

'Three.'

'Three.' The Greek's brow wrinkled. 'Do you not consider that excessive?'

'Perhaps.' He shrugged. '*Inshallah*.' He nodded to the door. 'But if I had one such as yours . . .'

'Indeed.' Theon decided he had had enough of the exchange, and was not sure he had got the better of it. 'And now, shall we get to business? What is it that you wished to discuss with me?'

Hamza smiled. 'Discuss? This meeting is more in the way of getting to know you. And what better way to know someone than . . . this.' He reached again into his satchel, drew something from it – a rectangular board made of dark brown wood. It had alternating slim pyramids of teak and ebony, each tip surmounted by a crescent of mother of pearl. The board's raised surrounding edge was studded with brass stars, inset with small rubies.

'Do you know this game?'

Theon studied the board. He suspected it was worth more than the contents of his rooms. 'Of course. We call it *tavli*.'

'And we call it *tavla*. So just one letter divides us. Is that not . . . significant perhaps? The little that divides us, Greek and Turk?' When Theon did not reply, he added, 'Do you play?'

'I have done.'

'Then shall we play now? The good thing about *tavla* is that one can talk as well as throw.'

'As you wish.'

Hamza dipped again into his bag, pulling out a smaller cloth one, tipping black and white wooden counters from it onto the board, setting them swiftly up. Four dice were amongst them.

Hamza picked them up, held them out in the palm of his hand. 'Choose,' he said.

Theon picked the two white ones. They were heavier than he'd thought, ivory not mere bone, and as he rolled them, something glittered. He looked at the one. It was a diamond. 'Exquisite,' he murmured, as Hamza swung the board so that he was black.

The Turk gestured down. 'Please.'

Theon threw a four and a deuce. A good beginning, and he covered up his fourth pyramid. Hamza did not roll. 'Something else?'

'We have not decided the wager. *Tavla* must always be played for something.'

'But does not the Qur'an forbid wagering?'

'You know our holy book?'

'I have studied it. I know it speaks of various . . . sins.'

' "They will ask thee about intoxicants and games of chance," ' Hamza declaimed softly. ' "Say: In both there is great sin as well as some benefit for man; but the evil that they cause is greater than the benefit that they bring." ' Then he lifted his dice and added, 'But what is life without a little sin?' He smiled, gestured down. 'The board is beautiful, is it not? Shall we play for that?'

'I have nothing to offer that could compare in value—'

Hamza interrupted. 'You have friendship. You could offer me that.'

Theon raised an eyebrow. 'You would win my friendship . . . with a game?'

Hamza laughed. 'You are right. Perhaps the playing will do that on its own. All right.' He sat back. 'If I win, I will take that magnificent cat.'

Theon considered. Everything his wife possessed was his – even the cat he hated. Hamza knew this. He was offering a bribe . . . and a challenge. Theon was always happy to accept both. 'Very well,' he said. 'It is your roll. And I already have the advantage.'

He pointed to his first roll. Hamza frowned. 'I had not considered. My father always said he raised a fool. Allah bless me,' he said, and rolled.

They played for a while in silence. Theon had the luck, continuing to move safely onto points, occupy them, fortify them. Hamza tried to run, was hit, returned, was hit again. Theon placed his counter on the side of the table. 'Sodomite donkeys,' Hamza exclaimed. 'Your wall rises strong against me. As the wall before your city does.'

'Indeed. As it always has. Our protector, ever.'

'And yet a wall always has a weak point.' He pointed. 'If I throw double fours, I will find yours.'

'You would need the luck.'

'One always does – in war and in games.' Hamza rolled. Both men drew breath as Hamza returned his counter to the table and moved it four up to hit and dispatch Theon's.

'So.' Theon placed his dice on the table, leaned back. 'Do you think you will have such luck before the walls of Theodosius?'

Hamza placed his dice down too. It was time to concentrate on the other game. '*Inshulluh.* But as in *tavla*, we will seek ways to reduce our reliance on luck and rely instead on things we can control. On men. Many, many men. And guns.'

'We have guns too.'

'Some. But not like ours.' Hamza was about to speak, took a sip of water instead. He'd already decided, in his wait outside the house, not to belabour the man before him with the blunt weapon of tallies and armaments. There was no need, not when both knew them.

Theon reached down, picked up his dice, rolled. It was a good throw. 'Yet you forget one thing,' he said, as he brought his man back on, covered him. 'We have a power on our side that all your men, the largest guns, cannot overcome.'

Hamza frowned. 'What power?'

'We have God.'

'But, my friend,' Hamza laughed, 'so do we.'

Theon studied the smile. The Turk was not there to tell him what he already knew. He was there to make an offer. Both men knew it.

'So we come down to the will of God,' Hamza continued. 'You believe as fervently in your faith as we do in ours that God will decide. You know we say "*Inshallah*". "As Allah wills it." We also both know that in every battle, victory usually goes to the side that is larger.'

'Not always.'

'Agreed.' Hamza leaned forward. 'But why fight at all? Your faith abhors it. Allah forbids the shedding of blood unless absolutely necessary for some holy cause.'

'Why fight?' Theon fingered the dice against his palm. 'Because you are coming to take our city.'

'Then why not just give it to us? Save all those lives. And join us in the new city whose glory will eclipse even the brightest days of Byzantium.'

'*Join* you?'

Hamza leaned even closer, his eyes glowing in the firelight. 'Aye. Look at us, sitting here playing *tavla*, in our silken robes, in our slippers. We are not like these others . . .' he gestured outside, 'these men of Europe, with their filth-covered boots, their brawl-filled taverns. Their grudging generosity. We are men of the East. Civilised, open-hearted men. It is in our lands that the prophets arose – Moses, Isa, Muhammad, praise him. Praise them all. The Levant winds have always filled our sails and driven us to glory. We have more in common with each other than you have with . . . them.'

'We worship Christ, like them.'

'Like them? How do you worship him? You of the Eastern Church? What are you being asked to give up, to gain the begrudging aid of Rome?' His eyes shone. 'Only the essence of your faith. Your people hate the union you have made with the Romans. They shun your churches and riot in your streets. And when they stand on your ravaged walls as our huge army advances, they will doubt that God will hear their prayers, because their leaders have betrayed . . . Him.' He raised his hand to the heavens, then let it fall. 'All for a thousand Genoese, and the princes and bishops of Europe looking the other way.'

Theon didn't move. Much of what the Turk said, of faiths and peoples, was true. But Hamza was not there for a theological discussion. 'What are you suggesting?' he asked.

Hamza shrugged. 'That we do not fight. Mehmet will be disappointed that he cannot conquer. But we will have other wars. We always do.' He smiled. 'And he will be hailed as a holy leader for gaining all, and shedding no blood. While you of the city, men . . . and women, you will stay on and see it great again I have been there. I know it is a ruin, that scarce one-tenth of the people who lived there once do so now. Help us restore its greatness, as the centre of an empire it once was and can be again.'

'A Muslim empire.'

'An Eastern one,' Hamza countered. 'And as for your faith, keep it. Keep it as you want it, not . . . compromised by Romans. In Islam, we do not force any to convert. You may worship as you please – though you will have to pay a little more in taxes. And what man wants to do that?'

'Few that I know.' Theon found he was grinding the dice between his fingers. He set them down. 'And how do you think I can help you in this? Should I choose to?'

It was there. A hook baited, dangling before the eel's mouth. Hamza took a breath. 'There are those already in your city who know, if it comes to war, that you will lose. Align with them. Raise your voice when the time comes.' He leaned forward, placed a hand on Theon's. 'Come, man of the East. See your destiny. Save your faith, your city, your family. Help us.'

Theon let the hand rest for a moment, then gently lifted it, turning the Turk's palm upwards. With his other hand he reached, picked up the other's dice, the ebony ones, and placed them in Hamza's hand. Closing the fingers over them, he said, 'It's your turn to throw.'

Hamza leaned away. 'Mine? I thought I just did. No, you are right.'

For silent minutes, they took turns. At one point it looked like the Turk might escape. But then the Christian rebuilt the wall six deep, impossible to jump over. With a counter off the table, Hamza could only watch as Theon threw – and remember the subtlest weapon he had not yet used. 'If only the Hexamilion had been so strong,' he murmured, not too softly.

Theon, who was enjoying the conquest, held his dice. The mention of the Hexamilion, that six-mile wall in the Morea that was meant to be unbreachable and that the Turks had destroyed with cannon in six days in 1446, brought memories he'd tried to forget. Of terror. Of betrayal. But Hamza was staring, so he swallowed and spoke. 'Were you there?'

'I was Murad's cupbearer. I was always at the sultan's side.'

'Always?' The slightest smile came, but Hamza did not let it provoke him.

'Were you?'

'I was. Beside my emperor as well.'

'I see.' Hamza studied the board. 'And your brother?' he added softly. 'Was he beside your emperor too?'

'My brother?' The smile vanished. 'What do you know of him?'

Hamza looked up. 'Little enough, sure. All I know is that brothers can be problems. I have five, and they compete with each other in stupidity. They . . .' The look on Theon's face halted him. 'But I can see the mention of your brother causes you grief. We will not talk of him.'

'Not grief, I . . .' He stopped himself. Why had Hamza brought Gregoras up? He needed to know, spoke carefully. 'My brother . . . was deemed to be a traitor at the Hexamilion. Some say he betrayed the wall to . . . you. A postern gate left open at night.'

'So he is dead. A double sadness to you.'

'He may be dead now. Not then. Then he was . . . disfigured. Battlefield justice by men crazed with anger. I arrived

50

in time to save his life but, alas, too late to halt his . . . punishment. To . . .' Theon paused. He'd been drawn into a conversation he did not want. Been forced into lies when he did not even need to discuss this.

'Disfigured?' Hamza said, his voice all sadness. 'How?'

Theon made his reply casual. 'The usual way. They cut off his nose.'

Hamza watched the Greek's eyes. He had taken him off guard. But it was enough, for now, to know the wound was there. He did not need to probe it . . . yet.

'I am sorry for your sorrow.' Hamza let pity show on his face, then picked up his dice. 'My throw again? No, your Hexamilion still stands.'

'Yes.'

Theon won swiftly. But thereafter he did not seem to be fully concentrating, and his luck was not as strong. Hamza took the next two games with ease. When he swept the last of his counters off, Theon leaned back, throwing his dice down. 'This victory is yours,' he said.

'And what was the stake? Ah yes.' Hamza grinned. 'That beautiful cat.'

Theon stood. 'I will call my wife.'

Hamza rose too. 'A moment.' He leaned in, rested his hand on Theon's arm. 'I am glad we have had this chance to get to know each other a little. Friendship will be a good thing in the days that lie ahead. If it comes to war . . . well, perhaps I will be able to help you and yours when the city falls.'

'*If* it falls.'

'If indeed. But *if* it does, there will be the customary three days of pillage. Have you seen a city taken?' On the other's head shake, he shuddered, continued. 'It is horrible, to watch men turn to ravening beasts. To slaughter. Despoil. Enslave. Ravish.' The glance to the bedroom door was slight but clear. 'Should it come to that . . . should luck and guns and above all Allah, most exalted, be with us, it would be good to have a friend among the conquerors.'

Theon squinted at the man so near him. 'And what must I do for this . . . friendship?'

'That shall be as you decide, *brother* of the East.'

The word was barely inflected. Just enough. 'Well, I will think on this.' Theon moved away a pace, turned to the door. 'Sofia,' he called.

She came out, cat in her arms. 'Good, he is there,' Theon said, gesturing to the board. 'I wagered your cat at *tavli*. I lost. Give him to our guest.'

She could not restrain a shudder. But Hamza marvelled at the speed with which she mastered herself, diving behind the veil of her long lashes. She crossed the room. 'Here, sir,' she said, holding him out, 'he is yours.'

But Hamza did not reach to take him, just stretched out a hand and scratched the purring animal between his eyes. 'Nay, lady. I won him – and now I offer him as a tribute to your beauty.' He bowed. 'He is yours. I just wanted to see Ulvikul once again.' He picked up his satchel, went to the door, took off his slippers, put on his boots.

'You have forgotten your board,' Theon called.

'I have forgotten nothing. It is a poor return for your hospitality,' said Hamza, 'though I . . .' He crossed back, bent and picked up the ivory dice. 'I will take these. They are my lucky ones. I am surprised that you won even once with them.' He held them up. 'Traitors,' he murmured. Then he crossed the room, bowed and left.

Theon followed him down the stairs, but the Turk gave him nothing more save a smile as the door was unbolted, opened. Silently, he left.

Theon returned. 'What did he seek?' Sofia asked.

'Hmm? Nothing. Nothing that need concern you. Leave me.'

'Our city concerns me—'

'Leave me,' he roared, so loudly the cat was startled and jumped from Sofia's arms to scurry under the table. For a

52

moment, Sofia's brow wrinkled in anger. Then she turned, and walked slowly into the bedroom.

Theon went to the chest, pulled out a flagon of wine. He wasn't going to drink wine if his guest didn't. Now he was alone he would probably drink it all. He sat, gulped, stared at the board before him. It was exquisite, as beautiful and expensive an object as he had ever possessed. Yet the Turk had given it to him as if it were a bauble. No, thought Theon, taking another deep swig of wine, this Hamza had known exactly its value. And he thought he knew Theon's, the price of board and man, matched. The only thing he hadn't left were his dice. But he'd left a word in their place.

'Traitors,' he whispered.

He felt a push against his leg. Ulvikul was there, nuzzling, purring. Picking him up, Theon turned to the open window and hurled the cat through it.

— FIVE —

Masks

Ragusa (Dubrovnik)
Early December 1452

It was not unusual to hear a woman scream on the streets of Ragusa.

Yet what she screamed was. For it was actually a curse, in Osmanlica, language of the Turk. Before it was cut off, her assailant was being encouraged to perform a deviant act on a camel.

It made Gregoras smile, even as he turned to find a different route home. Then it made him stop, and look at the flagstones. It was unusual for him to care. But he'd spent the night alone again in a tavern . . . and suddenly he decided he'd like to hear how the curse ended.

He did not have to go far. He heard a grunt of pain, hissed words: 'Hold her legs, damn you.' He leaned round the wall, glanced, leaned back.

Five of them, if you included their prey, who was held off the ground by the biggest man there, one arm wrapped around the woman's chest, a hand around her mouth. Her legs were flailing, trying to land kicks, obviously succeeding with some.

He considered. Four men. All of them young. Him coming swiftly from the darkness. Four was not bad odds, he'd faced far worse. Still, he hesitated. What was this to him – a Turkish woman, raped? Even if he succeeded in helping her, he could be hurt, which would hamper him in his mission, the one that would change his life. Why risk his future? For what? Instinct told him to walk away.

Then, from round the corner, he heard a louder yelp of pain – and the curse completed, as if the woman had held her breath this long only for that purpose. Smiling again, he drew his cudgel and stepped round the corner.

The big man had dropped the woman. He was clutching at his ear, trying to stem the blood flowing there.

It was his time. '*Heya*,' Gregoras called softly, moving forward.

The one who turned swiftest to his call was the one Gregoras hit first, a blow delivered with half-force but at the temple, dropping the man on the instant. The youth on the left was reaching to his belt, but the one on the right cleared his scabbard. Grabbing the sleeve of the man on the left, Gregoras jerked it down hard, off-balancing him, at the same time sweeping his cudgel in an upwards arc and hitting the other man's dagger hand just as he was thrusting the weapon forward. There was the crack of bone, a wail, steel clattering against the alley wall.

Gregoras still had the sleeve in his grip. He braced and pulled it again, swinging the youth into the one whose fingers he'd just broken. They locked together, tripping and falling in a heap, clearing the space before Gregoras and the last man standing, the biggest one, with the bleeding ear, just now drawing a sword, bellowing as he raised it above his head.

There were three paces between them. One too many. He raised his cudgel for a throw . . . and then before he could, the last figure before him moved. The woman leapt, dagger leading, its point entering the man's arm just as it was beginning its descent, just above the elbow, the force of the two blows driving the steel in to the hilt.

The man screamed, kept screaming as he dropped his sword, reeled back against the wall. 'God's mercy! Help, help, for a son of Ragusa. For Christ's wounds, help!'

His voice was high-pitched for a large man, but it carried, and shutters were flying open. The three youths on the ground were untangling themselves, screaming too. 'This way, and swiftly,' Gregoras commanded, stepping past the sprawl.

'A moment.' The woman answered in the language he'd used, the one she'd cursed in. She bent to her assailant, who slid down the wall, raising his arms to protect his face, whimpering. But she did not strike him. Instead she grabbed the hilt of the dagger Gregoras saw was still buried in the man's arm, and jerked it out.

The cry was piteous. More were coming from windows, from the labyrinth of alleys ahead. 'Come now,' Gregoras said, turning away. If she did not, he had done all he could.

She came. They did not run. Cries sounded from behind them. 'Thieves! Murderers!' When iron-shod feet came towards them, Gregoras stepped into a doorway, throwing his cloak over both of them, pulling her close. She did not resist, as four of the town guard ran past. And she did not move away as their steps receded.

'Here,' he said, setting off again, turning left, right, right again, left, climbing ever upwards. The uproar faded, blended into the noise of a tavern, a drunken song, the clatter of dice on several boards. It was his local one and he'd planned to stop. But he was known there, as far he ever let himself be known. And he would not want to explain the woman.

In this, the poorer quarter of the city, there was no paving as yet, the city's new edicts not reaching so far. They squelched through the puddles left by the autumn squalls, climbing ever higher. When he felt the sea breeze on his face, saw the night-sky darkness ahead, he felt along the wall to his left. Stone gave onto wood under his fingers. Lifting the latch, he pushed the door in.

He was breathing heavily from the rapid steps, the sudden violence. Leaning against the table, he fumbled for the lamp, nearly spilling it. It was oil-fuelled, its wick kept low, and he turned the wheel that raised it, opened the metal gate. Flickering light made a passage between them. They were both masked. Between scarf and veil, between hat and doublet, their gazes moved, each over the other. The stillness, the silence lasted a few heartbeats before he broke it. 'Are you hurt?'

'No. You saved me from that. Thank you.'

'Well . . .' He was suddenly uncomfortable. 'A woman, alone on the street at night. Speaking in Osmanlica. It was . . .' He paused.

'Did it shock you? I have always been told my language better suits the barracks.' She laughed, a deep sound of sheer pleasure that had him staring harder.

'Shock? No. I have been in a few barracks myself.' He halted, surprised that he'd revealed something about himself. He never did. It was how he lived. 'Why were you alone? Unprotected?'

'I was not unprotected. As you saw.' She lifted the knife she still held. 'Have you water? I would wash that pig's blood from my companion here.'

The sight of blade and blood *did* shock him. And reminded him. It had been so long since anyone but himself had been in his house. 'I am sorry. Yes, water. For yourself. For your . . . friend. To wash. To drink. Or I have wine for that? Though you . . .' He shook his head. 'Being Turkish, you may not drink that.'

'Can I if I speak Greek?' She'd switched languages, her accent as faultless in each.

It was his turn to laugh – and to reply, also in Greek, though he wondered how she had penetrated that mask so quickly when he thought his Osmanlica as flawless as hers. 'Of course. And I will join you.'

He placed the lamp on the table. The room was small, and he barely strayed from its light-spill to fetch what was required. A basin for water, a rough cloth for drying hands and weapons, which she promptly used for both. A stoneware jug of wine. He poured some of that into his only goblet, handed it to her. Raising the flagon, he toasted her. 'To midnight adventures,' he said. Both lifted their masks to drink. Both let them fall again.

'So,' he said, placing the flagon down, leaning on the table. 'I must apologise for my city. It is usually a civilised place. But like most cities it has . . . uncivil elements. And young men are young men anywhere.'

'Young men like you?' she said, raising the empty goblet.

He refilled it. 'But I am not young.'

'It is hard to tell behind that mask.' She sipped, stared. 'Do you ever take it off?'

He pushed himself off the table. 'I have some bread. Some cheese.'

He reached to a bag suspended from the ceiling. From it he pulled a wheel of dense, rough bread, a round of pungent goat's cheese. 'I have no plates,' he apologised.

'It matters not,' she said, breaking off a hunk of each, taking bites. 'And you didn't answer my question.'

'Which was?'

'Do you ever take off your mask?' When he did not move, did not answer, she wiped her fingers on the cloth, then raised them to her veil. 'Come. We have broken bread, drunk wine and fought together on the streets. We speak each other's languages. Why, we're practically cousins. So I'll shock you with my face if you'll shock me with yours.' With that, she removed the silk. Laying it by, she leaned closer to the lamp.

He did not move, scarcely breathed. If she did not have Sofia's nobility, she was pretty for all that. Prettier perhaps, if less beautiful, her almond eyes deep-set, her eyebrows a plucked line of hair, her mouth full, the lower lip swollen as if bruised.

It was her nose he stared at. They always fascinated, their variety, their complexity, the ones that just sat upon a face, the ones that joined with the other parts in expressing the person. Hers did. It was large yet not overly so, her nostrils flaring the challenge that echoed in the raised eyebrow, in the dark eyes. In the words that came now.

'Your turn.'

Those words returned him to himself. He had never had a woman in his house. Had only twice *had* a woman since his disgrace, fumbling, drunken acts of brief satiation and lasting regret. He lifted the lamp, moved away from the table, causing the light to spill onto the horsehair mattress on the floor. 'You may sleep here,' he said, hanging the lamp from a ceiling hook, moving to the door.

'Where do you go?'

He did not turn round. 'Out. To the tavern. I can sleep in a corner there easier than on this floor.'

Her urgent words halted him. 'So I have driven you from your house, from your bed, all because . . . ' She took a step towards him. 'I am sorry. My mother warned me against my unceasing curiosity. There are many reasons why a man would want to remain masked. I shall not presume to find out yours again. Unless, somehow, I earn your permission.'

She had come close as she spoke. He'd turned back and she was there, as near to him as she'd been in the doorway of that alley. He breathed in – and caught her scent.

When the saw-toothed dagger had first descended to take his nose, and his wound clotted with blood and ripped cartilage, he'd believed he would never smell anything again. Eventually he'd discovered he could, if the scents were strong, as hers were. They were a mix of sweetnesses – cinnamon was there, clove. But there was something else too – sandalwood, he realised in a rush of memory. He had not smelled that since his last day in Constantinople, the day he'd set off for his first war . . . and said goodbye to Sofia. That same scent rising from this woman, fragrant, spiced, reminding him of all he'd lost. Her eyes were dark pools and he thought there would be nothing better than to dive into them, swim deep, never come up for air.

'What is your name?'

'Leilah,' she replied. 'And how are you called?'

He hesitated. Everywhere he was known as Zoran. It was a

mask, just like the other. Yet here, now, with her, he wanted to reveal the truth of himself. For some reason, for the first time in the six years since he'd put them on, he wanted someone to see behind the masks.

'My name is Gregoras,' he replied softly, and as he spoke, he reached up and pulled aside the cloth that covered his face.

Even in the shadows by the door, there was light enough to see. He waited for the usual reactions, those he'd seen on the few who'd looked before, the physicians, the whores, the mercenaries. Shock, followed by – depending on who looked – either pity, fascination or mockery. The last two he could handle. It was the first that he had never been able to stand.

He saw none of them now. All he saw was something he'd not seen in anyone's eyes in six years.

Desire.

'Well,' she said, closing the small gap between them, till their clothes touched, 'I have seen wooden ones before, but never . . . is it ivory?'

'Yes.' He reached up, touched the tip of the false nose. 'The carver was a sculptor of Thessalonica. He made me three, for ivory yellows. It is nearly time for me to exchange this one.'

'And it is held on by . . . ?' She looked to the side, to the twin leather straps that braced it high and low and went around his head above his ears. 'It looks tight. Do you ever take it off?'

'When I am here, alone. When I sleep. Sometimes when I fight, if I am not wearing a helmet.'

'A soldier? But of course I knew that.' She took his hand, raised it to her mouth, kissed it. Her eyes never left his. 'Take it off,' she said.

The shock ran through him at her touch, at her command. It was, for him, a mask within a mask. The last concealment. No one saw behind it.

He said nothing. Just bent his head, reached behind to the catches that held the leather straps, flicked them, put the ivory in a pocket. Searched her gaze again.

No shock. No revulsion. No pity. The excitement never wavered in her eyes.

She still held his hand. She tugged it now and, wordlessly, led him to the bed.

Leilah woke to shuttered sunlight striping the man beside her, his face buried in a sprawled arm. She raised herself to stare . . . and smiled. Not at the memory of their lovemaking, intense though it had been. No, it was something else, something even more powerful.

For how often does one gaze upon one's destiny?

She'd had the dream again, in the brief time of sleep. A man, cloaked and hooded, leading her. A locked door. 'Do you have the key?' she'd ask. Only then would he turn to her. Within the hood, he was masked. 'Here,' he would reply, reaching up, pulling the mask away.

Mask falling, door opening, she'd stumble forward, past him, fall onto her knees, reach, finally touch what she'd sought from the moment she'd heard of it, in another man's bed – Isaac's, her previous lover; Isaac the Alchemist, his grey eyes lost to a greater lust than he'd ever felt for her. Lust for the manual of alchemy written by the great Jabir ibn Hayyan, whom others called Geber. The Arab's hand-written notes in the margin. Answers to questions that every alchemist sought. Answers to life itself.

It was in a monastery in the city known as the Red Apple. It would reveal to her the secrets of the world, secrets she could sell to some man for the fortune that would free her of all men. And this one, who stirred beside her now, was going to get it for her.

She always woke from the dream wet with desire – of every kind. '*Heya*,' she called softly.

Gregoras woke. Had he slept? A stronger light was in the sky than the last he remembered and she was against it, her face in shadow. He could see her hair, unbound and flowing over her bare shoulders. See one breast, silhouetted against slats.

She bent to him now, breasts falling onto his shoulder, brushing his bare chest as she kissed him. Her nose pressed into his cheek . . . and he remembered. He was naked before her. Not unclothed, he was not concerned about that. Unmasked.

Yet before he could slip from the bed and seek his protection, she had slid down, curved around him, drawing the covers they'd thrown off over them again. 'I'm cold,' she whispered. 'Warm me.'

Then he remembered that with her, he didn't care about masks.

Their lovemaking was sleep-laden, half a dream, gentle, unlike the fury of the night before. He was aware now of each part of her he touched, when last night they had passed before his eyes, under his hands, his mouth, in a trembling blur of delight. Now he took his time to explore them all. Her breasts, their wine-dark nipples growing, responding to his tongue and teeth. The slope of her belly, its rise and fall, down to her loins, which flooded her thighs like a stream its banks at his stroke. He consumed her, tasting in her the same scents he'd received before, fragrance of spices, of cinnamon and clove. With that scent behind them all: sandalwood, its memories ignored now, the past conceded to the delights of the present. While she took an equal delight in him, moving now above, now below, up him and down, tracing his many scars with different parts of herself, running the length of him with fingers, tongue, with the firmness of a nipple, exploring his varied hardnesses.

In the end, their cries came together, but softly, as if daylight restrained their voices, though there was nothing held back, nothing not given.

She lay for a while with her elbows on his chest, studying him. There was a different kind of hunger in her gaze, disturbing him. Despite her protests, he managed to untwine himself.

There was a small porch at the back of his hovel, walled in, but open to the sky. He kept his water there, and a pail to relieve himself in. He did so now, aching slightly, smiling at the ache. Stood there afterwards, staring at the blue sky, despite the chill breeze — until he heard her call from within. Filling a flagon with water from the brimming rain barrel, he returned to the room.

He was disappointed to see her in her shift. 'Do you leave?' he said.

'Soon. And it was cold in here without you.'

'Well, now I am back. With water,' he said, lifting the jug.

She was taming her hair, catching it up with pins. 'Ah, that I would like.'

He rinsed his one goblet out, throwing the dregs of wine out of the window, refilling it with rainwater. Bringing it to her, he said, 'Shall we return to the bed?'

'I would like that.' She pushed the last pin in. 'But I must go.'

'Must?' he asked.

'The tides. My captain swore he'd abandon me if I was not back at the harbour by noon.'

'Captain?'

'Of the ship I came on. I am on my way . . . elsewhere. We were blown into this port by the storm. I was seeking an inn last night when those men . . .' She shrugged.

'Oh.' He bent to his discarded clothes, fetched out the ivory nose. With practised hands he secured it.

'You need not do that for me,' she said.

'I do it for myself,' he replied, reaching for a shirt.

Silence came as they sipped. Of course she is leaving, Gregoras thought. Why would she stay? He didn't like the feeling he had. Wanted her gone now, so the feeling would go too. But he found himself asking something else. Opposite.

'Do you have to go?'

'I do.' She laughed as she saw the look on his face. 'But I can return soon. If you would like me to. I do not travel far.'

'I would like you to,' he said, too swiftly. Then he remembered. 'Yet I must also travel today. I will be gone a . . . a few months. And then I will return.' He hesitated – then said it anyway. 'Will you meet me here?'

She considered him – and remembered her dream. 'Here? Perhaps we could meet somewhere . . . warmer?' She looked around and smiled. 'With furniture?'

He looked around also, saw the room as she saw it. Lost in lust, they could have been anywhere. But in the morning light . . .

'Come with me,' he said suddenly, putting down the water jug, taking her hand. He led her across the room to the other shuttered window. Throwing it back, he said, 'Look!'

'At what?'

'At the view.'

She laughed, looked. It was indeed a sight. They were high up in the town. To their left it fell away in swoops of red-tiled roofs, houses leaning over the alleys that threaded the town. Directly below them, a stone's throw away, the walls of the city followed the land, dipping straight ahead, giving an un-interrupted view out to a sea that sparkled in the winter sun. Xebecs, with their slanted red-striped sails, and tall-sided carracks tacked against the wind, making for harbour. In the near distance, an island thrust pine-covered slopes toward the sky.

'I own the house, but it was this,' Gregoras said, 'that I paid so much gold for. Now I need much more, and I will build something worthy of it.' He swept his arm against the expanse of sky and sea. 'There was a poet who lived in Byzantium near a thousand years ago. His name was Paul and he said, "A room with a good view is a surer possession than virtue."' He laughed. 'Since I possess few virtues, I will settle for my view.'

Byzantium, she thought, content that he'd mentioned the place of her dream. 'Why here?' she said. 'Why not there?' She leaned closer to him, continued softly, 'For you are of Con-stantinople, are you not?'

His eyes narrowed above the ivory. 'How do you know that?'

'I live my life from knowing people,' she replied. 'Your accent is from the East, its tone refined. I would guess you are from the city, and well born.'

He grunted his reply. 'Perhaps.'

'Then why not return there? The views your poet speaks of are there.' Her eyes searched his. 'So is your heart, is it not?'

'No!' He was surprised at the savagery with which he shouted it – until he remembered what he'd already revealed to this stranger. And so he did not hold himself back, as he had not held back before. 'That city took my heart and crushed it. It took my face and destroyed it. It is a sickened place, it is about to receive its mortal wound and I . . . I could not be happier.' He turned to gaze out to the east, his voice quietening, yet losing none of its intensity. 'I will never return there, not even to gloat among its blackened stones. Never!'

Passion again, of a different kind. Leilah liked her men to be passionate. And she was always interested when a man declared he would not do the very thing he must.

In the silence after his storm, a bell tolled. She counted ten. 'I must go,' she said, turning.

Anger passed from his face. 'As must I.' He reached, caught her hand. 'But I meant it when I said I would like you to return.'

'And I was serious when I said I would like to.' She squeezed his fingers hard, then stepped away. 'Do you have anywhere for my . . . relief?'

He gestured to the back door. She picked up her bag, went out onto the walled porch. She squatted, then used rainwater to wash herself, shivering the while.

By the time she returned, Gregoras was dressed. She finished dressing too, and finally they both donned their masks. Once done, they drew back and stared at each other. 'Well,' she said finally, 'I prefer you bare.'

He chuckled. 'And I you. But the stone merchants I go to meet might not.'

As he opened the door, he stooped beside it to pick up a bag and something else. She smiled. 'Will the stone merchants appreciate a crossbow?'

He laughed again. 'There is good hunting where I will visit.'

She studied the weapon. It was a fine example, plain, unadorned. Purposeful. She had one much like it upon the boat. 'Are you good with it?'

'A journeyman, merely.'

They did not speak again as he guided her down the alleys to the harbour, along the docks to her vessel. The captain eyed them suspiciously before taking her bag.

Leilah turned back, but Gregoras was already walking away. 'You know where I am,' he called. 'Return, if you will.'

She did not mind that his farewell was gruff. Besides, she enjoyed seeing the vision from her dream so clearly realised on a sparkling Ragusan dock. She was almost tempted to follow him, to see if he would lead her right then to Geber's book. But then she remembered: destiny awaited in another city, the one he swore he would never return to, the one that he was walking towards now – though by what path, for once, she could not see.

SIX

The Rescue

'There is only one way for a gentleman of Scotland to face death, you coo's arse,' John Grant declared, 'and that is, once he has made his peace with God, to get completely, utterly and overwhelmingly drunk!'

He spoke it in his native Gaelic, letting his tongue and throat shape and expand the guttural qualities that his audience loved to hear. They presumed him German and would not believe anything else. But as he lifted his goblet high while declaiming it, they took it for the latest in a series of incomprehensible toasts and pledged him back with roars and the draining of vessels.

He sat down heavily. It was getting harder and harder to stand. Next pledge he'd do sitting down. The one after perhaps prone. When he could speak no more, when his eyes closed and his head finally fell onto his arms, someone would come along and cut it off.

It was getting close to that time. He could tell by the way the room shifted to his gaze, and because the dozen faces in the cellar had begun to blur into just one – round, sweaty, flushed with aqua vitae, creased with tears. They were a sentimental lot, the pirates of Omis. They had grown fond of him. Stanko repeatedly declared that he loved the German like a brother, like a son. But Grant knew the pirate leader had killed several of each. They had grown even fonder of what he made them in his captivity – for distillation was an important part of his alchemical studies and he was fond of a dram himself. So now the pirates shed tears for both, liquor and life, coming to an end. They had given him a week, to complete one last batch. It was up.

Moving his head slowly to the left, Grant squinted at the fire beneath the cauldron. Closing one eye, he focused – and saw that the flames had got low. He checked the seals around the main glass vessel, and especially where the alembic joined the stag's horn; grunted with pride. He had fashioned a fine still. Even Geber, the Arab master whose few writings he devoured, might have been impressed, considering the poverty of the raw materials he'd worked with. Yet now there was only a little more distillation to be had from the fermented oranges in the vessel's belly. His life would be measured in one last burst of steam collected, in the drops that . . . dripped.

Life was irksome. He was ready.

He leaned, toppled. Giggling, he righted himself and shoved hunks of wood onto the fire. Bending, he blew exaggeratedly. Stanko, the chief, bent beside him, blew as well, covering the Scot in spittle. Flames grew, lapped wood. 'Still more?' the pirate yelled.

'A little.'

'Good. Drink!'

They clattered mugs. 'Craigelachie,' the Scotsman shouted. It was the war cry of the clan Grant, a rallying call for the men to gather on the hilltop so named and repel all enemies. He hadn't cried it in his life in recent years. His clan, his family, he was an exile from their lands, from their regard. But now that his life was about to end, he wanted to be connected to them in some way.

'I love you, German.' Stanko grabbed him by the back of his head, pulling him close. 'You are like a son to me.'

The words were kind. But Grant saw the cunning eyes, sunk in the sweaty face like olives in flatbread. Saw where they moved – around his neck, envisaging the cut that would sever. The head Stanko caressed would soon be floating in a pail of the liquor they all craved – though they would lament the waste – and on its way to the sultan.

'And you are a lover of pigs,' John Grant replied in English, smiling. He loved to insult them in languages, of which he spoke seven, and of which they understood not a word. He raised his mug again. 'Craigelachie,' he yelled, throwing on more wood

Gregoras was getting increasingly uncomfortable. Not so much with his perch in the bell tower of Santa Emilia, though it was colder than that saint's tits, the wind finding every scar and ache in his body and jabbing them. What jabbed most was that in the time he'd sat there, close to two hours, at least ten men had gone into the house opposite him and only two had come out. Each time one entered, he would hear bursts of singing, toasts, sentences of execrable Croat poetry. Heat would rise too, making him shiver all the more.

The night had come, perhaps even the hour. The victim's name was a secret and so, in the taverns he'd visited, it had been proclaimed in the loudest of whispers.

Johannes Grant, German, was about to die. And the site of execution was no secret either. Who was going to tangle with the pirates of Omis in their own nest?

Am I? Gregoras wondered. He'd begun to doubt it as the pirates' numbers grew with his stiffness. He knew what he should do: return to the vessel he'd hired, make sail for Ragusa. The odds were too great. He was too late.

And if he did? He'd be sailing back to a hovel. The ducats he'd been advanced had bought him the stone for his house. The finest came from Korcula and he had used that business as cover for this other. But he needed the balance for the masons to build it. Besides, the advance would have to be repaid if he failed. One didn't fail Giustiniani. He would lose all.

He had no choice – and could wait no longer. Cursing, he descended to the *ulica* and waited till two more pirates came swaying up the hill and went in. Cursing still, he followed.

At first he thought that he'd stumbled into an alchemist's den. An uncle had dabbled in the hermetic art, and he'd had equipment such as this. But Gregoras swiftly realised that the main scent was not of heated metals, but of oranges. It was not the philosopher's stone that was being conjured here, but what the Arabs called *al-kohl.*

He was in a small distillery.

From being near frozen, Gregoras was immediately – and unpleasantly – warm. Apart from the equipment, fifteen pirates were belching and farting as a musical accompaniment to the many toasts they gave. But at least the fug meant that he was not the only one masked. He would not immediately be spotted as an intruder. Besides, everyone's focus was on the room's centre. On one man there.

He had seen this before. Death's approach drew everyone's attention. Hell or heaven beckoned. There was life and soon there was to be its opposite, and the transition fascinated. No one wanted to miss a moment.

But this man would have been hard not to stare at. In contrast to the pirates, generally shaped like barrels, he was tall and slender. They were dressed in a motley collection of colours, he in soberest black. Their faces were as rounded as their bellies, his thin and long. What separated them most, though, was the colouring. The pirates to a man had the black hair and burned complexions of their race and trade. Their prisoner was so white he looked as if he had never seen the sun, but had spent his life underground, in places such as this. A pallor only emphasised by the long, curly red hair that fringed his face in a halo of flame.

In only one way was the condemned man akin to his captors – he was utterly, sprawlingly drunk.

Beneath his mask, Gregoras licked his lips. He could have used a draught himself. But vying for the barrel that the newcomers were even now tipping on its side, seeking dregs, would have drawn attention he would prefer to avoid.

It was hopeless. And he could sense that the bloody climax was approaching. The flames beneath the cauldron were lapping violently up its sides, steam was escaping from cracked seals, forming on the ceiling and running in sudden spurts onto men who yelped, then leaned closer. While the roundest, sweatiest pirate there had just taken his hand from the back of the prisoner's head and was now fumbling beneath his robes.

Hopeless. Gregoras turned to go. He had no desire to witness life's sudden end. He'd seen it enough, from very close at hand.

Then the prisoner spoke – and the language halted him. He had spent half a year shackled on a slave galley's bench with nothing to do but row, try not to die . . . and learn the tongue of the slave shackled next to him.

The words were spoken in English. And they turned Gregoras back into the room, with a little hope.

The words were: 'Come on then, ye bastard. At least I'll have some company at the gates of hell.'

With liquor, it was always a puzzling transition for John Grant. One moment he was happily laughing at the situation – in this case, the absurdity of him, a lad from Strathspey, dying in some cellar God-knows-where, at the hands of pirates, Christ on a carthorse, at the behest of the Turk, may his liver boil, for knowledge he was sure he no longer possessed. The next he was angry. No, not merely angry: red-eyed furious. He had it from his father. One moment the mellowest of drunks, the next, striking out at any he could reach for reasons he didn't explain.

Well, John Grant had his reasons. These fish-fuckers were going to kill him. He had little fear of dying and few reasons to linger longer in this world. He'd given up all he loved when he'd taken the exile's road. He had found nothing worth living for upon it. But that didn't mean he wished his death to serve this sea scum's purposes. And after he'd made them the finest aqua vitae seen in this desert of decent *al-kohl*?

Ingratitude, that was it. Ingratitude had always made him mad. Like the time he was expelled from the university in St Andrews just because he blew up a very small barn. Had he not been close to a major chemical revelation? And when he returned to his glen to share his discoveries with his family, his clan, they rejected him. Well, he'd show them too.

There was a toast they gave at home and John Grant spoke it as he slowly unfolded himself from behind the table. It was usually pledged to someone else, but Grant decided to give it to himself. 'May I be half an hour in heaven before the devil knows I'm dead,' he whispered in Gaelic.

Stanko had found what he'd sought in his robes and produced it now – one of the largest and dirtiest knives Grant had ever seen. 'What do you say, German?' he said, his piggy eyes narrowing as he tried to focus on the man rising before him.

John Grant looked down. 'This,' he replied, in Croat this time, pulling a small stoppered vial from his belt. 'And for the last bloody time, I'm Scots, you pig's arse.' Flicking the plug off, he lifted a seal from the still, squinted against the sudden gush of steam that exploded out, and tipped the contents of the vial in.

Gregoras was already moving. He had been in his uncle's cellar once when a mistake had been made. Something added in incorrect proportions. The results had been devastating.

He heard the whine of the still, saw froth bubbling from its seals. Stanko saw him coming. 'Who are you?' he said, starting to rise, turning to his men. 'Who's this cunt?'

Gregoras grabbed an edge of the table. It was not huge, but it was solid oak and he had to bend to tip it over onto its side. Then he jumped over it and yanked the red-haired man over it too.

There was a moment of silence. Silent men anyway, for the equipment was still frothing and emitting a low, almost animal groan. Until Stanko leaned over the table and stared blearily down. 'What are you doing?' he asked.

Gregoras peered up. He couldn't think of anything to say. And then he didn't have to, because the room exploded.

The force of it drove the table back, tipping it against them. Men screamed, some in terror, some in instant agony, as pieces of metal and glass drove into flesh. There had been a few lamps, but all of these were blown out save one that hung from a hook on the ceiling. It wasn't dislodged but swung violently from side to side, shafts of light piercing the acrid smoke that almost instantly filled the room. Those who weren't screaming were coughing.

Someone must have got the single door open, because there was a sudden rush of air, the smoke sucked away. Gregoras shook the cloak, dislodging the debris that had accumulated. His face and the Scot's were about a hand's breadth apart.

'And who, by Christ, are you?' John Grant asked, in Croat.

There was no time to reply before another voice interrupted. 'That was my question.'

Stanko was looking down at them again, the same bemused expression as before in the too-close-together eyes. Only one thing was different, Gregoras noticed. The pirate chief now had a large shard of glass sticking through his neck. He seemed to notice it too, the moment Gregoras did. He squinted at what protruded just below his chin, reached fingers up to explore. When he touched one jagged end, his eyes rolled up in his head and he fell away from their view.

Gregoras was up on the instant, dragging the Scot to standing, assessing the room. Those who were not badly wounded or dead were dazed, coughing against the lingering smoke, staring wide-eyed before them. 'Come, and quickly,' he said, and tugged the other man around the table and over the writhing pirate chief.

'A moment.' John Grant dipped down and snatched up a satchel that had spilled to the floor. He straightened. 'Guud. Now, where are we going?' Grant was staring amiably at the havoc they were stepping through. His ears were still ringing with the explosion, which had also driven out his previous fury. A man was leading him somewhere. Speaking English of all languages. He thought it unlikely that a demon guiding him to hell would be speaking English. Or perhaps the words of his last toast were being honoured: the devil didn't know he was dead yet, with so many more obvious sinners to deal with.

No one stirred to stop them as they crossed the cellar floor. It was only when they reached the foot of the stairs that a voice came out with more than moans. 'Stop them,' Stanko said, lifting himself off the floor.

He was used to being obeyed, and swiftly. Stunned though they were, those who were still alive in the cellar rose to do so. 'Go,' Gregoras yelled, pushing the other man hard, drawing a small dagger at the same time. As the Scot stumbled up the stairs, the first pirate lunged at Gregoras. Ducking, he jabbed up, putting the blade swiftly, shallowly into the flesh just beneath his attacker's chin. The man collapsed in the doorway with a cry. It was not a mortal wound, but he had lost blades in men when he had struck too deep and he had a feeling he would need all the weapons he had in what lay ahead. Besides, a blood-gushing pirate in the entranceway might slow the pursuit a little.

He turned to the stairs. The Scot was sprawled across them. 'Ma legs dinna seem to want to work,' he giggled. Bending, Gregoras got his arms around the other man's chest and heaved him to his feet. Grant was all height and little weight but he was still not easy to drag up stairs. Gaining level ground, Gregoras ran the two of them down a small corridor, shoved Grant hard against the front door, reached round him to the handle, turned it and threw the Scot into the street, where he fell straight down, curled himself up and sighed.

Gregoras looked both ways. No one seemed yet to have reacted to the explosion – though from behind him he could hear Stanko roaring, the man he'd knifed screaming and feet crashing onto the stairs.

He bent to the prone man. 'Listen,' he hissed. 'If those men catch us, they'll kill us both. I have no intention of dying in this fleapit town. So either you get up and run, or I'll let them spill your guts into the gutter.'

John Grant rolled onto his back. 'Beautifully phrased, my friend. For did not the great Homer say . . .' He belched extravagantly, assumed a pose to declaim.

'Fuck Homer,' Gregoras shouted. 'Run!'

John Grant ran. The first few steps were to one side, the next to the other. But with Gregoras seizing an arm, the two of them began to make progress up the narrow, wet, steeply ascending street. They'd gone twenty paces before the first pirate emerged, and bellowed, 'There! They are—'

His last word was cut off. Something took him in the back, throwing him forward. The two men ran on.

Leilah wasn't sure why she shot. Instinct, she supposed. She had heard the faint crump of an explosion, then seen Gregoras bursting onto the street, accompanied by another. Relief at seeing him was mixed with puzzlement – she'd watched him go in from her vantage in the abandoned house. But who was that with him? Then the two had begun running, a pursuer had emerged and she had shot. It was only when the man fell that she looked again at the fleeing men – and caught a glimpse of this other as he passed beneath a lamp above some better-off-citizen's door. His hair was red. A brighter red than she had seen even sported by the whores of Aleppo. It was not a red you saw often in the Adriatic; it belonged more to northern races than the darker locals.

And then she realised who he must be. When she'd rapidly left the tavern Gregoras had entered the previous night, she'd guessed he'd been there for the same purpose as she. Now they were bound to each other, did it matter which of them got the Turk's reward? But the swaying, fleeing figures told her different – he was there to rescue the German.

She'd wasted her bolt. And her quarry had turned a corner. Snatching up bag and crossbow, she ran down the stairs and opened the door onto the *ulica* just as more pirates ran out of the house. A large man was shouting louder than the others, one hand clutching a long, curved sword, the other clamped to his neck.

She counted three, and followed.

It was not easy manoeuvring a drunk over slick cobbles. Shouts behind pushed Gregoras on, and the two men soon stumbled into the main square. It was at the top of the hill, the town built below and around it. Over the square loomed the bulk of the cathedral, St Marka, and Gregoras ran into its shadows, pausing for breath and thought.

Streets ran off down the hill from the square on both sides. In his brief stay there he had learned that the former lords of the island, the Venetians, had taken advantage of its siting to construct a unique system of air flow. For when the harsh winter *bura* blew, it could chill the stone balls of a statue. So the streets on the side of the town that faced it were curved to minimise the wind's chilling effect. But the other side of the island would receive the mistral. In high summer heat, that wind could cool. So the *ulicas* that faced it were made straight to air the town.

If he ran down one street, the way curved. Far harder to shoot the bows that many of the pirates would carry. If they ran down the other . . . they would be easy targets all the way to the water.

But as he stood in the shadow of the cathedral, pursuers' voices getting ever closer, Gregoras could not remember whether the curved ones were to the left or the right. Nearing shouts meant he had to choose. And the decision could cost his life.

He poked the man beside him, and got a snore in reply. Putting one hand over the man's mouth, he jabbed harder with the other. 'Listen, Englishman,' he whispered in that tongue, as Grant's eyes opened, 'we have to run now, and run fast, or we die. If you wish to do that, you can stay here till they find you. But I am going.'

'And I'm coming with ye.' John Grant had only slept for one minute. But he'd woken with an awful pounding in his head – and the equally vivid certainty that, despite the pain, he wanted to live. 'By the by, I'm not bloody English, all right?'

The two men got into a crouch. Yelling pirates burst into the square. Gregoras seized an arm and moved. Right.

Wrong. As soon as he entered the *ulica* he knew it. He could see lights in the distance – ship lamps on water. The alley ran straight to it.

Shouts came from behind them. 'There!' they heard Stanko cry. 'A gold *hyperpyron* for each of their heads!'

'Run,' Gregoras yelled.

The two men ran. Almost immediately something glanced off the left wall and skittered down the street. 'Arrows. Weave!' Gregoras commanded, darting to the side.

'What, you mean like this?' John Grant muttered. He always woke up sarcastic after too much aqua vitae. Wet cobbles, slickened from an overflowing gutter, and smooth leather boot soles took care of his swerving. As it was, he had to fight to keep upright and moving, his long body jerking up and down for balance, more sliding than running, like a boy on ice.

He fell and Gregoras, grabbing for him, went down too. Arrows flew overhead where they'd been. Judging from the cries behind them, men were tumbling there too.

Behind them all, at the top of the *ulica*, Leilah halted. She regarded the sliding, slipping men, the pursuers and the pursued, and smiled. Yet she did not dwell on the humour of the spectacle but pulled a bolt from the quiver and placed it in her mouth. Unslinging her hunting bow from her back, she put her foot in the stirrup, bent, breathed deep and with three fingers smoothly drew the string up till it notched. She took the bolt, moistened her lips, drew the feathers over the wetness, evening the flights, then lifted the crossbow and laid the bolt in its groove. A near-full moon gave her light enough to see. And since the *bura* was blowing on the other side of the island, wind did not affect the straight street. The men's jerking movements did, the way they blended together and suddenly flew apart. She had to be careful. She did not wish to shoot her man of destiny.

She saw the German fall again, heard the pirates whoop as they ran faster, closer. She believed that Gregoras would survive, because she had seen him in that dream, in her charts. The other, the engineer that Mehmet feared would thwart his conquest, she had no mystical thoughts about. She only knew that to aid that conquest, and all that it would bring her, he must die.

It was in Allah's hands, as ever. As the men below merged into a mass, then separated out again, she breathed out on one word – '*Inshallah*' – and shot.

Gregoras snatched at the German or Englishman or whatever the hell he was, who was falling again, with two of their pursuers less than twenty paces off. Another group of five, including the shouting Stanko, were the same distance behind.

Thinking briefly that he'd had better odds in that other alley in Ragusa, cross-handed he drew his dagger and falchion – the short, heavy-bladed weapon ideal, for the *ulica* was narrow. The two pirates skittered, slowing, curved swords appearing from beneath folds of cloak. He braced himself, wondering which of them he should take first.

A hand closed over his dagger hand. 'Gie me one of them,' John Grant cried. 'I'll show 'em, murderin' bastards.' As he fumbled for Gregoras's dagger, he raised his leather satchel high like a shield and cried, 'Craigelachie.'

'Let me go.' Gregoras wrenched free of the other man's grip, and turned – too late to do more than lift his blade against the one that fell. Steel clashed on steel with a force that sent pain shooting through his arm. The second man arrived a second after the first, his sword about to fall too. Gregoras threw up his dagger blade square across his head, though he was sure the scimitar would snap it.

The curved blade never fell. Something opened in the assailant's throat like a second mouth, spewing forth steel. A crossbow bolt, barely hindered by neck gristle, slammed into Grant's still-raised satchel, knocking him over.

The other man stepped back, giving himself room to swing. Closing, Gregoras punched him with the falchion's curved finger guard, straight and hard on the nose. The man went down, wrapped in his dying companion. Beyond them, the other pirates had caught up. Yet their eagerness had increased their speed. Trying to stop before their fallen, writhing comrades, the first two lost their feet, slammed onto the ground, slid into what became a mound of bodies. Those behind them, Stanko leading, fared no better.

A flesh wall blocked the alley It was a chance. 'Go,' Gregoras yelled, lifting and turning the stunned Scot, pushing him from stumble to run.

Leilah had just raised the crossbow, loaded again and brought it to sight, when the two figures disappeared round the corner. She lowered the weapon, watched the pile of pirates finally separate, rise, run, leaving the man she'd killed by mistake on the cobbles. She considered pursuing, taking another shot. But Korcula's citizens were stirring, roused by the mayhem. Doors were opening, voices screaming for the night watch. She would find it hard to explain her armed self, once they discovered she was a she. It was time to vanish.

As the yelling pirates rounded the corner, Leilah aimed into the sky, pulled the trigger. It was a waste of one of her beautifully fashioned bolts, but she couldn't remove it to shoot; it was too hard on the weapon, all the energy that should have launched the projectile jarring to the stock and bow, while straining the braided rope that bound them together.

As she turned back into the square, filling with the first of the townsfolk, she shrugged. She would have another chance to catch up with this German, if Allah willed it. If not . . .

'*Inshallah*,' she said. Pulling the crossbow over her shoulder, covering herself and it with her cape, she headed down one of the curving alleys towards her vessel.

Gregoras had left his skiff in a cluster of similar fishing boats, indistinguishable each from the other. But he had told its Ragusan captain to hang a red lamp from his mast, and it was this that he spotted as he burst out of the water gates and onto the docks. 'There,' he yelled, shoving his companion towards it. Glancing back, he saw the pursuit emerge from the gateway, halt, spot them, start running again. They had barely a hundred and fifty paces of lead. He could only hope that the considerable purse he'd given the captain had bought obedience. His order had been to keep the sails furled on the mast, oars in the rowlocks and the vessel on a single tie, ready to cast off fast.

They reached the boat. The captain rose from behind the gunwales. In a glance, Gregoras saw that he had not been obeyed. Three ropes held the vessel to the dock. The sail lay in folds upon the deck.

Shouts came from behind them as he and Grant scrambled aboard, the small vessel tipping with their weight and velocity. Steadying, Gregoras bellowed, 'Cast off!'

The man shook his head. 'Feel that?' He tipped his head into the breeze. 'You know what they say: "When the *bura* sails, you don't."'

Instead of hot anger, Gregoras felt as cold as that wind. '*You* don't,' he said, and bending at the knees, he placed his hand in the other man's chest, stood straight and launched the captain over the side of his vessel into the water. Using his falchion, he slashed the three ropes in three sharp strokes. 'Row!' he yelled, then leaned over to the dock, giving it a huge shove. The boat moved away, as Grant gathered the oars and dropped them into their locks.

The first two pirates had reached the jetty and were running down it, screaming. The rest were close behind. Reaching over his shoulder, Gregoras lifted his crossbow above his head with one hand, the other delving into the quiver at his hip. Thrusting the front end onto the deck, he shoved his foot into the stirrup, pulled the string to its notch, had the weapon raised as he dropped the bolt into its channel. There was no question of aiming, no time to do so. The closer of the pirates was three paces away when he pulled the trigger.

The bolt sent the pirate flying back, his sword arm smashing into the other's face. Both sprawled on the dock. Grant had got one oar in, was struggling with the other. Dropping his weapon, Gregoras grabbed the second oar, leaned out and pushed it against the jetty. A big shove, and some current began to take them. There was now a patch of water between them and their pursuers.

An arrow smacked into the mast. Dropping the other oar into its lock, Gregoras shouted, 'Row,' and bent again for his bow.

Stanko had seen his dreams of Turkish gold explode in his cellar. Then they were running away from him down an alley. Now they were on a boat, drifting forever and finally beyond his reach. Unless . . .

Vaulting over his prone men, he leapt into the water.

Gregoras turned at the huge splash in time to see the pirate chief surface and, in three strong strokes, propel himself to the boat's side. When he grabbed it, his weight tipped it, and Gregoras thought they were going to capsize. Only by throwing himself backwards was that avoided. But now he could only watch helplessly as the man used the counterweight to haul himself up over the gunwales. Gregoras saw moonlight reflect in the jagged piece of glass still sticking straight through the man's neck. Why hadn't it killed the bastard? he wondered, as he reached for his dagger and waited for a chance to do just that.

Stanko had pulled his body half over when an oar rose out of its lock and the blade end was thrust forward. Not into the man's face. Not to smash his grip on the wood. Straight into the glass that protruded from his neck.

'And *that's* for calling me a bloody German,' John Grant cried.

It was surprising that the pirate had lived so long. It didn't take much movement of the glass to sever the artery, so close it must have been. Stanko looked as if he wanted to say something. But he didn't. Just lost his grip and sank slowly back into reddening water.

Gregoras was not so stunned that he did not leap forward to balance the boat again. When he finally did grab and load his crossbow, he did not shoot. The five left on the dock had no weapons raised, showed no desire for a swim. They were all just staring at the floating body of their former chief.

One at each oar, Gregoras and Grant steered their vessel between the tied-up fishing smacks. Soon they were clear of them and nosing into the choppy waters at the edge of the harbour mouth. Free of the shelter of the hilly island, the wind was blowing from behind them, bobbling them about. Without talk, the two men got the sail up, and Gregoras was relieved to see that Grant appeared to know more about it than he did. In fact, he soon left him to it and, finding that his legs were a little wobbly, sat down.

Something poked into his thigh. He reached, discovered the Scotsman's satchel and, sticking from it, a crossbow quarrel.

He jerked it out. Its steel tip was red with congealing blood, but it was the flights that made him stare harder. For they were not thin pieces of wood, slotted into curved grooves, as was most common. These were of feather – heron's, he thought, by their grey-blue tips. Feather flights had to be glued on, and the helix that would spin the bolt in flight required a fine judgement of both eye and finger in the making. He knew because it was a style of bolt he would fashion himself, before a campaign began, and save for a special shot. Once used up, he rarely had time to make more, would revert to their easily acquired, wood-fletched cousins. He'd thought such skill beyond a pirate's patience, to be sure.

He shivered, glanced back . . . but Korcula was lost to night. And so was the bowman, who, he decided, they'd been lucky to survive.

SEVEN

Rendezvous

John Grant leaned upon the railing, doing what most of the men aboard were doing — trying to disperse with prayer the mist that had trapped them for three days. The breath of Circe, it was called. The witch's exhalation blinded ships like theirs, luring them onto the rocks.

He licked his lips, as ever craving more than the wine that had passed over them on their three-week voyage — by skiff, fishing boat and, at last, this carrack — from Korcula. Something stronger might fill the void he felt whenever he thought of what was being asked of him. He was a good engineer, a builder-up and knocker-down of stone. A delver beneath the earth. He could wield a sword, if he must. Yet his life had been saved for quite a different skill he was rumoured to possess.

Anger came with the fear. The skill was to do with an ancient weapon of war. One that had saved the city of Constantinople more than once from Islam's assault. But it was a Greek invention. It was named for them. So why, by the Pope's shrivelled balls, did the Greeks need a Scotsman to rediscover it for them?

Grant sighed. Like the pirates, it was the chemist's art his new patrons required. As with a distillation of fruit or barley, there were elements to be mixed in precise measures to achieve the required effect. It was the proportion of those elements that had been lost. The formula. It was said that an angel whispered it into the ear of the first emperor of the city, for whom it was named: Constantine.

'Whisper it to me,' Grant muttered. Closing his eyes, he

again did what he rarely did, had done so little since he left his home. He prayed. 'Oh merciful and most just God, if it be Thy will, remove the scales from Thy unworthy servant's eyes. Help him to see.'

Head bent, eyes closed, he stood awhile in silent contemplation. Until someone stepped up to the rail beside him and spoke. 'At last,' said Gregoras.

Grant opened his eyes. It was as if that same Circe who had breathed it out was now sucking the mist back in. Shafts of sunlight pierced it from a winter-blue sky, and a steep-hilled island was before them, barely a quarter-league away. They were heading straight for it, moving fast towards a harbour that looked like a beech forest in winter, the masts of a multitude of ships like so many leafless trees.

Gregoras let out a whoop. 'He's even better than we thought, our captain. For there she lies, our destination, right before us.'

'It is?' Grant turned. 'You never told me where the rendezvous was.'

The other man smiled. 'Did I not?' He pointed. 'It is there.'

'Aye. And what is its name?'

'The island of Chios.'

'What? Chios!' Grant cried the name, joyfully.

Gregoras smiled at him. 'Our destination pleases you?'

Grant swallowed, nodded. 'Never has an unworthy sinner had a prayer answered so quickly. For if I'm to do what you all believe I can, I will need pine resin. And the best, the most stable gum, comes from *Pinus halepensis*.' He smiled at Gregoras's head shake. 'The Aleppo pine.' He pointed ahead. 'This island is covered in them.'

'Well, I am pleased also.' Gregoras nodded. 'I was concerned that my commander may already have set out. But there he sits – that banner at the largest carrack's masthead proclaims that Giovanni Giustiniani Longo is still here. So let's to him. You to get your gum, me to claim my gold.' He clapped the other man on the back. 'And may the new year bring you such answers to all your prayers.' He turned to the stairs that led to the hold and their meagre gear.

Grant did not move. 'The new year?'

'Aye, man. Today is the first day of it.' Gregoras smiled at the Scot, a man he'd grown to much like in their three weeks of journeying. 'Welcome to 1453.'

She'd stood on the terrace for a long time, wrapped only in a thin blanket; offered her discomfort as penance, staring at the mist, willing it gone, praying it gone. With the *lodos* wind strong in the sails, her city was only three days away. She had thought to be back there a week before, to have celebrated Christ's birth with her children. But someone else would have baked them the sweet chestnut cake, lit the festive candles, sung the songs, intoned the special prayers before the family altar. She was still on Chios, trapped in chill greyness. The room behind her blazed with flame. But it felt colder within than where she kept her vigil. For her husband was there, and he had not spoken to her in three days.

Sofia held her breath, leaned forward, not willing to hope. The mist had played games with her sight before; shapes had appeared in it, demons and angels. People. She'd seen Gregoras there, Gregoras from before, not . . . as she tried never to imagine him now, as she had seen him only in uneasy dreams. Gregoras as he'd been, laughing, always laughing, and her with him. What had they laughed about so much? She'd never been able to remember. People, she supposed, for he had a wicked mind and a voice shaped for mimicry. And she did too, though she found it hard to imagine, since she laughed only secretly now with her children and she tried not to be wicked with them.

Yes! It was true, the mist that had bewitched the island for ten days was lifting, like a veil drawn back by the hand of God. At its lifting, a vessel appeared, full wind in its sails, driving hard towards the land. She looked at the sky she had not seen for so long, its raw blueness, seeking some hint that this was mere caprice in a pagan god, that Circe would breathe out again and swamp the world once more in grey. But it was going, fleeing . . . gone. Almost as if it had never been.

She closed her eyes to the sunlight, feeling a bit of warmth in it though it was only the first day of a new year. Breathed deep of the clear, the no-longer-wet air. Then she turned and went back into the room.

'The mist has lifted.'

Theon, crouched over papers, spectacles on his nose, peered at her. 'Hmm?'

'The mist. It is gone.'

'Good.' He took his spectacles off, rubbed between his eyes. 'Then we can get off this rock and go home. We should have left while we could, before this damned fog trapped us.'

'Yes.' She stepped towards him. 'The Genoan was waiting for someone, was he not? That was why he delayed. Do you know if that someone arrived?'

'How would I?' he replied sharply. 'Do you think I make a habit of chatting with . . . mercenaries?'

The last word was spat with such venom. There was a time – the time of laughter with Gregoras, perhaps – when she would have spoken her feelings, born of several conversations she'd had with him – for Giustiniani liked the dinner-time company of women. She'd have said that behind his roaring surface, the Commander was a courteous, kindly man; that if he took gold, there were few who did not, and he was not one of those who fought only for that. Indeed it was said he had given away nearly all that was meant for his personal coffers to arm his men – his 'lambs', as he called them – for their better protection . . . and to better harm Christ's enemies. Raised in a family of politicians, married to one, she was bred to recognise deceit. And she could hear none when the Genoan declared, with tears in his eyes, that he would give his life for Constantinople's cause, which was Christendom's cause.

Once she would have said it. Not now.

Theon was dressing. Pulling on his boots, flinging a heavy

86

cloak over himself, he went to the door. 'I will go and make sure we have someone to take our things to the boat before the madness begins. Like all Italians, they will sit on their arses for weeks, then, when they decide to move, rush at it like rams at an opening gate.' He glanced around the room. 'Make sure all is ready,' he ordered, and was gone.

She followed him to the door he'd left open, put a hand upon it. Then, instead of closing it, she stepped out again onto the terrace. The boat she'd seen before had already dropped anchor, and as it did, a smaller skiff was being lowered from its side, men waiting at the rail above to descend a rope ladder and board. Closing her eyes once more to the weak sun, she wondered if the person whom the Commander had waited for had, at the very last minute, arrived.

'I promised you gold, Zoran. I never promised you where I would pay it.'

Gregoras took a breath. 'We had an understanding, Commander . . .'

'Did we?' Giustiniani swivelled to the two men, constant sentinels on each side. 'Do you remember any understanding, Amir? You, Enzo?'

The Arab shrugged. The Sicilian spoke. 'It's like any mercenary's wages. You pay when you can. You pay when it's possible.'

'I was not offered wages, but—'

'Exactly.' Giustiniani ignored him. 'And it is not possible, right now. I've spent all the gold I had.'

Gregoras fought to keep the anger down. 'On what?'

'On what?' The Italian's eyes widened. 'You know on what, Zoran. You've been on campaign enough to know. On more powder, more armour, more whores and more wine.' He glared. 'And on waiting for you to show up two weeks late!'

'There were . . . difficulties.'

'Oh, we heard.' When Gregoras stared at him, Amir smiled. 'A fast galliot brought papers from Genoa. They put into

Korcula for water and found the island abuzz. Someone had murdered one of their best-loved citizens.' The grin grew wider. 'You killed Stanko.'

'Stanko?' Giustiniani's laugh erupted. 'One of the most vicious pieces of pirate scum that ever drifted over the water. I believe he has six brothers, each as ugly and equally murderous as he. They will seek you out and delight in separating you into various pieces as slowly as possible. Strangely, that mask you wear for concealment makes you distinguishable.'

'They will not know me . . .'

'But they already do, brother,' Enzo said, shaking his head. 'Your name – Zoran of Ragusa – has been hailed as the assassin.'

'How . . . ?' Then Gregoras saw it, and cursed silently. That sea rat of a skiff owner, the one he'd tossed overboard. He'd known him, a little. The bastard hadn't drowned but had lived to give him away. 'Well . . .' he shrugged, 'gold buys good hiding places. I'll take my chances.'

'Suffering Christ!' The Commander threw his huge arms up towards the ceiling. 'I've told you, I have no gold left to pay you with. But I will have . . . in Constantinople, where we make for as soon as this tide turns. We have been prepared for departure for two weeks.' His arms lowered and he came round the table and placed them on Gregoras's shoulders. 'You know what they say of Constantinople, lad. Even the street signs are made of beaten gold. So my thought is this . . . you will accompany us there.'

Gregoras squirmed. 'I will not go.'

The Genoan's grip tightened. 'Come with us, help deliver the German and collect your reward.' He smiled, lowered his head so he could look directly in the other's eyes. 'This is not an attempt to recruit you. You will not have to sign the articles and I will feed and wine you out of the regiment's coffers and from the kindness of my heart. And it will be good to have my lucky token beside me as I take up my latest, my greatest, challenge – at least for a while.' His eyes moistened. 'What do you say, lad? Are we really such poor company?'

A part of Gregoras still seethed – from disappointment, from recognition of his own stupidity. From a virulent desire to stick to his vow and never again see the city that had taken his all. But he had been soldier long enough to recognise a fight he could not win. He would have to choose other ground. Besides, for all that they quarrelled, these mercenaries were the closest to family he had, and Giustiniani the nearest to a father.

'I will . . . accompany you.'

The other three cheered. Giustiniani changed his grip and hugged Gregoras to his huge chest. Enzo appeared with wine, and the four men pledged 'Damnation to the Turk' and drank.

Two flagons later, Amir leaned forward and refilled their goblets yet again. 'What sort of man is he, this German?' he asked.

'For the first three days he sweated out enough liquor to get three regiments of Switzers drunk,' Gregoras replied. 'After that, he shook and sweated but drank wine only when there was not water for his thirst, and then in moderation.' His audience gave a collective shudder as he continued, 'He talked a lot as well.'

'Of what?' Enzo asked.

'His home. His exile from it. His wanderings and his service to various courts and kings. He is a soldier too, though it seems his main skills lie not in weapon play but in the mechanics of war, especially to do with siege. In mine and counter-mine.'

'And in Greek Fire, Zoran?' The Commander placed his mug down and stretched. 'Is it true he knows the lost secret of it?'

'You will have to ask him that. From what he's said, he knows what it's made of, he is just not sure of the proportions.' He set his own mug down. 'Which reminds me, Commander. You may not be able to leave on the next tide.'

'What's that?' Giustiniani looked up sharply. 'We are already delayed . . .'

'I know. But the . . . German told me that one of the things he needs, and in quantity, is pine resin. This island abounds in the tree that makes it, apparently. So he will need to collect it.'

'Ah. Then our delay may not have been fruitless.' The Genoan gestured, and Amir rose to root among the papers on the table. 'This island has few things of worth, but we have collected what they have – a few girls to accompany us, more of this sweet wine and . . .' he squinted at the paper Amir handed him, 'twelve barrels of Aleppo gum. Will that suffice?'

'You will have to ask him. Shall I send for him?'

Giustiniani shook his head. 'Plenty of time to talk when we are aboard. And plenty to do before we sail with the evening tide. I have a sad farewell to take . . .' He smiled, his eyes misting. 'A widow of the island, a ravishing creature.' He collected his hat and sword and moved to the door. 'You'll sail with us, Zoran. It will be a little cramped, as we needs must return a few of the city's ambassadors to their home. But you're used to that.'

Ambassadors? For a moment, Gregoras stiffened as he wondered if he'd know them. But then he remembered that he would be masked, by both his name and the cloth before his face. And he would be thrice hidden, catching up with old mercenary friends.

When he followed the others from the room, like them he squinted against the winter sun, which seemed twice as sharp after the days of fog. Instinctively, he noted its position and glanced away, north, slightly east. If fortune and wind favoured them, their destination lay there, three days away.

He whispered the word. 'Constantinople.' He was disturbed to discover that the feeling it gave him was not, as formerly, all hate, and resolved to drown it forthwith in more wine.

EIGHT

Yaya

As the exhalation ended, the wailing began.

It was his daughter, Abal, who breathed out. She had been named for the wild rose that overran the southern wall of their house in the spring. Now, in the deep of winter, she was as withered as last year's blooms.

It was his wife, Farat, who keened. She was named for the sweet water, the first of the ice melt that flooded their dried-out ditches, filling their hearts with hope and, eventually, their fields with golden wheat. But that was yet months away, and the water that fell from her eyes was bitter.

Achmed was at the door with no memory of having got there. Jerking it open, he stood for a moment on the threshold, looking back. His wife had fallen over the corpse, voice shrill in denial of what they'd known was coming for weeks. The dead girl's brothers, Mustaq and Mounir, looked at their mother, at each other, helpless, tearless. He knew he should go to them, console, wail, weep. But he also had no tears, no words, had never found much use for either. Instead he stooped under the lintel, crossing the threshold into the weak winter sunlight.

Behind the glare, shapes. He raised a hand and saw villagers, relatives. They questioned him, with word and look, but he could not answer them, could not move, just stood, and the women had to squeeze past him, for he was big, taller than the doorway, near as wide. The men formed a half-circle before it. There was space for him there.

He pushed through it, brushing aside hands that sought to detain him.

It was warm, so strangely warm. It happened, one January in ten perhaps. The wind had veered, blew from the south now, passing through deserts, not from the north and cooling snow peaks. While it blew, it ate the snow on the ground, and began to warm the frozen earth.

It is the one blessing in the curse that is my life, he thought.

He knew what he must do. The previous winter had been harsh and lingering, the spring too wet. They'd planted late, the crop sparse as a result. All of them starved, a little, enough. Enough for his Abal, his wild rose, flower of his eye, light of his darkness, to be too weak to resist the sickness when it came. And since he had no excess, he had nothing to sell or trade in Karseri for the food or remedy that might have saved her.

As he moved to the side of the house, the wailing inside it became a choir, and he knew only one thing: no one else he loved would die because he'd been too poor to feed them.

The two oxen stared at him from their pen, grinding chaff. Like him, they were leaner than they should have been. But they would still do their job, better now perhaps than in their normal time after another three months of hunger.

Achmed opened the gate, moved past the beasts, put his shoulder against the wall and lifted the plough from it. It was heavy, made from the Y of a beech where two branches forked from the trunk. He hardly felt the weight, nor that of the single-log harrow and the straps he scooped from the ground. He did not look at those. Abal's first sewing had been to put blue beads the length of the leather, ward against the Evil Eye.

He clicked his tongue. If the oxen thought it was early to hear such a sound, they did not show it but obeyed, and moved out of the yard.

Some men had followed him. Some called, 'What are you doing, Achmed? Has a djinn taken you, Achmed?' He ignored them. If he was to do what he must do, then he had to do this first. Once he went away, there was every reason to believe he would not return. Yet if he prepared the land now, at least his widow and his orphans would be able to sow when the season came.

Inshallah. It was all in God's hands, as ever. But His will could be manifested in man's efforts.

Achmed guided his oxen with whistles, with blows from a switch he picked up. The weight upon him made him plod like them. Slowly man and beasts climbed from the bowl of the village and onto the hills beyond it.

He had a patch of land that he'd never ploughed, with only grass and his goats upon it. If any land would give his family a worthy crop, it would be there. Reaching it at last, he set down his load and let his oxen root among the dead leaves of a stand of poplars while he began to walk in straight lines, bending to scoop and throw aside the smaller rocks, stooping to lift and carry the larger to the edge of his land.

He did not think. He did not feel. He did not remember.

'*Ya daim. Ya daim,*' he chanted, as he would at sowing, at reaping. The chant to keep going, to keep life as it was, to keep someone alive. And though it had not helped before, it helped now when the ache came, helped him carry beyond the ache, through the day, into the darkness, pausing only to pray, and afterwards to break the ice crust on the small pond and suck upon shards.

The ground was white with starlight and moon-spill when he noticed the figures standing near the oxen. His two sons. Mounir, the elder at seven. Mustaq, near as tall but only five. One held a goatskin of milk, some cheese in a cloth, a wheel of hard-baked bread; the other Achmed's sheepskin coat and a bag of chaff.

He took them, drank, ate. After a while, his elder son spoke. 'Come back. She needs you.'

Achmed didn't reply. Just shook his head and turned back to the field.

For two days more he cleared the land of rocks, large and small, piling them into cairns to mark the perimeter of his field. At night he slept under the poplars, between his two oxen, dreamlessly. On the third day, his sons returned with more supplies, enough for them too, and for two more days they watched as he drove the plough across the earth, which, if it was not full winter frozen under the still-warm wind, was still hard enough to the ploughshare. Yet its tip, which he'd seasoned in fire while still green, only fractured on the fifth day, and by then he'd ploughed three-quarters of the land. Good enough in a good year, which this would be, *inshallah*.

Unharnessing the plough, he fitted the beasts with the harrow, a log wide enough for the boys to stand upon, their weight forcing it down upon the clods the plough had turned over, breaking them up.

It took a day and then it was done. The harrowing would have to be repeated perhaps if the warm wind died and the land froze again. But the worst of the work was finished and his wife had brothers who were the boys' *dayi* and as such would have a special responsibility. Should Achmed not return.

He left the broken plough at the edge of the field, the harrow propped against a poplar, carried the harness, whistled the oxen home. The boys ran ahead, and by the time he reached the village many lingered on the roadway to see the madman and perhaps glimpse the djinn who had driven him mad.

Looking at no one, Achmed made straight for the house. From a distance he saw his wife in the doorway. Closer, he let the beasts go on, the boys coming to take the harness and drive them to their pen.

He was ten paces away when Farat spoke. 'We buried her,' she said, her face pinched around her mouth. 'We could not wait.'

Wordless still he moved past her into the house. She closed the door. 'What have you done, Achmed? Have you gone crazy? Ploughing in January? Are you going to sow now too and kill us all next winter?'

He moved to the back of the room. He was tired and yet he could not rest. He reached into the chest, lifted out the sack of seeds and, for the first time in days, spoke, his voice rough with disuse. 'You know the time. Mounir helped last year and Mustaq will this, but get your brothers to watch them.' He replaced the bag. His axe hung on the wall before him. He took it down.

'And where will you be when that time comes?'

Her voice was trying to show anger. It only showed her fear. He moved to her, stopping close. 'I will be where Allah guides me. Seeing that we never lose another child to hunger,' he replied.

Her eyes shot wide, tears filling them, flooding out. 'How? How?' she wailed.

He reached a hand, caught a tear on his finger as it fell. He raised it to his lips, tasted it, her. It was sweet, and he remembered how well she was named, for the sweetest of spring waters.

He bent and kissed her – brow, both cheeks, lips. Then he moved past her to the door, out of it, between the lines of staring villagers again. At the edge of the village, his sons caught up with him, thrusting another cloth of cheese, another half-wheel of bread into his hands. He knew he should talk to them, counsel them, but he could not. So he just hugged them, turned and left.

He walked half the night, slept in a ditch, walked another day. It was early evening when he reached the town of Karseri. He had been there before in the good years to sell his excess and knew it a little. But it was not hard anyway to find the inn he sought. An *alem*, verses of the Qur'an cut into the steel spear point, marked it out, as did the noise of many men within it.

Achmed crossed the room to the man he recognised. Men leaned away to make him a path, for he was the largest there by far.

'Ah, so you have come!' Raschid rose from behind the table and limped round it to stare up. 'What changed your mind?'

Achmed looked down. Did it need explaining? 'When you passed through our village you spoke of gold.'

'Gold, yes, so much gold.' Raschid's wide smile glimmered in the reed-torch light. 'The streets of the Red Apple are cobbled with it, the walls of their sacrilegious temples studded with precious stones. Our sultan, balm of the world, peace be unto him, has promised us three days of looting when the city falls. Three? The place is so wealthy that a poor man will be rich in one day. And then he'll have two more to indulge other . . . delights, eh?'

He laughed, poking Achmed in the stomach. The bigger man frowned. 'Other delights?'

'Slaves! We can turn every one of their citizens into slaves. To sell. To use.' He winked and looked around at others who were listening. 'For does not a good female slave need breaking in, eh?'

Men laughed. Achmed did not know what he was talking about. And then he did. He knew that if he died in this holy cause, Allah would reward him with one hundred virgins in paradise for eternity. He had not heard that such a reward could be taken this side of death.

He shrugged. Raschid studied him. 'You are huge, my friend. I think Allah will be pleased with me that I have recruited you.' He grinned, lifting a bottle from the table. 'Come, drink some *boza*. And do not look shocked, my big man. There are special dispensations for warriors. Eat. Drink your fill. Our shepherd the sultan, praise him, looks after his *yaya*. And then sleep, for we leave with the sunrise.'

Achmed ignored the bottle. He turned, then turned back. 'This place we go?'

'The Red Apple?'

'I heard it has another name.'

'It has many. It used to be called Byzantium. It is hailed as the Rome of the East. We of the true faith have always seen it as that delicious fruit waiting to drop into our hands. But the

Greeks themselves, the world, know it by another name – Constantinople.'

'Constantinople.' Achmed mouthed the strange word, hard on his tongue. Then he nodded, turned again, seeking a corner for sleep.

It did not matter what it sounded like, where it was, who held it now. All that mattered was that he go there. Die in the holy cause, if Allah so willed it. Or live to get the gold that lined its streets, then return to build a bower of wild roses over his dead daughter's grave.

NINE

Persuasion

Edirne, capital of the Ottoman Empire
January 1453

'It is time.'

Ignoring the voice, the gardener glanced along the raised bed. Every ten paces, from the terrace to the pond, a sapling stood in a mound of freshly turned earth. Swivelling, he checked again that this last he'd planted was directly opposite another across the mosaic path. Each would grow as Allah willed. But this much he could control, their precise placement.

He raised a hand. Hamza pulled him up. He bent to rub his right knee. He'd been crouched a while and his leg had never been completely free of pain since Kossovo four years before. He had commanded the right wing of his father's army on the Field of the Blackbirds and a Serb had hit him hard with the boss of his shield before he'd ridden him down.

'They call it *Cercis siliquastrum* in the Latin. I have heard there is an avenue of these in the palace of Constantinople. There it is known as the Judas tree.' He glanced over. 'Do you know why?'

'No, lord.' Hamza's tone made it clear he did not wish to know, that other matters pressed. He even turned towards the direction they must take.

Mehmet did not follow. He had spent a precious morning doing what he loved, here in the garden that was his joy. And even though the path that Hamza urged him along could lead to an even greater joy, he did not want to take it. Not yet.

'Judas is another name for the betrayer of the prophet Isa,

praise him. It is said that after the betrayal he hung himself from this tree; the thirty pieces of silver he'd been paid spilled at his feet.'

Hamza looked down. 'Is it not a little small for hanging?'

Mehmet laughed. 'It can grow to three times the height of a man, though the branches are ever thin. Yet strong enough to bear the weight of a traitor.' He looked down the avenue. 'My *bostanci* tell me that it will grow fast, that the flowers are pink, bountiful and fragrant. Perhaps in ten years we shall walk beneath these Judas trees, Hamza, and breathe in their scent.'

'*Inshallah.*' Hamza shook his head. 'Or perhaps the scent will be from the bodies of traitors dangling from their limbs.'

Mehmet noted the hint that was there. But he was in too good a mood to join his adviser in his fears. 'Well, it would be a convenient place. Since my *bostanci* . . .' he gestured at the five kneeling gardeners, 'are not only janissaries but also my executioners.' He turned to the waiting men. 'Water them down, then report to your barracks.'

Hamza wiped the mud from his master's hand onto the sleeve of his *gomlek.* 'There is water also for you to wash,' he said, as they began to move down the path.

Mehmet stared at his fingers, the nails like black crescent moons. 'I think I will not. It will be good to see the mark of the soil on my *belerbeys*' faces after they have paid homage to me.'

He laughed, and Hamza's concern increased. His master was yet young, his emotions . . . variable. 'This talk of trees and traitors, master,' he murmured as they climbed the steps up to the *saray*'s rear entrance. 'Do you fear . . . ?'

'I fear nothing.' For the first time colour came into Mehmet's voice. ' "Traitor" is too strong a term for these men, my father's men, grown fat and lazy and cautious. But they are as bad as traitors, for they stand between me and my mark. And now they must duck else my arrows go through them.'

The other grunted. 'And this talk of Isa . . .'

Mehmet halted, his voice lowering. 'I know that many find my interest in other faiths troubling. Suspect that I may even be . . . drawn to the mysteries of the Sufi, or the salvation offered by the Christ.' He stopped before the door, laid a grubby hand on the older man's sleeve. 'But do not fear, Hamza. Today they shall see only what I am – a *gazi* of Islam.'

They continued, reached the *saray*. The robing room was where Mehmet had donned his gardening clothes. It was also where a very different type of clothing awaited.

'Arm me,' the sultan commanded the men who waited, raising his hands. 'And Hamza?' He waved at the table. Parchment rolls covered it. 'Once more.'

Hamza felt he did not need to look at any page, so inscribed were their facts on his mind. Yet there was something reassuring about the inked lines, the lists of forces, the disposition of ships, the signatures on treaties. He named them all now as Mehmet was armed, his voice measured.

He was not close to the end when Mehmet halted him with a word. 'Look.'

Hamza looked. Studied. Nodded.

They had argued long about what Mehmet should wear this day. To exalt the status of a sultan, without setting him too far above those he needed to serve him. To remind them that he was, though young, a soldier of some experience from a tradition of military men. That he was also what he called himself – a *gazi*, a warrior of the faith, taking up the Prophet's banner in a jihad eight hundred years old.

Mehmet was muscled from years of training at arms and on the wrestling floor. His armour emphasised that, the mail coat raised over padded shoulders, his chest plates lifted slightly. These were clearly old, dints visible, though polished to a brightness that would dazzle in the sunlight. Only in the helmet was there any ostentation, for though it was in the simple style of a metal turban, with more mail descending to protect the neck, a type that all his *sipahi* horsemen would wear, the metal was silver. And on its surface had been etched, in cursive Arabic lettering, a well-known *haditha* of Muhammad: 'I will assist you with a thousand of the angels, ranks on ranks.'

Hamza went to Mehmet. Though as tall, he felt dwarfed by the shining bulk. Which was how he wanted to feel, what he hoped all would feel. 'And your sword, master?' he asked. 'How did you decide?'

Mehmet opened his hand and an armourer placed a weapon in it. Mehmet pulled a hand's span of steel from the battered sheath, to glitter in the sunlight. 'I know what we discussed – a new sword, perhaps, so they would see a new leader and not . . .' he hesitated, 'a father's insufficient son.' He drew the sword fully now, dropped back into fighting stance, free hand out and forward, curved blade high and back. 'But the men we are to persuade saw this sword melt the Crusader ranks at Varna, saw it scythe the very air upon the Field of the Blackbirds.' He stepped back, swung it in a high cut that was yet low enough to have men ducking. 'I decided that a small touch of my warrior father's memory will not go amiss this day.'

It does not go amiss with me, who loved him, Hamza thought, but with you, who did not? Still, on balance he thought the choice was right. Murad had been one of the greatest warriors the House of Osman had ever produced. He had nearly always won.

Mehmet swept the blade through the air. 'So what think you, Hamza? Am I not Achilles?'

Hamza nodded. His master considered the text of the *Iliad* as a near equal to the holiest of books. Achilles, the fearless, ruthless supreme warrior, was his model. 'Every fibre of him, master. And are you ready now to go and mock the strutting Achaean lords?'

The younger man smiled. 'I am ready. Stay by me. Guide me if I falter.'

'I shall be your rock ever, master. Though you will need nothing from me but my praise when you have won them.'

'Your lips to God's ears.' Mehmet lifted the sword into sunlight once more before sheathing it, then sliding it into its strapping at his belt. '*Inshallah*,' he said, and led the way to the door.

He needed no fanfare, just the tent's flaps thrown back. The hour had been judged precisely so that the sun, low in the west, shone through the *otak*'s aligned front entrance and made his armour dance with flame. Other servants had instructions to keep that canvas spread till Hamza signalled them to lower it. He did not do so till Mehmet had reached the centre of the raised platform and even the most reluctant had their noses pressed to the carpet for three full breaths.

'*Allahu akbar!*' Mehmet roared.

'God is great!' came the echo from fifty voices.

The flaps dropped, faces came up, men rose, and saw their sultan clearly for the first time. Saw too, just behind and to the side, the plain contrast of Mehmet's imam, Aksemseddin, the cleric in sober brown and grey, a gold-leaf-covered copy of the Qur'an in his arms.

The Prophet's warrior let them study him for half a dozen breaths before he beckoned. Only a few had been allowed the honour of kissing his hand.

The grand vizier, of course, would be first. The two *belerbeys* next – as governors of the larger provinces, it was expected. Other *beys*, only just below them in prestige, would follow. Every one of them he and Hamza had, in endless night-time analysis, named for animals. As each approached, Mehmet spoke the alias along with the name inside his head.

The Elephant came first, his grand vizier, Candarli Halil Pasha. The Ox and the Buffalo followed closely, Ishak and Karaca, *belerbeys* of Anatolia and Rumelia, who would command his Turkish and European levies respectively. Each bent, kissed, avoided his eyes. Mehmet watched them waddle back to their factions. Old bulls, he thought. Devoid of seed. Lowing for peace.

He had a different smile for the two men – the two animals, Cheetah and Bear – who came next. Zaganos was an Albanian, a convert, more fanatical for the faith than almost any born to it. He was lean, fast, young, ambitious. The other man was huge and also well named. Baltaoglu was a Bulgarian, a former prisoner and slave, who had embraced Islam only to rise as fast as he could, his skills at naval war matched by the brutality with which he pursued it. They worked as a pair, a young Balkan alliance against the old Anatolians.

A last man came when they retreated – Imran, *agha* of the janissaries. His bow was brief, his kiss likewise, his leaving swift. He and his sultan had little love, for he had been Murad's man entirely. But Mehmet knew as he watched the man walk away and stand directly in between the camps of war and peace with the other undecided, the majority in the room, that he could be persuaded. Janissaries got restless with too much peace and made trouble. Like cheetahs, they needed the hunt.

He looked at all who'd greeted him, at the others behind grouped mainly in the middle. Suddenly he felt uncertain. What was it he was going to say? In what order? He turned . . . and Hamza was right behind him. In his adviser's stare, he found certainty again. And when he looked again at the upturned faces, sought out those of the men he must persuade or overcome, he saw that he had marked them all. Mud, that had been on his hands, was now on their faces. His grand vizier was wiping grit from his lips. It made Mehmet smile – and then he was speaking.

'Lords of the horizon,' he said, lifting off his great silver helmet, 'pashas of lands that stretch from the mountains of the Tartar to the seas of the Greeks, all united under Allah, praise Him . . .' He paused as 'Praise Him!' was shouted in response, then added, 'Welcome, lords, to the end and the beginning of history!'

Some men, already aligning themselves with him, cheered. Most did not. He lifted a hand, and received immediate silence. In a quieter voice he continued, 'You know why we are gathered here. And since it is not a secret . . .' he turned to Hamza, nodded, watched his adviser leave by the back of the tent, turned back, 'let me remind you where we seek to conquer, why we seek it and how. Let me shout the name, so that it goes to God's ears as tribute, as prayer.' He threw back his head and yelled, 'Constantinople!'

He looked down again. 'Constantinople,' he repeated softly. 'We also call it the Red Apple. How many times have the sons of Isaac camped before its walls, waiting for that luscious fruit to drop into our hands? In the memories of men gathered here are visions of my grandfather, whose name I bear to my honour, packing up his tents and stealing away from that prize. My own father, Murad, an incomparable warrior, could not cut the fruit away from the tree. So why do I, grandson, son of such esteemed warriors, believe that I can do what they failed to do?' His voice dropped and he smiled. 'Because prophecy is the voice of destiny – and it is prophesied that it is time for the Red Apple to fall. Did not the Prophet, most exalted, say: "Have ye heard of a city of which one side is land and two others sea? The Hour of Judgement shall not sound until seventy thousand sons of Isaac shall capture it." '

He stared out, letting the Prophet's words rest in their ears a moment. 'You know that we have already assembled the number of the prophecy,' he continued. 'You have brought them yourselves to gather beneath my tug. More are coming. Many more. Yet what size of army will face us? Our enemies have never been weaker, nor more disunited. We will fight only those impoverished few who live there. No one will come to their aid. Oh, they will make great noises, they will clash their arms – but they will not lift them. I have treaties signed with the dread Hunyadi, the White Knight of Hungary. With Brankovitch of Serbia. The Pope weeps . . . and does little more. And if conscience does finally strike them all and they set out, it will be too late.' His voice dropped and men leaned closer. 'Too late. For we will already have turned their temple, the Hagia Sophia, into a mosque.'

More cries of 'God is great!' came then, from more voices. He could feel a shift in the room. Not enough, yet. Soon perhaps. After other persuasions.

He took a breath. 'Isolated, alone, weakened? Yes. But if we leave Constantinople now – now when we are so strong, when stars and man align – who knows if some other power will not come and make it strong again? Our enemies the Venetians, who held it once. Our enemies the Hungarians, always seeking to hurt us. As long as its gates are closed to us, they could be opened to an enemy who could do what these Greeks can no longer do – use the best-placed harbour in the world, the city that cuts our lands of Anatolia and Rumelia in half, to stab us in the back.'

Another murmur came, more uncertainty in it. Mehmet pressed on. 'Now, as never before, we have a chance to end that threat for ever.'

He could feel the change under the canvas. Men beginning to make up their minds. Yet he sensed that too many still balanced on the dagger's edge.

It was his time. The moment he and Hamza had discussed. The moment of hazard. He turned to the one man who could yet tip it either way. 'What do *you* say, my grand vizier, most esteemed of all my father's and my advisers? Doubt still rests upon that venerable brow. Speak it. We would be honoured to hear your wisdom.'

Candarli Halil Pasha blinked. All knew that the young sultan could move no enterprise without his help. So to consult in open council was to invite him to sway the waverers back. It was a challenge, there was danger in it, and he chose his response with care. 'Asylum of the world, guide of all nations, I hear you. Your words are wise, your preparations clear, your courage and skills undoubted. Yet you have talked already about the great warriors – your own unparalleled grandfather and father were two of them and I stood beside them both – who came to this place and failed.'

He paused, so Mehmet's words were not exactly an interruption. 'And why did they fail so, old warrior?'

'There are men here perhaps more qualified than I to speak of this. But I believe two things have always thwarted the sons of Isaac whatsoever their numbers and faith. Two – water and stone.' He looked around, licked still gritty lips. 'The seas that lap the city on two sides and the triple walls that seal off the land.'

Assenting murmurs came. It was the moment Mehmet and Hamza had foreseen; the time for two strokes, swift as sword thrusts. One in words. One in . . . something else.

'I thank you, uncle, for your wisdom. They are both questions I have long pondered, as many have pondered before me. Water and stone indeed.' He looked behind him. Hamza had returned to the tent. He nodded and Mehmet turned back. 'We are *gazis* and prefer to feel God's good earth under our hooves than shifting planks beneath our feet, do we not? Yet, as you have stated, a city surrounded by water needs command of that water to be taken. I will take command of it.'

He opened a hand. Hamza placed a roll of parchment in it. Mehmet began to read. 'Know that in boatyards up and down my empire, men have been hard at work, building, repairing. The day we march on Constantinople is the day our fleet will sail from Gallipoli. A fleet of one hundred and twenty vessels.' There were gasps at that. 'There will be twelve – *twelve!* – full war triremes. Eighty *fustae* each armed with cannon. Thirty fighting transport ships. Even if renegades of Venice and Genoa sail against us, how many will they muster? Twelve? Twenty? The seas, Candarli Halil, will be ours.'

The grand vizier was not the only man who looked shocked as Mehmet rolled up the paper and tapped it against his breastplate. 'Now . . . what else was it that has always thwarted us, uncle?'

'The walls,' the old man stuttered. 'The walls that . . . that . . .'

'The walls that defeated every army that camped before them, including my father's? Including Eyoub, the Prophet's banner-bearer, whose grave I would seek beneath them and raise a temple over it?' Mehmet nodded. 'But neither of them had what I have,' he added.

'And what is that, lord?'

It was time. 'Something to take away stone as easily . . . as easily as I can take away canvas.'

He did not look back. Simply lifted his hand, held it high, let it fall. Hamza, holding the fold of the entrance, looked outside and did the same.

The pavilion was not the largest. Indeed, it had been chosen for the purpose it was put to now. Four big men rushed to the centre to grasp the thick pole there. As soon as they had a firm grip, Hamza beckoned again – and the canvas walls vanished, drawn up fast and away by a system of pulleys, men and horses.

One moment his council had been standing sheltered in a tent. The next they were in the open air, shading their eyes against bright winter sunlight, blinking at what they had not seen before – that the tent they'd entered from the city gate behind them had been set atop a hill; that from its summit, a valley dropped and rose gently to another summit perhaps a mile away. That the distance between the two was lined by thousands upon thousands of soldiers in two huge bodies, a wide avenue between them. Finally that they shared their hilltop with the largest cannon any man there had ever seen.

Cradled by wooden blocks, settled into the ground like a huge black worm, it wasn't just large. It was monstrous. Five tall men lying toe to fingertip could not have equalled its length. Its vast girth tapered to a narrower end that no man would be able to wrap his arms around.

It was the drawing of Mehmet's sword that drew their eyes back to him. He had donned his helmet again, and once more his armour shimmered in light. He raised the weapon high into the sunlight, brought it scything down, crying out one word: 'Now!' As a man who seemed all soot thrust a glowing taper into the breech, Mehmet sheathed his sword, raised the forefinger on each hand and spoke again. 'You may wish to do this,' he called. And he put a finger in each ear.

Some did, most were too stunned, too slow, and so were

destined to hear the cannon's roar for weeks afterwards. To some it was as if hell itself had gaped, exploded forth flames and the screams of all who had ever died. To others, to Jew, Christian or Muslim gathered near, it was as if Armageddon had finally come.

Sound was one thing. Sight another. From monstrous flames a comet shot, trailing fire and smoke, soaring the length of the valley between the massed ranks of men to finally, with a sound more of animal than of man, bury itself in those slopes a mile away.

The cheering from the army went on for a while, funnelled up to them by the valley's contours.

Mehmet stepped to the edge of the pit. The smoke that filled it slowly cleared, and once more the monster could be seen. Men swarmed around it, using soaked bales of cloth to cool it down. In their midst was the man as black as his creation, though his colour came from gunpowder and not brass. 'So, Urban Bey?' Mehmet called to him. 'Are you happy at your child's first cough?'

The black-clad man spat before he spoke, in heavily accented Osmanlica. 'I am, lord,' replied Urban the Transylvanian. 'But I would see the afterbirth.'

'Then let us go and see it.' Mehmet turned to Hamza, standing a little back from the crowd on the emplacement's slope. At his master's nod, he beckoned other waiting men forward.

'Lords,' Hamza called. 'Will you ride?'

There were horses for all, and even the most venerable, like the grand vizier, mounted. If a Turk could still walk, he could still sit on a saddle.

Mehmet led them sweeping down the valley, a bolt of mounted light that passed from him onto the steel ranks that lined his path, and back again. His tens of thousands of soldiers cheered, ululating their loyalty in shrill extended cries.

They galloped the whole way, all freed of the confines of the tent and most from their doubts. Reaching a small cluster of men, Mehmet reined in, dismounted. The mob opened to him, admitting him to what they were grouped around – a rough-edged tunnel, about half as wide as a man is tall, dug straight into the earth. Perhaps straight through to hell itself, for smoke rose in wisps from the jagged entrance.

When the rest of the horsemen had gathered around him, Mehmet signalled to one of the men, prostrate before his sultan. 'Brother, you look the tallest here. Slide in and tell me how deep it is buried.'

The man bowed, swallowed and then slid feet first into the earth. He disappeared – and then the wiggling tips of fingers were thrust out.

Mehmet could not check the murmuring, did not want to. 'Content, Urban Bey?' he said. The begrimed gunner's black face showed white in his smile. Mehmet turned away from him, back to his council. He looked straight at Candarli Halil Pasha. 'Your last question, Uncle, was how I would do what my father and grandfather and eight hundred years of the Prophet's followers have failed to do.' He pointed into the hole. 'The stone down there is granite. I will fire stones like it, every day, every hour. Until the walls collapse. And then I will lead the heroes of Anatolia and Rumelia, the Kurds of the mountains, the Arabs of the deserts, the janissaries of my heart . . .' he turned and smiled at their commander, 'over those walls. And I will take my war standard and the Holy Qur'an and pluck out the core of the Red Apple.'

Those who doubted could doubt no more. Those who still opposed could not be seen to be doing so. All the men of the Council could do, from the grand vizier down, was cheer. The cry spread back again into the valley and the soldiers drawn up there, whose ranks melded into a mob that rushed now to the base of the slope, held back by the household guards, triple-ranked. The cry filled the valley, doubling, if possible, when Mehmet leapt onto his horse, drew his father's sword and once again gave the war cry of the Faithful.

'*Allahu akbar!*'

From the walls of Edirne, through the slits of her veil, Leilah watched. She knew she could have dressed as a boy and moved closer. Or even donned the apparel of the Bektashi she'd once been, the janissary's girl, and gone with her hair unbound, braving men's stares. But that would have required her to pay elsewhere the attention that she only wanted to focus forward. To the man at the valley's far end, the destiny he was shaping.

His. Hers. God's.

She did not truly watch with her eyes; though she kept them open, all was a blur at that great distance. Her sight was better close to – and best of all when looking in. There all was clear. Her two men of destiny – one was on that far hill, no doubt raising his father's sword as he started the shout that thundered down the valley and swept them up in its noise, even the huddle of women, who'd come from the town to watch their men, caught up in it, shouting it.

God *is* great, she thought as she turned away. And though everything was His will, she had helped shape it as only she could. Only Allah could assure victory – but man could be aided by stars and portents. By those gifted like her to read them.

She headed to the house of her father's sister's daughter. Her disguises were there; her weapons too. She would shed the concealment of the woman, don that of a youth, strap her breasts down beneath a tunic, cover her slim legs beneath billowing *shalvari*, push her long hair up inside a turban, mask herself. The dagger at her waist and the crossbow on her back deterred most. She could pass unchallenged. Even into the city she would set out for this day. Constantinople had a Turkish population still, for trade continued even as all prepared for war. One more young man come to see a merchant relative would not receive too much scrutiny, even now.

As Leilah hurried down the twisting alleys of Edirne, she was excited that one task was complete, another beginning. It was not without its dangers. But the man she sought now, her other man of destiny, was more blurred to her than Mehmet had been at the valley's far end. It was for that reason she had to go. She had to find him again.

Gregoras.

There was a time for people. Each important man in her life, the janissary and the Jew, had come when she needed them and they, in some way, needed her. It was vital now to find him again, one more time, before all that was to come. Place guards around him to keep him safe.

To be certain he is mine and not another's.

The thought halted her before her cousin's door. She leaned on it, did not push it in.

This . . . other. Leilah had seen her in the chart she'd drawn up after her return from Korcula. In whispers before dawn, in the drowsiness that followed lovemaking, she had got the information she needed to map him. And she had found *her*, in his conjunction of Venus and Neptune, a certain place for the entanglements of love.

She is why I must find him, she thought. I would bind him to me one more time.

She was surprised at how her legs gave slightly at the thought, how the ache came between them. Smiling, she took a breath, and pushed open the door.

— TEN —

City of Ghosts

Sofia watched him through the shutter, through skeins of rain. They had deluged the city for a week, dissolving even the short distance between their house and the one opposite, making sight and stone insubstantial. It was a ruin, and when she'd first glimpsed the figure within its tumbled timbers, she'd thought it a ghost from the family who'd lived there, parents and three sons lost to plague five years before. She'd crossed herself, gone to pray before the house altar, returned . . . and the figure still stood there, shrouded head tilted up, the face within lost to rain and shadow. Despite the ceaseless storm, he was there an hour later, a steadfastness most un-ghost-like, for she had encountered spirits before – of her mother once, of a dead brother – and they flitted, came, stared, went if spoken to. They did not stand for hours staring up.

She knew who he was. When she'd named her ghosts he had made the tally. And that was the most disturbing thing of all: the realisation that he whom she'd assumed was dead wasn't. That he who was banished from the city for ever had returned despite the threatened instant death. That the man she'd loved and forsaken was standing ten paces from her.

'Mama!'

The cry startled her, so lost had she been. Yet it was not a surprise. Since she'd returned to the city three weeks before, her daughter had not left her, was always touching her. 'What is it, lamb?' Sofia bent and stroked the five-year-old's soft cheek.

'You said you would tell me a story, Mama.' The girl thrust

out her lower lip, reminding Sofia instantly of Theon. Minerva took after him in many ways: in her strong will and calmly voiced demands. While Thakos, lost in books in another part of the house, was more like her. Tall for his age. Quick to laugh or cry.

'A story?' Sofia knelt, took her daughter in her arms. 'What kind of story?'

'A lovely one,' Minerva said simply, snuggling in.

Lovely? Sofia glanced up at the window. There was a story out there, standing in the rain and the ruin, but it was not lovely and it did not have an ending, which her daughter would not like. She'd thought once that it had a tragic one, fitting the plays of gods and heroes enacted in the Hippodrome on feast days. Now she realised that she did not know the ending, that what had gone before was only a break in the acts. And she knew, strongly, certainly, that she needed to know, and know now.

She hugged her daughter, lifted her as she stood, kissed her. 'I have to go out, my cherub. Athene will tell you a story.'

The child squirmed. 'Athene's stories are terrible. And her voice is like a crow's.' She snuggled in closer. 'I will come with you.'

'No.' Sofia set the girl on her feet, extricating her limbs. 'I have to . . .' She glanced at the window. There seemed to be a lightening out there. The hammering of rain on the tiled roof was slackening. 'The storm is passing. The market will be opening. I need to buy provisions.'

It was not entirely a lie. It gave her an excuse to go out anyway. Athene could be trusted with the cooking of food but not its purchase; she would always be cheated, and they could not afford that now. She would go to the market. But there was somewhere she needed to go first. A place she loved more than any other on God's earth.

St Maria of the Mongols. The saint for whom it was named was a Byzantine princess, sent to marry a barbarian centuries before. She had returned to found the chapel and Sofia had loved her story and the place since she was her daughter's age. Now she could not remember a time when she needed the consolation she found there more.

It was not far. She would go by narrow streets that she knew well. Streets that had plenty of shadows to step into and watch a shrouded man pass by.

Fool!

So. Another title earned. As if 'Rhinometus' and 'mercenary' were not disparagement enough. Only a fool would have stayed there staring up, hour on hour, under a chilling rain. Anyone else would have done what Gregoras should have done the hour Giustiniani told him, three weeks after they'd landed, that he still could not find him his gold: head to the docks and take a ship leaving . . . for anywhere else.

But his foolishness stretched back long before this cold night. Why? Why, in all the scenes he had played out in his head, had he never thought of this? What had he expected Sofia to do, once news of his disgrace reached Constantinople? Take holy vows? Live alone and only for his memory? He had forced himself not to think of her. In the main, lost in war and wine, he had succeeded – at least when awake. But what he had not expected her to do – earning him his new title – was to marry his brother.

When he'd slunk through alleys in the twilight to look at the home he'd grown up in . . . there she was. Worse, with children too, returning with a boy and a little girl. But worst, far the worst was when his brother opened the door . . . and pulled her sharply to him.

Theon. If the first sight of her had brought desolation, surges of longing and a jabbing loss that had him bent and clutching his stomach, the sight of his brother had brought something clearer, single, certain.

Hate.

Once it had been little more than distaste, for a twin who was nothing like him – cool to his heat, intellect to his emotion.

114

Their rivalry had been delineated early, ground chosen, ceded: Gregoras would not challenge him in the libraries; Theon would not attempt to rival him in the open air. It was a kind of grudging truce, had worked, after the first excitements of childhood had passed. They ignored each other, made their different ways. But what had happened at the Hexamilion, and after, destroyed all neutrality. Gregoras had begun to loathe his own memory, for the way it would throw up his brother's face before him – like his, not his, unlike especially in this regard: Theon's was not disfigured. Elder by a moment, he had not been savaged, marked with disgrace. Still, for the time they were apart, Gregoras could imagine him alone and mostly leave him there. Until . . .

Until he saw Theon's hands on Sofia, pulling her to him. Not as a lover, though she must have been; the brats attested to that. As a possession. And suddenly, savagely, he knew: Theon possessed the only person Gregoras had ever loved. There had never been a truce, there had only been a biding. And seeing the victory, knowing his defeat, his hatred, like a newly forged blade, almost had him running across the road, dagger in hand, to slaughter them both before their children.

Yet he had not. Nor could he leave, despite a night of rain and cold and dawn's light bringing the peril of discovery. Could only stand there, staring up. And now, when she emerged and walked off, an hour after his brother, alone for the first time, all he could do was follow.

For a fool could not help himself.

And yet . . . to simply watch her walk! In the time of youth, he had often followed her unnoted, delighting in her sway, the voluptuousness of her gait that was such a contrast to the stiff and proper manners she displayed when he visited her in her father's house. And in following now, he remembered the last time he'd done so. A different kind of day, sun making warm the new armour he wore so proudly. It was the day before he departed for his first campaign. While she . . . she had managed to lose her maid within the church she loved, abandoning her watchdog to her devotions. She had burst from the chapel, surprising him waiting outside, then had led him running to a slab of rock on the shore of the Golden Horn. They had spent the day there, dipping toes in the water, telling stories, laughing. And when the sun sank and darkness shrouded them from any eyes, he had kissed her for the first time, a youth's fumble that became, under her command, something smooth, timeless. Devastating.

Gregoras shook himself. Memory was making him careless. A crossroads lay ahead, and the right fork would take him back to the only place he was truly safe in Constantinople – the barracks of the Genoese mercenaries. His maiming and exile had come with a final penalty: instant death if he should ever be caught within its walls again.

Yet now . . . now, at the crossroads, Sofia went straight ahead. If he'd been oblivious before, focusing outward on her walk and inward on his memories, he now realised where she was going. To that same church, the one she loved, St Maria of the Mongols. And when it was his turn to stand where four ways met, he did not hesitate. He followed, not far.

There was a small archway in the church's red surrounding wall. As he passed through it, he saw her cloaked shape enter at the chapel door. The courtyard was ten paces across. He crossed them, and the atrium beyond.

The church was as he remembered it. Small, more a square than a rectangle, its whitewashed walls and three ribbed-vault ceilings a simple backdrop to the splendour of the oaken altar screen, carved with biblical scenes, and the tall ikons set against it, their exquisitely painted faces gilded with real silver crowns and vestments. One, St Demetrios, had thrilled him as a boy – a soldier-martyr, clutching a large bejewelled sword. He'd seen him as a chivalrous knight; and one day, seeking a boon of love, he'd thrown a scroll of paper with his name conjoined with Sofia's into the narrow gap between ikon and screen.

A service of communion was in progress. To the chant of male voices, the faithful approached, knelt, received the host and the wine the priest brought down from the altar only he could see. The small space was crowded and he did not think she would recognise him, so changed was he from the city's warrior who'd last seen her here seven years before. He would not partake of the sacred mystery, had not since the last – the only – battle he'd fought for that city, the day of his disgrace. But he crossed himself by reflex, bent his head, lulled by harmonies in half-forgotten prayers.

Perhaps it was the exhaustion of his long vigil beneath her window. But when his head jerked up, the crowd was dispersing and she was gone.

He pushed through dawdlers at the door, ran to the archway, through it into the square. A glimpse of green turning a corner, not the way they had come, the way they'd gone that day, towards the Golden Horn. He ran. Another turn, another . . . and he had lost her! He ran to one more crossroads, saw nothing but streets of leaning, ruined houses every way, doorways boarded beside the crumbled walls. Cursing, he took the one that led straight on, the one they'd taken all those years before. He was three paces along it, passing the first portico, when a voice came from the shadows.

'Gregoras.'

He whirled. Thoughts cascaded. Discovery, the penalty of revelation, had his hand upon his dagger and his thoughts on running. But he'd been lost in memory and it was memory's voice that softly spoke his name.

'Sofia.'

Other voices from behind them. A hand reached out and drew him into the darkness.

Time dissolved. He was a youth again, pressed against his greatest desire. Yet he was himself too and the one he looked at was not a girl but a woman with lines of care carved around her eyes. 'Sofia, I . . .'

'Shh.'

A finger on his lips as voices grew louder. Two men, coming

down the alley. One yelped as he saw them. 'What make you there?'

Death if he was unmasked. Gregoras was about to turn, brazen it out, prepare to fight or flee. But Sofia held him fast, leaned over his shoulder, spoke. 'A husband off to sea. Give us some peace, will ya?'

She used an accent from the harbour, the fishing fleets. The two men laughed, one bowed and they moved on, ribald suggestions echoing down the cobbles till a corner cut them off. 'Gregoras,' she said again, differently, wonder in her voice. 'How . . . ?'

He stepped away, remembering – this alley was a shortcut between squares. 'Not here,' he said. 'Come.'

She did not hesitate, came out of the doorway. He led her now, down the steeply descending alley, through the square, into a lane that twisted down to the water's edge. A house had collapsed, jagged timbers in the path, and he stopped to take her hand and help her over them. A patch of open ground crossed and he found the gap still there that he had found before and squeezed between still standing walls. A tower stood sentinel on the shoreline but no one was in it, and bolts on the sally port to its side slid back easily despite their rust. He led her onto the slab of rock, into sunshine spilling through cloud rents.

She looked around them. 'But this is . . .'

'Yes. I could not think of anywhere else.' He pointed past her. 'If you would rather . . .'

'No.' She blurted it, stopping his step towards the doorway. She shivered. 'It is colder here than . . . than before.'

He reached up to his neck, unclasped his cloak. 'Here,' he said, and swept it around her shoulders.

'Thank you.'

Silence, and stares. There was so much to say and neither of them could think of one thing. Then they spoke together.

'I thought you were—'

'You have not changed—'

118

Falling silent again. When she saw him breathe in, she spoke. 'I thought – we all thought – you were dead.'

'We?'

The word carried a weight. She did not pick it up. 'Your mother. And I. She is . . . She , , ,'

'I know. I did not until I returned.' He looked away, across the open water to where the Genoese colony of Galata rose to its highest point, the Tower of Christ, insubstantial in the misting rain. 'Did she die well?'

'I . . . I think so. She became a nun, died in a convent. In her sleep, I heard.'

'A nun?' It was the usual way for widows, to retire to a life of prayer and contemplation. But his mother had always had a raucous laugh. He could not imagine it contained in a cell. 'And did she take the vows after the rumour of my death? Or on the revelation of my treason.'

Sofia flinched at his tone. 'She did not believe . . . neither of us did. And when Theon returned and said there was doubt—'

'Theon!' He shouted the name, interrupting her. 'My loving brother. My . . . tardy brother.' That hatred he'd felt in the doorway surged again and he had to turn his masked face away from her, feeling the absence of his own nose as clearly as he saw hers.

She stepped to him, placed a hand on his arm. 'No one who knew you believed that the Turkish gold found in your bags was payment for treason.'

He turned to her, spitting words. 'Well, the soldiers who found it believed it! Wanted to believe it was treason that had caused the Hexamilion, that six-mile unbreachable wall, to crumble in six days. Not Turkish guns. Not someone's carelessness with a sally port. So the coins I'd pillaged from the enemy camp in our one counterattack confirmed their belief – and the battlefield court passed its sentence. While my brother . . . my loving brother came just in time to stop them acting beyond the first half of the sentence.' He gave a wild laugh. 'Oh, we both know his persuasive ways, do we not? He pleaded for my life and won it. Commuted my sentence. Sent me out into the world without a name. Without a . . .'

He coughed, broke off. For a moment he was not there, but back in the place and the time he'd see now only when he slept. Felt again his helmet ripped away, the arms that pinioned him, the hands that twisted his face up to meet the butcher bending down. No dark oblivion to fall into, then or since. White agony only that he sometimes still felt, even though the place for agony was gone. As if the saw-toothed blade never stopped grinding down, half drowning him in his own blood, shredding the cartilage, severing his nose.

She stepped to him, fingers on his arm. 'Theon said that Constantine . . . that if our future emperor had been well and not lying in a ship in a fever, he would have come too, stopped it . . .'

'Well, he would also have been too late,' Gregoras said savagely, ripping his arm free of her. 'For I would already have been marred. And no amount of pleading would have given me my nose back. Or my name. Or my city. Or my mother.' He was shaking as his voice rose still higher. 'Or you.'

It was there, spoken, somehow the worst of accusations. She'd known, from the moment she'd realised he was not a ghost, that she'd have to answer it. 'I had no choice, Gregoras. You must know that. The pact was forged between our families, contracts drawn . . .'

'And what of our pact?' he roared. 'Our contract?' He threw his arms wide. 'Sealed here, on this rock. Vows made to God, bound by our joined bodies.' She turned away but he got in front of her again, taking her arms now, seeking her eyes, which darted wildly about. 'Does he know of *that* vow, your husband, my tardy brother?'

Her eyes settled on his. She ceased to struggle against his grip. 'He does not. Though sometimes . . . sometimes I think he suspects.'

'Why? Why would he?' He could not help more savagery now as he shook her. 'Did you confess it?'

'Why?' She echoed him, freed herself, stepped away, turning from him to face the water. The panic in her left as swiftly as it had arrived. She had always known that, if by some miracle he had lived, she would have to say this one day. She had said it silently to the Holy Mother. To St Maria of the Mongols. To no one else. Now she would say it to him. 'Because we made something else, Gregoras, when we made love here that day.'

The rain was falling harder. It was cold again. But not the cold that smothered his anger like sudden snow. 'What . . . what can you mean?'

'Only that sometimes when he looks at our son, I think he sees a ghost.' She turned back to face him, to see his eyes above the mask. 'Your ghost.'

Gregoras's legs sagged. He sank down upon the rock. 'You mean . . . ?' he whispered. 'But how?'

'How?' The faintest smile came to her lips. 'You know the how. Sitting where once you lay, you must remember it.' The smile went. 'And when Theon was sent back early from the war with messages and the . . . the news, I was not close to showing the life within me. I was young and did not recognise the signs. When I did, when I knew . . .' She broke off, looked above him. 'We had already been married a week. And when the child was born, he was small enough at birth to pass for one sent before his time.' She came, knelt behind him where he sat, his head now on his knees. 'And he is beautiful, our son, Gregoras. As beautiful as his father . . .'

When she broke off, he raised his head. 'Was. You were going to say: was.'

'Is,' she replied. She lifted a hand, laid fingers on the edge of the mask. 'Let me see.'

'No.' It was too much. Suddenly he remembered the other woman he'd taken off his mask for, in Ragusa, two months before. Leilah had looked at him like no other woman had looked at him . . . since the afternoon he had last sat upon this rock. She'd had a hunger that had startled him. She'd looked with curiosity – but with no pity. He could not bear to see the pity he knew would be in Sofia's eyes. Anything was better than that. So he caught her reaching hand, pushed it aside, stood. She rose with him as he spoke. 'You have another child, do you not? I saw her at your window.'

'Minerva. She is five.'

'Theon's child?'

'Theon's . . .' She broke off. 'Of course, Theon's child. What do you mean?'

He saw the fire spark in her eyes, anger there. His rose to match it. 'I mean that you married one man while carrying his brother's child. I mean that betrayal can take many . . . physical forms. This one here . . .' he gestured at his face, then pointed at her belly, 'that one there.'

She let out a shriek, raised a hand as if to strike him. He grabbed it, held it as she tried to pull away, then let it go suddenly. She stumbled backwards, just kept her balance, looked down, as if seeking for shells upon the rocks. Only when she was sure she could speak did she raise her head and look at him again. 'I will pray to St Maria for you.'

'Pray to the devil,' he shouted, 'for he has me now.'

She stared at him for a long moment. 'You have changed, Gregoras.'

'Really? Do you think so?' he spat. 'I assume you are not referring to my disfigurement. You are too noble a lady to say that. But here, you wanted to see?' He reached up and ripped aside his mask. 'I bow to your request.'

The fingers he reached to the knot did not fumble. In a moment, with the flourish of a street mountebank, he pulled the ivory nose away. He did not know what he saw in her eyes, but he took it for pity, used it to focus his anger, and his voice came low and hard. 'Do me one kindness, Sofia. Remember me in your prayers just once as you remember me here that day. Then forget me for ever and pray for me no more.'

She turned away, shrugging off the cloak, which folded onto the rocks like a crouched body, moved to the door, through it, while Gregoras turned to the water, lifting his head to the ceaseless rain, feeling it fall *into* his face though his mouth was closed. He choked, coughed, looked to the ships. I want to be on one, he thought. But first I need paying. This city has taken everything else. It can give me that.

He was Gregoras no more. That man had died here upon this rock, there under a saw-toothed knife. From now on he was nothing but Zoran the mercenary. And he wanted his gold.

— ELEVEN —
Walls

Theon dropped the scrap of paper into the basket on his right and moved three more beads upon his abacus. He stared at their ranks, wondering. Had he made a mistake? It was not impossible. He had been at the task from two hours before dawn, when the first reports came in, and had continued, without pause, with barely a moment to eat, drink, relieve himself, until long after the matins had sounded in the nearby monastery of Christ Pantocrator. It was the sort of work that once he would have delegated to a clerk; but with this census that was not possible. Two men had been charged with the task by a third, and it did not matter that the two were *megas primikerios* and *megas archon* respectively, two of the highest ranks in the land. The third, the man they must report to, was the emperor himself, and only the three of them could know what secrets the abacus tallied.

He looked again, with some disgust, at the man next to him. He had been asleep for close to an hour, and was beginning to leak – from eye, from nose, from mouth. George Sphrantzes may have been the most venerated historian in Constantinople, at the centre of everything important that had happened to the empire for the last fifty years. Yet to Theon he was a barely living symbol of all that was wrong with that empire, an old man with an old man's cautions and compromises. Who cared now that he had once been the confidant of the last truly great *basileus*, Manuel? Or that he wrote the most elegant of begging letters to the kings and powers of the world, letters that were read, admired and ignored? Ink might flow from his pen like rheum now flowed from his eyes, but he, and men like him, had reduced that once mighty empire to essentially what was contained within the city's walls, that impoverished little.

And that impoverishment had been made all the clearer by this task that Theon had largely accomplished alone. Even if the old historian would get the credit, Theon did not envy him that. There was a time when messengers who brought such news could be executed on the spot. The emperor would not do that to the old man he loved. But there would be no reward for this night's work.

Theon watched the man begin to slouch towards him. He was about to move an arm in danger of becoming wet when Sphrantzes's elbow slipped, and he jerked his head up, stared wildly around, moist eyes focusing at last. 'Eh?' he said, wiping a cuff over his face. 'What did you say?'

'It is nearly done, Megas Archon,' Theon replied, though he had not spoken. 'There are only those for you to tally.'

He pointed to the basket at the older man's left, the scrolls curled in it. At his right, another, fuller basket awaited with the papers he had already checked. Sphrantzes rubbed his wispy white beard. 'I must have . . . Can't remember . . .' He peered at the first basket in the line, which had but one scroll in it and sat on Theon's left. 'You have been swift, young Lascaris. But your family always was. I was at school with your uncle . . . No, it must have been your grand-uncle, Theophilus. He beat everyone in the running games.' He smiled. 'Is he still alive?'

'No, Megas Archon.' Theon tipped the half-filled basket that was between them. 'Do you wish to check these?'

Shaking fingers reached, withdrew. 'I think I will trust your additions now, young Theophilus. And you have one last one to add, do you not?'

Theon didn't correct him on the name, just reached for the last piece of parchment. Like all the other monks they had used for the census, this one from the area near the old Bucoleon palace had exquisite penmanship. But beauty could not disguise the poverty of the figures the monk had written down.

Theon let the paper curl, dropped it into the other basket, reached, moved three beads. Sphrantzes squinted at the abacus, swallowed. 'It is done?'

'Done. Would you like to know?'

The older man glanced nervously around. The nearest others were through thick doors and walls. 'Write it for me, my son,' he commanded in a whisper, putting on his thick spectacles. 'Write it in Latin. Few can read it these days.'

Theon looked at the abacus, dipped his quill, wrote the numerals out. Then he blotted the sum, folded the paper, passed it over, waited.

Sphrantzes did not open the paper straightaway, holding it as if he'd been handed a dead, noisome insect. Then, taking a deep breath, he did.

Theon was watching him closely. There were thirteen characters on the page; they would take no time to read. But the older man pored over them as if they were a newly discovered fragment of Homer, reading, rereading. Only a slight tic under his left eye betrayed his reaction, and that could have been there already, unnoticed amongst his others.

Folding the paper, Sphrantzes took his glasses off, pinched between his eyes, spoke. 'Where is the emperor?'

'He meets the leaders of the defence upon the walls.'

The old man nodded, reached for the table, pushed himself up. 'Then let us go and tell him how many men he will have to defend them.' He swayed, grabbed for wood again. Steady, he glanced down to the curl of paper in his hand. 'Burn this,' he said, holding it out. 'Burn the blotter too. And the paper you rested on.'

Theon took the scrap of parchment back. 'Do you not need it?'

The old man's roar took him by surprise. 'Do you think, having seen that figure, that I could ever forget it?' he shouted. 'It is branded here . . .' he pointed to his head, 'and here.' He jabbed a thumb into his chest. 'I may be an old fool to you, Theon Lascaris, but I can read doom as well as one as young and swift as yourself.' He grabbed the staff that lay against the table. 'Give me your arm,' he muttered, fury fading, 'and let us go and break an emperor's heart.'

'You are like a centipede wedged under my breastplate,' Giustiniani roared, 'and me in the middle of the fray, unable to strip down and flick you away!'

'I am sorry to be so wearisome, Commander,' Gregoras replied, 'but you said you would speak to the emperor . . .'

'On the rare times I converse with Emperor Constantine, my son, we have a few other matters to get through before finding payment for a mercenary.'

'Nonetheless, you did promise . . .'

'Nonetheless? Nonetheless my arse. I promised I would try, and I will.' The big Genoan glared at him, and his voice came mockingly. 'Forgive me, Zoran, if I have been a little distracted. I am trying to figure out ways to save this fucking city from the Turk!'

Gregoras opened his mouth, closed it again rapidly. It was the third such conversation they'd had, each more heated than the last. All he'd do was provoke still more rage if he spoke. The problem was that Giustiniani was no longer merely the leader of his own band of mercenaries, concerned only with their well-being. When he'd arrived, he'd been greeted with more than just the acclaim bestowed on any strong body of reinforcements. His vast experience in war had led Constantine to immediately appoint him supreme commander of all the city's defences, and all forces within its walls. Since that time, finding gold to pay off promises was far from his mind.

Giustiniani raised his arms and his body servant came and strapped his huge sword round his waist. 'Still raining, Amir?' he called.

The Syrian at the window turned. 'Like the flood before Nuh called the animals. Wait much longer and we will have to row to the rendezvous.'

'I wish we could. I prefer a deck under my feet than my

rump in a saddle any day.' Giustiniani bent so that the servant could slip the thick wool cloak over his shoulders, then grabbed a broad-brimmed hat off the table and crammed it onto his head. He turned back to Gregoras. 'I'll tell you what, Zoran. I am going to meet the emperor now on the walls. If you come with us and stand in the corner of my eye like some bedraggled crow, I may find the moment to ask Constantine for a little gold. Though they say he is as poor as a mouse, he did order that all his richest citizens bring half their wealth to him forthwith. If they have, which I doubt – for these Greeks have pockets as long as their beards and arms as short as their cocks – then maybe he can spare two hundred ducats to silence your cawing.'

'It's three hundred ducats, Commander,' Gregoras said, through his teeth. He considered. He did not really want to leave the barracks, let alone be close to the imperial party. Too many around the emperor – including Constantine himself – knew Gregoras Lascaris of old. And even if some doubted his treason, he was still an exile, under pain of death if he returned. However, he also knew that if he did not stand within his sight, Giustiniani would forget him instantly. And then he would never get out of Constantinople with what he needed. So he sighed, nodded. 'I will come.'

'Good,' the Genoan said, clapping him on the back, the thunder vanished from his face. 'And since you've been in a few sieges in your time, perhaps you will favour us with your advice? For a few extra coins?'

'If it gets me out of this city faster, Commander, you can have that advice for free.'

'Christ have mercy!' Giustiniani staggered back, clutching at his heart. Then he turned and bellowed, 'Enzo! Fetch this Samaritan a horse.'

It was like riding through a solid wall of rain, driven hard into their faces by a gusty north-west wind. Still, as the four of them rode from their barracks in the Genoese quarter, out through the forums of Constantine and Theodosius, and into the land beyond, Gregoras was able to glance between hood and mask and see, yet again, how run-down the city was. Only every third house showed any sign of occupation. The shrinking population had moved to the seashores, occupying houses that the richer folk must have fled. Beyond the ancient ruins of the walls of the first Emperor Constantine there had always been open fields, villages, vineyards. But the fields were a wasteland of mud, half the villages deserted. Only as they neared the great Theodosian walls did he see activity, swarms of labourers moving over the stones, bearing others.

Tying up their horses, the Genoan led his party up circling stairs and out through a low door, onto the flat floor of the gate tower of Charisius. The wind and rain, which the walls had partially deflected, hit them full force now, causing all men there to secure hats and cloaks about them with one hand, and press the other against the crenellations.

'Have you been up here before, Ragusan?' Giustiniani had stepped close and still had to bellow to be heard above the wind singing in the battlements.

He had. His father had first brought him and Theon here under pretext of inspecting the never-ceasing works that kept them in repair; really, to tell his two sons tales of his service upon the ramparts, at the great siege of '22, when the present sultan's father, Murad, had come to conquer. It was not something to share with Giustiniani. 'Never, master.' Gregoras looked about. 'It is an impressive sight.'

'Aye, is it not? Not one wall. Not two. Three.' The Commander lifted his arm and swept it before him. 'This is the highest point of the defences. You see how it falls to the south, then rises again?' Gregoras looked, to the steeply descending slope of walls and small towers that then rose to the bulky grey blur of a larger tower close to a mile away. The other man continued, following his gaze, 'That's the civil gate of St Romanus, and that valley . . .' he swept his hand straight before him, 'that almost funnels towards us here, is known as the Mesoteichion.' He sucked at his lower lip. 'From all I have read and heard, this place has always been the focus of any attack. I have no doubt it will be again. This, between the gates of Charisius and St Romanus, is our heel of Achilles. This is the weak spot.'

'Weak?' Amir whistled. 'By the Prophet's beard! I have seen cities that were justly proud of one wall such as is before us. But three?'

'Aye. Built them a thousand years ago. Yet still they stand.' Enzo shook his head. 'How is that possible?'

'Because we . . . those old Greeks knew how to build,' Gregoras muttered. He remembered his father's description of the killing ground before them. 'They are . . . perfection.'

'Nothing is perfect in siegecraft, Zoran, as you well know,' Giustiniani said, 'but this is as close as you will ever encounter. Come, let me tell the Ragusan what he will miss if he leaves before the fight.' Clamping his hat to his head, he led them from the more sheltered rear of the platform to its blustery front. 'We stand on the highest, the landward inner walls. Some say we should fight only upon them, cede the rest of the ground to the enemy. I say they are wrong.'

'Why, master?' asked Amir.

'Many reasons – and this the main.' Giustiniani reached forward and, with some ease, pulled a chunk of rock from the crenel. 'The inner walls have been most neglected over the years. This is one of the better-kept ones and, as you see . . .' He crumbled mortar between his fingers. 'They are far worse either side of us. But the second wall . . .' he pointed down, 'has had most of the efforts expended upon it. Its towers are smaller but it stands above that open space they call the Parateichion. Since that can only be reached by a scramble up from the deep ditch and over the last, smallest of the walls, the Parateichion is one of the finest killing zones I have ever seen.' He leaned over the edge. 'From up here, our best archers, crossbowmen and culverin men can rain hell into it, over the heads of our defenders at the outer wall. Those few of the enemy who survive will be chopped into separate parts by our soldiers.'

Gregoras leaned out too. 'A perfect killing zone indeed, Commander. I shall envy you your fortunes,' he said. 'So where is this Achilles heel?'

Giustiniani sucked his lower lip. 'Out there. They are bringing it with them. No,' he snorted. 'You cannot bring a heel, can you? But you can bring the poisoned arrow to shoot into the hero's flesh.'

'You mean guns, Commander, do you not?' Enzo, the blunt Sicilian, said.

'Aye. Cannon. If our spies' reports are true, such cannon as have never been seen before. Forged by devils to spit fire straight from hell.' Giustiniani leaned to the side and spat himself, angling it into the wind, a fat gobbet that was caught and splattered into the granite behind them. 'Murad had some guns but they were boy's slingshots compared to what his son is said to be bringing. If he places them and hits these walls somewhere between here and St Romanus, again and again by day, and our efforts to repair them at night prove insufficient . . .' he shook his head, 'then the breach he makes will widen and widen and the fanatics he throws at it to die for him and for Allah, of whom he has so many, will keep coming and coming . . .' he cleared his throat, hawked again, 'until eventually even the finest killing ground in Christendom may not prove enough.'

'What will then, Commander?' As a boy, Gregoras had dreamed of fighting these walls like his father had. The idea of them ever being taken . . . 'Prayer?'

'Of course. We pray for a miracle. God will dispose, as ever.' Giustiniani raised the medallion of San Pietro round his neck and kissed it fervently. 'Yet until His will is revealed, we strengthen our walls, we sharpen our blades, we place our best men where they are most needed and, yes, we pray – not for lightning bolts from heaven perhaps, but for something a little more plain.' He pointed out to the valley again, beyond the valley. 'We pray that the powers of the West, from the Pope to the Roman emperor, from bishops to barons, realise that if they do not stop the Turk at these walls, they will have to stop him at their own. We pray that we can hold these crumbling stones long enough for them to act on that realisation and send a relieving army or fleet. And that,' he said, crossing himself, 'will be miracle enough for me.'

Enzo imitated the Commander and made the sign of the cross. Caught up in the moment, Gregoras did too. Yet his return to his city had affected him this much: his crossing now was the opposite to the Catholics before him, three fingers, not two, and moving right-left across his chest. All saw it, the division between allies. In many ways, Amir's obeisance to Allah was less disturbing. 'While that,' said Giustiniani, 'is another matter.' He spread his arms wide, herding them towards the stairs. 'Now let us go and meet the emperor. He awaits us down there, at the Romanus gate.'

'May I accompany you?'

The four men, warriors all, started, flinched back – for the black figure that suddenly loomed up behind them did not appear human; or had been once, only to recently crawl from his grave. It was Gregoras who recognised the skinny, mud-clotted frame, mainly by the Italian words that seemed wrenched from the back of the throat. 'Grant,' he cried, easing the grip on his dagger. 'Are you living in a hole?'

'Aye, most of the time.' The Scot reached up and scraped muck from his face. 'The emperor has had me exploring the ground near some of the bastions. To foresee where the Turks will mine, so we can countermine 'em. I think I've found a few likely places. It's why I want to see him, ye ken.' He tipped his face into the rain. 'Man, I could use one of these baths the Greeks are always taking. Though no doubt I'd catch my death from such an effeminate practice.'

He shook his head and Gregoras laughed. He was fond of the Scotsman, after their time at sea. 'I will take you to one, if you like.'

Giustiniani frowned. 'I thought your task was to provide me with the weapon called Greek Fire?'

'It is. And I have been experimenting. But I need more naphtha, a combustible oil found most in some place name of Irak. Men are searching the town for it.' He shrugged, spat mud, 'So I'll dig and delve until they find some.'

Giustiniani moved on towards the tower's entrance. 'You may report your findings to Constantine. Come, German,' he called over his shoulder.

'That's Scots, your wor— Och, why bother?' As they followed the Commander through the archway, Grant leaned in and whispered, 'I've set up a distillery too, while I wait. First batch will be ready end of the week. It won't be smooth but it will slake a thirst. Will ye come?'

'Perhaps.' Gregoras would have been happy to partake of his friend's *al-kohl*. But if he could keep in Giustiniani's vision, and goad him into asking for his gold, he hoped he would not be there at week's end. And having the Scot beside him as a reminder of the contract he'd fulfilled would not hurt. He clapped his hand onto a sodden shoulder. 'Come. Let us to the emperor.'

TWELVE

Old Friends

Constantine had changed.

The vigorous warrior Gregoras remembered had been the Despot of the Morea, a land not without troubles but with options and allies. Now he was Emperor of Constantinople – and the burden of that ancient title, in the empire's greatest crisis, had stooped him. Taken the hair from his forehead, greyed his beard, etched lines around his eyes.

He stood in a white cloak, head bent, at the centre of a swirl of black-clad figures who squabbled around him like crows around a dove. It was clear that the leaders of the Genoese and Venetian colonies still hated each other. Nothing new there, Gregoras thought. Centuries of struggle to become the greatest trading power in the world, conflict on sea and land with the city as a regular battleground – and sometimes victim – made unity in a cause near impossible. Even if that cause was their own survival.

Gregoras and Grant placed their backs against the wall near the gate and watched as Giustiniani took a deep breath before pushing into the crowd within the Peribolos, the space between the inner and outer walls. His presence – not to mention his girth and height – brought some silence. A little cluster of gesticulating, cursing men did not see him. But a horn was raised, sounded, its shrill blast bouncing off the stones, making men duck, wince, look around for the source – which Gregoras finally saw as the mob shifted. 'The devil,' he gasped, taking a step forward.

The man lowering the horn from his lips was Theodore of

Karystenos. Champion bowman, captain of archers for the Imperial Guard . . . and the man who had taught Gregoras everything he'd known about war, and not a little about life.

Gregoras had presumed him dead. He was ancient when he'd taken the young Greek on as a pupil fifteen years before. And the man who now stepped up beside his emperor *was* old, his long beard pure white, the lines of easy laughter that had always danced around his eyes deep furrows now. But he was not bent by age, and if its pains afflicted him he did not show it, slinging the horn over his shoulder, drawing his sword. Muscles thrust out the surplice he wore, marked with the double eagle of the city. 'Cry silence for our lord,' he bellowed in a voice near as loud as his bugle blast.

Theodore! Of all in the city who would have heard of Gregoras's 'treason', the aged bowman would have been the most hurt. He'd regarded Gregoras as his sixth son, and knew him to be the most gifted, of a gifted brood, with the bow. And it was not just a love of feathered flight that bound them. It was to Theodore that Gregoras would come to hear the old tales of war and adventure, and plan his own share of them.

Gregoras looked down, away from the memories. If any man in Constantinople could persuade him to stay and fight for it, that man was Theodore of Karystenos. He would have to keep masked and far from the old man's still lively gaze.

To his relief, men swirled before him, taking his old teacher from his sight. When they cleared, Giustiniani was stepping forward. 'Our *basileus*, Constantine,' he declared, using the ancient title of supreme general, 'who has honoured me beyond all measure by giving me the disposition of his forces, has asked that I speak of them today.' He paused, looked over the whole crowd. 'You all know me. I have fought beside many of you standing here. I have fought against many of you too – yes, I see you lurking there, brothers Bocciardi of Venice . . .' this produced a shout of denial from three men who stepped around others who blocked their view, 'and you, most of all,

Girolamo Minotto, *baillie* of the Venetian colony. How many times have we exchanged quarrels upon the sea?'

A tall man, with twice the lace to his doublet than anyone else, swept off his plumed hat, revealing styled curled hair, and bowed. 'Twice, most excellent. And only the wind saved you last time off Crete.'

A chorus of jeers arose at that, laughter too, in which Giustiniani joined. 'I will concede that,' he replied, 'if you will concede the wind you emitted when I drove you onto the reefs of Lesbos.'

More acclamation, denial, laughter. But Giustiniani cut it off with a wave of the hand. 'But whether we have always been friends or worthy adversaries in the past, on ships and other battlements,' he continued, 'what is certain here and now is this: today we are united as soldiers of the beloved emperor. United in our hatred of the infidel. United in our faith under God, and before the face of the Blessed Virgin.'

Nearly every man crossed himself, murmured amen. After a moment, in a quieter voice, Giustiniani went on. 'Since my arrival three weeks ago, and in the company of our exalted sovereign, I have studied the rolls of our forces. I have walked the walls – these we stand upon and those that line the shores of the Golden Horn and the Sea of Marmara – to see how we should disperse those forces. Now each of you who are not native to the empire – you of Venice and Genoa, of Crete and Chios, of Spain and Catalonia – are used to being only under your own command, going where you will, fighting for as long or as little as you think fit. Yet since we are now so united, in faith and fervour for our cause, I ask that you consider these dispositions, and hold your allotted place as long as a single comrade, of whatever nation, holds the one next to you. Let no man fail his neighbour.'

He turned. Enzo and Amir were standing behind him, each at one end of a large cloth pinned to the stones of the inner wall. Reaching, they pulled it down.

Gregoras and Grant, like everyone else, stepped forward for

a better view. Etched in chalk was the unmistakable dog's-head shape of Constantinople. The land walls, against which it was drawn, were a vivid red slash down the neck. Small banners marked different sections, some containing symbols, others names. Both were too small for even Gregoras's keen eyes, but not for those who crowded closer. Once read, they provoked many oaths and exclamations, and a rising babble of dissent.

One voice was clear above the others. 'Why are all these Greek names by the harbours of the Golden Horn?' the Venetian *baillie* Minotto called out. 'While the Venetians are here and here and here.' He jabbed his finger at various points. 'Why do you separate sailors from their ships?'

A Genoan voice came from the thick of that city's merchants. 'Isn't it obvious? To stop those sailors sailing away at the first whistle of Turkish shot.'

'You lie!' The body of Venetians surged, shouting, around their leader, who stepped toward the Genoans. Hands gripped daggers. 'And you are all safe because of your colony of Galata just across the Horn,' someone cried. 'You are the ones who will scuttle for your homes when the first sword is drawn.'

The babble became a roar. Men stepped closer, as Giustiniani shouted in vain . . . until the bugle's blast sounded again.

'Enough!'

It was Constantine who called, his cultured voice hoarse with use. He stepped forward with arms raised, and men turned to listen to the emperor. 'Enough, lords, gentlemen, citizens of mighty Genoa and proud Venice. Remember where your enemy is.' He threw his arm back behind him. 'There, the other side of the walls. Not within them. There!' The hubbub died a little, and he continued in a softer voice. 'This is a preliminary plan only, and we will listen to all your concerns. If some Venetians want to stay with their ships, why would we object? You have all sworn to stay and fight, and the oaths of such men are their honour and so are unbreakable.' His gaze swept over the crowd, his voice grew stronger. 'But do you not see why we have suggested this disposition? It is *because* of Venice's honour. You can do good service at the harbours, sure. But the main fight will not be there. It will be here.' He turned, placed his palm at the top end of the dog's neck, against the red painted lines. 'Here would stand the intrepid Bocciardi brothers of your city, here where the walls are thought vulnerable. In the lion's mouth.'

Three men, almost identical behind their thick beards, swept off their hats and bowed. 'We will die there to protect it,' they declared in chorus.

'I know you will,' Constantine said, smiling. 'But there is a more dangerous spot even than that.' He ran his hand up the red line, stopping where it seemed to bulge inwards. 'For here is my palace of Blachernae – and there is only one man I thought to ask to defend it.' His eyes sought and found that man. 'Will you yourself, Minotto, *baillie* of Venice, protect my home?'

The Venetian ran a hand through his coiffed hair, then bowed. 'It is a great honour, majesty, and I thank you.' His dark face flushed. 'And, as leader of the men of Venice, I declare that not one of our number shall desert you, while there is life in your body and while the banners of Constantinople fly.' He turned to glare at his fellow countrymen. 'Not one!'

A huge cheer came. Constantine waited for it to die down, and in a quieter voice went on, 'And I will stand sometimes here at my palace, or here at the gate of Charisius, that some call Adrianople. Wherever the action is hottest,' he said, a slight smile coming, 'for since my winters in the mountains of the Morea, I have always craved the heat.'

There was some laughter. Hands were withdrawn from hilts, as men peered closer at chalked lines and words.

'And have you a place of honour for an old servant, sire?'

The man who said this was as old as Theodore. But he did not look half as vigorous: gangly, stooped, rain running from the rim of an old-fashioned steel helm like water from battered eaves. His voice piped high, and though one hand rested on the basket hilt of a sword, the other was more heavily supported by a servant's shoulder to his right.

'Ah, my good Don Francisco de Toledo.' Constantine smiled, 'Do you not wish to wield the famed steel of your city beside your compatriots?' He gestured to a group of sunburned men to the Spaniard's left.

'My liege,' replied the don, bowing slightly, 'if you are referring to the detachment from Catalonia, then no. Castilians and Catalans make the rivals of Venice and Genoa look like children, squabbling over dice.'

No one was quite sure who was the most insulted. Before they could decide, Constantine stepped forward and offered the old man an arm. 'How would you like to fight beside me, Don Francisco? I could use Toledo steel to guard my back.'

The Castilian unfolded himself from his stoop. 'An honour to me and my country, sire.'

As the emperor led the don to a barrel beside the wall, Girolamo Minotto stepped away from it. 'I have a question, Giovanni Giustiniani Longo,' he called. 'Where will you be? You and your seven hundred men? I do not see your name in chalk. Are you leaving us so soon?'

The Commander, who had stepped back when Constantine spoke, laughed as he advanced again. 'We will go wherever we are most required. But I suspect we shall be here, or close. Between the palace and this, the Fifth Military gate.' Amir came and whispered in his ear. Giustiniani nodded, then raised his voice again. 'Take note of this, all of you. I am reminded that it is a custom of war here to name the military gates after their nearest civilian one. That is a confusion to me, and battle is confusing enough.' He shook his head, continued. 'I am here not to jiggle with names but to fight. So know that this gate we stand before will henceforth be known only as St Romanus. When I summon urgent reinforcements, let them not go to the wrong one.'

He gestured at the tower atop the gate. 'Now. I have studied the land, spoken to men who withstood Murad's siege in '22. And I know the Turk. He will attack the length of the walls. He will raid the shoreline. But his cannon will mostly pound here. His finest troops will attack here. So I will be here.'

A murmur arose again. Men crowded ever closer to the wall and its chalk. One of the brothers, whom Gregoras had heard named Bocciardi, was having a loudly whispered debate with his siblings. At last he threw a restraining arm off himself and turned. 'There are many Italian names here,' he called. 'Mainly from my own city of Venice, a few less from Genoa . . .' his voice rose over the dispute he'd provoked, 'others from the Papal States, from Tuscany, Sicily, Umbria. But where are the Greek names? I see hardly any. This *is* a Greek city, is it not?'

Others voices loudly joined the call. Constantine raised his hands. 'You see only some names – Loukas Notaras, the *megas doux*, for example – because these are the men we know are in the city. Others are on embassy or soldiering beyond our walls. When they return, they will command our imperial forces . . .' He broke off, looking suddenly above the heads of the throng, just to Gregoras's left. 'And here are the men who will be able to tell us what those forces are! Come forward, old friends. Come.'

Gregoras looked. The first man to come through the gate masked the other, and that first was George Sphrantzes, court historian and friend to emperors past. He cleared . . . and Gregoras saw the man he'd concealed.

Theon Lascaris.

Gregoras's first thought was his knife. His hand dropped onto the hilt, but instead of drawing it, he swung away, turning his head to the north. When he glanced back, his brother had gone past, eyes fixed on the beckoning Constantine.

He let go of his knife. Theon, he thought, but the name sounding in his head did not bring with it the clear, bright hatred it had brought for so long. That had become muddied by Sofia's revelation the day before – that beside Theon, raised as his own, would be Gregoras's son.

My son. Mine! He thought of him now, as he had not thought of him till this moment, too stunned to consider, as if from a mace blow to his helmet. What does he look like? he wondered suddenly. And then: does he have my mother's laugh?

He tried to focus again on the group of men before him. The aged Sphrantzes had drawn Constantine aside to whisper in his ear, and Gregoras watched as such colour as there was fled the emperor's face. He beckoned Giustiniani, who stooped to hear and go pale in his turn. Questions were being asked that Gregoras could not hear. But he could hear the words that came from beside him, though he had not heard the approach of the man who spoke them.

'I know who you are,' came the whisper. Fingers tightened on his arm. 'And I had to feel that you were alive and not a ghost.'

Gregoras turned. It was a rare man who could take him unawares. But Theodore of Karystenos had always been a rare man.

Gregoras looked up into watery grey eyes. Saw no danger in them, no threat that the traitor and exile was about to be unmasked. Only the same amusement that had ever been there, mixed now with curiosity. 'How did you know me, master?'

'By the way you stand, my young man. Even when you wielded a bow, and despite the years I spent trying to beat it out of you, you always stood that way, ever forward, like a heron about to strike. Once I'd finished calling on the Virgin to protect me from ghosts and demons, once you did not vanish into stone or rise into the air spouting flame, I had to know for sure.' Fingers like small iron bars kneaded Gregoras's forearm. 'You are with these Genoans?'

'I am. I sought refuge in their company. Have fought with them on a dozen ventures.'

'Fought?' His hand settled again on Gregoras's arm, higher up. 'But not with the bow, certain. You have the muscles of a girl.'

Gregoras smiled. 'They use the crossbow.'

Theodore spat. 'An assassin's weapon! And you, an archer of the guard, one of the elite! What's become of you, boy?'

His smile vanished. 'Treason and exile, master. One must make one's way as one can.'

Sadness replaced the humour in the old man's eyes. 'I know. I know,' he said, gently shaking the arm he held. He stepped closer, his voice lowering further. 'You have to know, Gregoras, that none of your comrades believed . . . that *I* did not believe in your villainy. No one who truly knew you did. But when those bastard Turks brushed aside our wall in the Morea as if it were gossamer, and some poured through that sally port that was left ajar, well . . .' He shrugged. 'Many sought to quell their despair in God's fury, or treason. I was unconscious for three days from a sling stone to the head.' He sighed. 'By the time I recovered, it was too late. The first part of the sentence . . .' he gestured vaguely to Gregoras's face, 'had been carried out. And you were gone.'

Gregoras grunted. It meant something, a little anyway, that his mentor had not thought him a traitor. But it was still too late.

Theodore continued, 'You were unlucky, lad. Wrong place, wrong time. And the Turkish gold in your pack . . .'

'I found it. In our one counterattack on the Turkish camp. I came back through that sally port and I locked it. Locked it!' Gregoras was a little startled by his heat. He thought he'd cooled it in a thousand wineskins.

'I am sure.' The older man patted his arm, looked away. 'At least your brother was there. To plead for you. To save you from a worse fate.'

'Worse?' The heat flared higher. 'You think there is something worse than this?' He pressed his face out against the mask. 'Than exile and dishonour? To be "saved" by a brother? A brother who then . . .' He broke off. It was not something to discuss, even with a man who had once been a father to him.

'My young man,' Theodore said softly, raising his hand to the other's shoulder.

Then his words were interrupted. Constantine was speaking. 'I have had news I must attend to,' the emperor declared. 'We will meet tomorrow at the imperial palace to discuss further dispositions.' He held a hand against the questions that were being called out. 'All will be answered then.'

He began to move towards them at the stairwell, Giustiniani at his shoulder. 'I must away with him,' Theodore said. He squeezed Gregoras's arm again, half turned away, turned back, gripping harder. 'Why do you not come too, lad? The emperor did not believe the accusations against you any more than I did. But there was never time to reconsider them. A brief retrial. A decree issued from the palace. Your name restored to you.' He smiled. 'When he sees you here, returned to fight for your city . . .'

Gregoras shrugged the hand off his shoulder. 'No,' he said, with more force than he'd intended, startling the older man. He breathed deep, then spoke more softly. 'Not now. There are . . . affairs I must attend to first. Leave me now and I will join you later. When the time is right.'

Theodore studied him for a long moment, then nodded. 'Very well. But do not delay too long. If you were recognised and . . .' he hesitated, 'unmasked, it might go ill for you before we could intervene. There are many in the city who, as before, seek vengeance to assuage their terror.'

'I will be careful. And I will come soon.'

'Do so. The crisis is nearly upon us.' He smiled. 'And it will take me some time to break you of all your crossbowman's bad habits.' He punched the arm he'd lately held and followed Constantine.

The men that passed through the archway had their own concerns. They were not seeking traitors. Even Giustiniani did not glance at him. So Gregoras was able to study, unobserved, all the faces – those he did not know. Those he did.

Theon. His proximity caused a cramp in Gregoras's stomach,

a surge of bile to reach his mouth. His hands rose, not to grip a dagger this time, but a throat. In sleepless dreams he had considered a thousand ways to kill Theon. Strangling, watching life slowly leave the hated face, had always seemed the best.

And yet that face! With Sphrantzes whispering in his ear, his brother nodding, tight-mouthed, suddenly Gregoras saw another mouth there, a different face, far younger. An imagined one, for he had never properly seen the boy that Theon called son.

His hands dropped. From their looks he knew that the discussions ahead would be long and stormy. It would give him time to ride back into the city, to stare up again at familiar windows, to glimpse, perhaps, the product of love and hatred.

John Grant tried to delay him. 'Will you take a cup with me?' the Scot asked.

Gregoras was already moving past him. 'Later,' he replied. 'I will find you.'

He would. The Scot was one of the very few he still cared about in doomed Constantinople. Another was his commander. But if Giustiniani did not pay him what was promised, Gregoras would wish him to the devil. And the city with him.

He ran back along the battlements, descended the stair. His horse was there. He mounted. 'Yah,' he cried, and galloped into the rain.

THIRTEEN

The Love of Two Brothers

By the time he reined in at the Genoan barracks, the steam from his galloping mount had almost warmed him. Leaving the mare with a groom there, he went into the tavern. It was too late for some of the mercenaries who would frequent it, too early for some others, and he had it to himself. Slowly he drank his way through a flagon and rid himself of his last chill by the fireplace. Then he left, hunched against the rain, and walked towards the gate of Theodosia, and his old family house close by it.

He was not there for his ghosts now. He saw lights, shadows moving against whitewashed walls within. Hoping one of them was the shadow he sought, he stepped up to the door, lifted the brass knocker, struck.

Sofia knew who it was. She had been expecting his visit from the moment they'd parted three days before. She knew he would not be able to keep away. Not after what she had told him. But who would come? The Gregoras of their youth? Or the one she'd just encountered? The laugher or the avenger? When she was not attending to her duties, she would kneel before the household altar and pray. Not for one to appear and not the other. For the grace to handle whoever came.

She was praying when he knocked. Crossing herself, she rose swiftly, bent for a moment as the blood returned to her legs, then descended the stairs. 'Who's there?' she called.

'I.'

She shot the bolts, opened the door. She could not see his face, but his voice was quiet within its shroud. 'Do you open your own doors? Where are your servants?'

'We have just one. I sent her out. Let her go visit her sweet-heart. Times are . . . different now.'

'They are.' He did not move. 'And your children?'

'My daughter is asleep upstairs. My son . . . is elsewhere.'

'Did you send him out too?'

'No. He . . . he visits a tutor. Mathematics. He is . . . not gifted.'

'Like his father, then.'

She did not know whom he meant. And still he made no move. 'Will you enter?'

'I will.'

He followed her up the familiar stairs. They opened onto the large central room where his family had always gathered. It had changed, different furniture, an altar against one wall. Yet it was the same room.

'Will you . . . ?' Sofia pointed to some slippers beside the entranceway. Some would be for guests. Some would be her husband's. After a moment's hesitation, he bent, removed his boots, put on a soft pair.

'Would you . . . ?' She opened her hands, to chairs around a table before the fireplace, its funnel-shaped chimney dis-appearing into the rooms above.

'Yes.' He moved slowly to it. He had come with demands. Here, in a room of ghosts, he could not remember any of them.

He sat, she stood. They looked at each other. The silence extended. And then a cat jumped into his lap. 'Jesu!' he cried.

'Ulvikul!'

She came forward to shoo the cat away. But Gregoras had already found its weak point, fingers rubbing rhythmically under its chin, the animal bending to his touch.

'A handsome beast,' he murmured. 'And you call him . . . ?'

'Ulvikul. A Turkish envoy who came, he gave him the name. It is because . . .'

'Of this.' Gregoras changed his stroking to the spot. 'The "M" above his eyes. He is beloved of Muhammad.'

146

'Yes.' She bent, rubbed her hand up the belly that was now exposed. The cat, in double assault, purred in ecstasy. Their fingers touched. Both stopped rubbing. She turned, walked a few steps away and the cat leapt off to follow her.

'He has a limp, your beloved.'

'Yes. He had an accident.'

'What kind?'

'Broke his leg. Fell out of a window.'

'You and your animals, Sofitra.' He paused as he used her childhood name, then went on quickly, 'What was that dog you had, the bitch from the street? It had skin like a leper's.'

'Pistotatos!' she cried. 'I loved her.'

'I know. You were the only one. She had a litter of puppies, each even uglier than herself, fit only for drowning.'

'Which you did not do, did you, Gregor? You and Th . . .' She hesitated, went on. 'You found a home for each one.'

'We did, my brother and I.' He licked his lips. 'But it was I alone who found other beasts for you when you decided to build the Ark.'

She came, sat opposite him. 'It had rained worse than this, for months it seemed. I was sure the flood was coming.'

'What were we? Eight? You convinced me, enough to send me down rat holes and up trees to squirrels' nests.' He held out a forefinger. 'You see that? That crescent-moon scar?'

She took the finger, peered. 'Yes?'

'You needed a parrot. I tried to steal it from that Circassian trader's shop. It took the top of my finger off.' He laughed. 'I don't know which hurt worse. That, or the thrashing my father gave me for thievery.'

She laughed too, still held his finger – until the cat rose onto its hind legs, thrust its head up, seeking strokes, breaking the grip.

'My first scar for you. Not my last.'

He had meant all scars. Thought he had, anyway. She took it differently. 'Gregor, I am so sorry . . .'

He held up his scarred hand. 'As am I. For what I said . . .

the other day. It was not what I felt. No, it was, for it was my anger. But not my belief.'

'I know.' Sofia leaned forward. 'You have reason for your anger.'

'Yes. Yes, I do.' He sat back, the cat craning up to look at him. Gregoras was aware again of what was between them. Actually between them, the mask and all it hid.

It was as if she spoke then to his thoughts. 'May I see again . . . your other scar?'

She raised her hand, reached towards his face. He caught it. 'Why?' he rasped, his throat dry. 'Curiosity? Is it not said that it will be the death of cats?'

'Not curiosity. Perhaps I wish to see again what fate wrought for us.'

'Then see,' he said, and released her hand.

He had seen the shock there before, the pity. He had recoiled from it. Now, as she reached and slipped the mask down, he saw only study, a woman's concern. 'Does it hurt?' she asked, her fingertips hovering near the ivory replica.

'No. It aches sometimes. But that is from its absence, not its presence.' He closed his eyes, as her fingers ran lightly down the side, where ivory met skin. Opened them again, spoke part of the question that had been there from the beginning. 'Does he . . . *he* have my nose? Our son?'

'Oh.' She sat back, looked away, to the cat, busy with something in the corner. 'He is young. Seven. His nose . . . it is not yet fully shaped.'

'Is that so?' He shook his head. 'I know little about children. I have not . . .'

He broke off, as the cat gave a little jump, landed. They both saw something else there, something small that tried to dart away, then froze as claws descended fast.

'Look,' she said, 'a mouse.'

'Yes.' He watched the cat release the mouse, corner it again. 'He is fast, despite his injury.'

'Yes.'

'There was a time when you would have saved it.'

'Yes.'

She watched the death game. He watched her, her eyes in the fire glow, the lines that ran from them. There were things missing that he used to see there. Her joy, that could light rooms, was gone. But he had seen caring there before, when she looked at his maiming. She was the same person, for all her travails. He leaned forward, spoke low and urgently what he'd come to say. 'That mouse is this city, Sofitra. The cat is the Turk, except the Turk when he comes will not limp. He will toy with us for a while and then he will swallow us whole.'

'You cannot know this.'

'I can! For I know him, have fought him on a dozen grounds. He is hard to beat when the numbers are close to even. But when he is bringing ten, twenty times our strength, to a city that is already almost dead . . .' He shook his head. 'He will not be stopped. And he will come up those stairs, and he will take whatever he wants.' His voice dropped to a whisper. 'You and my . . . your children must not be here when he does.'

She stared back at him. 'Where would we go?'

'Anywhere but here. I would accompany you, if you let me. See you safe.'

'You would desert our city? Our home? Now when she needs you most?'

'It is not my home any more,' he replied, hotly. 'I owe her nothing and I did not return to fight for her.'

'So why did you come back?'

He did not answer. For a moment he thought it was because he was ashamed to say that he was there for gold. And then he realised – and the realisation shocked him – that gold may have been the excuse. But it was not the reason. The reason sat before him. The reason was her.

'It is strange,' she said after a moment. 'But though you are so different, your brother and you, you are alike in this.'

He stiffened. 'How?'

'You both want me gone. He has tried to send me from the city, as so many of the richer families have sent their kin. And I know that a wife is subject to her husband, how she should always obey . . .' She swallowed. 'But I could not in this. And nothing he could say or . . . or do would persuade me.'

'Why not? What can you do here?'

'Little enough, sure. But if the Turk batters down our walls by day, I can go to them at night and help to patch them. I can take care of the wounded, bring them water and solace. Most of all, I can pray.'

Gregoras sat back. 'Pray?' he echoed.

'God loves us, Gregoras. He will forgive our sins, even those of this sinful city. And Our Lady who watches over us closely, she will not let her own city fall to the heathen. At the last, in our hour of most desperate need, she will guide heaven's holy fire down upon our enemies.'

He leaned forward, took her hand. 'But, Sofia,' he said softly, 'do you not think that the Turk is praying for exactly the same thing?'

She took her hand back. 'You cannot liken an infidel's prayer to ours.'

'And if God, Whose ways are mysterious, has decided that we should be punished and not forgiven?'

She shrugged. 'Then His will be done.'

Gregoras did not reply. It was an argument he had given up having years before. His own faith had been taken along with his nose. But he knew that no words of his would convince a believer. He would have to try different persuasion. 'And your children? They cannot choose as you choose. And you know the fate that may befall them if God has turned His back.' He shuddered, for he had seen what happened when the Muslims took a town that had failed to surrender. He had seen what Christians did too. Exactly the same. 'What then?'

She rose, went to the fireplace, where the logs had burned low. Stooping, she piled two more on before she spoke again.

'My parents had a Turkish maid once. She always said, "*Inshallah.*"'

'It means, "As God wills it."'

'I know.' She rose, turned back to him. '*Inshallah.*'

She looked so lost. He stood, stepped close to her. 'Sofitra,' he whispered.

There was a hammering on the front door. 'Your son?' he said, turning towards the sound.

'No. His knock is gentle, like himself.' She bit her lip. 'It is my husband.' He started, turned. 'There is a back way. Take it.'

Gregoras took a step, then stopped. He had discovered earlier that there was one reason beyond gold he had come to the city. Now he realised there was a second. 'No.'

She came to him, anguish on her face. 'You cannot stay! You are an exile. It is death if you are found here.'

'It is death only if I am revealed.'

'But . . .' Her eyes grew wider. 'You . . . you will not hurt him?'

It was all his dreams, for years, the hurting of Theon. He shuddered. 'I will not hurt him . . . within these walls. That much I will promise you. You have my word. Open the door.'

She did not move. 'And you will not . . . not tell him what I told you upon the rock?'

He took a breath. 'I will not.' He watched her hesitate. 'It is not for me to tell him, Sofia, however much I wish to hurt him. It is for you, if you so choose. If you do not, well . . .' He straightened. 'You have my word again. Now, go and open the door.'

She looked at him for a moment, then stepped away. When she reached the first step, he called her. 'Do not tell him I am here,' he said. 'I want to see his face when he sees mine. Give me that at least.'

She did not turn round. But he could see her nod, before she descended the stair, as he tied his mask back in place.

*

Theon leaned against the door, but it was only his tired body that rested. His mind seethed, Roman numerals flashing within it, as if laid over the chalked, crumbling walls of Constantinople.

MMMMCMLXXXIII. Four thousand nine hundred and eighty-three. The number of citizens within those walls able to defend them.

He'd become light-headed with exhaustion on the ride back from the meeting at the Blachernae palace. He'd begun to focus on the last 'III' of the tally. Who were they, those three men that the monk of the area around the Bucoleon palace had added last? Were they, like so many of the total, not soldiers at all? Thanos, perhaps, a cobbler? Markos, the tanner? Loukas, the ropewright? Each able to pick up a slingshot or hoist a spear without any true ability in either? If there had been twenty thousand, as had been hoped when the emperor decreed the secret census, that would have been one thing. Twenty thousand citizens on the walls would have made a fair display. Even ten, if they were spread out enough. But fewer than five?

Sphrantzes had been right – it had indeed seemed to break the emperor's heart, to have it confirmed just how impoverished his empire was. It was news that had to be kept to the barest minimum of ears. If it got out to the foreign forces – who, by anyone's guess, barely totalled two thousand more men, albeit most with some military skill – that they would have so few Greeks beside them in the unequal fight . . . well, it was suspected that for all their loyal declarations, many would decide not to remain.

Theon continued to stare at wood. His wife was slow at answering, but she was probably asleep at the top of the house. It was the problem of getting rid of most of the servants, selling the slaves, all to amass as much money as possible. In the grain of the wood, he noticed a swirl, like the symbol of the *hyperpyron*, and it made him think of the money he had sent away, placed with bankers in Florence, used to buy land in Crete, in

Sicily. He had precious little left of value in the city, which was good, since that city, after tonight, looked more doomed than ever. The cobbler, the tanner and the ropewright would not save it, and each man must look to his own.

And his was . . . 'Sofia,' he shouted up at the windows above. He'd sold the glass within them, and his voice should penetrate the cloth that filled them if his hammering on the door did not. 'Open . . .'

'Peace, husband. I am here.'

The bolts were shot back, the door opened, a little light spilling out from the lamp she held. He saw a shape dart out, kicked at it, missed the cat, who limped off down an alley. He noticed something in its mouth. He had always hated the beast, was amazed when he'd shown up again, his leg set in a splint from his 'accident', nursed back to health on the voyage home.

'What took you so long?' he muttered as he pushed past her. 'Sleeping? Good for some.' He climbed the stairs. 'I hope you prepared some food before you retired, at least. Otherwise, there will be . . .'

It took him a moment to realise the room was occupied, that there was a masked figure standing by the fireplace. It took him another to realise who the figure was. He thought that surprising, and put it down to his exhaustion. Because, despite convincing himself that he was dead, truly, he'd been expecting his brother to appear every day for seven years.

'Gregoras,' he said.

'Theon.'

Sofia stopped at the top of the stairs to watch both men. For a long moment, only the rain beyond and the crackling of logs within disturbed the silence and the stares. Until Theon spoke. 'What are you doing here?'

'Here in Constantinople, or here in my old family home?'

'Both. But the first will do for now.' Theon took a step into the room, trying to keep his voice low and firm. 'You know it is death if you are found within the walls. And that . . . disguise will not shelter you for long.'

'Truly? Yet it has sheltered me for the three weeks I have already been here. Even when I stood on those walls this day and watched you whisper in the emperor's ear.' Gregoras tipped his head to the side. 'What was it you told him, brother, that made him pale so? Rumours of treason, perhaps?'

Treason. Theon knew the word had not been chosen without care. Yet he was not ready to speak of it. Not yet. 'I told him of a census we had undertaken, that was all.'

'I see.' Gregoras gestured beyond the window. 'A census that tallied our strength? Or should I say our weakness?' When Theon did not reply, he continued, 'Come, brother! I have observed the empty neighbourhoods, the deserted streets. How many of our fellow citizens are there left to fight?'

'That is a matter for the emperor, and the very few he trusts.'

He knew he should not have used the word. His brother already had enough weapons. 'Trusts? There would only be a very few so honoured. You. Me, once. No more.'

Sofia ached. In her stomach, just above, came a jabbing pain. 'I will leave you,' she said, moving past Theon, crossing the room.

'Do not.' Gregoras's sharp command stopped her at the upper stairs. 'For at the moment, my promise not to kill your husband within these walls is the only thing preventing me doing it. If you leave, I may forget it.'

She gave a little cry, turned back to them, and Theon watched what passed between them. His *promise*? he thought. How often had he stood in this same room, watching them, with their secrets? And here, so long later, after so much . . . life, here they stood again, with things he could not share. It reminded him of all he felt then, felt all his life caught between them. Of all he still felt, and the fear that had seized him at the first sight of his brother passed.

'You will not kill me, Gregoras,' he said, taking another step into the room. 'You can, of course. I doubt I could prevent you. But you will never make Sofia your wife by making her my widow. If you don't know that about her, you do not know her. Her and her . . . God.' He went and sat in one of the fireplace chairs, two paces from his brother, head lifted, offering his throat. 'But there is another reason why you will not kill me now.'

Gregoras had not moved. 'What reason?'

Theon leaned forward. 'If you do, you will never know for certain what happened at the Hexamilion.'

Gregoras took a step towards him now, hands and anger rising, then stopped, stunned by the sudden collapse of years. Seven of them, since his disgrace, since his loss of all that was his life except life itself; of oblivion sought in wine or fighting and often found. All that gone, and he was standing again in his parents' house, confronting a brother who would not fight him, could not fight him, yet could defeat him again and again. With his words, with his coolness, with his . . . logic.

Anger, his keen ability to hurt, would not serve him here. He looked at Sofia, unclenched his hands, stepped back. 'Then you will tell me now, what happened there that day.'

'Tell you what?' Theon smiled. 'What could I tell you that you would believe, brother?'

'The truth.'

'Truth? Whose? Yours? Mine? Sofia's? I think they would be different, depending on where you stand.'

Gregoras grunted. 'Do not try to transform this into an exercise in rhetoric, Theon. We studied with the same tutors, and if I did not master the game as well as you, I can recognise it.' He bent, bringing his masked face closer to its unmasked twin. 'Let us be simple and clear.'

'And if we are? If you learn a truth that does not . . . slake your desire for vengeance?' He glanced at his wife. 'You may have made a promise here, this night, "within these walls", was it not? But a crisis is upon us; there are other nights of danger ahead, and other walls. How do I know that, out of her sight, vengeance will not be taken?'

She watched the twin faces, one hidden, the other masked. Time collapsing for her, the two brothers she'd known all her life before her still, fighting still, about this or that. She was fourteen before she realised that the fights had all become about her, she the prize. Yet here and now, the game was more specific, the stakes much higher, and it made her tired. 'Do not,' she said, coming close to them, 'make this about me once more. I cannot be won or lost. My life is what it is, in God's good hands. But what is between you both is between you alone. Speak to that.'

Theon looked at her, nodded, turned back. 'Can you do that, brother?'

Gregoras nodded. 'I can. I will.' He took a deep breath. 'When the Hexamilion fell and the Turks came through the wall, it was cannon that made the breach.'

'It was. Except for one section, where the wall had not been battered and a sally port was left unbolted.'

'The section I commanded.'

'Yes.' Theon shrugged. 'Carelessness or treachery? No one knew. But everyone was looking for someone to blame. Not the engineers who did not make their walls strong enough. Not the Turkish cannon that took them apart. Never God.' He glanced at Sofia before continuing. 'So when that bag of Turkish coins was found in your sea chest, everyone thought they did know.'

'We know what everyone thought. And we know what my fellow Greeks did.' Gregoras leaned down, the cloth on his face a hand's breadth from the other. 'And we know the story that followed. That once they . . . they had cut off my nose, you arrived suddenly to save me – from hanging.'

'I did.' A faint smile came. 'It is a good story, is it not?'

Gregoras felt his bile rising, swallowed it down. 'But that is all it is, isn't it, Theon? A story.' He stepped closer. 'Come! I *know* what happened. But I would like to hear you say it.'

The brothers, two fingers apart, stared at each other. Sofia did not understand. She shook her head. 'He spoke for you,

Gregor.' She lifted a hand towards him, dropped it again. 'Pleaded for you. Saved your life.'

Gregoras stood straight. 'So he did. But did he tell you *when* he pleaded? That his arrival was not . . . sudden?' He reached up, fumbling at the ties of his mask. 'For as the knife descended, before I became too busy trying not to drown in my own blood, I saw him!' He turned back to Theon. 'I saw you. There in the crowd of soldiers. Oh, you came to the rescue of your brother. But *after* this was done. After!' He let the mask fall. 'Deny it. Tell me I was mistaken. You were not there. You could not have intervened until you did. Tell me.'

Only silence came in reply. Firelight glimmered on ivory as Gregoras turned to her. 'And you think that this was not about you?'

'What can you mean?' Her hand flew up to her mouth. 'You are not saying that . . . that . . .' She dropped to her knees before Theon's chair, grabbed his shoulders, shook him. 'Tell him that it is not true. Tell him that you did not . . . *allow* this to be done . . . because of me?'

He'd always known he'd answer for that moment. That one when he'd stood there in the jostling ranks of soldiers he could have commanded, and didn't. Not . . . immediately. Yet now that the time was here, the remorse he'd thought he might feel did not come. Instead, exactly what he'd felt then returned. 'I have told no lies so far, my wife,' he said, the triumph clear in his voice. 'Why should I begin now?'

'What?' Sofia stared at him for a long moment, the one that passed as all her life crumbled before her. Then she pulled her hand back and slapped him.

With an oath, Theon leapt to his feet, his own hand a fist. With a yell, Gregoras stepped forward.

'Mother?'

The cry startled them, froze them, hands raised. They all turned, to the boy standing in the doorway. 'Mother,' he said again. 'Father! What is it? Why are you . . . ?'

'Thakos!' she cried, running to him. She tried to take him

into her arms but he avoided her, stepped to the side to stare at the two men.

'Who are you, sir?'

Silence, for three heartbeats. Sofia bent. 'This,' she said, reaching up to his head, which he jerked away, 'this is . . . your uncle. Your father's brother.'

Silence again, shorter. 'Yes! Oh yes!' Thakos's cry was excited. 'For I see his nose.' He pointed. 'I see the traitor.'

Until that moment, Gregoras could not have moved. Not when he was looking into time's mirror, the shade of the face he'd once had. Until the shade spoke, in the shrill voice of a child, shattering the glass . . . with a title. Not who he was. As he was known. It was the title that unfroze him, and his son's eyes – his mother's, his own – that had him stumbling towards him, past him, down the stairs, through the front door Sofia had forgotten to rebolt. Out into the rainy night. Seeking oblivion.

FOURTEEN

Gone

Leilah shifted, trying to find some angle of tumbled stone that the wind did not sweep around. Failing.

Someone else had waited here, in this freezing ruin. There were boot prints in the stiff, churned mud at her feet. Him? Had Gregoras watched for the woman who'd opened the door for him this night?

She felt her first flush of warmth, insubstantial as thought. Marvelled at it, at something she had never experienced. Jealousy! She knew this was his city; and the savagery with which he'd rejected it back in Ragusa had told her that there was something here for him, some passion, some hunger unassuaged. More, she had seen her in his chart, where Venus and Neptune conjoined. A woman. This woman who drew him into her house this night.

Even in the one glimpse, Leilah had seen that this woman was beautiful, in a way she herself was not – tall, noble, elegant. And they were not siblings or cousins. The way they'd greeted each other told her that. The way they did not touch.

She was used to gauging passions. It was how she lived. Those that passed between her man of destiny and this beautiful woman nearly knocked her down.

She had to know if he stayed. It was beyond judgement. She knew the heat she'd felt in Ragusa had been matched by his. But here he was, heated for this other woman.

Heat! She shivered. Yet she knew she'd wait till dawn if she had to.

Then she didn't. A man went in, then a boy. Just after,

Gregoras came out, almost running, hooded head bent into the rain. So she followed.

At first, he appeared undecided, took turns off the larger street onto smaller ones, then doubled back. He headed west, as if towards the walls, then south for a while. When he came to the great aqueduct that split that part of the city east–west, he stopped beneath an arch, breathing heavily, looking about him. She nearly called to him then, but he turned suddenly about, and she had to step into a doorway to avoid him, watching him pass by within an arm's reach, a reach she nearly made – until light from a window reflected in water in his eyes. He dropped to a slower pace and she followed from a little further back. At last, he seemed to know where he was going and stayed straight – back towards the districts occupied by the Italians, from Amalfi, Venice and Genoa. It was in the last that she'd found him, for only that night had she heard the rumour that the Genoan mercenaries had brought a German with them to the city who possessed, many prayed, the secret of Greek Fire. She hoped now that he would return to his barracks. She would see him safely there – and return with the daylight when the heat and the tears had left him.

A bell struck ten. Most of the city was behind its shutters, the streets near deserted. Yet as they progressed, more men appeared, then some women, with light spilling more frequently onto the cobbles from the open doorways of taverns and brothels. He was leading her into the Venetian quarter, the largest of the alien enclaves. The Venetians had once ruled the city, she knew, the only foreign army ever to conquer here – by trickery and betrayal, the townsfolk said. Some also claimed they ruled there still, so dominant in trade that Greeks struggled to compete in their own city.

He'd halted before an especially crowded tavern. Then, with barely a pause, he began to push his way in, jostling through the mob at the inn's door, ignoring the curses. She bit her lip. But she had no choice. She tied her hair back, pulled her wide-brimmed hat lower over her eyes, her cloak tighter about her.

Most of the drunkards would barely glance at the small, stained workman in their midst, not with the painted, flounced whores shimmering before them.

Slipping around the group that Gregoras had pushed through, Leilah entered.

He'd found a three-legged table in a corner, far from the fire and the light and so deserted. He'd found a servant who had brought him a flagon of wine and was given a Ragusan libertine, silver coins of whatever nation assuring that he would return often to check on its emptying. Now, disdaining the goblet provided, Gregoras raised the flagon and drank half of it off.

He was going to get drunk. He'd come to a Venetian tavern to do it because he did not want to run into any Genoans who might know him. He hated Venetians with a virulence near equal to his adopted comrades' – another reason he'd come to one of their taverns. If the wine slipped down as easily as he hoped, then it would have one of two effects. He would either fall asleep there at the table, or he would seek to fight the largest fucking Venetian he could find.

Neither oblivion nor a victim appeared in the first flagon. But a third of the way down the second, another face appeared and would not leave. His son's, with the only expression Gregoras had ever seen on it – horrified fascination. Amidst the babel of the inn – and there were three men by the fire who were making the noise of an army – one voice would seem to rise up, one word shouted in Greek: *prodotis*.

Traitor.

He pushed aside the flagon, put his head into his hands. Why had he not listened to himself? Why had he let the Fates blow him back to Constantinople? For money? Gold he knew he'd never get, as soon as the Commander told him that he did not have it in Chios? No. He'd come because of her. Sofia. Some vestige of hope he thought he'd drowned in a thousand inns like this one. Some memory, like an itch in the nose he no

161

longer had. The plot was worse than any of the comedies he'd laughed at with her on feast days in the Hippodrome. Yet who was the fool now, who the cuckold, who the gulled father?

Father! A title he'd never sought to own. One his brother *did* own. Falsely.

He lifted his head, took another swig. Theon had not denied that he'd . . . tarried. Let his brother be marred, let his own family name of Lascaris be for ever blackened, for . . . for what? Revenge for all the losses he'd had over the years to a twin brother who was faster, stronger, more beautiful?

Yes . . . and no. All that paled beside the real reason.

Sofia.

He pushed the flagon away, stood, wobbled. The wine had worked some magic after all. Not enough to bring oblivion . . . Good! For that would have interfered with his plan, his new plan. Vengeance wasn't something only one brother should own. He could master it too. Return now to his family home. Shout the truth in the street. That would change the expression on the face of his son – *his son!* A face so like his own, yet different too. Himself . . . but someone else as well. Someone else.

Sofia.

He fell back onto his chair. Reached for the flagon, brushed it, missed it, knocked it over. It did not matter, there was not much left. Just a thin stream of red to flow across the table and drip upon the floor, like blood from a sawn-off nose.

Gregoras began to slowly lower his head to the table, to the beckoning darkness.

Another eruption of shouts and oaths from the fireplace. Gregoras jerked up, focused, looked at the three men there. Boots off, feet up on chairs before the flames, bare toes wiggling through rents in their stockings. One was banging an empty goblet on the table; another had a pot boy by the collar and was shaking him. The third and largest was just rising and, in a strong voice from the Veneto, linking Giovanni Battista, patron saint of Genoa, in an unseemly act with a donkey. His friends, most of the tavern's other customers, cheered.

Gregoras reached up beneath his mask to his ivory nose. He'd told the girl in Ragusa – and where was she now, that girl? – that he only took it off for two things. He'd taken it off for her, and he took it off now because he'd left it on once in a brawl and been staggered by the pain when someone punched it; that and the blood. He slipped it into his pocket. It clinked there, and he withdrew what it clinked against, slipping the brass knuckles over his own with a smile.

He stood, and when he was steady enough, he walked across. By the time he reached the fireplace, his head was clear. Enough, anyway. As was his voice, when the men finally looked up. 'Your feet stink worse than your mother's crotch,' he said, in an accent located squarely on the docks of Genoa, pointing at the biggest man's toes.

Leilah had watched him drink his way through two flagons, watched him rise, sit, finally rise again. She'd hoped that he was about to leave, so she could talk with him. She wanted to find out more about the woman he had visited, what she was to him. She surprised herself at how much she wanted that.

But then he walked over to the three noisy men at the fireplace, spoke. They were getting to their stockinged feet now, and one of them was bellowing, loud enough to still the hubbub, 'What did you say, you Genoan turd?'

Gregoras took a moment, till all noise finally ceased, then repeated it. And Leilah was up and moving, grabbing the flagon she'd been nursing in one hand, pouring out the wine as she crossed, reaching for the dagger at her waist with the other. She'd covered maybe half the distance when the first man drew his knife.

'Bastard,' he cried, having to step round his bigger companion, his sight blocked until it was too late, Gregoras stepping into him, his arm coming up, over and hard down, armoured knuckles smashing the man's wrist. There was a snap, a howl, the man falling onto a table, bringing it with him to the floor.

As other tables and chairs were knocked over, men clearing to look or to avoid, the middle man moved, a long, thin-bladed stiletto before him now, reflecting firelight; moved fast for a big, drunk man, set Gregoras weaving to avoid three swift slashes. They drove him sideways, into the last of the Venetians, who was just bringing his own knife out.

Leilah stopped five steps away, bent back, and threw. The flagon's flight did not have the elegant parabola of one of her quarrels, but her aim was still good. The vessel took the man in the side of the head, hard enough to shatter, knocking him backwards and into the fireplace. Sparks flew, he screamed, everyone was shouting, the landlord running forward with two of his men, all three wielding brooms like quarterstaffs.

In the centre, though, all was quiet enough, if not still. The big, nimble man feinted, flicked, lunged, a forearm's length of steel thrust before him. But Gregoras had just had time to do what he probably should have done before he'd spoken – he drew his own dagger left-handed, cut down, putting blade to blade, guiding the other's past his left side. Then he raised his boot and slammed the heel hard down onto the man's unshod toes. As he screamed, Gregoras drove his right hand up his hip, curling his hand over, bringing the brass knuckles uppermost just when the force of the blow was at its height.

They took the man on the cheek, snapping his head across. He was big and heavy enough not to move for a moment, then when he did it was silently, and straight down, eyes already closing.

'Brutes! Ruffians!' The landlord and his men had arrived and were striking out with their brooms at other men who were lurching in, and at the sparks that had scattered from the fireplace. Chairs were flying too, aimed indiscriminately. Gregoras fended one off with one arm, just as the other was seized by a masked youth. 'This way!' came the hissed command, and seeing no more Venetians standing to hit, he obeyed, stumbling, laughing.

There was a back entrance, and Leilah found it. Men screamed behind them, a goblet smashed against the door as she opened it, and then they were through and running down an alley. Shouts pursued them and they took another alley to the left, then another. Somehow they ended up back on the larger street, near the tavern's doors, a crowd spilling out before it. 'Come,' she said, moving the opposite way. Gregoras followed for a few paces, then lurched suddenly sideways into a doorway. 'You know,' he giggled, 'I feel a little strange.' And saying it, he sat down hard on the step.

'Oh good,' she said, staring at him, then looking back along the street. Any pursuit had stopped. A crowd was still shifting before the doors. Someone within was wailing. A man. She looked down again. 'Can you walk?'

He squinted up. There was a shifting shape above him, speaking from a blur. It sickened him. 'Do I have to?'

'I know a place.'

She couldn't take him back to her lodgings in the Turkish quarter, to the bed she shared with the daughters of the house. But in her wanderings through the city, she'd explored some empty warehouses on the wharf. No one would disturb them there. 'Come,' she said, stooping to him.

He used her arm to pull himself up. 'Do I know you?' he whispered.

She did not reply, just half carried him down the street.

The Venetian quarter was flush to their docks, the warehouses she'd discovered not far. But it was no easy thing to aid a large man whose every third step was sideways. She leaned into him, like a restraining prop preventing the falling of a branch, and they made a crabbing progress forward. There was a gate, the Porta Hebraica, but being on the Golden Horn side and the docks beyond, there was no one to guard it. The refuge she had in mind was a short stumble away, the spill from the gate lamps faintly lighting its entrance.

Just before they reached it, she lowered a mumbling Gregoras onto a pile of stones on which, with some dignity, he managed to balance. She slipped ahead, turned the corner, found the unbolted door she'd found before. Beneath its archstone, she unslung the small satchel from around her shoulder and delved inside it, removing the objects, laying them by her feet: a purse of coin, blue beads against the Evil Eye, a jade amulet in the shape of a dragon's claw, a Christian cross, a pentangle made from mother of pearl, a rosary, her divining cards, all stock for her trade. There were two other objects – a quarrel, for she always carried at least one, and the feathers for its flights, to work on when she had time; and a tiny bottle. This she did not set down. She unstoppered the bottle, sniffed, wrinkled her nose. The fish oil was on the turn. Yet it was still essence of beast, and when she'd extracted it, certain incantations had been chanted. It had a number of purposes, for hex and the lifting of curses especially. But its prime use was the one she put it to now, the one her mother had taught her, for she had used it to make certain of Leilah's father, as her mother had before her, on and back to the time when her family first became sorcerers.

Swiftly she poured the oil into her hands, and while they dripped she rubbed them around the doorframe, making sure the smear was unbroken from lintel to kerbstone. As she did, she chanted: 'He is come and he is mine. Let him enter and let him never leave.'

She rubbed her hands on her cloak, corked the bottle again, replaced it in her pack. A groan came from round the corner, and she swiftly gathered up the objects she could barely see before backing away from the sealed doorway, making sure that no part of her, no swing of cloak, touched it. The spell would envelop the next person who crossed the threshold.

Gregoras had slipped off his pile of stone. 'Come,' she said, and with her aid he managed to scramble up and stagger forward the way she directed him. A few paces short of the door, she slipped from under him, giving him a little shove as she did. 'Go,' she whispered, 'enter of your own free will and stay.' It seemed to her that the entrance shimmered, blocked by a plane of light, which Gregoras broke as his hands met the door and he stumbled in. She watched the gloom swallow him. He's mine now, she thought, whoever you are, O beautiful bitch of Constantinople. Mine.

She followed him. Gregoras had found a pile of sacks to sink onto. She came and lay beside him, her hands reaching up to free the mask at his face and help his breathing, which had become laboured. His forehead wrinkled as her fingers passed his face. 'Stinks worse than those Venetians' feet in here,' he mumbled.

She laughed. 'Sleep,' she said.

'But you,' he grunted, reaching for her.

It was as she suspected. Her first lover, the janissary, had often been this drunk. He'd attempt to love her, have as little success as Gregoras had now. His hands moved over her even as his eyes closed.

'Sleep,' she said, taking a hand, kissing it.

'All right,' he replied, pulling her a little closer, laying his head to her breast.

She lay there as his breathing eased. He began to snore. She was a little disappointed. She had been surprised by the passion of that night in Dubrovnik. More than surprised, for with her other men, Jew and janissary, lovemaking had always seemed much for them, little for her. With Gregoras, though, it had not been like that; he had given as much as he had taken. And though she knew that the fish oil around the doorframe had bound him to her, she would not have minded the different spell further lovemaking would cast. Wouldn't have minded the pleasure he'd have given her either!

Then another thought came. She and her man of destiny together in Constantinople . . . along with the book of the Arab alchemist, Jabir ibn Hayyan. It was kept in the monastery of Manuel. But why wait for Mehmet to break down the walls to get it? Why not find out where it was, go with her lover and steal the book now?

167

She laughed quietly. She'd heard that the city was just about to close its gates, break its bridges. She had to leave, and soon, or be trapped. But she could stay one more day, and wait for him to be sober again.

His snoring grew louder. She pushed him, and he grunted and rolled onto his side. Pulling a few sacks around them, she curled around his back. She felt the strength of him through his clothes. Perhaps, she thought, if he is not too fouled with wine, we will satisfy both my desires in the morning.

Gregoras awoke alone, to voices and flaring light. He did not know where he was, but wherever he was was dark, though light flickered through gaps and splits in what had to be a wall. He had a vague memory of being brought here, led by some masked youth after the fight, which he remembered only a little more clearly. He knew he'd tackled some Venetians . . . and it was Italian with a Venetian accent that had woken him now. He sat up swiftly, could not restrain the groan, feeling as if someone had driven a spike through his forehead. He pulled out his dagger and stumbled to his feet.

His first thought was that the men he'd attacked – or more likely their unhurt friends – had tracked him down. But as he managed to bring his senses into wakefulness, he realised that the conversation beyond the wooden walls was not about him. When he caught a word, he leaned forward till his head touched the wood of the wall. It cooled it a little, and he listened.

The word was 'escape'.

'Because the place is doomed, that's why,' came the voice again. 'You want to stay and be a dead hero, you can. But all the other captains are agreed. We get out and we get out now.'

'All of Venice? What of our city's honour?' the other man said.

'No, not all. Only us of the Black Sea fleet who were caught here by winds and fate. Most Venetians will remain.'

'I thought *all* must remain. Didn't the Council so order?'

'I piss in the water the Council drinks! Most of them don't have holds full of silks and spices that will make each of us captains a fortune back home – and nothing if the Turks seize them when they take this place. As they will.'

'I don't know. I . . .'

The other man must have walked away, because his voice came from further off. 'Well, it's up to you, Enrico. But in another few days the Greeks will have put their damn boom across the Horn and we'll be trapped. It is agreed. My crew's already aboard the *Raven* and we just await the dawn tide. Which comes soon, for there is light in the east already. I only came to find you and give you the choice. You decide.'

'Wait!'

Boot steps receded, along with low voices. Gregoras sheathed his dagger, sat, placing his back against the wall. So the Venetians were fleeing, he thought. Some of them anyway. Before the boom went up and they had no choice but to fight. He lowered his head into his hands. And he? He, who had returned to the city he hated, that had taken everything from him, that he had desired never to see again? And what had he found on his return? A son whose life he could have no part of. A woman he once loved, lost to him for ever.

He was close enough to the docks to hear commands being given. Hissed, not shouted, urgent for all that. He heard oars going in the water, boats setting out for larger boats offshore. Venetian rats were deserting a holed vessel. And who could blame them? Was it their fight, after all?

Was it his?

He lurched to his feet. There was nothing in the city that he needed – except perhaps his crossbow. But he could always get another of those, while the gold he'd come for he knew he'd never see now. That could be found too, probably when he found that crossbow and a war to use it in. Any war but this one.

As he stepped out through the door, he stumbled on

something. It glimmered in the faint light of the approaching dawn and he bent to pick it up, gasped when he saw what he held. A quarrel. A bolt for the crossbow he was going to seek. It seemed like a sign . . . and an odd thing to find in a doorway near the docks. Odder still when he brought it close to his eyes and saw that not all its flights were there, but the ones that were were made from heron's feathers – just like the one he'd plucked from John Grant's satchel in Korcula.

He slipped it into a pocket, where its head clinked against something. He delved, found coins, brass knuckles – and his ivory nose. It reminded him of the fight, and his rescue by the strange masked youth. Had he even been real? Where had he gone? He would have liked to have thanked him.

He heard more voices from the docks. He had no time to wait for his benefactor. But in case he returned, he stepped back to the entrance of the warehouse and threw a silver Ragusan libertine onto the pile of jute sacks. A reward, should the youth come back and find it.

He tied the false nose, then his mask, into place as he walked the short distance to the docks. Men were holding a rowboat close to the jetty. 'A place for one more,' he said, adopting the accent he hated.

One of the holding men looked up. 'What ship?'

What was the name the captain had said? 'The *Raven*,' he answered.

'That's her weighing anchor now,' the man said, nodding to the water. 'But we'll likely rendezvous in Chios or Lesbos. You can catch up with her there.'

Gregoras nodded, took the man's hand, stepped aboard, dropped onto a bench. Two men came running down the dock, and when they were seated too, the boat shoved off. They made good speed across the waters of the Horn towards the black shapes further out. It was light enough now to make out the city walls behind him. A little west of where he'd embarked was the gate of Theodosia. If he looked hard, he would have been able to spy a little platform of rock before it. Ghosts upon it. His. Sofia's. Who they'd made there.

Gregoras closed his eyes.

Leilah watched the last of the seven ships dance as it entered the waters where the Golden Horn, the Bosphorus and the Sea of Marmara all met, causing chop that was called *anafor* in the Turkish tongue. If Gregoras had woken as wine-heavy as she expected, his stomach would not relish the lurching.

It was the ship he was on; she'd seen him board it, her crossbow eye spotting him, recognising his black cloak and hat as he climbed up the rope ladder. When she'd returned to the warehouse, found him missing, she'd run where she'd thought he might go, in search of what she'd gone to fetch for his awakening – water, in a skin under her arm. But he wasn't in the shack of a tavern on the dock. He was already upon the sea.

The ship rounded Acropolis Point and was gone. Still she didn't move, stood squinting against sunlight reflecting off water. The sun had cleared the rain clouds away, and sparkled now on the rooftops and towers of Galata across from her. All was bright – except in her heart.

With a curse, she shut her eyes to the sunlight, tried to think. She'd been foolish to consider stealing the book now. It was clear, in the charts she'd drawn – her own, Mehmet's, Gregoras's – when it would be hers. After the city was taken, not before. But still Gregoras had to be there for that. He was not meant to leave.

And yet? That he had gone did not mean he could not return. Ships put about. Ships . . . sank.

She smiled, as her shoulders eased. He had walked through the door lined with fish oil. He was hexed, was and would for ever be hers. And there were other hexes she knew, to do with everything from love to finding a lost comb. Curses too, which could be laid on man or anything he wrought. Including what he sailed in.

All she needed was something of his, something from his hand. In her trade, silver was always preferable.

She opened her eyes, turned away from the water to the land, into the sun. Laughing, she spun high into the air the coin she'd found where he'd lain, watching as it flashed and sparkled, rose and fell against the walls of doomed Constantinople.

FIFTEEN

The Laughing Dove

Constantinople
11 April 1453

It was such a familiar sound. Yet it always surprised her, that chuckle right outside her window, high-pitched, staccato. 'Ha ha *hu* ha ha ha,' it came again, caught between a call and a croon, the middle of the laugh as if the joke had only then been fully realised.

'Swiftly! Minerva! Here! Here!' Sofia called softly.

Her daughter looked up from the floor and the sprawl of wool poppets she had there. 'I am teaching,' she said, frowning at the interruption.

'And will again, my duckling,' Sofia whispered. 'But come here now. I have something lovely to show you.'

Minerva rose, danced over. 'A sweetmeat?'

Sofia shook her head. Since the bridges were broken, and the boom drawn across the Golden Horn, little new food had come into the city. Sweetmeats were in short supply. 'Something better. Something wonderful. Shh!' She put her finger to her lips. 'And look.'

She drew her daughter a few paces towards the centre of the room, into the rectangle of morning light that came from the open window. 'There,' she said, pointing.

Minerva sucked in a breath. 'Ooh! So lovely.' She stretched up, put her lips close to her mother's ear, whispered loudly, 'What is it?'

'It's called a laughing dove. Listen!'

That call came again, a series of notes, another joke understood. Minerva giggled. 'It thinks it's funny!'

'Yes. They come every year. It means spring is truly here at last. I was beginning to doubt it would come.' The bird was rooting in a box of earth Sofia kept on the window ledge. 'See the head? It's your favourite colour, pink.'

'Oh yes. And it has spots on its throat. Black spots!'

'It has. And though the wings are red, can you see the blue and grey in them too?' Sofia sighed. 'So beautiful. It doesn't care about anything . . .' she faltered, 'out there. It only wants to laugh. And find someone to laugh with.'

Minerva looked up. Her mother had stopped smiling. There was some darkness in her eyes. Minerva wanted it to go away. 'I'll get you the funny bird,' she cried. Leaping up, she ran through the sunlight towards the window.

The startled dove took off. A flash of chestnut underwings and it was gone.

'Oh.' Minerva stopped, fingers up and into her mouth.

Sofia rose from her knees, went and put her hands on her daughter's shoulders. 'Do not worry, child. It will return.'

She stared out of the window, at a sky clear of clouds, a vibrant pigeon-egg blue. Few sounds came from the street, unusual on such a day and such a busy route to the wharves. But she knew where most of the people were – where she would be, had not Theon forbade it. Upon the walls, looking at what else the spring had brought her beloved city. Waiting for a sound that had no laughter in it.

The laughing dove flew north-west. Seeking open ground beyond the stones of men, his call changed from coo to the cry of flight, which he hoped would bring him to others of his kind. When he reached the Blachernae palace, an avenue of Judas trees in full bloom within its walls caught his questing eye. He dropped down to settle on a branch, and laughed again.

Theon glanced up, but could not see the source of the

laughter within the pink explosions, or what it was that was mocking him. Yet it seemed fitting that the sound should accompany him as he walked the last stretch of ground before the battlements, deriding his failures. Failures emphasised by the armour he had been forced to don, the weapons he now carried. His true skills – in diplomacy, subversion, manipulation – were to be put aside. The ones he had little skill in were called upon now. He was *kavallarios*, a knight in the imperial service, of the noble family of Lascaris. The fact that the lowliest *bashibazouk* in the Turkish forces could probably strip him of his father's sword and kill him with it was of no consequence. He must be seen to swing it at his emperor's side.

His father's sword! It was a heavy monster, not like the elegant scimitars even Theon could lift and many in the city used. But old swords, like ancient loyalties, had to be borne. It swung from his belt now, slapping his greaves with a repetitive and annoying clang.

He paused to catch his breath, pulling away the gorget from his throat. Despite all the sewing and padding that Sofia had done, the armour – and especially the domed helmet – chafed. His brother would love this, he knew, would be bounding up the stairs ahead, eager for the fight. Where was he? He had not glimpsed him since the night of their reunion three months before. Was he now part of the desperately thin line of men that ran the length of the land walls? One of two or three men watching from each tower along the sea? Or had he already slipped away? That was most likely. He was still a fugitive, after all.

Theon wished he could have slipped away too. Vanished at the same time as his last hope: that Constantine would take his very subtly delivered advice – for it would not have done to be caught advocating this line too strongly – and accept Mehmet's terms of surrender. The city would have been saved from pillage, its women from rapine, its children from slavery – and Theon could have accompanied Constantine into some very comfortable exile in the Morea. Or stayed, and seen what accommodations could be made with the new masters. Instead . . . well, he had never had much hope. Constantine was too proud of his family name of Palaiologos, of his title. And too lacking in imagination to heed subtlety, or recognise a good offer. He was a blunt soldier only, entirely without imagination, without any of the true qualities of leadership. He was of the type that had presided over the steady erosion of all Byzantium's power. And now, lacking the wit to do anything else, he would preside over its inevitable fall.

'And I,' Theon muttered to himself, 'lacking the wit to do anything else, will fall with it.'

He heaved himself onto the first of the battlement stairs. Behind him, in the Judas trees, the bird mocked him all the way up them.

When he emerged onto the palace's main turret, he was at the top of a flight of three steps and so able to see above the men who crowded at the crenels. See – and gasp.

He had not been on the battlements since the day, three before, when the word had come that the sultan had himself arrived with the bulk of his army. Theon, like most in the city, had come to view them – and had only seen a blur of movement on distant hills.

Now he could see men. Faces. Armour. Banners. Thousands upon thousands upon thousands of men.

The Turks had advanced to within two hundred paces of the walls. Behind a trench and a raised wooden stockade, a vast throng that looked a hundred ranks deep spread all the way to the Horn to the north and no doubt over the hill and all the way down to the shores of the Marmara sea. If there were not a hundred thousand men before the walls, he knew it would not be far short. Facing them – and he knew this because he had helped to compile the figures – were fewer than five thousand Greeks and around two thousand foreigners.

'Impressive, are they not?'

The voice, which seemed always to be gurgled from mud caught in the throat, came from beside him. Theon turned. It was the man all knew as 'the German' – all except the man himself, for he would protest that he was from some other, equally barbarous, place. Theon had had dealings with him, because he had been charged with trying to recreate a saviour of the city in previous sieges – Greek Fire – and Theon had tried to find him some scarce, and strange, ingredients.

John Grant pointed. 'His Highness is there at the front, as ever. Giustiniani's renegade Arab has been describing who are ranged against us here. Their strongest forces against our weakest point, or so our leaders say.' He turned, and spat over the edge of the turret, though a contrary wind took the sputum and flung it back onto his cloak. Theon watched him with distaste as he rubbed at the material, swearing unintelligible oaths that sounded like gravel in a drum, before he looked up. 'Did you find me that supply of saltpetre yet?'

'Perhaps. Come and see me later. You will excuse me.'

Theon moved down the stairs, though he tripped the last step when his scabbard swung between his legs. The German's chuckle came, as mocking as any bird's, but Theon ignored it as he tapped backs and pushed his way through to the emperor. He arrived as Amir, Giustiniani's tame Musselman, was describing the standard that flew in the distance before a huge tent.

'It is Mehmet's tug. As sultan he is entitled to nine horsetails to dangle below the golden globe and the half-moon of Cibele. There are bells too. Silver, with a sweet chime . . .'

'Balls to bells,' Giustiniani grunted. 'We've all seen a tug before. Can the keenness of your infidel eyes see what stands before the standard? As near as straight opposite us?'

Amir grinned. 'My infidel eyes, gift of Allah, praise Him, and my memory of such things, tells me that it is a gun emplacement.'

'Of course it's a fucking gun emplacement!' Enzo, the Commander's right hand, growled. 'But how many are emplaced there?'

'In the centre? I see but one eye. One big, most evil eye.'

A murmur arose, warding gestures were made, halted instantly when one voice spoke. 'Is that the one our spies told us of? What did they call it?' The emperor turned. 'Ah, Lascaris! You are the scholar amongst us. Was it not a scholarly name?'

Theon shrugged. 'The Turks named it, so I do not think so, *basileus*. But they named it in Greek. They call it Heleopolis.'

' "The Taker of Cities," ' repeated Constantine. He stared in silence for a long moment. 'Well, that is hubris, I think. At least until we have seen this "taker" try to take. Will we soon, do you think?'

'Soon, highness.' Giustiniani raised a large arm, pointed. 'Even my aged Christian eyes can see that they are busy about it. I wasn't sure which weak point they would commence at. But they chose to start here, at your palace, where the walls are only two deep and shaped like a dog's leg, leading up to the Horn.' He looked that way, towards the right, then straight down, frowning. 'That door there. The sally port. What is its name again?'

Reluctantly taking his gaze away from the gun and its preparations, Theon stepped forward till he could also peer down, over the battlements, see the small wooden door set into one wall, just where it joined the other.

'The Kerkoporta,' Constantine said. 'It was walled up till recently. Some old men remembered how useful it could be to sally out and strike at invaders. The Bocciardi brothers proved it so again, when the first of the Turks arrived.'

'Glory to our Venetian allies,' Giustiniani commented drily. 'It is sealed again?'

'Triply so, Commander.' It was Enzo who replied. 'Though we could have it open again in minutes when you order the counter.'

'See that it remains sealed. The days of the sally are passed. And we do not want any doors opening to our flanks, however small.' Giustiniani looked again to the front. 'They seem to be getting busier there, majesty. Will you retire?'

Constantine shook his head. As protests came, he raised his voice over them. 'My friends, if God chooses to kill me with the first shot of this fight, then He has already given this city over to the infidel. We will see many shots before our deliverance. I will not flinch from first to last.'

In a new, uneasy silence, all men turned again to stare at the one eye gazing back. But it took only a moment for the silence to be broken – by a screech of laughter. Everyone looked up, shocked – except for Constantine. 'A laughing dove,' he said, smiling. 'It is a little late. But spring is finally here.'

'Do you hear her, big man?' Raschid whispered. 'It is the laugh of the first virgin of Constantinople who sees you unsheathe your manhood.'

Achmed looked down, into a grinning mouth, isolated teeth standing out like yellowed rocks in a red sea. One had grown in before another had left and stuck out through the gum above it. For some reason, his recruiter had never accepted Achmed's first answer, that he was there for the glory of Allah. Nor his second, given when pressed once on the long march to the city from Edirne – that he needed gold to make sure his family never starved again. For Raschid, these reasons were important, but secondary. What lay within the conquered walls of Constantinople were Greek women, whom he could take at will. Slaves he could use brutally, repeatedly and then, when they were worn out, sell. He could not believe that all others did not share his lust. Especially the big silent man whom he had chosen as both his bodyguard and his butt.

'Think of her, Achmed.' He gripped the man's arm. 'Laughing at you, the bitch. She will laugh a different way when you take her, eh? They are all wild, these Greek sluts. Animals, groaning in the dark. Begging us for it. Not like our wives, lying there like stones.'

Farouk, their *bolukbasi*, hissed at them, pointing with his *bastinado*, which he would not hesitate to bring down upon any recruit's back when the order of silence was upon them.

Raschid closed his gaping mouth, and Achmed returned to his search of the sky. He knew the little man had no wife, had never had one. But he had, and he had thought of Farat immediately when he heard the dove's cry. It had been at this time of year that their families had agreed that they should marry. He knew her, of course, for she was his father's cousin's daughter. But he had only thought of her in that way at the time when the doves passed through their village, flying west.

There! He heard it again, then saw it as it flew up from the stockade before them with a different type of call, a shriek of outrage at a soldier's flung stone. He followed the bird's flight over his head, remembered his little Abal's delight when he'd brought her one he'd managed to snare in a flung net. His wild rose had cooed in imitation, and cried when the little bird had died. He had promised her another. He had promised to save her life. He had failed in both.

He turned again to the walls before him. The mortar between the stones was not gold, as he had been told, but he still believed the streets beyond would be full of it. Yet though he had stared at them for several days now, still he could not believe that man could have built anything so enormous. And he knew that he was going to be ordered to climb them soon, a feat that would be difficult enough without all the men he saw raining stones and shot upon him as he tried.

He licked his lips. He was tall and could see over many of his fellows, above the forest of spear tips, up to a hill. It seemed to be the only place where there was movement, men scrambling down into a wood-lined hole and back out again. There had been talk about a fire-mouthed dragon there, that some called a basilisk. Perhaps the wooden structure was its cage. Perhaps they would unleash it, let it tear the walls apart with its claws before he had to climb them.

The cry came again. Six notes, the third emphasised. 'Ha ha *ha* ha ha ha,' went the bird. Achmed turned and looked at the walls once more. I'll laugh too, he thought, when I am over them.

It is good to be about my trade, Hamza thought, as he dismounted and moved towards the covered wagon. Good to be out and hunting on a day that feels, at long last, like spring. It made him almost forget everything else, all that awaited him beyond the crest of the hill, all his other roles and duties. For now, he was only *cakircibas* – chief falconer to the sultan.

Only. Hamza smiled. As a boy in his father's dingy warehouse in Laz, tanning hides all day, he had dreamed of being free in the sun, chasing game across sun-blessed valleys. He could never have dreamed that he would be doing it while holding one of the most important ranks in the empire. But his skills with birds had been noticed by none other than Murad Han, Sultan of Rum. As had his intelligence. As had his beauty. And somehow he had managed to survive the old sultan's death and retain his position with his heir, his son, Mehmet.

The smile left him. He glanced back, at the sultan astride his horse, in the middle of his *belerbeys* and pashas. No one was smiling there, no one talking, though he was sure they had all mumbled their complaints – out of Mehmet's hearing – as to why today, now, he had chosen to go hawking. They wanted to be with their clans, with their soldiers on the other side of the hill. Now they were finally there, and any choice was over, they wanted to be fighting.

Hamza knew why they were not. His master, for all his education in science, religion and philosophy, believed absolutely in signs and prophecies. One year ago on this day, a sorceress in Edirne had told him that if he fired his first shot on this day, at this hour, success would be his. The closer it came, the slower that hour had approached – and Mehmet wanted to show his army that he had no cares. So he had called for horses and hawks.

Hamza halted by the wagon. It was beautifully crafted, black leather stretched over bent willow wands, divided into compartments. Inside each one, separated from his rivals, a bird perched. A groom was just putting one away, hooded now, a saker called Aisha who had flown from the sultan's fist and returned to it unblooded. It was the latest of three birds to do so. It partly accounted for the frown on Mehmet's face. All knew that with a foraging army camped nearby, any game would be swiftly netted, trapped, shot. Still, Mehmet was a man for signs and portents. At the start of a lot of killing, a kill would be propitious.

Hamza studied the leather compartments before him. He knew the bird in each one, had trained most of them himself in the happy days of leisure. Each had its skill, each was more suited to a particular terrain and type of game. In this land, with most of the wood cover chopped down to build the stockade that faced the city, he had thought sakers would have the best chance. But each had failed. It was time for something different.

'This one,' he said, pointing, and as the groom hurried to part the leather straps, Hamza pulled on his glove. It had never ceased to give him pleasure, the feeling as his fingers slipped into the supple leather, his eyes pleasured too by the craft of the glove and, more, the words carefully stitched onto it in gold thread. He murmured them now. ' "I am trapped. Held in this cage of flesh. And yet I claim to be a hawk flying free." ' When he had taught at the *enderun kolej*, a student of his had made the glove for him as a gift. An exceptional student, a prince no less. Vlad Dracula. They had been . . . fond of each other, for a brief time. But that Dracula was lost now, either already dead or dodging assassins in Hungarian alleys, no doubt, having failed to hold his throne of Wallachia. While his younger brother, Radu the Handsome, was one of the men clustered around Mehmet, still the sultan's occasional lover, still his confidant.

The straps were undone. The groom stepped back. Hamza called softly, 'Easy, my beauty. Easy.' Then, moving the flap aside, reaching in, he placed his hand beside the bird called Baz Nama.

The goshawk struck immediately, and even through the

thickness of the glove, Hamza felt its piercing strength on his thumb. He moved his hands under the perch, took the tresses in his fingers, pulled, and the bird, without relinquishing his beak's grip, stepped onto Hamza's hand.

He was well named 'the king of birds'. A gift from the Khan of the Muscovites, he had been born in some snowy northern country and was of the same near-blinding whiteness as that land. His eyes were red, though they had not been at birth. It was said of goshawks that as they aged, their eyes reddened from the blood of all their victims. For, unlike other hawks, they did not kill just to feed and stop when that was achieved. They killed because they liked to, and stopped when they could no longer fly.

Yes, Hamza thought, crooning till the goshawk lifted its head so he could stroke between its red eyes, you are the one for this flight.

He turned, walked back to the mounted men, halting at his sultan's stirrup. The frown on his face was gone, replaced by a big smile. 'Baz Nama!' Mehmet shouted. 'Yes, Hamza. Yes! You are right.'

He bent, so his falconer could transfer the bird. It moved, settled, bit down as it had bitten before. 'Aiee!' Mehmet cried. 'He is keen for the kill, as ever.' He looked around at his noblemen. 'As am I. 'Tis almost the hour. Let us ride.'

Hamza mounted. Setting heels to flanks, Mehmet led the way up the hill. They crested it and saw before them the slight valley filled with soldiers and the next rise crowned with more. Beyond them, the walls of Constantinople loomed. For tens of thousands of men, the order of silence was strikingly obeyed. They could all hear the snap of banners upon the battlements, the snort of horses, even the faint chime of the silver bells upon the tug set before the sultan's command tent to their left.

And Hamza, who was scanning the clear sky, not the crowded land, heard something else – the faint but clear sound of a laugh. 'Ha ha *ha* ha ha ha,' it went, and he realised it wasn't human, just as he saw what had made it, rising over the ranks on the hill opposite. 'There, *effendi*,' he yelled, in his excitement forgetting all of the sultan's more august titles. 'There!'

'I see it,' Mehmet yelled back. Standing in his stirrups, he flung the bird from his hand. It dipped low towards the ground, then rose fast, powerful wings bearing it swiftly up, powerful eyes already fixed upon its prey.

'It's some kind of pigeon, master.' Hamza leaned in, laying his gloved hand on Mehmet's, lost in the hunt. 'Look at its swoops.'

'Yes. But it is not weaving yet,' came the reply. 'Has it not seen my king?'

The laughing dove was flying straight along the line. Sunlight sparkled on the helmets below, a thousand points of light, a brilliant dazzle. Only at the last, when a flash of white appeared just beneath him, did he focus. By then it was too late.

The men watched the familiar goshawk kill. Five beats and then a glide, and then, because it was a pigeon, Baz Nama flipped onto his back to come at it from beneath. At the last, the dove made a desperate lurch to the left, but not fast enough to escape the claws that caught, held. For a moment it seemed they were frozen in air. Then the birds descended in a slow spiral towards the ground.

Hamza and Mehmet still clutched each other as they watched the descent. Then a slight cough from beside them broke the spell. They looked down. One of the sultan's scribes was at his stirrup. 'It is the hour?' Mehmet said, refocusing. The man nodded. Mehmet removed his hand from Hamza's. 'Fetch the bird, *cakircibas*,' he said. 'And bring it to me there.'

With that, he spurred his horse down the slight slope, through a gap in the troops, and up the other hill.

Hamza went to the hawk. He had only just begun to tear at his prey so was easily distracted with fresh chick flesh and lured from his kill onto Hamza's glove. Putting the dove into a pouch at his side, he rode the short distance to the wagon, replacing the goshawk on its perch, making sure the groom placed plenty of meat beside it. It was time that Baz Nama had a good gorge. Hamza suspected they would not be flying him again for a while.

He joined the leaders of the army on the other hilltop. As at Edirne three months before, they were all dismounted and gathered around a large scoop in the ground. In the base of it, wedged in with barrels filled with earth and upon wooden rollers, lay the basilisk. Though Hamza had seen the great gun many times before, it had lost nothing in its monstrosity by the familiarity. Whatever was needed to be done had been. Only one man was down in the pit with the monster – the Transylvanian gunner, Urban, as besmirched with mud and soot as ever. His eyes shone from their black surround, matching the head of the taper he blew on, keeping the red glow alive.

Hamza walked up beside his master. 'Balm of the world,' he said, and offered the dead dove.

Mehmet took it, looked at it a moment, then held it up so all could see. 'A good omen,' he said in a loud, clear voice. 'The first kill. But not the last. And the next comes fast upon it.' He stretched out his hand, still with the bird in it, and pointed straight ahead. 'There, right there before us, is the imperial palace. It stands within the Rome of the East. The Red Apple. Fabled Byzantium. Now is the time to fulfil the prophecies of Muhammad, praise him!' A murmur came, praising. 'Now is the hour appointed by Allah, all merciful, and prepared for with such care. Never have so many sons of Isaac gathered before these walls. Never have they brought with them such means to turn those walls to dust beneath their feet.' He gestured down to the cannon below him. 'Let no man falter, let no sword be sheathed, until the banner of the Prophet, all glory unto him, flies from the highest tower. Until the muezzin calls us to prayer from the minaret we shall plant in the heart of the Hagia Sophia.'

Reaching to the scabbard at his side, he drew his sword,

lifted it high. 'Let Constantinople fall,' he shouted. '*Allahu akbar!*'

He swept the sword down. It was the signal the gunner had been waiting for. Urban touched his glowing taper to the breech, made sure that it flared there, before scrambling from the hole. All moved back a pace, all except Mehmet, who stood unmoving, with sword raised once more. And then the sound came, in a flash of flame and a cloud of thick black smoke, a roar such as few men had ever heard, a sound that, if anything could, could have woken the dead.

Sofia heard it, a mile away in her house, knew what it was, even as she clutched her startled daughter to her, palms to little ears, too late to keep out the terror. The men before the walls heard it, and there was not one in the whole vast army, from elite janissary to wild-eyed *yaya*, and however fierce a warrior, who did not duck in the sudden shock. The men upon the palace walls heard it but had no time to duck before they were fighting for balance as the great ball slammed into the outer walls and the ground shook.

It was a sound perhaps to wake the dead. But the first man to die in Constantinople was torn apart by flying masonry and so beyond recall. While the laughing dove, still resting in a sultan's hand, did not stir.

— PART TWO —
Kappa

See me, Turk.

See where I stand. Upon walls that have defied every assault for a thousand years. You claim they will be reduced to sand by your monstrous guns. You cry that once they are, your army, innumerable as pebbles on the strand, will sweep away the weak few who would keep you out.

Shall I tell you what you cannot see? You cannot see into my heart. You cannot . . . because it is armoured better than I am. Steeled with a certainty no weapon can penetrate.

You doubt? Then let me tell you of that certainty, of what material it is made. Like the mortar that binds these walls, compounded of lime, sand and water, my certainty is made of three things. History. Faith. Love.

History is not our burden. It is our eagle standard, and when we gather beneath it, an army a hundred times greater than yours gathers too. Then we are not the impoverished few you deride. We are legion. A good word – for it was the legions who marched from Rome to the conquest of the wide world. And when they were done, the first emperor to recognise the glory of Christ Risen came here. Came with the first Rome's glorious past – and saw its future. Constantine gave the city his name. But he could have called it New Rome.

It is said your sultan wishes to be Caesar, but does he not see that Julius stands with us? It is also said that Mehmet wishes to conquer all that Alexander did, and at as young an age, but does he not know that Alexander was Greek! As are we. Greek and Roman, both.

If you could see through these walls, what glory would you behold? Not simply in stone, though the city is formed around its towering columns and splendid forums, its life-giving aqueducts and purple-walled palaces. Not only in art – golden trees filled with golden birds that sing . . . bejewelled silver ikons that grace both home and church . . . a ten-thousand-piece glass chandelier that holds the very light of heaven.

For there is another glory – that of our words. Texts translated from every language in the world, including your own. Ancient and new, alchemy and love poems, history and medicine, philosophy and geometry, copied in the coloured inks and the beautiful script of monks and scholars. Knowledge discovered and rediscovered on every subject that concerns man. Laws codified as they were on the orders of the Emperor Theodosius nine hundred years ago and used to this day wherever man is civilised.

Words are God's intention, made plain by His chosen people. Yet perhaps the true reason He chose us was that He knew that only we, of all the world, could build Him a house worthy of His majesty.

So know this. Even if you do manage to lay these walls low and reach God's dwelling, you will go no farther. For at the very height of your triumph, you will be brought low, by the Archangel Michael wielding his fiery sword at the head of the heavenly host. If you are fortunate, in the moment before He casts you into damnation, perhaps you will glimpse His glory on earth. See the immeasurable dome entirely covered in mosaic of infinite variety and colour. Hear the thousands who can fit beneath it sing the perfect harmonies of His praise. Smell the sweet scent of a thousand years of richest incense, impregnated in every stone.

This is the Hagia Sophia, the Church of Divine Wisdom. God lives here, and He will not let you drive Him out.

I know you cannot see this. All you see are walls to knock down, and too few men in impoverished armour. So let me tell you of the last thing you cannot see. What it is that makes this city unconquerable.

You cannot see my love for it.

It is not solid, like stone. It is not rousing, as history is, nor sustaining as only God's words can be. My love is made of air itself, of the breath I take from east and west and the scents they bring in each season. Of the sun I watch pass directly over me down the line of the Bosphorus, setting the dome of Divine Wisdom afire, falling on every column that marks our history, transforming the waters that surround and sustain us from the blue smelted steel of our swords to the green of an empress's eye. In its daily course the sun casts an even light upon the whole city, lingers like a lover reluctant to part . . . then flees suddenly, unable to look back, anxious to swiftly return, as it always does.

As shall I. If I am too tired to lift my sword, I will lay my body in the breach to trip your foot; and if my sacrifice is not worthy enough to mitigate my sins, perhaps it will yet be enough for God to grant one prayer: that I spend purgatory as a stone in Constantinople. Under that light, breathing those scents, part of that history. Part of the greatest city on earth. As was. Is. For ever will be.

I am Constantine Palaiologos, emperor, son of Caesars. I am a baker, a ropewright, a fisherman, a monk, a merchant. I am a soldier. I am Roman. I am Greek. I am two thousand years old. I was born in freedom only yesterday.

This is my city, Turk. Take it if you can.

SIXTEEN

Shipwreck

And Gregoras thought . . .

A noseless man drowns faster than any other.

He had assumed it would be so. Here, at the end of life, he had proved it. Where man had maimed him, there the waters gushed in. A last consequence of the violation that had destroyed his life. He tasted the sea, even as he drowned in it, an equal mix of salt and gall.

He, who once had loved to swim, had avoided it for seven years. Yet he had courted death in so many other ways. If there was a petard to be laid at a gate, he would lay it, as the fuse spluttered. A breach held by some vast Turk, he would challenge him, fell him, lead the charge in. Wrapped in darkness, he would steal into the enemy's camp, to learn the secrets spoken at their fires. His body was ringed in scars, worms of raised flesh from sword cuts, pits made by ball, the jagged line of arrowheads. Any one of these could have brought his quietus.

He saw them all as he drowned. Something else proved – for Theodore, who had commanded an imperial galley, had told him many fantastical tales of the sea; among them, that every event one had lived returned as one slipped beneath the waves. So the old archer had been right. It was one part of Gregoras's last, most bitter thoughts. That, and this: having sought to avoid a death upon the walls of doomed Constantinople, he had found one fleeing them.

The water closed over his head, filled his ears as it had filled the rest of him. In the sudden silence he heard a laugh. He wondered what dryad was darting through the waves to steal him. Until he recognised the laugh. Sofia's. He had stolen a parrot for her. The bird had bitten him. She had laughed. And now she'd come to laugh at him again, this noseless man, drowning fast.

These were to be his last thoughts, then. This, his unmarked end.

No!

This thought came, clearly: I have lived in bitterness for so long. I will not die in it.

A little air left. Enough, just, to push the arms, risen above him, up. One hand breaking the surface, jabbing into wood. Something floating there.

Gregoras used his last, tiny piece of air to kick up to it.

It was a spar. Rounded, it still had some rope and heavy canvas attached that stopped it rolling as Gregoras flung himself over it, wrapping arms and legs round as waves tried to dislodge him. Taking three deep, hurtful breaths, he vomited a stream of water, coughed violently, then, in a slight lull between waves, reached out and snagged a mess of rope, wriggling his head and chest through a gap, reaching underneath the spar to bind the ends tight. He was just in time, for the next wave crashed big and tried to suck him clear. But his swift knot and returning strength to his arms held him, and further turns of rope made him fast. Now all he could do was cling hard and pray. He thought he'd given up on prayers a long time before. He was wrong.

The storm, which had come so suddenly and sunk the Ragusa-bound vessel, as suddenly abated. It seemed to Gregoras a living beast that, once it had realised that it could not kill him, drew off and went in search of other victims. Huge waves reduced till they were no longer submerging him each time, but buoying him up. The cold rain that had pounded down for days ceased and the sun returned.

Gregoras lay still, letting the swell take him. There was little he could do. One swift look about had told him that his was one of the very few pieces of driftwood upon the water, and the only one occupied. Two days out of Crete when the storm struck and there was nothing but water stretching to every horizon. He examined other pieces of wreckage. Not far away there appeared to be a wider tangle of it. He tried to paddle his spar towards it, but made little progress, each swell pushing him back. Finally, he untied himself, slipped into the water, stripped himself of his sodden clothes and started to swim on his back. It took a while, as waves pushed him now nearer, now further away. When he thought that exhaustion would halt him, he was suddenly within reach and then upon it.

He lay on a mesh of wood rope and three part-planks that the storm had shaped into a half-circle. Some broken glass flagons were caught up in the ropes, and a swathe of canvas was bound to it, spread over the sea, steadying the whole. Briefly making sure that the ropes that joined everything were secure, Gregoras lay shivering on the wood and let the sun warm him.

He woke, opening his eyes, to others, staring back at him. His start startled the gull, which took off screeching, circled him once then flew away. He pushed himself off the planks, lifted his head – and wished he hadn't. It felt as if it was a drum being beaten, while his mouth was a desert, rimmed in salt from the sea water he'd swallowed. He was tempted to swallow more, he was so thirsty, but he took some in only to rinse, spat it out. Kneeling on the planks, he shielded his eyes from the sun and looked about him.

He was no sailor, though he had fought enough times upon the sea. From the height of the sun, he guessed it was about midday, but at all points of the compass and to the limits of sight there was only water, water and nothing else. He sat again. There was little he could do, but that little he did. Unbound the piece of cloth from his face, which somehow had remained tied fast, and retied it over the top of his head, where the sun was burning the worst. His ivory nose had fallen from his face to admit the sea, but it was still attached to its cord and hung round his neck. He let it lie.

There was little he could do now but think. Why had he been the only one spared? Had God decided drowning was too easy a death for such a sinner? Falsely marked and maimed as a traitor, was he truly not one now for deserting his city when she needed every mother's son? He'd been still drunk, still furious when he'd chosen to leave with the Venetians. In the two months since, in Chios, in Crete, he had tried not to think of the city or anyone in it. Of Giustiniani, Amir and Enzo. Of the emperor or his old tutor Theodore. Of the Scotsman, Grant. Especially of Sofia and . . . and his son. Back in his hovel in Ragusa, perhaps Leilah waited for him. There was other gold in the world to be earned to build his house with a view. Other wars to fight.

As the sun rose higher in the sky, thirst tormented him, yet not so fiercely as memory. He'd been offered a war and turned it down. Offered redemption and spurned it. *Inshallah*, they said, but he'd ignored God's will. Now, to give him time to consider his manifold sins, he would be tortured before he died.

It was a while later, a time when sea water became more appealing by the moment – to drink, to sink into – when the gull returned. A gull, anyway, with three companions, which Gregoras thought strange so far from any land. What were they seeking? Perhaps him, recognising a meal. If it came to it, he knew he would prefer to become fish food. Sofia's parrot would take the only chunk of him a bird would get.

Then something else made him look up. Some faint noise that just pierced the shrieking. He looked all around, squinted into a sinking sun . . . and saw them. If he had been studying the horizon the whole while, he would have seen them as specks upon it. As it was, the four ships were clearly distinguished – one long barge and three high-sided carracks. At the main mast of each of these he could even make out a flag. He knew it instantly. He had fought under it often enough.

It was the red cross of St George.

'Genoese, by God,' he muttered.

He knew that he would be a fly upon a vast blue wall to them. They were moving slowly, for the wind that caressed his face was weak, barely stirring the huge sails. Still, he could see they would pass far enough away from him to his left, beyond the sound of his voice and the waving of his hands. Yet if his hands were filled with cloth? His headscarf was too small, so he looked at the canvas that floated beside the planks, bent to it, tugged. It was thick, waterlogged, and he could not rip a piece from it. And then he noticed again the broken bottles caught in the mesh. They glinted as they rose with the swell.

He reached over, grasped, jerked till one came free. He held it by the neck, turned the wide, jagged edge to the sun. It flashed, dazzling him. Ripping the scarf from his head, he waved it, and directed sunbeams at the ships.

The ships came slowly closer. Soon he could make out figures upon the rigging. His arm grew weary from waving and he had to rest it for moments. But he always found the sun and kept the bottle flashing.

The first ship was passing him. His arm sank. And then he saw something as it passed. A small shape that had previously been hidden against the ship's dark side. A boat was making towards him, its smaller sail angled to the breeze.

He kept flashing, kept waving until he was certain. Soon enough he could hear the plash of oars, and he lowered both arm and glass and sank onto the raft. He just had strength to tie his nose into place, and the headscarf over it.

'*Ragazzo!*' came the call from the boat, a man half standing at the aft, his hand upon the tiller. 'Where are you from?'

Gregoras had swilled a mouthful of sea water so at least he could reply. Reply in the tongue and accent of the question. 'From Genoa,' he yelled, his voice a rasp. 'Bound for Ragusa.'

The tillerman steered his skiff skilfully alongside the raft, three men on the nearest side shipping their oars. 'A country-man,' he said, 'saved by God's good grace.' He stared at the mask, then glanced down the naked, scarred body. 'You'll want this,' he continued, handing over a flask, which Gregoras uncorked and drained, before holding out a cloak. 'And this.'

Two oarsmen helped Gregoras, part covered, cross from raft to boat. He settled on the strakes near the tiller as the sail was adjusted, oars were put into the water again and men began to pull.

He reached a hand up and the tillerman clasped it. 'Thank you, brother,' he said.

'It was a rare fortune you were spotted,' the man replied. 'A miracle. God must have you in mind for a better fate than drowning.'

'*Inshallah.*' Gregoras smiled as the man's eyes narrowed at the term. 'And whither is this fine fleet bound?'

'We are about God's work, sure, brother. We are bound to bring succour to our fellow Christians and damnation to the infidel.' The man stuck out his chest. 'We make for Constantinople.'

The sailor kept a firm grasp on the hand he'd shaken, even leaving the tiller to grasp the other's shoulder. He wasn't as concerned about drifting as about the man they'd rescued, who was laughing so hard that his whole body shook, and for so long that he feared they were all going to be tipped into the sea.

SEVENTEEN

The Standard

Night of 17/18 April

It had been the same most nights since the first firing of the great gun. Achmed and his fellows would press right up to the Turkish stockade, a vast mob of men beating their scimitars upon their wooden shields in time to the hammering of a hundred *kos* drums, the whine of seven hundred trumpets. The cries would erupt from a thousand throats – 'God is great!' 'Muhammad is His Prophet!' 'Mehmet, lead us to glory!'

While they cried, over them would fly the balls – great ones of stone, flung with explosions from cannon or hurled from the huge slings called mangonels, smashing into the city walls with a crack like thunder or disappearing over them to destroy whatever lay behind. Smaller balls from smaller guns, from what were called the *kolibrina* and the culverin – Achmed had learned some of the language of war – were aimed at the heads of Christians glimpsed briefly between the crenels.

The noise, the incredible level of it, the hours that it lasted, was something he had had to get used to. The loudest sound he had experienced before was that of the men of his village gathered for prayer. And the first night had nearly sent him running mad. But then, after perhaps two hours, his mob was withdrawn, another took its place with fresh throats, and arms to hammer upon drum and shield. Every third night they rested. And Raschid explained what Achmed had already come to understand.

'We can sleep, my farmer,' he'd said, lying back in their trench, settling his twisted limbs upon a sheepskin he'd stolen, 'but the Christians? If they do, it is standing up and with armour upon their backs, for they do not know if we will come.'

Yet this night was different. Even a farmer could see that something else was being prepared. Cords of wood great stacks bound with rope – were brought up. Scores of ladders were leaned against the stockade. Finally archer after archer, their great bows slung over their shoulders, pushed through the mob of *bashibazouks* to crouch upon the shooting step of the great wooden rampart, melding with crossbowmen and others who blew upon twines of red-glowing rope, their guns beside them.

'It is an attack, is it not?'

'You were ever quick, giant.' Raschid squinted up at him. He had managed to buy or, more likely, steal a thick-quilted coat, along with a dented turban helmet. None of his fellows had more than the small wooden shield for their protection, though the coat would have fitted Achmed better and the little man was trying to fold up its width and length so he could still walk. 'A week of hammering the walls, and that above us.' He pointed his fingers at the sky, a waxing moon directly overhead. 'We will be able to look into the Greeks' eyes as they die upon their walls. And see the plunder lying in the streets beyond once we take them.'

Achmed grunted. He moved to the top of the slight rise, where he could see over the stockade. The walls in the moonlight looked battered indeed, yet still high and solid enough. The week of shouting, of praising God and ducking guns, of endless waiting, had begun to annoy him. He had come to fight – for his sultan, for God's victory . . . and for what that victory could give him. Life and riches – or a martyr's death and a swift journey across the bridge of Al-Sirat to paradise.

Raschid was tugging at his ankle. 'See,' he said, 'who comes.'

Down the little valley between the hill of the stockade and the higher one of the gun battery came a procession of walking men. Some bore torches, their fire reflected off armour and helm, off spear blade and shield boss and swinging scimitar. Much of the light seemed to gather in the man at the centre of the throng, one of the biggest men there, whose steel armour was aflame, whose turban helmet burned. A dozen men his equal in size hedged him in a wall of halberds. Closest and on either side of him, their fingers on their bowstrings around a notched arrow, walked two archers.

'The sultan!'

Raschid was only one of several who spoke the title. It rippled back along the mass of men on the slopes. The party halted around an upturned barrel, and before that was cut off from sight by the gathering of men, Achmed saw a large piece of parchment raised and placed upon it.

'The men with the halberds are the *peyk*, his bodyguard. It is said that they have their spleens removed to make them more temperate.' Raschid was always keen to air his experience of soldiering, and he told Achmed things in the tone of a father to a dull child. 'The two archers are ever beside him. Did you notice how one drew to the left, one to the right? Of course you did not, ox that you are. Well, he needs left-handed bowmen too, to ward him on that side. And those men, coming in now? They are the leaders of the Anatolians, the *belerbey* Ishak and Mahmoud. *Our* leaders, for their divisions are behind us here, waiting to follow us over the walls.'

'Follow us?' Achmed looked across to the other slopes, filled with ordered ranks of men in armour. 'Should not they go ahead, since they are so well dressed for it?'

'No. They will let us do the first attacks.' When Achmed looked to object, Raschid continued, 'No, it is good. For when the sleepless Greeks fall to our thrusts, we will be the first into their city. We will have the first choice of the plunder.' He licked his lips. 'And their virgins. Besides . . .' he pointed to the next large body of men on the slope, set slightly apart from them by a space of earth and by their darker clothes, their longer beards, their hatless heads, 'I warrant that our sultan who loves us will dispatch those first to die. Christians,' he hissed. 'Mostly scum and mercenaries drawn by the promise of booty to fight against those of their own faith.' He hawked, spat. 'Let them take the brunt of the first fury. Then let you and I take the glory and the gold.'

'*Inshallah*,' was all Achmed could manage, his mouth suddenly dry.

A loud shout drew their eyes back to the flames below. It was one cry of assent from a dozen throats. The group split up, the *peyk* with their halberds lowered, parting the ranks of Anatolians to allow the sultan's party to climb the hill back towards the guns. Other officers came the other way towards them, including the leader Raschid had called Ishak. Still more men were moving through the mob, each bearing a staff from which they were unfurling a long banner. They were shouting out words that Achmed struggled to hear at first above a rising acclamation, and then did, just as he saw the Prophet's name. He could not read, but he knew Muhammad's symbol, his *tugra*, shining silver in the moonlight on the nearest banner.

'A hundred pieces of gold for the first man to raise one of these upon the Greeks' second wall,' came the cry, rising above the tumult. '*Allahu akbar!*'

'God is great!' came the echo from thousands of voices, as men struggled to grasp one of the dozen banners. Achmed took a step forward. A hundred pieces of gold were more than his farm would produce in his lifetime. But a tug at his sleeve delayed him.

'Do not be in such a hurry to die,' another voice said. It was Farouk, their *bolukbasi*, the officer to whom they, and a hundred of their fellows, had been assigned. He was a Karaman, who had fought against the Turks and now fought for them. He was distinguished by the body parts he'd left on various battlefields – an ear, a thumb, an eye. He stared out of the unpuckered one at Achmed now. 'The first who bears the banner will be killed, as will the second and the third, joining him swiftly in paradise.' He grasped the big man's shoulder, pulled him lower so he could speak in his ear. 'This is your first battle, farmer boy, and it will be different than you think. Stay close to me.'

Small fights had developed between men who did not have such cautions spoken to them. Officers stepped in and wielded *bastinados* till the banners were in one grip only. Then everyone moved up towards the top of the hill.

Farouk halted them about twenty paces behind one of the great gates that punctuated the stockade. 'Far enough,' he said, drawing his scimitar.

Achmed did not have a sheath to draw his from. He just laid the back edge against his shoulder, clutched the small round shield to his chest and stared at the white-clad back before him. Defend me, Allah, most merciful, he prayed silently. And if it is Your wish that I should die this night, let me die well, for Your glory.

Other men muttered beside him. Then all fell silent as the trumpets called. In that silence, a great *kos* drum was struck – once, twice, again. Its echo died away, all eyes fixed on the wooden wall before them. In its middle, directly before the gate, Ishak Pasha drew his great scimitar. '*Allahu akbar!*' he cried, stepping aside. The gates were swept back.

'God is great!' yelled thousands of voices as, up and down the Turkish line, men charged through the gaps.

'Keep your head down,' shouted Raschid.

There was little Achmed could do but obey. He watched the back before him, trudging a few paces when it moved, halting when it briefly did. His sight was that patch of white cloth, the sweat stain, like a lamb's kidney, already expanding upon it, although the night was cool. His hearing, though, was full. The mad beating of the drums, the wail of the horns, the hammering upon their shields of the warriors up and down the lines was joined by new sounds – the constant thrum of arrows as the archers upon the rampart step notched, pulled, released, notched, pulled, released, a near continuous glint of arrowheads rising into the moonlight, falling into the darkness beyond. Interspersed with them, other men would raise and point what looked like thick sticks, sticks that gave a sharp crack and then ejected flame, the shooter's head instantly hidden in a small cloud of smoke that joined with others to form a bank along the ramparts. A cloud that Achmed now pushed through, coughing on some sharpness in the smoke, as he and Raschid finally made the gate.

They had been moving slowly; now they moved fast, stumbling down the slight slope. Achmed placed his foot on something that first moved, then screamed. He had stepped on the body of a man crawling across his path. He saw something feathered sticking from the man's neck and, without thinking, he bent, grabbed the man with one huge hand by the back of his shirt and dragged him to the side of the rush.

'Good, good,' said Raschid, one hand on the man's leg, not lifting at all, 'helping a brother is good.'

Screaming men kept rushing by them as they laid the man down upon his side. With one hand he was clutching the crossbow quarrel, with the other he clung to Achmed's shirt, mumbling feebly, the words lost in the blood that bubbled over his lips. Achmed stared, helpless, until Raschid tugged him away. 'Come,' he said. 'He is either for paradise or the surgeons. Come,' he repeated, pulling him forward.

The slight slope ended in a lip of stone, and over it, a huddle of men were pressed together in a ditch and in the lee of a stone wall that rose from the far side to twice the height of a man. They slipped down swiftly, their feet finding the piles of bound wood that had been thrown down to fill the ditch, and leaned into the bodies there, as more quarrels, arrows, shots fell from the flaring darkness above.

'The walls of Constantinople?' Achmed said.

Raschid snorted. 'This?' he said, glancing up. 'This is a mere breastwork over the fosse. The Christians won't even defend it. The walls are beyond. And we shall be at them soon enough. For look!'

Achmed looked. Another rush of men came, every second one bearing a ladder. These were passed overhead to the men right below the breastwork, one end held and steadied on the wood of platforms or the mud of the ditch. There was a moment's pause, as the other ends clattered onto the stonework above. Men leaning against the wall peered into each other's eyes, waiting. Then the drums began beating double time and, with a great surge, the *bashibazouks* began to swarm up the ladders. Some made it, many did not, knocked back by bolt and flung stone.

'You!' Farouk was poking him with his *bastinado*. 'Big man. Strong with it, eh? How about hoisting some of your friends over the wall?'

Achmed nodded. '*Effendi*,' he said, handing his sword and shield to Raschid. He interlaced his fingers, stooped. A man stepped forward, placed palms on his shoulder and a foot in his cupped hands. Immediately, Achmed stood straight, flinging up his arms. With a yelp, the man flew over the breastwork and disappeared.

'Sodomite donkey!' the officer laughed. 'Not so hard! They are warriors, not pigeons. Just get them to the top.'

Achmed stooped, a man placed his foot, he rose carefully this time. The man grasped the stonework, pulled himself up and over. 'Good,' Farouk said. 'Another.'

Achmed bent to his work, Raschid content beside him in his role of sword-bearer. A half-dozen men lifted, and the crowd was thinned, more making it over on ladder top as well – ladders that were now being pulled over the walls. 'Enough!' Farouk commanded, stepping forward. 'Me, then him. You can climb up after.' He placed a foot, was lifted, scrambled over the wall.

Raschid propped Achmed's sword against the wall, sheathed his own. 'That was a blessing from Allah. With His grace, there will be too many people between us and the Greeks. Lift me! I'll wait for you the other side.'

Achmed lifted him till he could sit. Raschid pulled his one bad leg over and disappeared.

Achmed looked around. The first assault had passed, leaving

a mess of men who hadn't made it, still or writhing in the ditch. Above him, arrows were flying fast over the walls, from a mass of archers who had run down from the stockade. Another massed mob came with shovels and mattocks and began to dig at the ditch's walls, filling it in. Grasping shield strap and sword hilt in one hand, he jumped, grasped a jutting stone above him and hauled himself, by various promontories, to the top.

And into mayhem. The noise had been lessened by the wall. Here it hit him like an open-handed slap. The screams – of men falling as ladders were pushed off the far higher wall ahead of him, of other men slashing and smashing blade onto blade, onto shield or helm. The cries of the attackers: 'Allah!' Of the defenders: 'Christ! Holy Mother!' There they were, the first time he had seen them this close, his enemy, the men he'd come to kill. His enemy, men just like himself. Some in armour, striking down with swords, axes, spears. Others, like him, in nothing more than shirts, hurling stones and oaths. Lit by flames from torches that flared upon each tower and at spaces along the walls between each one. He saw an archer lean through the crenels of a tower and shoot down into the mob, saw the man he plucked from a ladder top with his shaft, saw that same archer knocked flying back by a slingshot stone to the face. Everywhere he looked, men were striving to kill, striving harder not to die.

It was hell, and he was staring into it. Frozen atop the wall, with missiles flying around him, Achmed found he could not move, could only stare. Something tugged at his leg, jerking it hard; he forced his gaze down and saw Raschid there, face twisted in rage, mouthing words he could not hear. He looked away from him, to the mobs and the madness beneath the high wall beyond.

And then he saw it. The banner of the Prophet. It was being carried forward through the crowd and appeared to be drawing the worst of Greek metal and stone. A bearer would fall, the pole would slip, the banner sag, and then another would snatch it up, to fall in his turn. Somehow it was always kept aloft.

The Prophet. It was why he was there, to serve him in this holy cause, to glorify him and Allah, most merciful. To be a martyr for him if he so chose. Yet the banner was something else too, something that had been cried out before the attack began – that it was worth more gold than he would see in a lifetime of labour in his fields. Gold could not return his little Abal to him. But it might return the smile to Farat's face when she realised that no more of her children would die because they had no food.

Gold he could have – but only if he were the one to plant the banner of his saviour on the walls of Constantinople.

He slid down. Raschid's words were clear now, cursing him for a fool for sitting there, a giant target for every Greek archer and slinger. Achmed began to push through a crowd that was beginning to thin near the back, as the wounded dragged themselves rearwards. But there were yet enough of the crazed or the ambitious hurling themselves at the walls, and ever another man to take up the banner when it dropped from life-fleeing fingers.

'What are you doing?' Raschid was limping beside him, striking his arm. 'Keep your shield up! Raise your sword!'

Achmed ignored him. He had reached the point of the solid mass, men pressed six deep to the wall. He began to move them aside. They protested, looked up, then moved. There was something in the giant's eyes.

He reached the banner as it fell, this time from a height, for the latest martyr to carry it had got halfway up the ladder. Achmed dodged the falling body, caught the pole as it passed him. Jabbing its butt end back, he took the wind from the protesting Raschid's chest. Free of him, he began to climb.

For so much noise, there was such a silence in his head that he could hear his own prayers there, words of praise for Allah, most merciful, and for Muhammad who was His Prophet, peace be unto him. But other words came too, the first his little daughter had ever spoken. 'Gobe,' she'd said, pointing at a goat. 'Gobe.'

Something passed through the flap of shirt at his chest. A stone glanced off his shoulder. There was a man right above him on the battlements, raising an axe. Achmed lifted the banner of the Prophet to protect himself . . . and then watched the man loose his grip on his axe, reaching up to the bolt that protruded from his arm. He tumbled from sight, his weapon fell, Achmed felt its edge open his side as it passed. But he did not feel pain; there was not time between the clear space suddenly before him and his stepping into it.

He was standing between two crenels. Before him, the body of the axeman was still sinking onto the flagstones. Either side of him, Greeks fought to push back ladders that had Turks on their top rungs, men who stabbed and jabbed and fought not to be dislodged. But already others were turning to him, to this giant suddenly stood amongst them. He had a moment. One.

'*Allahu akbar!*' he cried, and swept the banner left to right, Muhammad's name unfurling from the cloth in flaming light.

The moment passed. Something struck him hard in the forehead and he fell, the pole whipped from his grasp as he tumbled back, down, his fall broken by bodies, some of which broke in their turn, until he was lying on the ground, watching flame reflecting in a widening pool of blood. He saw a shadow reach into it, knew that someone was thrusting their face close, screaming more words he could not hear. Then he felt hands on him, thrust into his armpits, one at the back of his neck, all dragging. He began to move, slowly at first, then faster over the slick ground. When he stopped, it was suddenly, and he vomited, just as sound came back.

'Up, fool! Up! Or you die!'

Raschid was beating him, shouting in his ear. Achmed looked up to see men flinging themselves up and over the first wall, low enough on this, the city side. He lurched up, fell onto it, over it, sliding down onto a crush of mud and stacked wood. He was in the ditch, and then he was clawing up its mud sides, crawling out of it, stumbling forward. The gate in the stockade was wide open. There did not seem to be the crush to get in that there had been to get out.

Men were marching forward, men in plate and mail and helm with big round shields and spears slanted to the sky. He was slid out of their path, dragged into the lee of the wooden walls.

His eyes were closing. Just before they did, he saw a familiar face. It had one eye, and that eye shone with amusement. 'Well, well, farmer boy. You are a *deli* and no mistake.' Farouk thrust his hand forward in the traditional gesture to banish the mad. Then he let it fall onto Achmed's shoulder. 'Still, once we've cleaned you up a bit, I have no doubt our sultan will be happy to see you. To reward you. To reward us all.' The one eye narrowed, as the hand stroked. 'For we are comrades, are we not? All *gazis* for Allah, praise Him, yes?' He rose, smiling. 'So all will share in the sultan's bounty, is that not right?'

He moved away. Achmed wanted to understand more clearly what was being said. But he found that he could not stay awake, even with the cold water thrown in his face, even with the pain the rough cloth brought.

Oblivion found him. He sank into it, gratefully.

EIGHTEEN

Exile's Return

20 April: two weeks into the siege

It was a Greek upon the Golden Gate who saw them first. He was one of several stationed there, at the southernmost towers of the land walls, who were gifted with long sight. He did not stare, as the rest of the garrison did, at the mass of Turks two hundred paces away behind their stockade. His duty, for the length of his watch, was to look to the sea, to its horizon. Though it was optional, he was encouraged to pray.

Which he did, in a way, when he first glimpsed them. 'Christ's hairy balls,' he muttered, rubbing his eyes, trying to dislodge what had to be motes of dust. He raised a hand to the side of his face to shelter his vision from the sun, halfway up its climb through the sky. Sunlight on water, seabirds, a school of dolphins had all had him reaching for the bell rope before. He had even pulled it once in his excitement, just once, stopping when he realised that the sail he saw was single and slanted, just another Turk making for the Bosphorus.

This time he'd wait. This time he'd make sure he was spared his comrades' mockery. Even when the single blur resolved into four distinct ones, even when he saw the sails were not lateen, like most Turks, but square-rigged, he did not pull and shout. But he did begin to pray, correctly this time. And even when he was certain, he still took a breath before he grasped the bell pull, closed his eyes. For a moment, he was the only one in the city who saw its deliverance, and it filled him with a power that he'd never imagined.

The bell rang loud at his pulling. But it was his voice, the words, that brought men running. 'Sails!' he cried. 'Sails from the west, and the cross of Christ upon them.'

A lieutenant ran up the flight. 'How many ships?'

'Four that I can see, master. But mayhap they precede the many.'

'Four will do for now.' The officer turned to two men just appearing, both booted and spurred. 'Ride – one for the Commander, one for the emperor. Tell them of four ships, and more to come.' He laughed and clapped his hand upon one messenger's shoulder. 'Tell them that salvation is here.' He turned back to the man with long sight. 'Keep ringing that bell, brother. Soon every bell in the city will ring the glorious news.'

More men came, and he sent them all off, on foot along the ramparts, on horseback into the city. They must have cried the news as they went, because as the first bell ringer fell back in exhaustion, another in the nearby Church of St Diomedes began his peal. St John Studius was next, and then the monastery of Gastria, and on, like flame in a forest leaping from tree to tree. It was different from the alarums that signalled an attack and brought defenders to the battlements. The toll had a joy to it that the city had not heard in weeks.

Theon, showing papers to his lord, heard it just before the panting messenger was admitted to the emperor's chamber. As soon as the news was blurted out, Constantine was calling for boots and cloak. 'They will be making for the boom. We must make sure it is ready to be raised. To horse.'

Sofia, picking over the meagre produce at a stall upon the Hippodrome, heard the wave of bells, waited as they appeared to pass overhead and crash into the Hagia Sophia, whose deep voice joined and drowned all others. A messenger galloping into the oval was surrounded, and not permitted to pass till he had barked his news. It came back to them in ripples of voices.

'What is it, Mother?' said Thakos, looking about at the running, smiling people.

Sofia gathered her son and daughter into a hug. 'A fleet approaches. Relief for the city, perhaps. Come!' She began to lead her children where everyone else was going, up the hill to the Splendome, beneath the tower of St Irene, one of the highest points in Constantinople.

Her son dragged. 'But I am to go and practise my sling with Ari,' he said, holding up the rope weapon that all boys seven and over had been issued with.

'Perhaps this means you will not need to use it,' Sofia said, adding, when she saw his pout, 'and you want to greet our rescuers, don't you? We can see almost everything from up there.'

Less reluctantly, her son followed. They were still early enough to get a good spot near the summit.

The Greeks were not the only ones with long sight. On the shore of the Marmara sea, Turks were stationed for the same purpose. Only the tower's height had meant that the defenders had seen the ships first.

The bells had woken Mehmet, resting from a long night of carousing with his favourite, Radu. The younger Dracula was snoring softly beside the divan when the sultan heard the horse gallop up to his tent, heard the shouted news. Such was his hurry that he was already dressing himself, while bellowing for servants, when the officer of the guard entered. 'I heard,' the sultan said, strapping his sword belt round his waist, throwing on his long cloak. 'Send your fastest rider ahead, to Baltaoglu. Tell him to make ready the fleet. Tell him not to cast off until I have spoken to him. I will be on the messenger's heels. Go!'

He ended on a roar that finally woke Radu. 'What is it, beloved?' He yawned as he spoke.

Mehmet kicked him, not gently. 'Get dressed fast, unless you wish to be left behind. A Christian fleet is coming. And, by Satan's testicles, we have to sink it.'

He had last seen it lit by a single sunbeam that had split the clouds. He'd hoped it was for the last time. Now the dome of the Hagia Sophia glistened in full morning sunshine. No Turkish crescent flew over it; the men who lined the walls waved banners of the city and the other nations who defended it. The enemy was still outside, and he was in time.

The young voice came from right next to him. 'Is that where God lives, sir?'

Gregoras looked at the boy beside him. A son of Genoa, and so of the Roman faith. 'Perhaps. There is some dispute about it.' He smiled. 'Though I would prefer he lived with us this day, upon the water.'

The nine-year-old looked around, as if seeking. 'But do we not make for land, sir?'

'We do.' He reached out and rubbed his hand through the boy's thick hair. 'But someone is going to try and stop us getting there.'

'Who, sir?'

He turned the boy forward. 'Them,' he said, and swallowed. He had seen Turkish fleets before. But never one of the size that approached now.

It was close enough to study in detail. Suddenly so, for his own ship, *Stella Mare*, and its three companions had just rounded the curve of Lighthouse Point, St Sophia looming above it, and entered the stretch where three famed waters met – the Sea of Marmara, the Golden Horn and the Bosphorus. Clear of sheltering land, the sea became instantly choppier. *Anafor*, thought Gregoras, giving the swell its Turkish name. Yet his vessel – its three masts of sails filled with the same south-westerly wind, the *lodos*, that had driven them fast from Chios – seemed to leap forward in the rougher sea, flying between wave tops like a dolphin, as if she sought safe harbour as eagerly as those who sailed her.

'Are those the infidels, sir?'

'Aye.'

'S . . . s . . . so many?'

Gregoras glanced down. He could see the terror in the eyes of the boy, who was probably little older than his and Sofia's son. The lad, Bartolomeo, had adopted Gregoras ever since he was plucked from the sea. 'Aye, they are many. But look at them.' He knelt so his eye was level with the child's, rested one arm on the rail, lifted the other. 'That one ahead is a trireme. It has a mast but no sail raised, for we have the wind. Still, it is driving hard towards us, propelled by men on oars.' He shifted his hand. 'Those beside it are biremes, smaller, fewer oars, and those on either side, still smaller, are *fustae.*'

The boy laughed nervously. 'They look like water bugs.'

'That's it!' Gregoras threw his arm wide. 'And look at us, how tall we stand in the water, how high the sides of our ships. Those we do not crash through we will squash . . .' he stood, stamped, 'like bugs.'

'Bartolomeo!'

The call came from the boy's father, a lieutenant on the ship. He was beckoning his child to shelter below. Behind him, on the raised aft deck, another arm was waved – at Gregoras. 'Come! We are both summoned.'

He rose, the boy did not. 'I wish to stay with you . . .' his eyes went wide, 'and watch the fight.'

'I think you will see enough of it, wherever you are. But arrows are about to fall like rain upon us, so you need something over your head.' He walked, the boy following. His impatient father muttered a curse, grabbed him roughly by an arm, started to drag him below. Bartolomeo glanced back to Gregoras, who quickly raised his mask, giving a flash of ivory. It had never failed to delight the lad, and it brought a smile now.

As the boy descended, Gregoras climbed the steep stair to the aft deck. Bastoni, master of the *Stella Mare*, the man who had summoned him, lifted his head from the straps of his breastplate. 'So, Greek, it begins. Are you ready?'

'I am.' Gregoras had left his Ragusan name and mercenary history upon the vessel that had sunk. 'Where do you want me?'

'At the start, here beside me. There may be some parley and

you speak Osmanlica better than any here.' He cursed, fumbling with the strap. 'Can you aid me with this?'

'With pleasure.' Gregoras bent to the straps, swiftly securing them. 'And after the talk?'

'Where you will.' The man grunted. 'I would not take lessons from you in how to sail my ship and I would not tell a hunter where to position himself for the kill.'

He gestured to the crossbow, propped up against the rail, amidst a pile of armour. Gregoras glanced, reappraising. He had won the weapon from the captain himself in a shooting challenge the second day aboard. Other Genoans had rushed to avenge this insult to their leader's prowess, and each further challenge had given him the pieces of armour he needed to protect himself. They were mismatched, and nothing like his fine set that someone in Giustiniani's company would have stolen by now. The sallet was impressive, near new, with the visor that was becoming more the fashion. The bevor was less so, and he knew he would not want to expose the gap between them too long, offering the chance for a keen-eyed Turkish archer to put an arrow through his neck. The breast- and back plates had belonged to a smaller man, and stopped well short of his waist. He would need to be standing behind something so that his bare legs were covered.

Gregoras jerked his thumb over his shoulder. 'How long?'

The master looked past him at the enemy, up to his own sails, down to the waves. 'A half-glass.'

'Then I had better arm. Would you help me?'

'Aye. If you'll finish with me. There's little I can do now except run at the whoresons.'

Each aided the other and both were soon done, the master standing in a beautiful suit of blackened armour, Gregoras in his motley. He reached into his visor, under his mask, as if to remove his ivory nose. Reconsidered. His sallet had a visor, so he was unlikely to get hit in the face. He dropped his hand.

Bastoni had seen the gesture. 'You never told me the story of your nose,' he said.

'No. I never did.'

After a moment, both men smiled. Each took a deep breath. The Turks had got so close, heads could now be seen. 'Go with God,' Bastoni said, then turned and marched to the front of his aft deck.

Gregoras picked up his crossbow. It was a foot bow, a hunter's bow, which he preferred, certainly for a sea fight. A bigger bow, wound with a crannequin, would send a bolt farther, harder, but it took too much time to fit the winding mechanism, draw up the string, unlock, aim, shoot. More to carry too, and heavier, when he shifted positions. A foot in the stirrup, a pull using the back, it was ready in moments. Turning it over, he studied the face plate. The decoration was nearly always the same – the Huntress, a naked version of Diana with long flowing hair and high-set apple-shaped breasts. It made him think of the last woman he'd seen naked, Leilah, a memory that brought a smile as well as a question: where was she now? Awaiting him in Ragusa? Would his change of heart cost him her?

The quarrels rested head up. He reached past the smooth sharpness, grasped a shaft, pulled one out. It was not as beautifully fashioned as the one he'd found outside the warehouse doorway in Constantinople, nor the one he'd pulled from the Scotsman's pack in Korcula. Both those had curved flights of heron feather, could have been made by the same careful hand. Even though he knew that was impossible, he'd wondered briefly if some vengeful crossbowman had been stalking him. No, good bowmen made good quarrels, that was all. He would, if he'd had the time, for they flew that much more truly. Unfortunately, these flights before him were of curved leather, ordinary. Still, they would do the task at the range he would be shooting. But there were only twenty in the quiver. He would have to choose his targets carefully. Unlike arrows, quarrels were hard to scavenge in a fight. Once these were gone, he would need to rely on other ways of killing.

He checked that now – the falchion at his side. He liked the weapon, with its thick, slightly curving blade; shorter than most swords, it was perfect for the close combat he would soon be seeing. Sliding it back into its sheath, he checked that his small, round buckler was equally secure on his other hip, then rose, just as the master shouted his name.

'Gregoras! They come!'

The distance had halved again. The Turkish vessels were spread out ahead in the shape of a buffalo, a thin, wide crescent like horns, the bulk in a body in the middle. Close enough now for Gregoras to notice at last what the stiff south-westerly propelling them had prevented till then – the music. The wind still kept it faint to his ear, though he knew it would be loud enough, and soon. It was the same on sea as on the land – the Turk fought to a constant, frantic wailing accompaniment of horns and drums.

The enemy had shipped oars, most of them now rolling in the swell. Only one kept coming, the biggest of the triremes, oars on both sides rising and falling like mechanical wings, the big *kos* drum keeping time – that, and the man Gregoras now saw striding the *histodoke* that ran the length of the ship like an exposed spine, bellowing commands. He carried a long whip, furled for now, and Gregoras winced at a memory. Six months a slave upon a galley before his escape, and weals like white worms crawling across every vertebra of his back.

'Does he expect me to stop?' Bastoni was pointing at the largest man on the trireme's raised foredeck; the best dressed, too, with a suit of full mail and a huge helmet crested with peacock plumes.

'No,' replied Gregoras. 'But he will make himself heard.' He looked to his left. There sailed another of the carracks of Genoa. To his right, closest to them, was the one Greek vessel, a transport stuffed with grain from Sicily. It was wider, a little lower in the sides, though still sitting taller in the water than any of the enemy's triremes. He understood little of seamanship, could only wonder at the skills it took for all the Genoan ships to trim their sails to accommodate the slower vessel. Their strength lay in their unity, all knew. Besides, the grain in the transport's holds might be the difference between the city they sought to succour starving to death or not.

When he turned back, the halved distance had halved again. The Turks had masterful sailors too. The *kos* drum received a single, mighty thump. The man on the *histodoke* cracked his whip and all the oars upon the trireme's right side were lifted from the water. At the same time, three men pushed hard upon the tiller. The ship appeared for a moment almost to stop, and to tilt until the men upon their benches would have been able to dip their hands into the flood. But further shouts, further strokes of the left bank of oars jerked the trireme round and upright again. As the Genoan ship, its sails bellied, swept past, the drum began to beat triple time, the whip to snap and the oared vessel leapt forward alongside and perhaps fifty paces away.

'A clear shot, if a tricky one,' Gregoras said, placing his foot in his bow's stirrup. 'Shall I shoot him?'

Bastoni shook his head. 'There'll only be another sodomite to take over. Let's hear what this one has to say.'

The Turk commander raised a trumpet. 'You of Genoa! I am Baltaoglu Bey, *kapudan pasha* of the sultan's navy. What make you here?'

Gregoras translated. Bastoni nodded. 'Tell him that, if it is any of his business, we go to deliver goods to the city.'

'Which city?' Gregoras queried. 'Galata or Constantinople?'

Bastoni smiled. 'That truly is none of his business.'

Gregoras relayed the terse reply. Baltaoglu bellowed, 'That is forbidden. You will allow us to board you and take you with us to the sultan. There you may find mercy. But if you refuse, you will get none from me. Refuse and every man will die. Some quick, most slow.'

Gregoras shook his head. 'The man speaks with the most execrable Bulgar accent. Another renegade. But even with that, the message is clear: surrender or die. Slowly.'

Bastoni nodded. 'Tell him to insert one of his peacock feathers and twirl.'

There was no direct translation, but Gregoras anyway had a better way of answering. Throwing down the trumpet, he placed his foot in the stirrup of his crossbow, pulled the string to its catch, snatched two quarrels from his quiver, one for its groove, one for his mouth, raised the weapon, took swift aim, pulled the trigger. Considering the rise and fall of the sea and the still gusting wind, it wasn't a bad snatched shot. It snapped one of the feathers, the wind ensuring that it would never be used for the pleasuring suggested. With another bellow, Baltaoglu dived behind his rail, just as a line of Genoese crossbowmen rose above theirs and shot. Halfway between the ships, quarrels passed arrows loosed from Turkish bows.

'I think he understands,' said Gregoras, crouching, slipping the second bolt into the groove.

But Bastoni did not hear him. As an arrow glanced off his helmet, he raised his hand to his visor and, just before slamming it down, yelled, 'Ram the bastards out of the way!'

The battle was begun.

NINETEEN

Before a Dying Wind

At first it was too easy.

Every yard was filled with canvas, every sail thrust out like babies in a belly, hastening to be born. The wind that had swept them past Chios swept them on now, and the captains of some of those triremes, biremes and *fustae* not swift enough to manoeuvre out of the way were soon trying to remember if they could swim. Banks of oars were snapped as the carracks ran the length of them; the high, hard oak prows of the Genoese harrowing the Turkish vessels like clods of earth in a field. Most managed to evade the rushing doom, but some were left foundering in the larger ships' wakes, oars a-tangle, slaves fallen from benches to the deck, slavemasters wielding whips and curses to no effect.

Yet there were many, deeper into the pack, luckier, more skilful, and warned by the fate of their compatriots, who managed to evade, then turn to pursue. The fastest, with *kos* drums beating triple time and oars pulling dementedly, could keep up with the carracks for a while and their tillermen steered them close. Grappling hooks were twirled and thrown, and some bit into the wood of the ships' sides. But the moment one held – and even Gregoras, for that moment, could feel the slight slip of momentum – a sailor was there with an axe, the barbed head was severed and the ship surged like a hound freed from a leash.

From the shelter of an aft rail, Gregoras watched the sailors do their work. Though arrows flew up around them, he did not return the shots. There was little aiming in the buck and jolt of the *anafor* and it would be an unlucky seaman who was struck. He had nineteen quarrels left and he was determined to find a fleshy mark for every one.

And then the chance came. A hook landed, a sailor raised an axe, and an explosion followed that drowned the drum. The sailor reeled back, half his face torn away. 'Gun!' yelled Bastoni, beside him. 'What place do they have in a sea fight?'

Other sailors ran forward, to take away their wounded comrade, to strike again; the hook was severed. But more flew, and as another shot exploded a chunk of railing, Gregoras could see that they were attended to with less alacrity. He took a chance to peer over the edge. Upon the bireme's deck, men were readying a culverin with powder. He waited until the deck beneath him felt steadier, as the vessel crested a wave. Then he lifted his bow over the edge, breathed, sighted.

He'd been aiming for the chest. He took the gunner somewhere near the thigh, judging by the way he instantly doubled over, gun exploding as it fell from his grip. Ducking back, Gregoras watched sailors hack the grapple clear. The ship surged again and, looking swiftly to port, he saw that the others were equally free. Ahead, the bulk of the Turkish fleet had been passed through. A few of the smaller *fustae* were rowing hard out of the way. He looked up and saw the ruins of the ancient Acropolis, surmounted by the newer tower of the Church of St Demetrius.

'Acropolis Point,' he yelled to the captain. 'The Golden Horn and safety is round this bend.'

'I know it well, Greek,' Bastoni shouted back. 'We will sail to the boom and keep swatting these flies until your countrymen can raise it for us.'

Others had recognised where they were. From each of the four ships came the sound of cheering. All aboard knew they were close to sanctuary. From the Turkish ships still in pursuit there came a different kind of shout, a chorus of fury.

And then, as sudden as a man's last breath, the *lodos* wind died.

'What is it, Mother? What is wrong?'

Thakos tugged at Sofia's skirt. Minerva, who'd been dozing despite the shouting of the hordes on the Splendome, pulled her face from her mother's neck.

Sofia stared. She had cheered, as loud as any, the ships' sweeping progress and her mouth was dry. 'The sails. They . . . they . . .' she croaked.

The man next to her finished her sentence. 'They've lost the wind, boy,' he said, shaking his head. 'God help them now.'

All around, voices started up again. Not cheering now. These voices were low, words coming on whispers.

'Holy Mary, mother of God, help these poor sinners.'

There were ten, fifty, hundreds. Muttered prayers, sobbed out. Buried in Sofia's neck again, Minerva began to cry.

'By Muhammad's sacred beard, a miracle.'

Hamza marvelled at the suddenness of the change. Yet he'd always known that Mehmet was as changeable . . . as the wind, he supposed. Mere moments before, when the enemy's vessels had burst into view round the point of land, their sails full, their own fleet trailing like exhausted hounds about a galloping stag, their sultan had blasphemed both the Prophet and Allah in terms that had his closest advisers turning away to quietly pray. Now he was urging his horse closer to the water's edge, raised high in his stirrups, with nothing but reverence on his lips. The court – for all had followed Mehmet to this strip of sandy foreshore beneath the walls of Galata – moved forward with him.

'See!' Mehmet cried. 'See what Allah has given me.' He raised one hand to the sky, then swept it down, making obeisance. 'He has brought them here, cast them adrift right here before me, so that I may witness the triumph of my fleet. Is it not Allah's blessing, Hamza Bey?' He turned to grip the other's arm. 'Does this not, more than anything yet, show how our enterprise is holy?'

Hamza smiled, for show. He would gain nothing by crossing his master in this mood. But he had commanded ships at sea, and had fought Italians upon them. Even if they were becalmed, and the four vessels surrounded by twenty times that number, this was not going to be an easy fight. But he said, 'Undoubtedly. Is not one of your titles "lord of the horizon"? Why would the weather not act on your bidding?'

Mehmet laughed, turned. 'Bring me chairs, a table, food, wine. Let us feast and toast Baltaoglu the Bear's triumph.'

Men scurried. Grooms came to take their horses. Within minutes, a small pavilion had been set up, leather stools unfolded. Mehmet clapped his hands. 'Wine!' he bellowed. When he got it in hand, he stood and raised his goblet to the scene. '*Allahu akbar!*' he cried.

Only the imam and one or two of the more orthodox *beys* refrained from breaking Allah's commandments while pledging Him. Most, even those who did not drink, like Hamza, raised their wine to the scene before them and, like their sultan, called for God's victory.

For a while, they were just a spear's throw from the walls of Constantinople. But then the current began to draw them away, drifting them, almost imperceptibly at first, towards the Galata shore. The Genoese ships seemed to be barely moving – though this was not true of their enemy. Gregoras, snatching glances under what had become a rainfall of arrows, saw that the Turks were now hindered by their numbers, that someone – this Bulgar renegade he'd parleyed with, no doubt – was trying to order the chaos. Drums and trumpets were being used for signals now, not just for courage. And judging by the steadier flow of stone ball that was thudding into the ships' sides, Baltaoglu was having some success.

'What are they doing, Captain?' Gregoras called to the man a few paces away. Encased in full armour, Bastoni either paid no attention to the arrows dropping onto him, or swatted them aside like insects.

'They are readying for an assault,' the Genoan shouted through his visor. 'But first I see flames upon their decks.'

'They are afire?' Gregoras asked hopefully.

'No, they *have* fire. And here it comes.'

Gregoras heard the beat of the *kos* drum change, heard the crack of whip and the whoosh of oars in the water. Flicking the visor down on his helm, he raised his head to look. Several smaller *fustae* were charging straight at each of the carracks' sides. At the last moment, they veered parallel and he saw the flames the captain had spoken of – in large pots upon the deck and on spears, swathed in oiled cloth, dipped and instantly flung.

'Fire!' yelled Bastoni, at a crew who were already prepared. Sailors rushed forward with buckets of water, flung them wherever the lances latched. The sails had been furled as soon as they lost the wind, so there was little for flame to catch on to, and all that burned was swiftly doused. Gregoras watched ship after ship attempt the attack, and each one failed, its crews savaged by the soldiers on the carracks' decks, who shot crossbow bolts, flung rocks, snatched up flaming lances and returned them. Bastoni, for all his complaints before, had a few smaller guns, and these shot stones upon the enemy's decks. Yet still Gregoras did not raise his bow. Eighteen quarrels still seemed too few, and he was certain that other, more satisfying targets would present themselves soon.

He was right. Again and again the *fustae* attacked, throwing fire. Again and again they were driven back. Until Gregoras heard the drums' rhythms change, heard the different notes in the bugles' call. Heard a distinctive bass bellow, with a Bulgar strain to it.

'Board them!' screamed Baltaoglu Bey.

Gregoras tried to locate the source of the cry. There was some smoke, mainly from burning *fustae*. But he soon saw, among the many vessels, the Bulgarian's larger trireme; saw upon its aft deck three horsetails hanging from a pole beneath a crescent moon – the *kapudan pasha*'s tug, the same on water as on land; located just near it, that same gaudy helmet that now sported one less peacock feather.

It was time at last to fit a quarrel to the groove.

It was a long shot through smoke and the chop making for unsteady footing. At least there is no wind to compensate for, he thought, with a grim smile. Baltaoglu was armoured much like the Genoan beside Gregoras. But like him now, he had his visor up, the better to shout his commands.

A chance, then. Bending, he placed his foot in the stirrup and pulled the string smoothly up till it caught. Lifting it, he placed the bolt, then pushed the stock into his shoulder, leaned a forearm onto the rail, sighted. Then, as he breathed out, just as he squeezed up the trigger, a jolt ran through the ship, as wood smashed into wood.

When he looked, Baltaoglu was still standing, still raging, unharmed. He was directing his own trireme into the side of the wider, flatter Greek transport.

'Boarders!' yelled Bastoni, and Gregoras turned from what was further away to what was close – the bireme alongside, the men upon it whirling ropes and flinging them up, their heavy hooked ends latching onto the carrack's sides, binding themselves to the larger vessel. He heard the same thud upon the other side, saw ropes and hooks flying up there too. One landed right beside him. He saw the rope tauten as weight was put upon it. Carefully setting his crossbow aside, he untied his buckler from its straps, slipped his fingers into its grip, then drew his falchion from its sheath.

Arrows were flying over the ship's side, steeply angled. He leaned away from them as he would a spray of water. A hand appeared, clasped wood. Gregoras had time to notice thick scarlet hair on every knuckle before he cut it off.

A jet of blood, a scream of agony, the voice trailing away as the man fell, more cries below from those he fell onto. As three more hooks caught, bit, Gregoras glanced around. Men were standing at every part of the rail, swords, axes, daggers raised, waiting like hunters before a rabbit hole. If one fell back, struck by a projectile from below, another would immediately step up to take his place.

Despite the mass of noise – the drums, the trumpets, death cries, war cries – a particularly piercing shriek turned him. Above him, a Genoan had staggered back, dropping his axe, clutching feathers at his neck. Blood squeezed between his fingers, he fell – and at the hooks, hands appeared. The man next to him did not notice them, focused on his own stretch of rail. There was a gap, and suddenly a turbaned head was in it, the Turk vaulting the wood, landing with scimitar curved back.

'Captain!' Gregoras shouted, and Bastoni turned, dodging only just in time the swinging blade. He met its next stroke with his own and the two men spun away – from two more Turks hoisting themselves onto the ship.

A hand appeared on a rope beside Gregoras. Pausing only to slice off two fingers, and jerk his falchion from the wood it bit into beyond them, he charged. The slight slope to the aft deck made it feel like he was running uphill. The first Turk who was over snarled and slashed at him with his sword. Gregoras cut down, swivelling in his run, just enough to guide the razor tip past his breastplate on the falchion's edge. Bringing the buckler hard round, he smashed the small shield into the man's face.

Somehow the Turk did not fall. Blood streaming, eyes filled with water, he still saw enough to slash at Gregoras's hip. Throwing himself forward saved a deep wound, but he felt a burning there, where his armour did not cover. Spinning, he brought the buckler up and round, driving the shield's edge into the man's already bloodied face. This time he went down, stayed down.

But the second man over had his sword swirling before him, fending Gregoras away, the longer curved weapon keeping him at a distance. A glimpse told Gregoras that the ropes were taut. More men would soon be there. 'For the Cross,' he cried. He had to get close, within a falchion's shorter reach, so he brought his buckler high and hard across to knock aside the scimitar. At the same time he cut low for the man's legs, knowing it was a feint, that he was a hand's span short of his enemy's shin. But the man did not know, jumped back, half falling over the first man, still groping on the floor for his spear. For a second the scimitar was tangled in his stumble and Gregoras, using the moment, rose and stepped in, opening the Turk's chest with a tight swipe. The man screamed, stumbled back, and Gregoras closed, slamming the buckler into the man's chest, knocking him up and over the rail. The other had found his spear, was rising, shouting a curse between broken teeth. But he was half turned to Gregoras and the Greek placed a leg behind the man's front leg, thrust his sword arm around the man's neck. Grabbing that wrist with his other hand, he pushed his hip hard against the Turk's, bent, lifted and flung him after his comrade.

Two ropes before him creaked with weight. Dropping his falchion, he hoisted the axe the sailor had dropped, swung, chopped, swung, chopped again. Two ropes fell, to the sound of crashing and screams from below.

'Well.'

Gregoras turned, his breath coming in heaves. The captain was standing behind him, a dead Turk at his feet. Wiping his sword blade upon his cloak, he continued, with a smile, 'Shall I leave you command of my aft deck, Greek? You seem to have it settled.'

'I would . . . be obliged . . . if you would not.'

'Nay, then.' Bastoni turned, bellowed above the tumult, called more men.

As five ran up, Gregoras looked the length of the ship. A very few Turks had made it to the deck and now were lying still upon it. On each side, more attempted to climb and were thrown back. On they came, driven by drums and bugles, shouting their cries of Mehmet and the Prophet. Gregoras had never doubted the courage of his enemy. That and the skills of their leaders had led them to conquest far and wide. This assault seemed a hopeless task – yet there they were at the railings of their ships, crying out for the chance to climb and dare death. And Gregoras saw something else below, and at the sides of the carracks on either side – scores of Turkish vessels, riding the swell, waiting for their turn. Thousands of fanatics waiting to kill and die for Allah.

Suddenly he wondered who it was that faced the hopeless task.

Yet if the Muslim had courage, so did the Christian. At every rail, the men of Genoa and Constantinople stood and fought. As he would, as he did, turning to the sound of metal on wood and another hook biting deep.

On they came and on, and the deck was soon sticky with blood and studded with severed limbs. Gregoras's heavy-bladed short sword became more like a club, lifted and swung. He knew no reckoning of time except in the angle the sun made upon reddened wood. It passed.

And then, through the mist of effort and killing, came the captain's cry, 'The Greek founders!' and Gregoras raised his head to stare and see that the lower-sided grain barge, a mere fifty paces away and flying the eagle standard of Constantinople, was indeed so swamped with enemy ships, she looked as though they would pull her into the deep by sheer weight. He saw his city thus, like a stag with a dozen hounds at its throat. And the sight drove all tiredness from his mind.

'Can we aid her, Captain?'

Bastoni raised his visor, wiped sweat and sprayed blood from his eyes, and looked about. 'Aye,' he said swiftly, 'for each of is like a separate city under siege. Why should we not fight as one?'

A galley had just swept away from his right side, another waiting for it to clear before entering the fray with fresh men. 'Here, to me,' he called to Gregoras, dropping his sword as he did. The Greek did the same and joined the captain at his wheel. 'There's not much of a current,' Bastoni said. 'Pray Jesus it is enough.'

Both men heaved. The wheel turned . . . and so, almost

227

imperceptibly at first, did the ship. They heard Turkish cries
in the galley below, the crunch of snapping oars. And then a
shudder ran through the ship as its sides smashed into the
solid frame of the imperial barge. 'Make her fast!' yelled the
captain, leaning over the rail. The movement had shaken off
the galleys that had clung before. For a moment, no ropes
twisted with climbing men. Gregoras joined Bastoni at the rail
and looked down.

The Greek ship was wider, sat lower in the water, her huge
holds filled with life-giving grain. Men were already grabbing
ropes that the Genoans slung, anchoring one ship to the other.
'See!' Bastoni grabbed Gregoras's arm and pointed beyond the
vessel. 'They join us.'

Gregoras looked. On the barge's far side, the captains of the
other two carracks had seen Bastoni's manoeuvre and aped it.
Even now their ships were drifting in, to join upon the other
side.

He looked down again. He knew that their own vessel bore
all the scars of the fight. But it looked like the barge's wide
deck had suffered even more. Men lay around it, some dead,
some holding bleeding limbs. Such men as wore metal had not
the full dark plate armour of most of the Genoans but the mail
and steel turbans more akin to their Turkish foes. And they
had another mark that distinguished them – unlike the carefully trimmed beards of the Italians, those of the Greeks spread
over their breastplates.

Gregoras's hand rose to his own neat beard. He had fought
alongside Genoans for so long that he looked like them. He
could have been one of Giustiniani's company still, fighting
whom he was told to fight, just another paid killer. But looking
down upon his countrymen now, he remembered a little of
what he'd felt when he'd first gone to war, when he'd fought
for things other than gold: for country, family, emperor. For
God. Fate had not conspired so determinedly to send him back
to Constantinople merely to collect yet another war-wage.

Turning, he snatched up his crossbow and slung it over his

shoulder, sheathed his falchion, thrust the buckler's straps halfway up his arm. 'Captain,' he called as he armed, 'I go to join my countrymen.'

Bastoni raised his sword hilt to his face in a swift salute. 'Travel with Jesus, Greek,' he replied, glancing to the barge's deck. 'You'll need his care, down there. Tell the captain, Flatenelas, to hold firm. Genoa will not desert him.'

'Flatenelas?' Gregoras smiled. 'I know that old bear.' He jumped up onto the rail. The Turks had drawn off a little as the Christian ships joined together, so for a moment the arrows flew less thickly. 'I will give him your message. Farewell!'

The ships were locked together and the imperial barge's stays were a leap away. Gregoras jumped, landed in the linked ropes. Climbing up them led him to a spar, and along that a line trailed down past the furled sails. Gripping his legs around it, he slid down, slowly enough to avoid the burn. When he was two men's height above the barge's raised poop deck, he dropped into the middle of the group of men who stood upon it.

'Holy Mother!' 'Shrivel the Pope!' 'St Peter beat me bloody!' were just some of the cries his sudden appearance provoked. Weapons were levelled – and Gregoras lifted his visor and raised empty hands. 'May a countryman offer his services for the fight?' he said, in Greek.

'Have you dropped from our city's walls, boy, or from heaven?' The man who growled the question was the imperial commander, Flatenelas. Gregoras's father and he had been in business together, shipping silks.

'Neither, Uncle. Though I seem to have stepped into hell.'

The men shifted, staring at the newcomer. Flatenelas tried to peer through the mask. 'Do I know you?'

'You did.' He paused before he replied. 'For I am Gregoras Lascaris.'

The older man whitened. 'Gregor . . . but you are dead!'

'Not yet.' He tipped his head towards a sudden blast of

trumpets, the increased tempo from the *kos* drums. 'But I may be soon enough. Can I die by your side, Uncle?'

The captain's mouth opened and closed, no words coming. His gaze shifted to the prow of his barge, the enemy ships approaching head on. One of his lieutenants leaned in. 'The traitor, master?'

Flatenelas looked back. 'That story stank worse than his father's feet – and they were a legend.' He smiled, looked up at Gregoras's shoulder, pointed at the crossbow. 'If you are the man behind the mask, then why do you carry that skilless toy? You!' He yelled at the man who'd just spoken. 'Give him your bow. For if he is indeed Gregoras Lascaris, then he is second only to his tutor Theodore of Karystenos in his skill. And we can use that now.'

A shudder ran through the ship as something smashed into it. From the shouting, and where the axes and swords were rising and falling, the Turk had rammed them head on. 'Follow me!' Flatenelas cried, lifting his sword.

His officers descended the stair after him, running the length of the main deck to join the crowd at the ship's prow. The last of them thrust a bow and quiver at Gregoras, muttering something he did not catch, before following.

He took a step in pursuit . . . and stopped, stunned by what he held, realising now what the man had said. For he had handed over a treasure, and he would want it back and in one piece.

A bow. Yet to call it a bow was akin to calling the Hagia Sophia a church. And to Gregoras, heedless of war cry, death cry, flying barbs and flame, it was as holy. With reverent eyes, he traced the whorl in the polished maple from tip to tip, gazed on the tendons of buffalo sinew that had been gently simmered for weeks to give it strength and suppleness. He whistled – one as fine as this took over a year to make, and would last two hundred years! The wood seasoned, fed daily with oil of linseed, the horn for the grip boiled till pliable, then moulded, the horsehair string saturated in precise proportions of resin, beeswax and fish glue that turned it into resilient silk.

Gregoras closed his eyes, then, folding his fingers one by one upon the grip, sighed. He had wielded one near as good as this from youth, the only way to learn such a weapon, for the strongest men could lack the specific muscles required, formed over years of hard training. But when he'd been maimed and exiled, he'd given up his name and everything that reminded him of his loss – including the weapon he loved. He knew he was proficient with the crossbow, the champion of his company. But he'd always known that it was simply a tool of death. This bow, all it meant, was like a limb he'd lost, restored. He felt . . . whole, in a way he had not for years.

Reaching into the quiver, he found what else was essential – the bow ring. It fitted loose upon his finger, measured in sealing wax and crafted as it was for another man; but it would do for now. Turks were calling him. Yet though he notched a bone-tipped arrow, he did not seek an immediate target, not yet. Not because the string was a touch slacker than he would have liked – he was slacker too for the years of neglect. He did not shoot because he knew that when he did, the life he'd lately lived was finally, and completely, over. He would be mercenary no more, exile no more, but again Gregoras Lascaris, archer of the Imperial Guard, returned to fight for his name and for his city.

He eased the string back, unnotched the arrow. He would not waste even one, while enemies lived. Besides, his crossbow was still on his back, hampering his draw. He unslung it and its quarrels, laying them carefully aside, replaced it with the bow quiver. Then, looking about the ship, he spotted a little platform halfway up the main mast. Exposed, but with the space he required.

Stripping off his helmet, laying it beside the crossbow, he pulled the bow string over his head, jumped, caught a rope, hauled himself up it to the platform. He'd been right, it was a good site. Through tangles of rigging, between cones of canvas, he saw clearly onto the main deck of the enemy ship. It was a trireme and large, perhaps the largest of the attacking fleet. And he had seen it before. Seen the man screaming commands upon its main deck who wore a distinctive steel helmet that was missing one of its plumes because Gregoras had shot it out.

He smiled. He had missed Baltaoglu Bey, *kapudan pasha* of the Turkish fleet, twice before. But both shots had been with a crossbow. Now, a reunion of hand and horn grip, the restoration of a name, the reclaiming of a cause, demanded a third attempt. So he reached again into the quiver, seeking, by touch. He needed two arrows. One, bone-tipped, to clear the path ahead. The second, metal, blunt-headed, fit for purpose – to punch through mail armour or steel helm.

He found both.

TWENTY

God's Breath

Screaming obscenities, the sultan rode into the water.

Hamza did not follow, nor did any of the other leaders. Mehmet's anger was indiscriminate, and though it was all focused on Baltaoglu now, clearly visible on his trireme's deck a medium bowshot away, the object of it could easily change to those nearer to hand . . . and to sword; for the sultan had drawn his father's scimitar and was swirling it round his head, chopping to left and right as if he were in the midst of his enemies.

'How many men do you need, you Bulgarian pig-lover?' Mehmet shouted. 'How many of my motherless ships will you let sink before you prove you have any balls? Cowards!'

Hamza allowed himself the minutest shake of the head. He had fought Christians upon the open sea, knew how hard it was to take their ships. The advantages of being on high, of being able to drop, shoot and throw downwards, were immense. Even as he looked, he saw some of the enemy heave a barrel over their carrack's side. It plunged into the *fusta* that was grappling it, crushing an archer too slow to scramble aside, smashing through the deck planks. In a moment the ship began to list, the next men already throwing themselves off her – those who could, for slaves were chained to benches and the free men did not have time to loose them, so fast did the *fusta* go down. Hamza closed his eyes, but could not clear the image of arms waving above the water, snatched away. When he looked again, another ship, despite the fate its crew had just witnessed, was racing to the gap left to renew the attack.

The sailors had to be aware of their sultan upon the strand behind them. His tug was clearly visible, his figure, at this distance, distinct. But Hamza was grateful that the furious sounds of the battle would keep his words from them. They were anything but cowards, these men. And Baltaoglu, for all his blunt ways and indiscriminate cruelties, was in the forefront of the fight and doing the best he could.

He glanced to the sun. It set fast and was already low in the sky. Darkness would aid the defenders, making assault all but impossible. And he could see on the other side of the boom – that great linkage of chains that closed off the Golden Horn and so one-third of the city walls to Turkish assault – the gathering of more vessels ready to come to their fellow Christians' aid. He saw flags of Genoa, of Venice, of Crete, even of Constantinople. They would not risk lowering the boom when Turks could pour in. But under the cover of night?

Still, there was time. The gallant Turkish fleet continued to attack, fresh ships coming to replace the mauled or sunk. Christian arms had to be tiring. Christian arrows, barrels, stones had to be running out.

He felt it then, the barest caress on his cheek. Looked to the south, then up to the horsetails upon the sultan's tug. Did they move? Did he hear the faintest of chimes in the tiny silver bells beneath them?

'Allah, most merciful,' he prayed, 'hear the prayer of a humble servant. Send not these unbelievers Your sweet breath.'

'Baltaoglu!' raged Mehmet. 'I will find your mother and fuck her!' He had ridden up to his horse's middle. The sea was soaking his cloak, the sinking sun striking it, water and light turning the russet cloth a deep and bloody red.

Gregoras wiped his right hand on the cloth at his neck, then drew the two arrows from his quiver. The bone-tipped one he notched, having drawn its flights through moist lips, steadying it with his finger where shaft met the tortoiseshell guide. The second, its metal head like a miniature turban helmet, he licked too then placed, slanted almost straight down, inside the strap across his chest. Raising the bow, drawing the string back in the same fluid motion, he waited till he felt the ship crest a wave, sighted and shot.

The arrow flew true, between rope and rigging, and took the partially armoured archer, covering his commander's right side, in the armpit just as his own bow was rising for a shot. Gregoras did not watch him fall away, his hand pulling the second arrow from his chest, notching it without looking, keeping his eye on Baltaoglu. The Turk, his visor raised for clearer shouting, had turned in shock at his guard's sudden plucking, at the gap in the wall of flesh and steel that had covered him. Another was already stepping forward to that gap. Gregoras had a moment while the ship rose upon the next wave, to draw, to sight, to expel breath and then release, aware as he did of the slight change in the target, unaware what it was . . . until he focused again and saw that some instinct had made Baltaoglu flick down his visor at the same moment Gregoras shot.

A barbed arrow would have shocked but not penetrated. Gregoras had better hopes for the blunter head. But some mischance of angle, some tilt of helmet rim, some shift of sea or touch of wind – for he felt it now, cool on the sweat of his face – made the arrow strike the metal mask, but not straight on. The man's head jerked back, his feet shot up, Gregoras could almost feel the shudder as the big body hit the deck of the ship to which his vessel was joined. Then the Turk was lost to his protective wall of guards – and Gregoras was distracted by cries from below him. The latest wave of enemies were leaping back over the rail, leaving behind more of their dead and dying.

'Christ's . . . bones,' wheezed Flatenelas, slipping down to kneel on the deck, 'but I am . . . old!' He tipped his head to the rail above him. 'Do they come again? Look you, someone.'

Gregoras, from his height, had the best view. He looked – and if he could have found words and a faith long missing, he might have prayed too.

Baltaoglu's vessel had already cast off, bearing away the exhausted and the maimed leader. But another was waiting to slip into its place, filled with eager, unbloodied men. Beyond that another, and another, ships circling everywhere in sight, wolves pacing while the prey was weakened for the next assault. He looked to left and right, to the Genoese carracks lashed on either side. As many boats surrounded them. He looked back to his own again, to the Greek bodies among the Turks. How many more could they lose and live? How long could exhausted men go on fighting the rested?

Grasping a rope, Gregoras slid down onto the deck. 'Captain . . .' he began, stopped, trying to figure out the way to tell such news.

But Flatenelas was not listening anyway. He had raised his visor, thrust his nose into the air like a hound scenting. He tried to rise. 'Help me!' he called. 'Get me up.' Three men rushed to his aid, lifting him. He looked all around, licked his finger, thrust it into the air. 'God's breath,' he cried.

'Amen,' someone answered.

'No, man.' Flatenelas was grinning now. 'The wind. It has returned.' Gregoras turned, to the south, the way they had come. He did not need to raise a wet finger, he felt it on the sweat on his face. The wind that had driven them fast from Chios, that had abandoned them to the enemy within bowshot of their destination, was indeed blowing again. 'How do we use it, *kyr*?' he said, turning to his captain.

'How? Like this?' Flatenelas shook off the arms that still supported him. He stepped to the front of the aft deck, looking down into the belly of his ship. Cupping hands over his mouth, he bellowed commands. But Gregoras, standing near him, found them hard to hear over the tumult of war, the still pounding drums, the blare of trumpets and the shrieks of fighting men. Flatenelas realised, turned and shouted at his officers, 'To your men! Get the sailors aloft and every length of canvas flying. Let every man who can use one wield his bow to keep the bastards down.'

His officers ran. All along the vessel men were tapped on the shoulders, commands shouted, heard, obeyed. Soldiers became sailors again, shedding cumbersome armour the easier to climb. Some men needed to stay, armed upon the rail to guard it, though it appeared that, with their commander felled and the assault on the aft driven off, the Turks were pausing for a moment.

Gregoras knew that Turks never paused for long. Many were already shooting arrows at the new targets of men scaling up masts. He was tempted to follow and retrieve his bow, but he would impede men about their work – and anyway, his cross-bow was still to hand and he could shoot it near as fast. Throwing the quiver over his shoulder, he placed his foot in the stirrup, heaved the string to its notch. A quarrel for its groove and a second for his mouth and he was raising the weapon, sighting on an archer, pulling his trigger. He barely saw the man knocked back, was heaving again, placing, scan-ning, pulling. It was a flow he was long used to, and he did not think beyond the marksman's thoughts. Only when he was groping in an empty quiver and found nothing did he pause, his arms and back afire. Noise, which somehow he had not heard despite its volume, returned full force. Yet it had a dif-ferent feel to it now. Most of the drums had stopped and the trumpets' blare sounded . . . sounded somehow desperate to his ear. As did the enemies' cries. He reached up to wipe sweat from his eyes, raised them to see . . .

The sails! They were filled again, almost as one. On either side of the barge, Bastoni and the other Genoan captains had made the same choice as the Greek. Every Christian vessel was under full canvas, and men on each had hacked away the ropes that had bound them into one floating fortress. Separated now, they surged forward. The despair he'd heard in the enemy's voice redoubled, as their oars were smashed into kindling, their sides stoved, their grappling ropes ripped from hands.

Gregoras peered over the side. Their ship had caught up with, and was passing, the largest of the triremes. On its deck, raving useless commands, stood Baltaoglu. He had a bandage crosswise round his bare head, and over his eye a second eye had formed, marked in blood. He was passing within a stone's throw of Gregoras, but the Greek did not move. He had no quarrel left for him, and his arms were suddenly so tired, he was not sure if he could have raised the weapon anyway. Besides, it seemed that fate was not offering him the Turkish admiral's life. Today, his eye would have to be enough.

Brushing aside the clinging enemy, tacking, the four vessels passed before Galata, making the turn toward Constantinople. As they did so, in the sudden silence of his enemy's despair, Gregoras heard another voice raving. He crossed to the far side of the deck, looked to the strand of sand under the Galatan walls. He was close enough to hear, and easily close enough to see, the man on a horse that he was almost forcing to swim. The man wore a silver helmet that made Baltaoglu's look plain, while spewing forth a stream of obscenities that would have made the abbess of a brothel blush. Behind him on the shore stood a nine-tail tug.

'Mehmet,' Gregoras breathed, reaching into his quiver again, still finding it empty. It would have been a long shot anyway, with a crosswind. Perhaps a better chance would come.

A little later, with the sun low upon the horizon and the Turks rowing frantically but failing to catch up with their sailed ships, Flatenelas and an officer found Gregoras staring up at Constantinople's walls. 'You will be ashore soon enough,' the older Greek said. 'When night falls, the Turks will realise that they cannot entrap us, and a fleet of my countrymen already gather at the boom to lift it and see us safely to shelter.' He reached out, took Gregoras's arm. 'I am glad that my old friend's son has returned in the hour of his country's need. We need the strength I feel here. Need the skill I saw you display in the fight. You took that shot at the Turk commander, did you not?' On Gregoras's nod, he squeezed, continued. 'And I will tell all, from the High Council to the lowest courtesan, that what I saw this day were not the actions of a traitor.'

As eminent a man as Flatenelas could certainly help restore his reputation, and smooth the way to the rescinding of his exile. 'Well,' Gregoras nodded, 'I thank you for that. I am not sure about the Council, but it will be good to have the whores on my side again.'

Flatenelas laughed, turned away to the running of his ship. His lieutenant did not follow, stepped closer. Gregoras had not noticed what he was holding, saw it now – the bow that he had used and left on the platform above. 'It was my father's,' the man said, 'but I never had his skill with it. And I most certainly do not have yours.' He held it, and the quiver, out. 'I would be honoured if you would take it and use it. For our city.'

Gregoras looked at the wonderful weapon for a moment, then reached and took it. 'It is I who am honoured,' he replied. 'What is your name?'

'Archimedes. My father was Tanos, of Therapia.'

'I remember him – and his skill. I will endeavour to live up to it. And I will return this to you, Archimedes, when we have triumphed. If I live to do so.'

The lieutenant smiled, nodded, walked away. Gregoras turned to look at the city again. The sinking sun was setting it ablaze, the dome of St Sophia a vivid crimson flash. Our city, he thought. He had fought the Turk for gold and he had fought him for Constantinople, and though he always fought well – for fighting was something he loved – he had rediscovered what truly made his heart strong and his bowstring sing.

A cause. *The cause.*

The ships had bunched again, waiting for the sunset and the

lifting of the boom in the darkness. The imperial barge was close to the *Stella Mare*. Close enough for Gregoras to hear a high-pitched laugh. It was the boy, Bartolomeo, safe after the battle, on the aft deck of the carrack, making his father dance with a scimitar, a spoil of war. And looking at father and son, and holding a weapon that had belonged to a father and a son, he remembered that there were other causes within the walls above him, and that he was, at last, ready to seek them out.

TWENTY-ONE

Consequences

The sultan's *otak* was hot, for its canvas roof and walls still held the day's sun, and night was not yet far enough advanced to cool them. But heat radiated from within the huge pavilion as well. Not from the braziers, which remained as yet unlit. This heat came from men, from their fear, sweat running freely inside their *gomleks*, dripping down their legs within the folds of their silk *shalvari*.

Mehmet's rages were known to be indiscriminate. So all the *beys* and *belerbeys*, the pashas, even the imam kept their noses to the floor. Those who had their eyes open could study the intricate patterns of the Izmiri kilims that covered the ground. Most did not even venture so much.

Their ears they could do nothing about, though most would have preferred not to listen to the obscenities, many deeply sacrilegious, that gushed from their leader's mouth. Though in some ways they were preferable to the softer-spoken words that followed, that began to chill the rivulets of sweat upon their skin.

'It is not simply your failure, Baltaoglu,' Mehmet hissed. 'It is the abject manner of it. There, with all the Christians watching from their walls, there, you failed! Because of your stupidity, because of your cowardice, our men who watched now begin to doubt, to fear Allah's judgement, to think of all the times the sons of Isaac have attacked this place and failed to take it.' He bent to the man lying on the ground before him and thrust the *bustinadu* under his chin, using the short wooden stick to pull up his bandaged head. 'Do you hear them, pig? Do you hear the infidels' bells tolling their joy?' He tilted the head still further up, angling it towards the city. All in the tent could hear both Baltaoglu's groan of agony and the distant, constant, joyous peals. 'You have given them a gift. Though you outnumbered them ten, twenty to one, your stupidity, your cowardice, has given them the one thing I have tried to take away: hope!'

He let the head fall. It landed with a thump on the carpet before the sultan's slippered feet, and Hamza, taking the chance to peer up from the floor, saw fresh blood ooze from the Bulgarian's bandage. It would have to be changed soon, like three others before it. Something had smashed Baltaoglu's visor into his eye, and removing the metal had taken the eyeball too.

Now Mehmet turned to the only other man standing, and his command to him meant that sight was not going to be a worry for long. 'Execute him,' Mehmet said softly. 'I want his head on a spike before my *otak* so the world sees what happens to those who fail me.'

The huge man behind Mehmet stepped forward. Hamza had last seen him wielding a trowel in the gardens of the *saray* at Edirne. But the *bostanci*, the gardeners of the palace, were also the sultan's executioners, and he had the tools of this trade about him. It was these that caused him to hesitate, and to speak, the first voice other than Mehmet's to sound within the *otak* since the disgraced *kapudan pasha* had been dragged in.

'The bow or the sword, oh balm of the world?'

Mehmet stared incredulously at him for a moment, then exploded. 'I want his head cut off, you fool. Are you going to do that with a horsehair string?'

'Lord of lords.' The *bostanci* picked up the huge, heavy-bladed sword behind him, bent and seized the Bulgar by the hair at the back of his neck, eliciting another groan, a babble of words, 'mercy' being one of the only ones that passed the blood clearly.

'Not here, idiot!' Mehmet struck the man hard on his

shoulder with his *bastinado*. 'These kilims cost a fortune. Do you think I want them further stained?' He used the stick to point to the *otak*'s entrance. 'Out there! Where my army can witness the fate of traitors.'

Perhaps it was the word. Baltaoglu was many things – a failure, certainly, though Hamza knew that few would have succeeded that day upon the waters when wind and God intervened – but a traitor he was not. Nor was he a coward. And Hamza was also conscious of the ripple that ran through the tent, the low murmur of protest from men who dared not raise heads or voices. They would feel *their* cowardice later, at not protesting. They would resent the young sultan, so new upon his throne, who made them feel thus. And Mehmet, for all his rage and certainty, needed these men. He could not take Constantinople without them.

'Asylum of the world,' Hamza said, coming off his knees, crabbing forward to press his forehead against Mehmet's curled slipper, 'I crave a chance to speak before this just act is done.'

Mehmet glared down. 'Do not plead for this traitor, Hamza Bey. Only a fool defends a fool.'

'Yes, lord. And I do not plead for him, but for something else of far more import.' He risked a look up. In the year of preparation, the new sultan had taken his advice more than any other man's. He saw him hesitate. 'Come, master,' he hurried on. 'Killing a man is thirsty work, and there is sherbet here.'

He gestured to the latticed section of the tent, where more intimate conferences could be had. Since they had ridden back from the debacle before the walls of Galata, no one had drunk anything, so immediate was the sultan's anger.

Mehmet scowled, looking along the rows of backs before him. 'Well, that makes sense. Come.' He gestured to the executioner. 'Lay your blade upon this wretch's neck, so he feels death's approach.' He turned, and strode behind the screen.

Hamza took a deep breath, rose and followed. A servant was

already pouring from a jug, and both men sipped the sweet-
ened, frothy juices before Hamza spoke again, carefully. 'The
fool deserves to die.'

'He does.' Mehmet nodded vigorously.

'He failed you, lord. He blundered about the sea and let the
prize slip away.'

'You would have done things differently, Hamza. I would.
Anyone but a fool would.'

'Indeed, master.' Hamza was not sure how, but proving
Baltaoglu unlucky was not his goal. He was happy to see the
cruel Bulgar fall; it cleared the space around the young sultan
for abler men such as himself. However, he had recognised the
mood in the *otak*. Divisions had existed from the beginning
over this project, this dream of conquest, and half the men out
there had had to be compelled to assist in it – and needed that
compulsion still. There was already dispirited talk amongst
them, barely two weeks into the siege, the walls battered yet
standing, and the Greeks still obdurate. The party that had
always opposed the war, led by the grand vizier Candarli Halil,
seized on rumour and expanded on it – the Pope had organised a crusade, Hunyadi and the Hungarians had torn up the
treaty and were marching overland to join it, the Italian states
were sending a fleet. Even these four ships would be used as
evidence that once again the nation of Islam should retreat
from the place that had always defeated them.

But Hamza was not of that party. His continued success, his
rise from tanner's son to *bey*, could only be sustained, he knew,
if Mehmet sat on the throne. And he would not sit on it long if
he abandoned this dream. Conquer, and he would have the
success that had eluded the Prophet's followers for eight hundred years. Fail, and he would be gone, and Hamza with him.

Little things could change everything. War was cruel, and
cruelty was necessary on occasion. But it was like training
hawks. Sometimes you had to sit out in the freezing rain for
one whole night to bind a proud bird to the fist. But you did
not sit out two. You did not kill what would bring success.

'Master,' Hamza went on, softly, 'you have every right to take this fool's life. But I ask you, what would that achieve?'

'Achieve?' Mehmet's eyes flared. But his voice lowered too. 'It would achieve my satisfaction.'

'Undoubtedly, lord. But would it achieve your desire? Would it bring you nearer to tearing down the cross on the Hagia Sophia and raising a minaret?' It never harmed to remind the sultan of the holiness of what they were about. Seeing his eyes widen, he pressed on. 'It seems a little thing, master, to kill a fool. But many would think that though he was foolish, he was not afraid. He pressed the attack from the front. He has a bad wound to prove it. Not in his back, where cowards are struck. In his eye, which was fixed upon the enemy.'

Mehmet took another sip. 'Go on.'

'Make an example of him, master. Disgrace him. Strip him of rank. Expel him from your presence. But do not kill him. Alive, he would for ever be an example of both your wrath and your mercy, a goad to others to serve you better. Dead . . .' Hamza shrugged.

'Dead, he would have other fools rally about his corpse.' Mehmet nodded. The high colour had left his cheeks, cooled by sherbet and soft words. 'That is what you are saying?'

Hamza nodded. The sultan's voice was calm now. For all his sudden choler, Mehmet was also a thinker, a planner, considering even the minutest effect an action might have. Sometimes he agonised too much and slept too little.

Hamza watched as the young man turned to the table behind him, to maps and papers there. Laying down his goblet, he picked up a map, held it to the light. 'You know what we need to do, Hamza Bey?' he said calmly.

'What, master?'

'We need to make those bells cease their ringing.' He gestured towards the city beyond the canvas, its insistent tolling. 'The Christians think that these four ships mean rescue. That their triumph in this fight means that more triumph will come. We need to act now, immediately, to take away this little hope.' He looked up and, for the first time in an age, he smiled. 'Their despair tomorrow will be all the greater if it is contrasted with their joy today.'

Hamza stepped nearer. He had done what he needed to do. Now he must listen. For all his closeness to Mehmet, he was only one of several. The sultan would consult one, and not tell another. He delighted in secrets and surprise.

'Hold this,' the sultan said, handing over a map. Hamza saw that it was a close drawing of the cities, Galata and Constantinople, that faced each other across the Golden Horn. Mehmet pointed to a line that linked the two. 'Their accursed boom,' he said. 'Another failure of Baltaoglu's, for he tried and failed to force it. But it stops our ships entering the Horn, and so all these walls . . .' he ran his finger along the line of towers and battlements marked on the water's edge, 'need not be defended. They can put their few troops all here . . .' he tapped, 'on the land walls.' He looked up. 'Did you hear that our great bombard destroyed one of the towers, here, tonight, at the gate they call Romanus?'

'I did, lord. All praise to you for moving it there and our gunners for their skills.'

'But I was not there to order a general assault, because of that fool out there. And now the Greeks have filled the wall with rubble and barrels and all sorts of muck. And because they have the men, they can crowd a breach. But if they had to take men away from there, and guard these . . .' he tapped the sea walls again, 'our men would push through their weakness.' He looked at Hamza over the papers. 'We have to get our ships into the Golden Horn.'

Hamza looked down. 'The boom? A bigger assault?'

'I am not confident any would succeed. Remember also, the boom is as much part of Galata as of Constantinople. Those damned Genoese complain every time we attack it. They say they are neutral, but we know they supply their fellow Christians, while others of their country fight beside them.'

Hamza nodded. It was a constant problem. In fairness, the Genoese in Galata also supplied the Turks, making a great profit by the war from both sides. But their sympathies were clear. It was less to do with religion. The Catholic Italians had hated the Orthodox Greeks for centuries. But small Galata would not stay free for long once mighty Constantinople fell. Yet Mehmet needed them neutral, could not risk bringing an open war and a larger Genoese fleet than had already arrived.

Hamza frowned. It was a riddle he could find no answer to. 'I do not see, lord. How do we sail our ships into the Horn without breaking the boom and risking Genoese wrath?'

Mehmet was smiling now. All trace of the raging tyrant was gone. He looked like what he still, at least partly, was – a very tall and excited young man. 'We sail over the land, Hamza Bey. We sail *over* the land.'

Hamza, looking for traces of madness in the smile, found none. 'Lord?'

Mehmet placed a finger on the map. 'Here lies our fleet, at the Double Columns, behind Galata. But only the city and the foreshore belong to the Genoese. The rest is ours. And there is a path that runs from the columns, up this ridge and down the other side, along what the Greeks call the Valley of the Springs. That valley ends in the waters of the Golden Horn.'

Too many questions came into Hamza's head. He blurted one. 'A path? It would be wide enough for goats, no doubt . . .'

'I have caused it to be widened.' Mehmet's teeth gleamed in the lamplight. 'My loyal Zaganos, who commands my armies on the Anatolian shore, has been working at night, with soldiers making sure any curious Galatans have . . . accidents. Zagan has done well. And he sends me word this night that all is in readiness.'

Mehmet turned to the table. There were books there as well as maps, and he picked one up. 'You are not such a student of war as I, Hamza. So you may not have read what the younger Caesar did to take Antoninus and that heated bitch Cleopatra in her comely rear. Nor of a marvellous trick once practised by the great emperor Xerxes.' The smile widened. 'I will be Caesar. I, Xerxes. For on the morrow, I will lift half my fleet on slings from the Double Columns and roll it on greased logs over the land and down into the Golden Horn.' He pointed. 'And I will make those bells toll sorrow.'

Hamza was stunned. Partly by the fact that such had been the secrecy that he had heard nothing about an enterprise that must have been a while in preparing. Mainly by its sheer audacity. Mehmet just grinned at him until he found breath and words. 'King of kings,' he said, 'it is extraordinary.'

'Is it not? It will make me master of the waters. And soon after, I think, of the city itself.' He lifted the map with his *bastinado*. 'But I would have the shock of my fleet's appearance be very sudden. So I would distract the defenders.' He jabbed his finger down. 'Here my land batteries will fire ever more fiercely on the walls. And here . . .' he stabbed his finger at the line linking the two cities, 'the half of my fleet that does not sail across the land will make another assault upon the boom.' He sucked in his lower lip. 'But I have no *kapudan pasha* now to lead it.' He snapped his fingers. 'Yes, of course I do.' He pointed. 'You will be that leader, Hamza.'

'I?' If he'd been shocked before, he was more so now. 'Lord, I will, as ever, obey your every command even unto death. But do you think me suitable?'

'You have fought at sea?'

'I commanded a trireme for your father for a time, and yes, I raided a few towns, took a few stuffed carracks. But a fleet . . .'

'You know as much as most. We were ever a land people and are all learning new skills upon the water. Besides, what I want in my *kapudan pasha* is not just his knowledge upon the deck. It is judgement, it is courage, it is . . .' he let the *bastinado* fall onto the older man's shoulder, 'you, Hamza Bey. You, Hamza . . . Pasha!'

Hamza's mind churned. This swift rising would bring not only status but profit too. The *kapudan pasha*'s share when the city fell would be enormous. Yet extraordinary opportunity brought extraordinary risk. The *bastinado* resting on his shoulder had lately lifted the bloodied head of a man who had found that out. He swallowed, spoke his thought. 'And Baltaoglu?'

Mehmet turned away, swinging the *bastinado* through the air as if it were a scimitar and he was cutting. 'You were right, as ever. His death serves nothing. His courage will be rewarded by the sparing of his life. His stupidity punished . . .' he slammed the stick down upon a book, making a sharp crack, 'with a good beating.' He nodded, raised his voice so all could hear beyond the latticed screen. 'Let him be beaten, and then let him crawl from the camp. If he survives his wound, let him join the *bushibazouks* and try to regain his reputation in the breaches my cannon shall make in the walls.' He lowered his voice again, stepped close to Hamza, whispered in his ear, 'And let you and I rise early to watch our ships sail across the land.'

TWENTY-TWO

Ultimatum

22 April

The bell had not tolled in the Tower of Christ, but it was the only restraint the Genoans of Galata had shown in celebrating their fleet's victory. There was as much carousing, as much singing, praying, drunkenness, Leilah suspected, as in the larger city across the Horn. She had slept little, then woken suddenly to a silence more disturbing than the noise that had preceded it. She was out of the bed she shared with the daughter of the grain merchant and joining her at the window in a moment. 'What is it, Valeria?' she said, looking down at tense-faced men scurrying along the street.

'I do not know,' came the reply. 'When I came to bed, everyone was still laughing. Now . . .' She pointed down. 'Look, there is Sebastiano.' She threw open the window. 'Heh, Sebe! Sebastiano! Here! Here!'

The summoned youth hastened over, his face red with too much wine, and the effort of trying to buckle a sword belt round his large belly. 'Where is everyone going?' Valeria called.

'The walls,' came the terse reply.

'Mother Mary! Is it an attack?'

'Perhaps. There are Turks on the ridge, thousands of them. I must go.'

He staggered off. Valeria turned back – to Leilah, already dressing.

She joined a stream of people on the side street, which fed into a wider way and that surged like a river with a crowd – soldiers in the main, but other townsfolk too – headed to the western walls. The jabber was all of the sudden appearance of so many Turks, the fear of what it might mean – that they had decided to end the so called neutrality of Galata after the Genoese-led victory of the previous day. There was much bravado too, for Galatans were near as proud of their walls as the Greeks across the Horn were of theirs.

The throng became ever more tightly pressed as it approached the north-western edge of the city. Forcing her way to the side, Leilah took an alley cutting up. There was a gap between two houses high on the slope, a stair beyond. Others knew of it too; she was not alone. But with a shove and a slide she was able to squeeze against a crenel and peer over it.

Almost below her, a ridge ran at a right angle from the walls, its southerly slopes that swept to the water patchworked with cultivated fields and vineyards, the northerly ones largely wooded. Soldiers were spread in a double line along the crest, with a huge line in the middle thrust straight down over the fields, another thickness bulging across a short open space before disappearing into the trees. These centre lines, like the beams of a Christian cross, were abuzz, men in the middle engaged in some activity behind ranks of spearmen facing out. They were a bowshot away, and Leilah could see quite clearly, in the dawn light, the rise and fall of tools – mattocks, spades, poles – and hear both the thump of metal on wood and the underlying beat of a *kos* drum keeping time. Men were chanting too, a rhythmic call of one word: 'Heave! Heave! Heave!' Focusing on the cries, Leilah could see a ripple running through the line of men that led into the wood, as if they were one body, breathing out, breathing in.

A different ripple distracted her. Beyond the central bulge, the twin lines were parting, men falling to their knees, laying their foreheads on the ground. A band of horsemen moved down the gap created, at their head a man in gleaming armour, riding under the twin banners of the Prophet and his own *tugra*, slashed across a red sky.

'Mehmet,' she murmured. It was the first time she'd seen

her man of destiny since Edirne a year before, and she leaned closer to him over the parapet.

The horsemen reined in on a slight rise above the centre of the cross. Men knelt, made obeisance, rose. An officer came up to the sultan's stirrup, spoke, gesturing to the woods. Mehmet nodded, raised a hand into the air. All labour stopped, the drum ceased. The hand stayed up, as Mehmet slowly looked all about him, along the lines of silent troops, up to the walls of Galata; finally, across the waters of the Golden Horn to Constantinople. Leilah looked there also, seeing heads there too, crowding every crenel.

The hush held . . . then ended in the fall of the sultan's hand. Instantly, all was noise – the shriek of dozens of trumpets, the hammering upon scores of huge drums, the ululations of thousands of voices, all seeming to hail some triumph . . .

. . . which came, along with a gasp from every single watcher, as a ship sailed from the forest.

Though she had been born with the ability to see beyond the veil of things – from before, her mother would say, Leilah's rhythmic kicks of the belly answers to all sorts of questions – it still sometimes surprised her when her dream visions appeared quite so literally. For she had dreamed this – oars gouging earth, canvas among the trees. And there it was before her, a *fusta* with all its oars thrust out pulling at the air, its sail bulged by some breath of wind. An officer strode the *histodoke*, cracking his whip over the heads of the rowers. She could see that these were not the usual slaves, but warriors, armed with helmet and mail, laughing as they rowed. Indeed, all who watched on the Turkish side appeared to be laughing, at a sight so incongruous. She looked again at Mehmet, and he was roaring, his closest companions – *beys*, pashas and imams – joining him.

The vessel reached the crest of the hill. For a moment, it perched there, oars still moving above the land. Then, with a shouted command, the five pairs of oxen she now saw were unhitched, and the vessel moved forward again, tipping its prow down the slope. It moved as slowly downwards as it had risen, held, she could see now, by ropes attached to its thwart clamps, many men leaning at a sharp angle back and straining against the pull, letting it slide slowly down the front slope, through the fields. More oxen emerged from the woods, another ship followed, oars digging air, sail full, whip cracking, men laughing.

She could not help her own smile. But she smothered it when she glanced left and right, saw the shock on the faces beside her. Most were mumbling prayers, crossing themselves. Many had their eyes closed. She could not, of course, see more than the heads of people across the water, but she knew that if there was dismay in Galata, there would be terror in Constantinople. It did not take a Caesar to see that the Christians' flank was turned. Their boom bypassed, a scimitar now jabbed into their back.

As the second ship crested the ridge and began its downward slide, the first was already entering the Horn, rolling along a slipway made from logs. The oars dipped air no longer, but water, the trumpets blared loudly, drums doubled their beat and all upon the hill cheered. A third ship was just beginning to emerge from the woods when Leilah turned back to the stairs. Her time in Galata was over. It had been pleasant to become a Christian again for a while, to ply her trade where her unbound hair drew no mutters. But it was time to make her way back to the Turkish camp, and there she would go veiled again.

Her dreams had not told her what was going to happen next. A major assault upon men in despair that might force a breach? Surrender, when the Christian emperor realised his hopelessness? She must be ready. She had told Mehmet in Edirne a year before that she would come to him for payment on the eve of the city's fall. She knew what she'd need: a company of soldiers to shepherd her to the library of the monks of Manuel. But her daylight dreams *had* told her the next part: Gregoras already there, reading the ancient Greek, leading her to the aisle where the writings of Jabir ibn Hayyan waited.

'Geber' was what the Christian alchemists called the Arab, and more than any other he had illuminated their darkness. Her former lover and protector, Isaac, would shake with an excitement he never felt in her arms when he thought about the sacred text, the one annotated in Geber's own hand. The Jew believed it contained nothing less than the formula for *al-iksir* itself. And with that elixir, man would at last be able to turn all base metal to gold.

She did not understand the chemistry. But she smiled to herself as she walked. Because certain of the Jew's correspondents in Basle or Paris would pay a fortune for Geber's text. So paper would turn to gold – now that was a formula she *could* understand. Paper transmuting the base metal of her life, meaning she would never need to depend on any man again.

Any man . . . She slowed, her smile fading. She was surprised how the simple thought of Gregoras affected her. It was far beyond his use to her. She'd felt him close from the moment the Genoese ships had appeared two days before. She had mumbled verses to protect him during the fight, and cheered along with the Galatans when the Christians had broken free. Now he was back over there, she was sure. In Constantinople. Awaiting her pleasure. Her varied pleasures, she admitted to herself, the smile returning.

As she resumed her fast pace, pushing through the sullen, silent crowd, she heard the deep toll of a distant bell. From her brief time in the city of the Greeks, she had learned to recognise its solemn note.

The bell was summoning all to the Hagia Sophia to pray for deliverance.

'And so,' Hamza concluded, 'Mehmet, Sultan of Rum, liege lord of all of us, makes this last and most generous of offers to his brother emperor, also his vassal: that Constantine

Palaiologos leaves the city with as many of his followers as choose to go with him and embarks straightway for the Morea, to rule that fair land, with his sons to rule after him for ever. To live in amity thereafter with Mehmet, his sovereign lord and fellow emperor. To save, by this noble sacrifice, the most dreaded sacrifice of all within the walls of Constantinople, sparing its citizens the indignities that will come hard upon the refusal of such magnanimity – the loss of all they own, including their lives, the desecration of their temples, the ravishment of their wives, the enslavement of their children.' Hamza's tone softened, as he looked from Constantine to the noblemen and churchmen, the representatives of Venice and Genoa, who flanked him in the hall of the old palace of Porphyrogenitus. 'And know also that any who choose to remain will be treated with the dignity afforded worthy opponents. Free to keep their property and their gold, to trade as they would and enjoy the protection of that trade under the House of Osman. And to worship for ever as they see fit, in their most ancient and *orthodox* traditions.' He glanced at the papal legates as he emphasised the word, and away from them at the man he knew to be Loukas Notaras, hook-nosed and fierce-eyed, the *megas doux* and most strident opponent of the surrender to Rome. 'All this he promises,' he continued, his voice rising, 'and this besides: to honour the glory of Constantinople's history and to restore it to the dignity it once held, to make it again the foremost city in the world.'

He made the obeisance of head and mouth and heart, bowed in the style of the Christian, stepped back. Since he had arrived, the day after the launching of the fleet into the Horn, he had been treated with nothing but formality and courtesy. He did not expect outrage or defiance at his offer and he did not expect an answer. He knew he would have to wait for that.

He was a little surprised that Constantine replied himself, as he usually would only communicate through an intermediary, sometimes several. Their oft-impenetrable protocols had always complicated any dealings with the Greeks. But the emperor raised a hand to silence all others. 'We thank our sovereign lord Mehmet for kindnesses that his reputation only leads us to expect,' he said. 'If the most noble Hamza Bey would care to wait while we discuss his master's generosity, I am sure we will furnish him with a . . . suitable response, and soon.'

Hamza studied the emperor as he spoke. He appeared to have aged a decade in the year since the Turk had seen him last, his brown hair largely abandoned to grey, lines on his face like siegeworks. But the words of courteous reply were underlined with a determination that had not been there before, and a scarcely concealed anger. Hamza had always dismissed Constantine as a soldier promoted by family and situation beyond his talents, as a man capable of weakness. He looked anything but weak now, and looking in his black eyes, Hamza saw the answer he would get – which was truly the answer he was expecting.

Yet other men around the emperor looked far less certain. Many, Hamza could see, were already turning in to their sovereign, arguments forming on their faces. One of them he recognised. It was his opponent at *tavla* from Genoa, Theon Lascaris. It was his voice he recognised as a servant ushered him into the antechamber. 'My lord . . .' Theon said, and then the door closed upon him.

The room was larger than the one it served as waiting room. It contained the entourages of the men within – priests and monks in robes; secretaries in the cloaks of scribes; Italians in their more flamboyant garb; soldiers. One of these caught his eye for several reasons. His armour, which was a mismatch of styles and, indeed, sizes; the bow he held, which Hamza immediately saw would not disgrace his own collection. Mostly, he stared at an oddity.

The man had a false nose.

He studied him for a moment – until the man looked up and returned his gaze. Then Hamza turned away, to the table of sweetmeats. It was untouched, had been laid out for his benefit alone, and so was covered with a cornucopia of smoked fishes, meat kebabs, fruits, breads, stuffed vine leaves and pots of what smelled like lamb stew. He knew from his spies' reports that if the city was not yet starving, it was already running low on many items. And he could tell from the attitude of the men standing nearby, by the concentration of their stares, that none had seen such plenty for weeks. They were under orders not to eat. It was reserved for him, the excess to send a message that was a little insulting in its obviousness. 'Please,' he said, calling out so that all who weren't already turned to look at him. 'I am fasting, offering this small sacrifice to Allah, most merciful. But that is no reason why this magnificent feast should be wasted. Please.'

At first, no one moved. Then a man, a portly monk, took a step forward. Another followed. And then, at first trying to appear as if none were in haste, but all at once abandoning the pretence, everyone in the room rushed to the table.

Everyone except one man, Hamza noticed. The man with the false nose had not moved; he just continued to stare at the Turk. There was something unnerving about it, reminding Hamza of the gaze of one of his goshawks. Shrugging, turning, he knelt facing Mecca and began to pray, trying to shut from his mind the guzzling of some men, and the stare of another.

He was barely halfway through his third prayer when an opening door, and the blast of language that emerged with it, distracted him. He looked up – to see the diplomat he'd met in Genoa walking towards him. The man gave one dismissive glance to the table and the men moving away with food-smeared lips, reaching Hamza as he hastily murmured a concluding prayer and stood.

'I am to accompany you to the gate,' Theon said, in Osmanlica, and as tonelessly as if they were picking up a conversation broken off a few minutes before, 'and to give you the emperor's answer on the way.'

For some reason Hamza looked around the room, but the

fellow with the hawk's stare had gone. He focused again on the man before him – and on his own surprise. The rapidity of the response was unusual in itself. Its manner of delivery, unprecedented. There was a ritual to such negotiations. Especially with the protocol-obsessed Greeks. Hamza had expected to be called back into Constantine's presence at least once more, for debate, for counter-offer, for clarification.

Theon's next words, as he led Hamza to the outer door, spoke directly to these thoughts. 'The emperor is very clear. He will offer the sultan any amount of tribute he may demand—'

Since protocol had been abandoned, Hamza interrupted. 'He does not possess anything. And even if he did, there is no amount great enough that would be accepted.'

'Which the emperor knows.' Theon led Hamza down the stairs, the spurs on the heels of the six guardsmen clanking on the marble after them. 'Which is why he would not see you again. He is determined to triumph or die. Either rescue will come, by sea or land . . .'

'It will not . . .'

'Either it will come, or we will try our strength upon the walls of our ancestors. Die upon them if God so chooses. Conquer upon them if He so wills. We are in His hands.' Theon smiled slightly as they reached the lower floor of the palace. 'These are his words. He asked that I repeat them, exactly.'

Hamza was about to snap back at this diplomatic insult, that he should hear this from the servant and not the lord. But anger was not a weapon he reached for often. It rarely achieved what he wanted. So he took a breath, then spoke. 'Are they the words you would have chosen, Theon Lascaris?'

They had emerged from the palace's rear entrance, into an avenue of pink-petalled trees. The ground was covered in blossom, and Hamza watched a breeze shake more loose and let them fall like a blizzard. Memory came – of Mehmet in his garden at Edirne. The sultan-gardener had been planting trees that he said could be found in the palace grounds of

Constantinople. Before Theon could reply to the first question, Hamza asked a second. 'What is this tree?'

'This? We call it the Judas tree.' Theon stretched out an arm. 'Shall we walk?'

Without waiting for a reply, he barked an order for his guard to remain at the door, then set off down the pink path. Ah, thought Hamza, and followed.

'My words?' Theon continued as if there had been no interruption. 'Yes, they might have been different. Your ships in the Horn might have made them different.'

'You counselled your sovereign to go?'

'I did not.' Theon shrugged. 'You know as well as I that there are times when one can change a man's mind with words and others when you are merely wasting breath . . . and using up credit better spent in a winnable cause.' He stopped, looked at Hamza. 'Did you ever try to persuade the sultan against attacking us?'

'I did not. Easier to stick all these blossoms back to the branch.'

'There.' Theon began to walk again, slowly. 'As men of reason, we both know what is possible and what is not.'

'It is impossible that you can win this war, my friend,' Hamza said softly.

'No it is not. Unlikely, perhaps. Your cannon beyond this very wall – stand here for an hour, less, and you will feel the earth shake as a ball strikes. Your soldiers, that you can throw at us again and again. What matters if you lose a thousand? What matters ten thousand? Martyrs for Allah. But if we lose a thousand . . .' he shrugged, 'we lose. And then there is the magic of boats sailing over the hills. Clever of you.'

'Not me. All Mehmet's doing. He means to have this place. And he is skilled enough to take it.'

'It is likely. But it is not certain. As reasonable men, we both know this.'

It was the second time the Greek had mentioned reason.

Hamza looked away, to falling pink. 'So what do reasonable men do, when certainty is reached?'

Theon looked down, and brushed some petals off his sleeve. 'They consider their options.'

Hamza studied the man, who was not looking at him, who halted now in the middle of the avenue of trees, as far from soldiers at either end of it as possible. Carefully, he thought, and said, 'Do you still play at *tavla*?'

The other man looked up. 'My son does. On the exquisite board you gave me. He is quite gifted.'

Hamza laughed. 'It could ruin his life.' He nodded. 'Your wife. Is she still as beautiful?'

'She . . . is.'

There was a hesitation there. Something to do with his wife. Some tenderness to be probed. But not now. 'And does she still have that gorgeous cat?'

'She does, curse it. I hate cats.'

'Ah, my friend,' Hamza said, laughing and laying his hand on Theon's pink-petalled sleeve, 'you miss out on one of the true joys in life.'

Theon let the hand lie on his arm for a few seconds, then, glancing to the end of the path and the men there, he withdrew it. 'Then I will miss it.'

Hamza glanced too, then continued in a lower voice, 'I return to my question. What happens when a reasonable man becomes certain? Arrangements would have to be made. You would need a friend.'

Theon nodded. 'A friend who is, perhaps, close to the sultan?'

Hamza smiled. 'The best kind. One with the power to look out for your beautiful wife, your gamester son.'

'I see. And what would one have to do to earn such friendship?'

'Oh,' Hamza replied lightly, 'surely friendship is a gift bestowed, given without obligation?'

Theon's tone was not light. 'Like a *tavla* board. Yes. So what . . . gift could be given in return?'

They had begun to move again, drifting near as slowly as the petals at their feet, closer to the walls, the tower. Hamza looked at it, thought about what it contained – a door set low into the bastion's wall. A sally port, a way for the besieged to charge out and harass the besiegers. In the early days, before the bulk of Mehmet's army arrived, the Christians had issued forth and done much damage. Now it was sealed, triple-bolted, with barrels full of stone piled against it, only shifted to admit the sultan's embassy. Him. Impossible to storm by force.

But what if it were opened again, quietly, at night? Hamza thought suddenly, excitedly. His master was always talking of the fall of Troy – was not this a form of Trojan horse? 'This door, that I come and leave by? How is it called?'

If Theon was surprised by the change of conversation, he did not show it. 'The Kerkoporta,' he replied.

'Ah.' Hamza turned back. 'I have something for you,' he said, reaching into the satchel at his side.

'Another gift? Surely the *tavla* board was generosity enough?'

'This is far less valuable. And yet perhaps its true value is . . . inestimable.' Hamza pulled out a folded piece of silk and then, with a flourish, shook it loose.

It was a banner, a triangle of indigo silk the length of an arm. Emblazoned on it, rushing like comets across an early evening sky, were large silver letters in a cursive script. 'Do you read Arabic?' Hamza asked.

'Well enough to recognise your name. You call this your *tugra*, yes?' Theon replied. 'But this, I do not . . .' He pointed to other letters.

'It reads *kapudan pasha*. For I have been appointed to command the sultan's fleet.'

Theon sucked in a sudden breath. 'That is . . . an honour.'

'Indeed,' Hamza replied lightly, lifting the cloth to display it. 'And this was made for me only yesterday, to acknowledge my elevation.' In a swift move he bunched it up, held it out. 'I would like you to have it.'

Theon did not take it. 'Why?' he replied, bluntly now.

'Because,' Hamza said, 'my new *tugra* will mark anything I own. Any goods. Any . . . property.' He continued, his voice getting softer, 'You know what will happen if what is uncertain now becomes certain: if the sons of Isaac take this city by storm. As is the custom, they will have been promised three days of pillage as a reward for their sacrifice, their courage.' He shuddered. 'It is horrible to witness men turned to beasts. More horrible to suffer their . . . bestiality. Yet when lust and fury have been served, men remember that what they mostly want is money. And each troop will have such distinguishing marks as these, if more crudely made . . .' he raised the balled silken *tugra*, 'to lay claim to what is theirs. They will hang them from houses, and everything within their walls will belong to them. Women for their . . . pleasure. Men and their sons for enslavement . . . and worse.' He held out the banner again. 'But if the house was marked with the *tugra* of the *kapudan pasha*, no one will dare to violate it. Or any . . . property within it.'

Theon's fingers folded and unfolded. Still he did not reach. 'It is most valuable,' he murmured. 'What would a friend have to do to obtain it?'

'Oh,' Hamza said, letting the silk folds fall, beginning to roll the banner up, 'only act, as a reasonable man does, on a new certainty.' The silk had returned to the shape of a small cone, and Hamza pointed its end down the stairs. 'And leave a little door open for his friend to enter in the night.'

Theon looked away, at the steps that led down into the bastion. He could just glimpse the edge of one of the heavy barrels, pulled back to allow the Kerkoporta to open. Guards looked up at him from there. Without turning back, he spoke in a soft voice. 'Have you parchment in your satchel you can spare?'

Hamza frowned. 'I do, but . . . Ah! Ah, I see.'

The Turk replaced the silk into his bag, slipping it between two sheets of the terms Mehmet and he had drawn up for Constantine's exile from his city. He'd not been allowed to present them. But this is a better use, he thought. He raised the bundle, spoke louder, in Greek for the first time. 'Perhaps your sovereign lord will at least deign to read our offer?'

Theon took the papers and tucked them under his cloak. 'Perhaps,' he replied, as loudly. 'I make no promises.' He looked straight into the Turk's eyes. 'None.'

Hamza smiled. 'It is enough that they are considered. That is all a reasonable man may ask.' He made the obeisance, head to mouth to heart. 'Go with God, Theon Lascaris,' he said, and then turned, descended the stairs. The Greek guards looked at him with hatred. But they opened the door and he stooped underneath it, for it was low as part of its defence. His own guard awaited him just beyond, and under the flag of truce, they made their way the short distance back to the siege lines.

Theon stood and listened to the sounds of the gate being bolted, the heavy barrels shifted into place. One man can move one barrel, he thought, then turned and walked rapidly back down the avenue of Judas trees. The wind gusted, dislodging clouds of damp pink petals. Some settled on his clothes, but he did not try to wipe them off. There were so many, there didn't seem much point.

TWENTY-THREE

Reunions

Back in the emperor's chamber, the Council's debate had been distracted by the disappearance of one brother and the almost immediate appearance of another.

Theodore of Karystenos had met Gregoras at the door, brought him in, knelt, with some cracking of limbs, beside him before the throne. The aged captain of archers had insisted, when Gregoras had sought him out after the battle at sea, that he would not have the younger man lurk, unnoticed, on the battlements in the fight ahead. 'Your place is in plain view, lad, where the prowess of your bow will be an inspiration to all,' he'd said, adding, 'And for the same reason you will have to remove that mask.' When Gregoras had protested at this, Theodore cut him off. 'You cannot go masked to see the emperor. We are not Turks! Besides, who will care? War disfigures men, and there are plenty in service uglier than you. Besides that,' he'd concluded, taking Gregoras's face and turning it roughly side to side as he studied it, 'this one improves you. The nose of the Lascari was ever overlarge. Look at your grandfather. Your father. Look, Christ take pity on him, at your brother.' He'd dropped his hand, laughing.

And so, unmasked, Gregoras knelt before the throne, his head bent, his false nose displayed. Concealed outside, he had watched the councillors entering the palace, seen some new Greek faces but mostly the old – Loukas Notaras, George Sphrantzes and their ilk – along with his commander, Giustiniani, shadowed as ever by Enzo the Sicilian and Amir the Syrian. Churchmen came too, whom he did not recognise.

It was the Greeks who gasped now at his appearance, who looked to the guards for the immediate seizure of the exile, instant death the punishment for being discovered within the city walls. Only one was not surprised, for Constantine had been forewarned by his captain of archers. And it was the emperor who spoke.

'It is always a fortune when the prodigal returns. What did Our Lord say in the parable?' He raised his hand, smiling, as the two prelates both leaned forward to speak. 'Gentlemen, it is a rhetorical question. I hazard I know my gospels near as well as you. Forgive me, Archbishop Leonard, that I only know them in the Greek and not the Latin as our blessed father the Pope would have it now.' He closed his eyes. '"I have recklessly forgotten your glory, O Father." Is that not so?' He turned, still smiling, to the kneeling men before him. 'And let all witness that I welcome our prodigal son back to his mother, the city, as well as to another father in myself.' He looked down, gesturing to the marred face. 'I had always hoped to find you and make amends for . . . hasty justice. But word came that you were dead. Yet by God's good grace, here you are, restored to us. Prodigal and Lazarus both.' He rose from his throne and descended the few steps to lift Gregoras to his feet. 'And with this kiss, I remove the attainder and restore to you your name, Gregoras Lascaris.' He bent, kissed the younger man on each cheek and on the forehead.

There was not much that could daunt Gregoras, on burning decks or in a breach. For years he had maintained that Gregoras was the name of a dead man, Lascaris an accident of birth. So he was surprised now at the water that surged into his eyes and burst their bounds. Constantine, moving back from his kiss, was still close enough to see all. He smiled, squeezed the younger man's arms. 'You have returned to us, as you know, in a good time. A time for heroes. You were second only to my good captain, your tutor Theodore, in your skill with the bow. Now you will set an example again to all others. Just as I have heard, from our gallant countryman Flatenelas, that you did upon the deck of his ship in our recent victory.' He turned. 'And my good Giustiniani, most renowned of warriors, tells me that under the name of Zoran the Ragusan, you have become not merely a soldier but a fine leader of men. Is that not right, noble Genoan?'

'It is, lord,' Giustiniani said, stepping forward. 'And my company is bereft without his skills. If you would have me where the fight is hottest, then I would have him still at my side, if it pleases you.'

Constantine turned back. 'Does it please you, "Zoran"?'

'Majesty . . .' Gregoras hesitated, then continued, 'Since you have restored my name to me, sire, I would own it again . . . and my home. I am Zoran no more, but Gregoras of the Lascari. And I will fight for it and you, wherever I can serve you best. Beneath the red cross of Genoa or the double eagle of Constantinople.'

'Well,' said the emperor, looking around at the other men, 'perhaps there is a way to serve me and your old comrades.' He turned back to Gregoras. 'You are aware of the new threat to us, the Turkish ships in the Horn?'

'I saw them, my lord. Like everyone else, I could not believe the sight.'

'It is a threat that must be dealt with, and swiftly,' Constantine said, speaking now to the assembly, all his smiles gone. 'The enemy's guns have caused the land walls so much damage that we have been forced to erect, in places, a stockade of timbers and barrels. This is harder to defend and we need every man to do it. We cannot afford to divert men to the sea walls, yet already the Turks, sheltered by their new fleet, have begun construction of a bridge across the Horn to reach land, just here, near our palace.' He waved to the north. 'If they can assault us there too, the consequences could be fatal to our hopes.' He shook his head. 'No, indeed. We must drive their ships from our water. Our Venetian friends – their safe harbours as threatened as our city by these developments – are proposing some sort of secret action, and as soon as tomorrow. I go to the Church of St Maria in their quarter, to hear their plans, even now.' He opened his hand to include Giustiniani. 'Though he is of their rival, even they of Venice acknowledge our commander's great mastery in the arts of war. They will admit him to the conference. But if, as I suspect, they propose to use only their own countrymen, I will insist that we Greeks are represented too.' He smiled at Gregoras. 'You have already displayed your valour once upon the water, young Lascaris. Would you do so again, for your city's honour?'

Gregoras's stomach tightened. He had not thought to fight again so soon. The cut he'd taken on his hip was inflamed, and he was not moving so well. Also, he'd always much preferred to stand upon battlements than a deck. But he had won his reputation back with his actions in the last sea battle. And if this was a sort of test of his determination, he must not fail it.

'For my city's honour, for yours, *basileus,* and for my own,' he replied, bowing.

'Good. Then let us few away to the Venetian church and see what they propose.' He raised his head to look above Gregoras's. 'But let us first bear joyful witness to the reunion of brothers, our own Castor and Pollux!'

Gregoras stiffened, turned. Cain and Abel, he thought, seeing Theon caught in the doorway, watching shock pass so briefly over his face before a mask as impenetrable as the one Gregoras had discarded dropped back into place. Theon smiled broadly, came forward, arms spread wide. The rumour of Gregoras's return and his actions upon the imperial ship must have also reached him. But perhaps he had not expected his twin, younger by a moment, to be so swiftly welcomed back into the emperor's presence. 'I heard you had arrived, brother,' he said, putting his arms around Gregoras, kissing both his cheeks, 'and I rejoice both in your life and in the restoration of your – our – name.'

'Brother,' was all Gregoras said, could say. For now.

Perhaps Constantine, still standing so close, sensed what was unspoken. As the brothers broke apart, he changed the subject. 'And what, Theon, did Mehmet's emissary make of our response?'

Theon turned, relieved to be able to look away from Gregoras's challenging stare. 'He took our lack of civility ill, lord. And he fears that the answer we sent will rouse his master to fury.'

'Something to which he is prone, so it is said.' Constantine turned, beckoned his servants, who came forward, girded him in a riding cloak, fixed spurs to his boots. 'Well, shall we see if we can send him something else, and goad him into an apoplexy that will burst his heart?'

With that, he swept from the room, his entourage following. Giustiniani squeezed Gregoras's arm as he passed. His shadow, Amir, smiled and tapped his own nose. Soon all had left, leaving just the two brothers.

For silent moments, both men stared at the open door. Finally, without looking, Theon murmured, 'Our family house is open to you, brother, of course, should you choose to stay there.'

The offer was just a form of words, made without meaning. Gregoras turned. 'After what was said there last time, Theon? After what your . . . your son . . .' he paused, 'after what Thakos called me? How could you allow a traitor to sleep under your roof?'

Theon turned too, the two brothers face to face. 'He will learn that what he always thought was true isn't. He will learn a different story now. Now that the emperor and the city have taken you again into their hearts.'

Gregoras noted the taint of bitterness in the words, and could not help his smile. 'Our emperor did not quote the rest of the Bible story,' he said, 'and I cannot remember the words. But I do recall that the prodigal's brother was as unhappy about his return as you are about mine.'

For the years he'd believed Gregoras to be dead, Theon had scarce considered him. Now he was alive, he discovered that his twin still had the power to rouse fury in him as no other man. 'Perhaps you should ask my godly wife,' he hissed, 'for she will quote you chapter and verse.'

Unblinking, Gregoras stared back. Saw his brother's anger – but saw his fear too. And another's fear was what a soldier used, a weakness to be probed. 'Oh, trust me, Theon,' he replied softly, 'I will ask Sofia *many* things.'

Eyes so like his own narrowed still more. Then a voice at a door prevented further words. 'The Commander calls for you, Zoran . . . Ach, I shall have to stop thinking of you like that, won't I?'

Slowly, the brothers took their gazes from each other. Amir stood in the doorway, looking at each of them in turn, sensing what he could not know.

Gregoras came forward, and took his friend's arm. 'Then lead me to him,' he said. They left the room, and Gregoras never looked back to see Theon brushing pink petals from his sleeve.

28 April

Gregoras sat on a tumbled pillar, letting the strong afternoon sunlight work upon his wound. It was the way he'd healed many, as his bare torso bore testimony, a map folded in half and filled with rivers, clefts inked by bone tip, bullet and blade. His back was the worst, for it had taken the whips of slavers when he was chained before the mast. The new wound, curving like the scimitar that made it round his hip, would link the two surfaces and tell the journey of his life.

This latest was healing well, cleaned by an old family physician, the catgut stitching no longer an itching curse. And the delay of five days for what was meant to be the instant action to destroy the Turkish fleet in the Horn – decided upon at that night meeting – had given him the respite he needed to move freely again. He could pull his bow without pain. He could wield his falchion.

He twisted from the waist, felt a slight ache, nothing more serious. The frown came from the knowledge of what else the delay had brought – too many people becoming involved in the operation. An instant raid that first night, accomplished by the Venetians alone – and the odd Greek, for the honour of the city – would have had some chance of success. But once the other Genoese had demanded honour's share too – not Giustiniani, who was all for letting the Venetians take the losses *and* the glory if they relieved the threat – the chances of success diminished with every person told. Spies were everywhere, both sides of the wall. And Italians boasted more than any other nation of the earth. It would be a miracle if Mehmet had not heard of his danger, and arranged to counter it.

There was nothing Gregoras could say. His reputation, newly restored, was still fragile. He would join them in the darkness and sail out into the Horn. But he would not wear his fine armour, reclaimed from the mercenary company, just a few of his mismatched items, easily shed. He would not take his bow. He feared he would be swimming again before the light returned.

The thought made him shiver, despite the sun, the memory of his recent shipwreck still fresh. It would be good to stay in the wonderful late April sunshine, return again on the morrow, and bask, like the lizards that lived in the ruins of what had once been a fine house. Perhaps he would. Perhaps all would be well. Perhaps he would have the chance also to continue doing what he had never, in a lifetime of experience, done before.

Watch his son play.

Though 'play' was not quite right. When he and Theon, Sofia and others had escaped to waste ground such as this, the rare times their tutors freed them, they had done similar things to the boys before him now. Like these they had made slingshots and used them, in competition at targets, or to hunt birds – though Sofia wept the few times they'd actually killed one. But theirs *had* been play, children's games, full of shrieks and laughter. The six boys before him now, who ranged in age perhaps from seven to ten, were quiet, solemn. When the great Turkish gun fired and the earth, even this far back into the city, shook, they paused, looked up in sudden terror. The youngest cried once, till he was teased out of his tears. But all set more grimly to their work, which was not about targets, nor hunting sparrows.

They were learning to kill men.

The slingshot was the most ancient and the most simple of weapons, Gregoras knew. It needed little fashioning. A piece of rope, a patch of leather, a stone. It did not require the years of crafted strength required to pull back a bowstring. Even a boy with the littlest muscle in his arm and a lot of luck could kill a man with it . . . at, say, twenty paces. And since the city's strength was so small, the Council had ordered that boys be armed and practise with this simple weapon. If the Turks ran through the streets, maybe one or two more could be killed.

Gregoras shook his head. Once for the sadness of boys forced to be warriors before their time. And once for their ineptitude. The weapon may have been simple, but there was still a trick to it, and the boys before him had little clue what that was. Turks and sparrows would remain safe from them.

Suddenly most of the boys seemed to agree with him, for all at once five of them ran off. The sixth yelled at them to return. When they did not, the boy stood alone in the middle of the waste ground and lowered his head.

'Thakos,' Gregoras called softly.

The head came up. Thakos looked. He had seen his uncle from the moment he arrived to lie in the sun. It had caused a certain amount of whispering, some curious glances. But he had not ventured near. Now, when Gregoras called a second time, he did, stopping at the base of the pillar, gazing unashamedly at the map of scars. 'Uncle,' he said.

Gregoras looked down. The boy's light brown hair, his

271

freckled face, it did not remind him of . . . either of Thakos's parents, but of his own mother. The left eye was larger than the right by enough to make it noticeable, both wider now in their study. His mother had possessed a wonderful laugh, rough and coarse, that would echo round their house and of which his father would feign disapproval. He wondered if the boy had inherited that as well. He hadn't noticed much childish laughter on the streets of a city at war. It was as if the big gun had blasted it away.

He slid down the pillar to stand beside the boy. They had not spoken, since the night they'd first met and Thakos had called him traitor. He would have been told of the change in Gregoras's status – at least as far as his treason. All knew of the prodigal's return, the news broadcast widely in the city, a little light in the darkness that had settled after the Turks appeared in the Horn. But he would know nothing more and it was not up to Gregoras to tell him.

They stood staring at each other, Gregoras as uneasy. When had he ever had time for dealings with boys? His own childhood had been dissolved by harsh experience. More, he had no idea how to be a father. Yet an uncle had to have some advantages. 'May I see it?' he said, pointing to the slingshot.

'This?' Thakos looked down as if surprised at what he held. 'Of course.'

Gregoras took it, turned it into the light, turned it over and around, grunted. It was the simplest of weapons, but there were still rules to its construction. 'The rope's too long for you,' he said. 'It should be a little shorter than the length of your arm. It's why you are having some troubles. And this . . .' he pointed to one end of the rope, 'should have a loop in it.'

'Really, *kyr*? Why?' Thakos peered at what Gregoras showed him. 'Can it be fixed?'

'Yes, it can. If you will let me?' At the boy's nod, he held the rope up to Thakos's arm, took a measurement, then drew his dagger and cut a length from each end of the rope. He crouched, untwined one end into its four separate strands, twisted them apart two by two, held the tension while he formed a loop the length of three fingers, tied knots below and above it. The other end, he tied off with three tight knots to form one larger. He put his thumb in the leather cup, pulled the ropes together and tight with the other hand. 'Better,' he murmured, offering it.

The boy took it. 'Shall I try it, *kyr*?' he asked excitedly. He reached into a pouch at his side that clinked.

'Wait.' Gregoras rose and moved into the open ground before the tumbled walls. 'Before we risk our lives with way ward stones, let us see how you use it without them.'

Thakos came forward. Gregoras stood beside him. 'This loop is for your first two fingers, see? It is like . . . like the bow on my crossbow. It gives tension to the rope when you grip the other end, its knot so.' He pulled the knotted end up to press it against the loop. 'Now, push your thumb into the cup. Feel the pull? That's what a rock will feel like. Now, keep the tension . . . and fling it round!'

The boy did . . . and Gregoras stepped back, too late. Thwack, the rope caught him on his bare back. 'Ouch,' he cried.

'I am sorry, Uncle,' Thakos said, concern on his face.

'My fault,' replied Gregoras, rubbing, adding ruefully as he indicated his scars, 'You'd have thought I'd have learned to dodge flying rope by now!'

The boy burst out laughing and Gregoras joined him. Then, stepping away to a safe distance, he said, 'Now try.'

Thakos lifted the slingshot, swung it round. After a few swings the whirr came. 'Wait!' Gregoras called and, as the rope dropped, stepped in. 'Wider here,' he said, moving Thakos's legs until they were shoulder-width apart, squaring off his shoulders. 'He's your target,' he said, standing behind him, pointing at a piece of crumbling wall about twenty paces away, the faded shadow of a figure frescoed onto it. 'Swirl till you hear the hum. Two more, and fling the knot at it.'

'The knot?'

'If the loop is the bow, the knot is the trigger – and the sight

– of my crossbow.' He stepped behind Thakos, placed his hands over the boy's, the slingshot still stretched between them. Moving it slowly around the boy's head, he continued, 'When you are sighted, you throw the knot at what you want to hit.'

He stepped swiftly back. The boy swung, flung. The knotted end jerked straight out, then dropped. 'Good,' said Gregoras. 'Now with a stone.'

Excitedly, Thakos dug into his pouch and drew out a jagged lump of masonry. 'Wait!' Gregoras commanded again, stepping close. He took the rock, threw it away, began to search the ground. 'What you throw is near as important as how you throw it . . . Ah!' He stooped, picked up a stone, showed it. 'See. Smooth-sided, close to round, not too large. Like a dove's egg.' He tossed it hand to hand. 'It should fly true.'

'As true as your arrows?' Thakos's eyes were bright. 'My mother tells me that you are a champion among archers.'

Does she? Gregoras thought, but said, 'Perhaps.' He threw the stone over and the boy caught it. 'Let us see.'

Thakos pressed the stone into the leather cup, held the rope out to full length, swung. Gregoras winced – stones had been known to fly out at strange, wounding angles. But this held, Thakos flung the knot . . . and the stone hit the wall if not the faded figure upon it.

'Not bad,' Gregoras grunted. 'The Turk would have killed you, though.'

Thakos held the weapon out. 'Can you do better?'

The challenge was clear in the mismatched eyes. Gregoras smiled. 'I can try,' he said, reaching.

He found a stone that would do, fitted it, took his stance, swung, flung . . .

'Missed!' Thakos yelled in delight at the puff of mortar. 'That Turk would have killed you too, Uncle!'

Gregoras handed the weapon back. 'Then we had better kill him first. And see who does, eh?'

Thakos bent, scooped, loaded, shot. 'A hit,' he cried, delightedly. 'I win!'

Gregoras snatched back the slingshot. 'Didn't I say first to three?'

He smiled, then bent to the ground, seeking. Thakos bent too, a new game started, and both of them swept around trying to find suitable ammunition, bumping into each other, laughing. Through his own laughter he heard the boy's and thought, he does have my mother's tone! Then he pounced on a stone, a moment before Thakos, was up, swinging, flinging . . .

'A hit! A Turk apiece and the game's afoot.'

Thakos seized the weapon, didn't plant himself, missed. Gregoras, steadier, swung and hit. The boy breathed deep, took his time, waited till the air hummed with spinning rope, shot. 'There,' he cried, 'took his nose off . . .' He broke off on the realisation of what he'd said, mouth opening wide. 'I . . . I am sorry. I . . .' He swallowed, staring. 'Does it hurt?'

'Well . . .' Gregoras stepped close, his face a dark cloud. Then, laughing, he tapped the ivory on his face with one hand and grabbed the slingshot with the other. 'Not as much as the Turk's is going to – if only I can find the right stone to finish him.' He pointed near the boy's feet. 'There!'

Thakos dived, Gregoras shot a hand down, they both grabbed the smooth rock. It slipped between them. Laughing harder now, they stooped again, Thakos kicking it beyond reach towards what had once been the mansion's doorway – from which a voice came now. 'What are you chasing, Taki? Is it a mouse?'

They ceased their chase, looked up. Under the ruined arch stood Sofia, with her daughter held before her.

Boy and man stood slowly. 'Mama,' Thakos cried, 'my uncle has made my slingshot better, see?' He pointed, and Gregoras held it up. 'And now I am beating him with it.'

'Are you?'

Gregoras could see that Sofia's face was caught between a smile and a frown. 'Your son has a keen eye for a target,' he said, reaching out to tug at the boy's thick hair. Thakos gave a yelp of pain, snatched the slingshot, moved out of range, delighted.

'Has he?' Sofia said. 'Well, he also has a keen eye for his studies. Which he is late for. Again.'

'I am sorry, Mother, but I . . .' Thakos looked up at Gregoras, 'I am studying fighting.'

'Yes,' Sofia replied, 'and now you are going to study geometry.' Thakos groaned but took a step towards her. 'Wait! Show Minerva over your battlefield. I have to talk with your . . . uncle.'

Was there a slight pause between the last words, or did Gregoras only imagine it? Anyway, he watched as sister ran to chase her brother among the fallen stones. 'It is true, what I said,' he murmured, watching them run, 'he does have an eye for a target.'

'It is also true that he has a mind for studies. He is already gifted in rhetoric, in Latin . . .'

'Like his father, then,' Gregoras said, in a whisper.

Thakos was loading his slingshot, talking fast to a transfixed Minerva. Then he raised the cup, flung the rope round, shot. Mortar and dried fresco erupted from the figure's chest. 'Like both his fathers,' Sofia said softly. Gregoras turned to look at her as she stepped down beside him, continued, her eyes on her children, 'You have not visited us.'

'No.'

'And yet . . .' she gestured to her son, 'and yet you found him.'

'It was not hard.'

'But you have not told him,' she swallowed, 'what I told you?'

Gregoras shook his head. 'He has a father. The only one he's ever known. And I will not win him that way.'

She glanced at him. 'Do you mean to win him?'

'Perhaps. I do not know.' He stared at her. 'Perhaps I mean to win back more than him.'

She looked away then, from his hawk gaze, took a step further into the ruin. 'You have won your name back. I am happy for you. For your family.'

'And for yourself?'

She turned to him fully then, looked at him properly for the first time. 'Your name was never in doubt for me.'

It was his turn to be disconcerted by her stare. 'Well,' he mumbled, reaching up to the ivory tied upon his face, 'there are some things I can never get back.'

'Oh well,' she said, almost carelessly, 'would you truly want your nose back? *That* nose?'

'Why is it,' he burst out, 'that everyone keeps slandering the nose I have lost? My old tutor Theodore was doing it only last week. Was it so very unshapely then?'

'No. It was merely very . . . huge. Certainly not your best feature.'

'Oh really?' He laughed. 'Then tell me what is?'

Her eyes narrowed, her gaze flitting briefly over his bare chest before returning to meet his. 'I am a married woman, sir,' she said, her voice deepening a shade. 'How could I possibly say?'

She was there, finally there, back in the light in her eye, in the curve of her lips, the Sofia he remembered and hadn't seen in seven years. Teasing. Provocative. Alluring. Before he could summon words, she spoke again, in the same tone, with the same smile, 'You know I do not mean . . .'

'No. No, of course not.' Gregoras smiled. 'A woman who prays as much as you . . .'

'The mistake you make, sir, that most men make,' she said, as softly, 'is to think that just because a woman seeks the Holy Spirit, she must deny herself the human flesh.'

It was as if he was seeing her again, as she was that day upon the rock, before he went away to war and never returned. 'Sofia,' he said, stepping closer.

A shriek turned her away. 'Mama!' her daughter cried. 'Look! Look at me!'

They both looked. Minerva had the slingshot now, was whirling it above her head. Thakos was dodging in fear, but the girl let fly and her stone struck the wall.

'She's good,' Gregoras murmured.

'Minerva?' Sofia laughed. 'If my son is mainly mind, my daughter is all flesh and spirit. At five years old, you could set her down on the streets of a strange city and within the night she would have food, shelter and protection.' She raised her voice. 'Come, children. We must leave.' She turned back to him. Their previous conversation was only in the colour on her cheeks, not in her words. 'Do you go to fight the walls?'

'Not tonight. Tonight they have me in mind for something else.'

'Something more dangerous?'

Gregoras shrugged. Too many people knew of the midnight mission, and Sofia had enough cares already.

She stared at him. 'Be careful then. And visit us when you are done. Thakos would like it.'

The children were getting close. 'And you? Would you like it?'

The heat came to her cheeks again. 'I would,' she replied, then reached out and touched his arm. 'Walk with God,' she said, turning, moving through the doorway.

Thakos waved the slingshot as he went, and Gregoras lifted a hand. When they disappeared round a corner, and she had not looked back, he went and fetched his shirt, pulled it on, strapped on his falchion. 'Walk with God,' he murmured in echo of her, as he ducked beneath the ruined arch, 'but dance with the devil.'

TWENTY-FOUR

Into the Dark

29 April

'Can you see *anything*?'

'Am I a cat, Zoran, that I can pierce the darkness any better than you?'

Gregoras grunted. His friend Amir was one of the few things he could half see, and that was only due to the light colour of his cloak. It was saffron, an exact shade, and though it had been more beautiful in its youth, Amir would not give it up. He had worn it from his days as a spice trader, driving camel caravans across the Arabian sands, and during his time commanding a galley, which was where Gregoras had met him, for he had been a slave upon the vessel, Amir its master. Though they had not actually 'met' until the time when the galley caught fire in a sea fight off Trebizond and the chains were slipped so even the slaves could take their chances in the water. Gregoras had thought such chances small, he had seen the bloated corpses of too many drowned men, so when he'd noticed that the galley's captain – in his distinctive cloak – had not abandoned his vessel like the others but was staying aboard it to fight the fire, Gregoras stayed too, fought too. Somehow, luck, effort and Allah's blessing of a rogue wave had extinguished the flames, though the ship was much damaged. Two men could not sail her; so for a week they drifted with only each other for company and conversation, a long one they found they both enjoyed enormously as it ranged over the delights of God and the iniquities of man. When a Genoese fleet of mercenaries, commanded by one Giovanni Giustiniani

Longo, appeared to claim them, Gregoras presented himself and Amir as two swords for hire – if the Genoan would kindly provide the swords. They'd been taken on, and Amir had found the role of renegade as comfortable as any of his others – linked as ever by that distinctive fraying saffron cloak.

'I tell you what does pierce the darkness, man.' Gregoras leaned forward and clapped his friend on the shoulder. 'When are you going to wash this thing?'

A slight gleam came as Amir smiled. 'When the campaign is won, or ended, as I always do,' he replied. 'It would be an unlucky thing to wash its protection off me before that is settled.'

Gregoras shook his head. Soldiers were superstitious. Many wore amulets; others grew beards, or dressed for battle in a certain, unwavering order. He could hear, in the darkness around them, mumbled incantations of men trying to ward off the danger that the coming combat would expose them to, appealing to God, however they saw Him. Sofia would be angry with him for likening prayer to superstition. But from the day he was disfigured, he made no time for God in his life. He preferred to put faith in the falchion that hung now at his side, the crossbow that was within arm's reach, and his skill with them. He had reluctantly left his Turkish bow ashore, the closeness of the dark, hot work foreseen better suiting quarrel than shaft.

Dawn had to be an hour or two away, at most; and so the time appointed for the attack was upon them. He heard Amir slip onto his knees beside him and begin to pray, at the same time as he heard the pad of soft-soled shoes upon the central deck, the *histodoke*. The man upon it whispered, loud enough to be heard, 'To oar!'

Gregoras leaned closer to the saffron cloak. 'Say one for me, brother,' he whispered.

Amir paused in his Arabic to answer. 'Allah will look after His faithful child,' he murmured, 'while the devil has care of you, as ever, Zoran.'

Gregoras laughed, listened to the familiar sound of oars dipping. He was glad that he was not pulling upon one, that his position meant he had only to fight, not row *then* fight. For none of the men at the oars of this bireme were slaves; each had been hand-picked by Coco, its Venetian captain, as both sailor and warrior. It was true also, Gregoras knew, of the crews of every vessel in their small fleet, every man a free-born Venetian, Genoan or Greek; every one – save for Amir – a Christian. Slaves could find a way to hinder a vessel in combat. Muslim slaves could cry warnings. And their one hope of success in this mad mission was silence and, for most men there, faith.

He felt, rather than saw, the heavy shapes of the ships setting out from Galata's harbour. He had been at the meetings, knew what they were: two larger transports that had some oars and whose sides were thickly padded with wool and cotton bales to shelter the swifter triremes, biremes and *fustae*, which were filled with combustible agents and carefully nursed pots of fire. If the plan held, if they could get close enough to the Turks' eighty-strong fleet moored in a bay on the Asian shore before they were heard or seen, they had enough fire to destroy the enemy. If the enemy was unaware of their coming.

The last great 'if', Gregoras thought, and shivered, from the thought and from the breeze that swept him now they nosing into open water. And no sooner did he feel that than his eyes were dazzled. 'A comet,' said Amir, breaking off his prayer to murmur. 'A blessing on our enterprise?'

The light did not fire and fade straightaway, as a comet's would. It lingered, flickered long enough before it went out for Gregoras to mark where it flared. 'It is atop the Tower of Christ in the centre of Galata,' he hissed, 'and unless I am much mistaken, it is the light of betrayal. Someone is marking our departure. Someone is warning . . .'

He broke off, as a hiss came from the *histodoke*. 'Double speed,' came the command, and the oars quickened their strokes. 'That is not good,' said Amir, the former galley captain.

'It is not,' added Gregoras, the former galley slave. Both men knew the plan – to proceed as a fleet, so the padded high-sided transports could shelter the others from the enemy's land-placed cannon and the swifter vessels could dart out and cause their havoc. But Coco's *fusta*, which they were on, had seventy-two rowers and the build of a sleek greyhound. The transports had forty-eight and the bulk of an ox.

'We are leaving them behind, sure,' said Gregoras, rising. 'I will go and see the captain.'

He descended the stair from the aft deck, ran along the *histodoke*, passing the bosun there just as he hissed, 'Triple time.' The surge nearly threw Gregoras off his feet, but he found them, ran on, mounted the foredeck. He saw the bulked shadow of a group of men at the front railing. Spray was rising over the prow and splashing them. 'Captain,' he hissed, but not as quietly as he had spoken before, for he had to top the sound that triple-time oars made in the water, 'what are you doing?'

He was close to the men, who split apart at his voice, and alarmed that he could now make out their features – for that meant some light was creeping into the sky. 'Ah, Constantinople's latest hero,' said the smallest man there, his dark face darkened further by a beard that reached from high cheekbone to chest. 'Well, we have heroes too in Venice!' he said, sweeping his arm around his assembled officers. 'And we would be first among the enemy and claim the glory of destroying them!'

'Captain . . .' Gregoras began heatedly, then stopped himself. Though he had some status as the emperor's man, he could not let his exasperation show, not on the man's fore-deck. Pig-fucking Venetian braggart, he thought, and took a deep breath. 'Captain,' he went on in a more reasonable tone, 'the plan agreed was to approach as one, attack as one. There are upwards of eighty of the enemy ahead and they are protected—'

'Eighty times the honour, eh?' Coco interrupted loudly. 'The others will catch up soon enough. And they will engage an enemy we have woken rudely from their dreams. No!' He raised a hand and his voice as Gregoras made to speak. 'Do not counsel caution, Greek . . . or is it Genoan?' He sneered a smile. 'We of Venice do not know the meaning of that word. We—'

It was strange to be looking a man in the face one moment and staring into the stump of his chest the next. Strange too, the reversal of sound and sight, for Gregoras realised he must have heard the cannon's blast before he saw the cannon's effect. Blood hit him as spray had done before, and he had to wipe his eyes to clear them, in time to see the legs collapse, the stump fall. The Turks' remarkable first shot had cut Coco neatly in half, and taken most of his officers. Shocked, Gregoras shifted his gaze from the dead and the near-dead to the source of the next flash that came, from the east. This he clearly heard before he saw, before he threw himself down onto boards already slick with blood and entrails, though the ball probably struck the ship before he reached them. It made a great tearing sound, wood ripped aside by the entry of a stone ball fired, he realised, from less than two hundred paces away, undoubtedly from the shore. It accounted for the accuracy – and for the flare he'd seen atop the Tower of Christ. The Turks knew they were coming, and they had laid their ambush well.

He felt it through the soaked deck, heard it too – the timbers tearing apart. Screams confirmed it. 'Mother of God,' someone cried, 'we sink! Jesu, save us, we sink!' Rising, Gregoras looked back along the vessel. In the flash of the next Turkish shot, he glimpsed what had happened – the *fusta* had been hit amidships, the ball passing straight through, opening a hole on either side. In the dying glare he saw men already throwing themselves over the sides, most silent, some calling on God to save them. If I was a praying man, thought Gregoras as he stripped his little armour off, I would have time for just ten paternosters before this ship is gone.

Another thought struck. 'Amir!' But he'd left the Muslim praying on the aft deck, and the *histodoke* that had brought him there was already awash. Gregoras would have to leave him to Allah and hope to find him again in the water. Flinging aside his breastplate, the last of his armour, cursing that he could not even manage his falchion, he ran to a rail and launched himself over it. He did not have far to fall.

As ever, the water cascaded through the gap in his face. He rolled onto his back, spat it out. 'Curse them, curse them all,' he spluttered aloud as he trod water. 'Curse every captain who has had me on his boat and has tried to drown me. Jesu Christ!' He swallowed a mouthful of sea water, choked. If I survive this, he thought, I swear to St Anthony that I will walk wherever I want to go.

Other men were appearing from the broil of water where the ship had gone down. He did not know how well any of them could swim, so made sure he moved away from them. Men could drown others as well as themselves; he had learned that in his two encounters.

But which way should he go?

Another gun flashed. He turned about in the water. Where was he, other than close to the north shore of the Golden Horn? He looked away, opposite to where the muzzle flash had come. He must have been facing roughly eastwards, for the great bulk of Constantinople was slightly backlit by the rising sun, below the horizon. He squinted, spat more water out. They'd headed west up the Horn, rowing, in the end, at triple time from Galata harbour. So they could have reached . . .

He searched the gloom, and there, he saw it, or thought he did. Further down, away from the dawn, a slightly taller piece of darkness upon the Constantinople shore. The Phanar, the flame in the lighthouse tower extinguished for now to give no guidance to the enemy. It was maybe four hundred paces away if measured upon the land. The currents in the Horn were ever treacherous; but the nearer shore was held by the Turk, and Gregoras had not returned to his city and reclaimed his name to give himself up to the enemy now. To slavery, at the least. Probably to death.

He rolled onto his front, struck out, his arms sweeping before his chest, his legs driving. Though the waves were slight and he kept his head raised high, he had to stop every twenty kicks to breathe, to spit out water, to check. It was hard to tell if he was getting any closer, and a current was taking him down and west of the city. If it swept him past its walls, he would make landfall on the enemy's beaches. Taking a deep breath, he flipped onto his back, began kicking hard again, angling against the tug of tide. When he next looked up, limbs and lungs burning, the bulk of the lighthouse was more or less before him. He surged again, and soon his hand hit something solid, bringing pain, flesh scraped off on one of the rocks the lighthouse, in less warlike times, warned ships against. He pulled himself atop it, resisted the current's attempts to drag him off. But the cool breeze was making him shake near as much as his tiredness, and soon he had to plunge again.

He lost senses then, only keeping the ones he needed to propel him through the water, and spit it out when it flowed in. He wasn't even sure of direction now, could only hope that his last sighting still held, that he was moving toward the Phanar. Then, when he thought that he would have to just roll over in the water, was almost welcoming its embrace, a leg hit rock. He looked up and saw the tower ahead of him, and waves splashing over the foreshore it was built upon. With a last surge he pushed for the land, touched it, scrambled onto it, careless of jagged rock that cut and bruised him. Then he was out of the water, stumbling clear of the tide's final reach, falling onto sand.

He could have rested there, sunk into the silence that he'd nearly found under the waves. But every wall was watched, and on this morning even more so, with the city's hopes afloat upon the water. So he was not surprised when he heard a voice ask, in Italian, 'Are you alive?'

'Barely,' he replied, and closed his eyes again.

'It is over. They part.'

Gregoras sighed. He'd nearly fallen asleep, despite the discomfort of the stone corner he was wedged into and the constant cursing of the men alongside him. For the time he'd watched, the battle in the Horn had taken the same course as the one he'd lately been involved in – the swarming of Muslim vessels around their far fewer Christian opponents in higher-sided ships. The continuous attempts to board and their repelling. He'd lived it once and recently and did not need to see it again. He was also very tired.

But Theodore's shout – Gregoras had reached the shore near the palace where the old archer stood sentinel – made him drag himself up. 'Have we triumphed?' he said, rubbing his eyes.

'As you see,' Theodore replied, 'they did not capture any more of us. But their fleet still holds the Horn.'

Gregoras looked. The vessels were parting, the smaller Turkish *fustae* and biremes heading towards their new berths in the northern bay and the shelter of the shore batteries that had sunk Coco's ship. The Christian vessels divided, Genoans and Venetians making for Constantinople and their own harbours.

Gregoras looked, rubbed his eyes, looked again. 'Where's Trevisiano's galley?' he asked.

'Sunk, two hours since,' one of the men said. 'God save him.'

Others muttered similar prayers. Gregoras just shook his head. Coco had been a braggart and a fool and the city could suffer his loss. But Trevisiano, the expedition's other leader, was one of the foremost of the Venetian captains, the first to offer his sword to the emperor, 'for the honour of God and the honour of all of Christendom', as he had put it. And he had, according to report, wielded his sword with honour ever since. Not only his countrymen would be seriously dismayed. While enemy vessels in the Horn were a serious wounding to the city's hopes, the loss of two shiploads of men and this one gallant captain was perhaps a worse one. Gregoras could see in the faces around him what would be on every face in the city this morning: despair.

Another thought struck him, as he shrugged the borrowed cloak around himself. Though he knew it was ridiculous, he peered anyway, searching the Galatan shore that the enemy fleet was making for. It was possible to make out individual figures, so close was the land opposite. But he could not see a saffron-coloured cloak amongst the crowd. 'Allah watch over you, my friend,' he murmured, passing his hand from forehead to mouth to heart, thinking of Amir.

Theodore was staring at him. 'Have you turned Turk, boy?' he grunted irritably. 'You should be praying to Christ for deliverance. You should be calling curses down upon the traitorous curs who warned the enemy of our coming – that whoreson *podesta* of Galata, no doubt. You should—'

A shout, one that spread rapidly along the walls, ended the tirade, had them both looking. 'What can you see, boy?' Theodore asked. 'My eyes are not what they were.'

The ships had cleared rapidly, each to their respective harbours. Gregoras now noticed a small group of men sitting on the sandy foreshore, guards standing around them with spears and halberds. 'I see our ships' crews, those who survived,' he said, then looked above them, to sudden movement on the ridge. Mounted men were riding slowly over it. In their midst was a distinctive horsetail standard. 'And I see the sultan.'

Sound came to them, the ululation from thousands greeting their leader, the deep thump of *kos* drums, the shriek of the seven-note *sevre*. Mehmet was acknowledging the acclaim with a raised hand.

'What does he now?' Theodore queried, leaning towards the scene he could not see.

'He has reached the beach. He is dismounting. Men are kissing his feet. He is raising them up, reaching back. I think he is giving them something, gold probably. You can hear the cheers.' Gregoras licked his lips, cracked, swollen and salty from the sea. 'And now he is moving down to the prisoners.'

'Holy Virgin, guard them,' Theodore mumbled.

Gregoras rubbed his eyes. Now he would see just how important it had been to risk drowning rather than be captured. The war had been distinguished already by the slaughter of innocents, villagers in outlying districts, soldiers in forts beyond the walls, captured, killed. In raids before the vast army descended, he knew that some Greek captains had done the same to Turkish villages. It was one way of war, the terror of it. But there was another way, and many commanders practised it selectively – the showing of mercy to a captured foe. Besides, Christian galleys, like Muslim ones, were crewed mainly by slaves. He had been one himself. And sitting at Mehmet's feet were perhaps a hundred fine seamen from Venice and Genoa.

The crowds along the walls fell silent, save for muttered prayers. At a harbour to the side of the Phanar, a Venetian galley, fresh from the fight, had already docked, its crew lining its rails, looking to their countrymen across the water. All, on wood and stone, could see the flash of silver when Mehmet drew his scimitar. Those whose eyes were keen enough saw that sword rise slowly, curving toward the sky, then fall swiftly as if cutting a line through the middle of the prisoners. Immediately, Turks rushed in, parting the men either side of Mehmet's unwavering sword. To his left, the prisoners were driven at a stumbling run up the slope. To his right . . .

'Holy Father in His heaven,' someone muttered nearby, as a groan ran the length of the battlements.

'What?' snapped Theodore.

Gregoras tried to get some moisture into his mouth, did so,

spoke. 'Half the men have been taken away, half remain. And they are bringing . . .' he swallowed, 'they are bringing wooden stakes.'

Groans became screams, shouts of denial, of appeal to God, the Mother, her son. But it did not affect or slow the preparations opposite. 'What now?' Theodore whispered.

Gregoras turned to him. 'You know what now,' he said harshly. 'You have seen impalement, haven't you?'

'No,' came the soft reply. 'God has spared me that before and now . . .' he waved a hand over his rheumy eyes, 'He spares me again.' He stood straighter. 'Come, boy,' he said. 'We must hasten to the emperor. He will respond to this. He must.'

Gregoras was about to step away when he heard the drums suddenly stop, heard the first dreadful scream. He did not want to look back, could not help himself. Unfortunately for his sleep, he *had* seen impalement, so he knew there were two kinds – the slow insertion into a man's anus, a hideously prolonged death. Or the plunging through chest or back, brutally swift, a sudden, shocking end. Either way resulted in the stake being hoisted up, the victim to jerk out his life in the air.

He looked – and saw that Mehmet had ordered the swifter method. Wanting the shock no doubt, the screaming of the dying echoing in the screams of those watching them die. And he was not prolonging it either, must have decided that shock was best served fast. One man jerked and died, then five, then ten more, the stakes rising and being planted in the ground like a forest springing straight and fully formed from the earth.

He was about to turn away when he noticed something, like a flash of reddish light. Looked away, muttered, 'No, no, no.' Looked again. Saw.

He'd never had many prayers for himself, and he could manage none for his comrade Amir, hoisted now, bleeding and breathing his last, his saffron cloak flapping around him. Gregoras closed his eyes to the sight, tried to close off memory . . . of the way the Syrian would pull the worn cloak around him protectively and shrug off its detractors. No executioner had considered it worth stealing, and for just a moment, Gregoras considered that almost the saddest thing of all.

They did not have to go far to find the emperor. He'd been watching from the northernmost tower of his palace, above the water gate named the Xyloporta. But they could not get near him, so thick was the press of men around him. A babel of voices came, in screamed Italian, in the accents of Genoa and Venice, in Greek, shouting the unambiguous message.

Vengeance must be taken. Infidels must die.

Gregoras watched as the baying crowd pressed in, some getting too close, demanding too violently, needing to be shoved back by the halberd-wielding imperial guards. He could see Constantine trying to speak, failing to be heard. And then there came the sound that all in the city heard every day, many times a day. The great cannon had fired again, and its roar, which just preceded a ground-shifting thump as its stone crashed again into crumbling walls, brought a moment of silence.

Into it, Constantine shouted, 'Friends! Subjects! I know what you feel. I feel it too. Our sons, our gallant allies, must be avenged. But we are not barbarians, as the Turks are. Let our response be swift, but of a Christian nature.' Before anyone else could interrupt, he turned to an officer beside him. 'How many of the enemy do we hold in our cells?'

'More than two hundred, sire,' came the reply.

'Hang them,' Constantine commanded, 'every mother's son. Hang them from the battlements, one to each crenel, facing the place where our gallant martyrs gave their lives.'

Men acclaimed the response, followed the officer, who descended the stairs. The palace's inner gate swung open into another mob, their cry for vengeance identical. When they heard that their wish was to be granted, they absorbed the soldiers, turned and rushed for the city's prison.

As Gregoras and Theodore advanced, they saw that only a few men remained around the emperor. Gregoras recognised the aged Sphrantzes, the *megas doux* Loukas Notaras, with his bull's body and weasel's face. Between the two of them stood his own brother. Theon was engaged in a whispered conversation with both men and did not see Gregoras. The man who did was his old commander, Giustiniani, who leaned into the emperor and spoke softly. Constantine turned, saw Gregoras, and a brief smile passed over the careworn face.

'You were one of many we were already mourning, Gregoras Lascaris,' Constantine said when the two men drew near. 'By what miracle have you survived?'

Gregoras glanced at Theon, caught the brief flash of surprise before the politician's veil was dropped again. He related, briefly, the tale. 'Well,' said Constantine, 'God must have you in mind for another destiny to show you such favour twice in a month. Stay and share in our discussions now, for I would have men close to me who are so blessed.' A messenger ran up the stairs, knelt, offered a slip of parchment. The emperor took it, read, coloured. He beckoned his old friend Sphrantzes to him, and they had an urgent whispered conversation.

Giustiniani called Gregoras. To his left was Enzo. To his right, the space where Amir should have been standing. The Commander spoke straight to this. 'And where's my renegade?'

'Dead.'

'Drowned?'

Gregoras shook his head. 'His cloak now hangs from one of those stakes over there, and him in it.'

Enzo let out a cry, turned and buried sobs in his sleeve. Giustiniani went white but did not speak for a moment, his jaw moving as if chewing words. Finally he murmured, 'I commanded him to wash it. Ordered it a thousand times. Told him its stink offended. He disobeyed, the cur. Said that it was the stink that protected him.' He reached up, wiped a hand across his nose. 'Well, let's hope some Turk will wear it soon and choke on it.' He turned to the weeping Sicilian. 'Enough now, boy,' he said softly, reaching a hand to the man's shoulder, 'enough. We will mourn him later, and seek his ugly face in the bottom of a dozen wine casks. And we will be avenged. Not in this way . . .' he gestured into the city, where the ugly shriek of the mob could still be clearly heard, 'but in our own, as Amir would have wanted it: upon the battlements in the heat of the fight. And with the enemy in the Horn and the sea walls now to man as well, I think we will have plenty of opportunities.'

Gregoras nodded. They had suffered many a comrade's death before. Death was a soldier's lot. And the only way to mourn it was as soldiers – roughly, drunkenly. He would raise a flagon to a fallen friend. And he would kill the men who had killed him, to his own dying breath, and be mourned roughly in his turn – if any survived to mourn.

TWENTY-FIVE

'Give Me Mine'

3 May: twenty-seventh day of the siege

It began with such a small spark, the fire that almost consumed the city from within.

Two housewives fighting over a wheel of bread.

Sofia was there, in the Forum of the Bull, ten paces away from the front of the line. She had walked across the city because of the rumour that the monks of St Myrelaion, to honour their saint's day, were baking loaves from their private granary and giving it as alms to the poor. And as almost everyone was poor in the city now, Sofia fetched her own bread. She'd stood in one of the long lines for two hours, Thakos and Minerva at her side, the boy clutching his slingshot, proudly acting as her guard. But the closer she got to the three tables, the more what had seemed a mountain of flat loaves diminished. Each family was given one only, though time was spent with many pleading every excuse for one more. There had already been arguments, that family members had split up to get more than their share. A fight had broken out between two men who claimed the other had already been in line and returned. Everywhere Sofia saw the same expression on faces drawn tight by ever-present hunger – an angry glitter in the eye as others got what each desired, a sullen droop to the mouth, bitter thoughts hanging there as unspoken words. She knew her own face had the same expression, that she stared at those who had received and could not wait, stuffing their mouths with bread, needing to swallow repeatedly to suppress her gushing saliva.

Five paces away, Minerva crying her hunger again, Thakos sulking . . . as one monk behind the table turned to the other, who shook his head. Whatever was before him was the last of it. A despairing murmur moved through the crowd. Someone shoved her. Like many others, Sofia could only double her prayers that she was not this close and too late.

So she was near enough to hear everything, to witness the spark fall on the tinder of anger and hunger, to fan it into flame with her own breath. A woman at the head of the line had produced a small scroll of parchment. 'My sister,' she declared in a voice that showed she was an *archon*, of the ruling classes, from the airy villas by the water and not the fetid slums nearby, 'is too sick to come. She writes this note and prays that the good brothers will pity her and send her life-sustaining bread.'

It sounded like a speech, something from a play that might have been spoken in the Hippodrome in happier times. But it did not produce the laughter that might have greeted it there. A growl ran from just behind the woman and all the way back. In Sofia's throat, as in the others.

It was the monk who answered, his round pink face showing little of the privations of those he served. 'Alas, *kyra*, we have so little left, and those who have waited here—'

'Ridiculous!' she interrupted. 'Do you not realise who I am? My husband is Aris Noulis, the *megas primikerios*! He has given such bounty to your monastery. Speak to the abbot. And give me my sister's bread!'

The monk hesitated. But it was the woman just before Sofia who spoke, yelled, in the rough accent of the streets, 'Her sister is a whore and dances with Venetians every night in the Tavern of Scythia. If she's sick, it's because she's swallowed too many Italian cocks.'

Harsh laughter took the crowd, and Sofia glanced down, but Minerva and Thakos were still lost to their own woes. She could not know if the accusation was true. But it could be, and she felt her anger rise at yet another local woman carousing with the 'allies', who kept the best food to themselves and let the people they'd come to defend starve.

'I'll take what I deserve,' the rich woman declared shrilly.

'This is what you deserve,' shouted the other and, bending, she scooped horse dung from the cobbles of the forum and threw it full in the woman's face. More laughter came as the thrower shouted, 'Now give the bitch her one loaf and give me mine.'

The rich woman gasped, wiped shit from her skin, then hurled herself at her assailant, leading with her long nails. As they locked together, screeching, Sofia felt fury seize her, a surge that swept her forward like the others, the line dissolving in a universal cry of 'Give me mine!'

'No! No!' cried the monks, as the crowd rushed the table, grabbing the few loaves that remained there. Sofia, near the front, got her hands on one, only to have it snatched away by a snarling, toothless man. She slapped him, hard, grabbed for the bread, which tore apart in their hands. Stuffing what she held down the front of her dress, she turned to look for her children . . . but they were gone, dissolved into the mayhem. Everywhere people tussled for the precious rounds, and much ended up squelched into the dung and mud, where men and women snatched it up anyway and chewed without wiping. The monks' tables were overturned, so were the wagons that had borne the bread. The two women rolled in the muck, oblivious to all but their quarrel.

'Minerva! Thakos!' Sofia screamed, thrusting through the jostling bodies. Then she glimpsed her son. 'Thakos!' she cried again, and struck out for him, shoving aside any who bounced into her. 'Where is Minerva?' she yelled when she reached him, seized him.

'I do not know,' he sobbed, tears flowing. 'I had her hand and then . . .'

Sofia looked frantically around, crying her daughter's name. But her voice was lost to the roar.

Another's wasn't. Another's, loud and deep as a bull's

bellow, cut through the noise, and even Sofia, seeking everywhere, looked up to the large man in a stained butcher's smock standing on the fountain of Aphrodite, arms spread wide. 'Greeks! Greeks!' he shouted. 'Citizens! I know where there is bread. I know where there is bread!' The shouted repeated phrase diminished the noise enough so more could hear. 'The bastard foreigners have granaries stuffed with grain. They feast each night on roasted lamb and quail, while we starve!' A huge shout greeted this, as more and more stopped their scrapping to listen. 'It's our city, isn't it?' the man continued. 'Why should a Venetian eat my food?' He pumped a fist into the air. 'Give me mine,' he yelled.

It was the woman's cry from before, the cry taken up now. There were perhaps two hundred people in the forum, and they all rushed as one to its northern exit, the way that led to the enclaves of the foreigners. Sofia, clutching Thakos, did not move, hoping that when the forum was clear, she would see her daughter. But when the last yelling person had run out, only beaten monks, upturned tables and squashed bread was left.

'Come,' she said, dragging Thakos forward. There was nothing she could do but follow. Minerva had to have been swept up in the crowd.

'Mother,' Thakos said, pointing.

Sofia looked down. An edge of bread poked out from her dress. She pulled the piece out, split it into three, gave the largest portion to her son, tucked away the next biggest. They ate as they ran, catching up to the crowd where the main road, the Meze, crossed.

'Minerva!' she cried, again and again.

But the mob was larger now, men and women joining from the side streets of the poor quarter they came through, each taking up the cry that had turned into one chant of rage, drowning all other words.

'Give me mine!'

*

Theon was with Constantine, watching him pray at the tomb of his father in the Church of Christ Pantocrator, when the soldier ran in, his spurred heels clanging off the stone floor, violating the silence and seeming to cause the frescoed saints to frown ever more deeply. Theon drew him aside, and when the panting man had regained enough breath to tell his tale, listened to the barest minimum he required.

He went straight to the emperor. 'Majesty,' he said.

'Another attack?'

'No, sire. Well, in a way. An attack from within.' He relayed what he had heard.

Constantine listened, nodding. 'I feared this. How large is the mob?'

'A few hundred strong. But the soldier tells that more are joining it every minute.'

'Will they stop in the Amalfitian quarter, think you?'

'I do not. They know – all know – that the Venetian warehouses beyond it are the richest and best supplied.'

Constantine turned, headed for the door. 'They must be stopped. If we lose the forces of Venice . . .' He swallowed. 'I must stop them.'

'Majesty, please.' His tone halted the emperor, who turned. In a low voice, for others were near now, Theon continued, 'You are loved, it is true. But not by all. Many still think that the ill that befalls us is not just the greed of foreigners, but God's curse. Because we have forsaken our holy church and accepted the union with Rome.' He raised a hand as Constantine made to speak. 'Sire, I do not think so. But riots can turn on many causes, and if some agitators were to see you, blame you . . .' He shook his head. 'Let me go, majesty. If there is blame to take, let me take it.'

Constantine stared for a long moment, then nodded. 'You are right, as ever, *oikeios*.' He took Theon's arm, led him outside where a dozen men of his personal guard stood swiftly to attention. 'And you can take something more than blame. Take my guard. Their barracks is on the way. Stop there, gather more . . .' he squeezed, 'and crush this riot. Stamp its leaders underfoot like snakes upon the path.'

'I will, *basileus*.' He used the old military title for the empire's war leader, delighted that Constantine had used such a familiar one for the first time. He was happy to be the emperor's 'kin'. He had made himself useful since the siege began. But to rise even higher, he needed to prove his worth in matters other than lists and tallies.

I'll never distinguish myself tussling with armoured Turks upon the walls, he thought as he walked to his horse. Yet a rabble of gutter filth, rioting in the streets?

He mounted, then looked at the men mounting behind him, dressed in mail, bearing spears and swords. Constantine had already spoken to the guard commander, who now looked to Theon. The men were ready for a fight. And Theon was delighted to lead them to it, and watch them triumph – from a safe distance.

He dug spurs into his horse's flanks. 'Forward!' he cried.

Sofia had still not found Minerva. And the swelling crowd made it ever harder. She was torn – should she press on and assume that the little girl had been swept forward with the mob, or was she somewhere behind them now, lost? She knew she had joked with Gregoras that her daughter could be abandoned in a strange city and make her way. And Minerva did have a self-belief uncommon in a five-year-old. But it had been a joke, and beyond the narrow streets that surrounded her own home, Constantinople was as strange a city as one could find.

'Minerva,' she screamed, again and again, knowing it was useless, unable to stop herself. Beside her, Thakos sobbed still.

Glancing ever behind her, at men and women spat out by the crowd, carrying items stolen from looted shops, Sofia pressed forward. The mob was surging north-east now, and she felt she had no option but to follow it. It swelled at every junction, the wider Byzantine avenues allowing it to flow fast, and the warehouses that were sacked along the way did not slow it much. The Amalfitians, other Italians, did not have the wealth of their richer countrymen, and their stocks were not enough to feed the riot's hunger – which was not only for food. An old Jew was dragged from his oil store and beaten half to death. Though he and his family had probably lived in the city as long as any of his assailants, he was a foreigner and responsible for all their woes.

'Give me mine!' The cry of a housewife in the Forum of the Bull had become the voice of riot. They yelled it as they struck, beat, stole, wrecked.

They marched into the Forum of Theodosius. The other side of it, streets led to the Venetian wharves and warehouses. As Sofia was swept into the great plaza, she realised, with a sudden gasp of air, the folly of what she was about. She would never find her daughter while this mob ruled. And she was risking her son's life in the search. 'Thakos!' she shouted, pulling the boy by the arm she'd never let go. 'This way. We must . . .'

She tried to lead him left, to the edge and safety. But it was like swimming crosswise against a spring tide; for every step she took forward, she was pushed two along. She was being dragged deeper into the square, towards the entrance of the streets and all they led to – further riot, further wreckage, further harm. She struggled in vain – and then it was as if everyone halted at once, flung suddenly onto the person in front of them, though she saw it was more a ripple, those behind her moving and sticking all the way to the back of the square. The sudden stop caused a sudden cessation of sound, the whole mob pausing to draw breath, as did she.

And then a voice came, one she knew well, loud, commanding. 'Disperse!' her husband shouted. 'Disperse now, or it will go ill with you.'

'Theon,' she cried, the word getting out before the crowd's roar swallowed it.

'Give me mine!' they screamed, as one.

It was strange, Theon thought, as he peered through the raised lances of his cavalrymen, the axe-headed halberds of his infantry, that some woman should have recognised him when his face was half covered with his visor and he was astride his horse behind guards much taller than himself. For a moment, he was concerned that what he was about to do would be remembered as his doing. Then he smiled. It was good that they would remember his name, know it, fear it. If the city survived, when all the beloved warriors on the walls had hung up their arms, he would be beside his emperor, the risen man, and the city would fear him. Better that than striving unknown. Better far than being loved. If he was to thrive.

He glanced around the square. If he was not truly a military man, if he had always preferred Cicero to Caesar, still he had studied enough to lay this ambush well. At the entrances of all the streets that led off from the forum, sunlight glimmered on the steel tips of spears, double-ranked. Only the way they had come was still open to the mob.

He looked through his ordered men, to the swirl before them. Men and women snarled and snapped there like feral dogs, faces distorted by fury and hunger. Some mouthed curses, others still chanting the same ridiculous phrase, 'Give me mine!' What did they mean? What was theirs? Nothing, for they were the scum of the city.

He'd waited a short time for them to obey him. None looked as though they would. Indeed, the front of the mob, impelled by within and by the people still pushing into the square, was already pressing close and spitting on his double-ranked halberdiers. In a few seconds, soldiers and mob would be touching. That could not be allowed. He reached and tapped the commander of the guard beside him on the arm. 'Now,' he said.

'Over their heads, Megas Stratopedarches?'

Theon smiled. He liked being addressed as a military man, as much as he had liked being called 'kin' by the emperor earlier. And as a commander of soldiers, he had to make decisions. Hard ones, sometimes, though this one, truly, was not. 'No. We should not waste the bullets.'

The officer bit his lip, then nodded. Saluting, he turned to his men and shouted commands. His foot and horse guards swung to left and right, as he and Theon moved their horses aside. Perhaps the forefront of the crowd thought they were being allowed through, because they started forward with a shout, only to fetch up suddenly, the ones in front tumbling as the ones behind shoved, as what was behind the guards was revealed – twenty arquebusiers, their weapons on forked shafts planted on the cobbles, muzzles forward, glowing cords above the breech.

'Fire!' the officer shouted.

The blast, Theon thought, was loud enough to be heard across the square, even above the inane chant. It brought a near silence again, broken immediately by the wails of those struck, those who had not died immediately, the shrieks of those behind them shoving back. The smoke made Theon cough, blocked his vision for a moment. Waving it aside, he saw the bodies, the anger on the faces transformed to terror. It was the moment. 'Advance,' he called crisply, and as the gunners carried their still smoking weapons to the side, the mounted guardsmen behind them, fifty strong, formed double ranks again, lowered their lance tips and came at a walk.

Theon drew his father's sword. Only for show. He did not think he'd need to display his ineptitude with it.

'Thakos!' Sofia screamed.

The boy had been ripped from her grasp by the crowd as if they were the sea and a wave had taken him. She glimpsed his panicked face between two large, jostling men, and then he vanished as both were shoved opposite ways. She screamed again, tried to force her way back, stumbled as her feet struck something soft on the ground. She was standing on a body, the fallen woman screaming in agony, the scream suddenly cut off as a boot trampled her face. Sofia, ducking lower, trying to keep her balance and dodge beneath flailing limbs to where she'd last seen her son, was caught hard by an elbow in the ear. Instant agony, and ringing loud enough to reduce the shrieking all around her. Reduce, but not eliminate. She heard neighing, snorting, the clack of metal hooves on cobbles. Behind her, the crowd parted enough for her to see a horse rising on its rear legs, its rider lifting a lance high up, stabbing down. He was maybe a dozen paces away.

She fought for her footing, won, propelling herself off the body. 'Thakos!' she screamed again, praying her saviour that he was upright, beseeching the mother Maria to protect another's son, to return him to her.

Her prayers were answered. The tide that had ripped them apart flung them together again. His foot was trapped in someone else's fall, he was crying out as another tripped on his twisted leg, falling towards her. She caught him and, with a strength she did not know she possessed, wrenched him clear.

'My foot,' he wailed, and she held him up, looked around. There were three roads that led south from the square, and she could see that the main one, the one they'd come up, was blocked with the hordes trying to force their way through. They were closer to one that seemed to be letting some people run. An arm under his, she half carried, half dragged him towards it. Bodies bunching, sticking, a huge shove, the sound of limbs cracking and they went through with the surge, vaulting some of the bodies that rolled there, stepping over others. People ceased screaming, to run faster. She heard the hooves behind her, but her son could not run, so she cut sideways, beneath the flailing arms of cursing men, and stepped into the doorway of a shop.

Cavalrymen clattered by, interspersed with the fleeing crowd. She heard the steadier march of shod boots on stone, stole a glance back. Down the alley marched the halberdiers, beating the fallen and any who still stood nearby with the butt ends of their weapons.

'Can you run?' she whispered. But Thakos just shook his head, flicking tears onto her dress.

She hesitated . . . and then a voice spoke from behind her, through a grille in the door she only then noticed. 'Is there anyone near you?' came the whisper.

Sofia looked around. 'No,' she replied.

Bolts were shot, a latch lifted. 'Swiftly,' the voice said softly.

She shoved Thakos ahead of her, followed into the gloom. The door was slammed shut, quickly locked again. At first she sensed, rather than saw, shapes crowded there. Gradually the little light from grille and shuttered windows revealed a half-dozen people, mainly women. Some stood; some were collapsed onto the floor; some sobbed; some stared ahead.

'Welcome to my house. Remain until it is safe,' came the same voice from behind her.

She turned. An old Jew stood by the door, long grey-black locks hanging down his face, a cap in the centre of his head. 'Thank you, *kyr*,' she said. 'Thank you for saving me and my son.'

He smiled, nodded, turned back to look again through the grille. She bent to Thakos, crying on the floor, clutching his ankle. Gently she parted his fingers, looked, raised the foot. It was swollen already, sprained, she thought, but not broken. Clutching her son to her, she tilted her head, listened to the fading cries from the street, and prayed again for her daughter's deliverance.

It took a while for the cries to die away entirely. A while longer before the Jew threw back the bolts and cautiously looked outside. He stepped back in, nodded. 'I think it is safe,' he said, 'but you can all remain longer if you will.'

Some left, passing through the door without saying a word. Some stayed. Sofia could not. Helping Thakos to rise, she moved to the entrance. 'Thank you, *kyr*,' she said. 'You have saved us.'

The man shrugged, then looked down at Thakos's swollen ankle. 'Here,' he said, reaching behind the open door, picking up a walking stick there. He offered it to Thakos, who took it, stood on his own.

'Thank you again,' Sofia said.

'I have a grandson out there,' he said, nodding to the street. 'I hope someone, somewhere is perhaps giving him a stick.'

They left. She had no thought but to go home, leave Thakos there, send for her husband, begin the search for her daughter. Where was Gregoras? She had not seen him since the day before the failed assault on the Turkish fleet, though her husband had said he had survived it. Perhaps he could help, him and his mercenary comrades. But how to find him?

Mind churning along with her guts, she went as swiftly as her hobbling son would allow through streets that bore the scars of riot. There were bodies surrounded by bunches of gawkers, patches of blood on the stones. But they passed through these streets fast enough into others that bore no trace of what had happened. Wine stores were open, and men were drinking. Shops were selling a meagre supply of goods. In one square there was even a bread stall, a large but orderly queue before it. When Thakos could no longer walk swiftly enough, she found the strength to lift him onto her back.

She prayed unceasingly to keep the terror at bay until she was able to do something about it. And then all her terrors were swept away, as she rounded the corner onto her own street, by an angry cry.

'Where have you been, Mama?' Minerva was rising from the doorstep, on which she proceeded to stamp. 'I am hungry and I want my bread.'

Strangely, the last piece of bread from the Forum of the Bull was still tucked into Sofia's dress. But before she could hand it over, she half squashed it by pressing her daughter hard against her. Minerva, looking over her mother's shoulder at Thakos on the ground, stuck out her tongue.

'So it was achieved, *basileus*, as you commanded.'

Theon bowed, stepped back. He had given his report

bluntly, like a soldier, reining in his desire to elaborate. He had not removed any of the dust from his armour, the muck that had kicked up from hooves. In fact, he had decided he did not look quite dirtied enough and had added a little more from the stables below.

His words, his demeanour, had their effect. 'You have done well, Theon Lascaris,' Constantine said. 'Twenty dead and others with cracked limbs to be displayed through the streets will be a good example. The mob will not rise again.'

'And yet it might, lord.' The voice came on a wheeze from the aged adviser, George Sphrantzes. 'People who are always hungry, who either fight upon the walls by day, or spend the nights repairing them, who sleep little and eat less, will resent us of the noble class, those who have, perhaps, more than they and show it.' He gestured to his own ample belly. 'The Holy Father knows that we have few enough citizens to defend our own. And if these despair, lose all hope, how long may we survive?'

'I am everywhere, showing myself. And I sleep less and eat as little as any man in the city, I'd wager.'

Sphrantzes raised his hands against his master's fierce tone. 'I know this, lord. But people who are hungry are not apt to remember anything but empty bellies for long.'

Constantine sighed, running fingers through his greying hair. 'You are right, as ever, old friend. We must take action.' He looked up at a sharp report, a dull thud that caused dust to float down from the ceiling. 'We must address their resentment. We must husband our resources, make sure they are distributed equitably . . . and show that all defenders of Constantinople are the same.' He turned to another man beside him. 'Megas Doux, will you take charge of a committee of relief?'

'I?' The tall, grey-templed Loukas Notaras mustered all the disdain he could into the single syllable. 'I, act as a broker to the mob? What do I know of tallies and measures of corn?'

'We need a name, Loukas. You are the second man in the

city. Sphrantzes and Lascaris will organise everything. But you will sign your name to it, and appear before the people to distribute what is collected.'

Notaras looked as if he was about to reply harshly, rudely again. But Theon, watching him closely, saw the words withheld, the light of cunning in the eye. The *megas doux* was ever seeking to advance himself further. All knew he had always had designs upon the purple itself. And all could see – save perhaps Constantine, who, Theon had learned, was not attuned to all the subtleties of rule – that Notaras was being given a gift here. If, one day, he aspired to be more than *megas doux*, he would need the mob behind him, however much he despised it. The rabble of Constantinople had placed more than one emperor on the throne before – and torn others down.

The tall man folded his height into a low bow. 'As the *basileus* commands,' he said.

Constantine stared at him a moment, before turning to the two churchmen on his other side. 'Archbishop Leonard. Cardinal Isidore. You shall aid the *megas doux*, for it is to the Church we must go for the funds we need now. And we will begin with the heads of all the holy houses, the monasteries and nunneries of the city. I will approach them and personally seek donations. We will need gold to buy the grain in the foreigners' warehouses.' He raised a hand at the murmur that rose. 'Yes, buy. They are our friends and we depend on them for their arms, for their support. But they are merchants too. Do not fear.' He smiled, briefly. 'I know how to haggle, and will get a good price. Once the grain is ours, and the bakeries organised, we will produce a regular supply and distribute it fairly – and free. Yes?' He looked around, received the nods, continued, 'And what else was said here?' He paused again, pinched between his eyes.

Theon wondered when his emperor had last slept a night through. Back in the Morea, he suspected.

Constantine looked up. 'We were speaking of resentment and despair, were we not? How it saps the will of men to do

306

what must be done. The first . . . well, I can see how resentment would be fired by the sight of well-fed nobles and churchmen not doing their share for the defence. Examples must be set.' He turned again to Leonard and Isidore. 'We have a large body of men in this city who perhaps are not doing enough. The monks. When we speak to the abbots about gold, we will also talk about manpower. Let the monks become the main repairers of the walls the Turks knock down.'

'Would they not be better engaged, majesty,' Archbishop Leonard said, his tone cool, 'in moving among the people and urging them to pray correctly to the Holy Catholic Church and its father in Rome? To come to the cathedrals and beseech God for deliverance and not to avoid them as if they were houses of contagion?'

Constantine sighed. 'I think, if we are trying to reduce resentment, we will not do it by coercing people to pray in a way alien to them.' He raised his hand against the churchman's interruption. 'I have done all I can in that regard, for now. Let us address it again in time of peace, after our victory. For now, all our concern must be to secure that.' He turned away from the prelates. 'I think that our noble families must also be seen to be more active. My own dear sister went to the walls one night with her ladies and helped repair a breach. It inspired all who witnessed it. Perhaps some more of your families could do the same?'

Theon found himself nodding, along with other noblemen there. Unlike most of theirs, he thought, my wife will consider it her duty and be the first to go. Her ability to sacrifice herself had always irritated him.

'And now, as to despair?' Constantine went to the window. From it he could just see a section of the Horn, and Theon knew what he would be looking at there – the bridge that the Turks, in command of the waters now, were building. When it reached the city shore, close to the palace, they would be able to pour fresh men across it and assault the walls there too. The way they built, it would not take them long. 'We need a message of hope,' Constantine said without turning round. 'And since no vessel has brought one since our Genoese heroes broke through, it is time to go out and seek it.' He turned back, looked at his adviser, Sphrantzes. 'Let a fast vessel be prepared, crewed with able men and dispatched in dead of night and under Turkish colours. Let it seek the Venetian fleet that was ordered dispatched three months since. If they do not meet them in the Archipelago, let them venture as far as Euboea. And if they do not encounter them, let them return and tell us so . . . and we will find ways to manage our despair with knowledge and prayer.' He rubbed his eyes. 'I must sleep, my friends. Try, anyway. Let my orders be performed. And let us meet here early on the morrow so we can discuss them further.'

He lifted his hand, saluted them, turned away. They were dismissed. Though Theon was tired too, he knew he would get little sleep this night. Sphrantzes was already beckoning him into an antechamber, Notaras stalking ahead. He would need his abacus, he was sure, a weapon he wielded more assuredly than the sword he had drawn that day. Yet both were building his influence in the court. If they survived, he would have a new status in the city. And then . . .

'Give me mine,' he murmured, with a smile.

TWENTY-SIX

Hades

16 May: fortieth day of the siege

He had fought at the Blachernae palace most days since his near drowning, thought he knew its every stone and stairwell. Yet when Gregoras and his company of guardsmen, in that darkest hour before the dawn, were sent to seek out the Scotsman, and even though he was given directions as to how to discover him, still he wandered the length of the inner wall, calling out, 'Grant! Grant! Where are you, man?' and, for the longest time, heard no reply.

Then he got one, of a kind. He was lifting his torch high and peering again at what appeared to be just another ruined flight of stairs leading down, its crumbled steps filled with broken chunks of masonry, when there came an explosion, not another from the enemy beyond the walls, no cannon shot, but from the dark depths he stared into. It was preceded by, and accompanied by, a high-pitched and rising shriek of 'No, no, NO!' Then some portal was flung back below, smoke gushed forth and, a moment later, he'd found his man as John Grant came running up the steps.

On fire.

'St Peter take the Pope in the arse,' the Scot screamed, beating at his flaming clothes. 'Holy St Katherine, feast upon my . . .'

Gregoras had his cloak unclasped and swirling in a moment. He engulfed his friend, threw him to the ground, threw himself atop him. The curses saints and obscene acts quite ingeniously combined – still came muffled from within the heavy wool, along with the scent of singed flesh. When the thrashing and the cursing finally stopped, Gregoras slowly pulled back the top of the cloak.

Two eyes, dark holes in an oval of grimy white, stared up. 'Will you get off of me, you great Greek lump? You're squashing the future heirs of the Clan Grant.'

Gregoras rose, gently pulling his cloak off the prone man, who shakily stood. 'Good to see you too, Scotsman. Can you tell me why it is that whenever I see you, you are always blowing things up?'

'It's my job, do ye ken?' Teeth bared in a smile, splitting the almost solid grime. 'An' I love it.'

Gregoras peered closer. 'Well, this last accident has taken your eyebrows.'

'Ach, they went two weeks ago. No loss. I've discovered that it's safer not to have bodily hair. Less to burn.' He grinned again. 'What make you here?'

Gregoras gestured to the twenty men behind him. 'I was told it might be time, for . . .' He pointed down the still smoking stairwell. 'The Turk is close, is he not?'

'Aye. But not that close.' Grant slapped at an ember glowing on his doublet. 'Come,' he said, moving towards the steps. 'We have a little time.' He glanced back at Gregoras, who had not moved. 'Don't worry, man. Everything that can explode has exploded. For now.'

'It's the "for now" that concerns me,' grunted Gregoras, reluctantly following.

Grant halted, looked back at the guards. 'You can tell your men to rest up but be ready for my call. And tell them there won't be room down there for those great bloody halberds. Swords are too big really. Long daggers and short axes will do the trick.'

Gregoras turned back, nodded at his lieutenant, who had heard as well as he. The Scot always spoke as if addressing a parade ground. The men started shedding weaponry, and Gregoras followed his friend down into the smoking pit.

He could see nothing at first, but Grant obviously could, for a lantern was lit, its beam slicing through the clearing smoke which was being sucked up the stairwell. Coughing, Gregoras looked about a large stone cellar. Several barrels and various pieces of glass and metal equipment were scattered about, and his feet crunched on shards. 'Has the explosion destroyed much of your work?' he asked.

Grant was setting a table upright, picking up a stone bowl. 'Ach, no. This place looked much as you see. It was quite a small experiment, truly.' He held the bowl out. The bottom was scorched and smoked slightly. 'I thought I had the way of it sorted. It works seven times out of ten, but . . .' He sighed, broke off.

'The way of what?' Gregoras asked.

'Why, Greek Fire, of course.' Grant shook his head. 'It's the proportions that are difficult. How much of that resin we brought from Chios to mix with the oxidising agent . . .' He held up a plate; Gregoras got a whiff of foulness and coughed. 'Aye,' Grant laughed. 'Bird shit, lovingly scraped off rocks on the shore. Full of saltpetre but of a dubious quality.' He put down the bowl. 'If you want to clear your head, take a sniff at that barrel.'

Tentatively, Gregoras leaned down over liquid, inhaled . . . and his head whirled at the sharp scent. He had to reach to a table to steady himself. 'Aye,' laughed Grant. 'You don't want to sniff too much of it. Makes you feel drunk and gives you a worse headache than that aqua vitae I was distilling for the pirates.' He bent forward, sniffed himself. 'It's called naphtha, from some place east of here, name of Irak. It's what does the burning. But I didn't stabilise it enough, so . . .' He gestured at his charred clothes, then continued, 'Speaking of aqua vitae . . . could you use a drink?'

Gregoras's head was still whirling a little. But if he was about to fight, a tot of the Scotsman's liquor would not harm, but help. Just one. Two, and he'd want five. And then he might get careless. 'Where do you keep it?' he said.

'In my quarters. Here . . .' he replied, and led the way to a door in one of the walls. It gave onto a room of contrast to the one they'd left. Here was order, a bed, a basin, books and scrolls upon a table. The one thing out of place was the large glass vessel, the cauldron below it heated from a small fire, drops condensing and running through the alembic into a stoppered jar.

Grant lifted a jug and poured two measures. 'Death to the Turk,' he declared, and the two men shot the liquor back. It was far smoother than Gregoras had feared, and he was tempted to break his rule. But he put the mug down. 'Should we not get ready to kill them now?' he said.

'There's time.' Grant sat, poured himself another, smiled when Gregoras demurred. 'I have skilled men watching for signs.' He pointed to the room they'd come from. 'There is a door there that leads to a countermine that's dug about twenty paces before the bastion. I'm almost certain that the Turk mine has nearly reached it.'

'Almost? How can you know at all?'

'Well, it's a science, like the other,' Grant replied, lifting his mug to stare at it. 'If I were the Turk, I know where I would dig, for I have examined the soil all around and it's only fit, solid enough to support shafts, in a few spots along the whole length of these walls. Then it's a question of studying the lines over there, seeing where the Turk is trying to make us *not* look.' He put down the mug, jerked his thumb over his shoulder. 'He's about, och, twenty-three paces that way, by my reckoning. Except of course it's not Turks who dig, but our fellow Christians, Serbs from Novo Brodo, by the tongue I've heard a few times at night. I recognise it and know their skills well, for I learned the same trade beneath the same ground as they.'

'Twenty-three paces? And you twenty out?' Gregoras half stood. 'Should we not . . . ?'

'Sit!' commanded the Scot. 'My men will tell us in plenty of time. And for God's sake have another dram.' He poured another tot before Gregoras could cover his mug. 'You make me nervous with this abstemiousness. And I haven't seen you for an age.' He grinned as Gregoras sipped. 'So? What news of the world?'

Whenever the people of the city met, each would ask the other for news – whether the ship the emperor had sent out two weeks before had returned; whether the latest Turkish assaults on the boom had come close to succeeding, so the enemy's two fleets could unite; how many more attacks upon the walls the city could resist, for the Turks had come at night twice recently, once at the St Romanus gate, once at the palace, and had only just, and after long hours of hard fighting, been driven back each time. So Gregoras talked of his knowledge of this, and of something more recent, which he had witnessed himself at the emperor's side: Constantine, striding into a hall full of shouting Venetians and Genoans, and putting his body between the rivals, between the many who had drawn their daggers there, accusing each other of cowardice, of betrayal. Using his voice and his tears to calm them, to beg that they save their hatred for the enemy and not give him succour and their own people despair with their enmity. He had succeeded in forcing an accord. But there would be no love between the Italian rivals.

Gregoras paused to take a small sip and Grant interrupted. 'My friend, I have heard all this and more than perhaps even you know. This, my finest distillation,' he said, lifting his mug, 'draws all officers here eventually. There are nights when I cannot move and feel more owner of some dark bothy in my native Highlands than a man of science.' He shook his head. 'Nay, lad. I was asking after news of you. How's the girl?'

Gregoras was never quite sure which drunken night it was on their journey from Korcula that he had told Grant the whole tale. The drinking had also drowned his memories of what exactly he'd told. Not so for Grant, who seemed to recall everything, perfectly. He thought immediately of Sofia, that laugh she'd given when she'd surprised him with Thakos. That look in her eye. He had not come near her since. He was not sure what he would do when he did. Theon was the emperor's adviser as Gregoras was his soldier. He did not wish to see tears in Constantine's eyes, calling on two brothers not to fight and so aid the enemy, just as he called on the Italians.

'I have not seen her in a while,' he said.

'Not since Ragusa. I know.'

Gregoras frowned. 'What girl do you speak of?'

'The one you saved from those assailants. The pocket Venus who showed her gratitude by fucking your eyes from their sockets that same night.' He grinned. 'What was her name?'

Truly, Gregoras thought, I have to be more restrained in what I tell people when in my cups. But the memory the Scot conjured was not unpleasant; far from it. 'Leilah,' he said, with a quick smile.

'To her, then, lad,' Grant said, lifting his mug. 'And to a swift reunion of your loins.'

It was a toast Gregoras could not refuse. Draining the mug, he felt the liquor surge through him, bringing a question: where was Leilah now? Would she meet him again in Ragusa as he had offered? If Constantinople survived, would he even be returning there?

Grant raised the flagon. If he had kept his eyebrows, he'd have raised them too, so it was his brow that wrinkled in query. Gregoras considered another tot. He'd had two and they tasted fine. But then a man rushed in, one near as filthy as the Scot.

'M . . . m . . . master,' he said. 'They are close.'

'So soon? I doubt they'll be here yet awhile.' Reluctantly, Grant put the flagon down. 'But just in case, Lascaris, order your men down to wait here, close for our call. Let them breathe while they can.'

Gregoras moved swiftly through the wrecked cellar and to the bottom of the stairs. 'Come,' he called, and heard the order passed, his men assembling.

He turned back into the stone room, saw the Scot, a pickaxe

in his hand, standing by a now open door that led into a deeper darkness. His teeth glimmered in the torchlight. 'Welcome to Hades,' he said.

'Should I give you a coin, Charon, for the ferrying of my soul?' Gregoras muttered as he stepped past him into blackness.

'Maybe later. You may survive, if you listen carefully.' Grant moved in front of him as he spoke, and Gregoras followed, slipping the first two steps, for the ground he expected to be level sloped. And he found he could see, for there were torches every five paces, their flickering light falling on earthen walls and roof and the wooden props that supported them. The tunnel was narrow and low enough to make him uncomfortable, and Gregoras suddenly found himself yearning for the ship he'd vowed never to take again, the open space of its decks. Then the passage levelled, widening into a chamber that he could stand up straight in, and reach neither wall with outstretched arms from its centre.

It also ended in another earth wall, the man who fetched them pressing his ear against it. 'Are they . . . beyond that?' Gregoras whispered, hand going to his short sword's grip.

Grant laughed, replied in a normal tone, 'You do not need to whisper. They cannot hear us yet.'

'How do you know?'

Grant pointed. 'That tells me.'

Gregoras followed the finger. On a little shelf left untrimmed in the building of the wall, he saw a drum resting, a small one such as a child might use. 'Do you have time for music down here?' He could not help the whisper.

'Nay, lad, look closer.' Gregoras bent. 'Do you see the pebbles upon the skin? See how they move?' Gregoras nodded. 'They bounce with each stroke of a Serbian pickaxe upon the wall. They do not bounce too high . . . yet. But soon enough we'll have to turn from these stones to those.' He grabbed a torch from its bracket and brought it nearer to the wall. The light indeed glistened on other stones, larger ones, embedded in the earth. 'When the first one of those falls, that's the time not just for whispers, but for silence. The Turk will be just a few heartbeats away.'

His lieutenant coughed behind him. Gregoras turned to see him in the narrow doorway, waiting for orders. He swallowed. 'What would you have us do, Scotsman?'

Grant was bent, studying the pebbles on the drum. 'Hmm,' he said, more softly. 'Perhaps a little closer than I thought.' He straightened. 'Do? The Serb miners will be there, thinking they have some time yet before they get underneath our bastion. But they will be on guard for this countermine too, so Turkish soldiers will not be far behind. Their plan is to dig beneath the tower, prop up the walls with wood, then burn that down, causing the earth to fall in and the tower above with it. My men will do the same to their diggings, cut down their props, collapse their mine.' That glimmer came again, lips parted over teeth. 'All you have to do is drive the Turks away, fifty paces will do, and keep them away long enough for us to do that. Kill as many of their miners as you can, for they are irreplaceable . . . Oh, and listen hard for my call . . .' he pulled a small silver whistle from his doublet, 'above the dagger play. Because we cannot hold the earth up for long.'

'How long?' was all Gregoras got out before he heard the man at the wall hiss, 'Master?'

Both turned. The man was pointing at a stone in the wall. It seemed to jiggle and then, quite suddenly, it fell. 'Hmm! Yes. Swifter than I thought,' Grant whispered. 'Fetch your men.'

Gregoras turned, hissed a command down the passage.

Grant gestured at his man, who moved away from listening and snatched the torch from the wall, stabbing it into the ground, snuffing flame, putting them into the dark. All Gregoras could do, he did – unstrap his buckler from his back and slip his hand through its grips, draw his long-bladed dagger, listen. He heard his men's harsh breaths as they filed into the darkness, the sudden fear it brought making them inhale deeply in air that was already foul, and limited. He pulled at the shirt beneath the breastplate, freeing its grip from his neck. He felt a little faint, and reached a hand out to the earthen wall to steady himself. Behind him, men armed themselves. Before . . .

He could hear it now, the muffled fall of metal on earth. It was rhythmical, a steady time being kept, and he thought he could also hear something beyond that, some hum. When he listened more closely, he recognised it. The men the other side were singing a hymn, one he knew well. Serbs, he thought, of the Orthodox faith as they were. Kill as many of them as you can, the Scotsman had said. Well, Christians killed each other as regularly as Christians killed Turks. The sultan had thousands of Christ's followers in his army, while a Turkish prince, Orhan, a pretender to the throne of Osman, defended the walls with his infidels. And then there was Amir.

Gregoras leaned to the side, spat some of the foulness from his mouth that bad air and good aqua vitae had made there. He pictured his friend, his fraying saffron cloak flapping, and held his dagger a little tighter.

He listened, to the ragged breathing of his men, to the steady strike of metal on earth, to the praising of Christ the son, Maria the mother, their song getting louder or his hearing getting better in the dark. Other senses more acute too – the smell of sweat, for it was hot in a crowd beneath the ground, and of men's gases expelled, fouling the air further; the wetness on his palms, the drops running down his back. He heard his men behind him muttering prayers till a harsh whisper from the Scotsman cut them off. And he could not help silently mouthing the words to the hymn the men he was about to slay were singing. Christ in all his glory come, he thought. Lead us from the dark.

It was as if he'd summoned it. The perfect blackness ahead, pierced suddenly by a single shaft of light. The sound of the hymn slightly louder for a moment, then cut off with a harsh cry, part triumph, part fear. Serbian was not a language he spoke, the word hissed the other side of the wall unintelligible. Not so the whispered Turkish reply.

'Have you found it?'

John Grant did not whisper. 'Now!' he shouted, and swung his pickaxe hard into the wall. On the other side, his man did the same. Four blows were enough to shatter it, the cave flooding with torchlight as the wall collapsed. Gregoras was squinting now, till the blurred shapes before him coalesced into three bearded men stripped to the waist, tools held crosswise before their chests. Behind them, a man in a turban, eyes widened by a shock all felt, each enemy staring at the other for one single, endless moment. Broken by the Scotsman's next scream, the native war cry Gregoras had heard him cry before.

'Craigelachie!' Grant yelled, and swung his pickaxe again – into the bare chest before him.

All that was silent transformed to noise, all that was still into movement. Gregoras stumbling forward now, then finding his feet, then running, dipping to dodge a swung shovel, needing to reach the Turk before he cleared his curved dagger from its sheath. He did, one hand grasping the wrist, shoving the blade back down, the other bringing his own weapon up and slashing the steel across the throat just too late to stop the cry erupting from his throat. 'For the love of Allah, come!'

God's name was enough. Further down the well-lit mine, wider than the one he'd come from, men were moving. Miners rising from their rest; soldiers turning with weapons in their hands. As Gregoras dropped the dying Turk to the ground, he heard the cries of the miners he'd passed, falling. His men needed no commands, they were already running forward, his young lieutenant at their head. He pressed himself against the wall to save a trampling, and when the last of the twenty had gone past, he followed.

'Drive them! Drive them back! Further!' Grant was beside him now, his own miners in a body coming up. Some were holding shovels, pickaxes. Most seemed to be carrying clay pots in both hands, their necks stuffed with rags. As Gregoras ran forward, quite fast now because the miners ahead and the Turks had, to a man, turned and fled, he shouted, 'What is in those pots?'

'The product of my labours. At least, it will be. Far enough,' he bellowed, halting suddenly, his men and Gregoras with him. Grant whistled, pointed at what looked like a large bladder on the ground, with a long stick thrust into it that trailed off into the mine ahead. 'Look! A pump to cleanse the air. A fine example. I'm having that.' Bending, he ripped the device from the ground, then looked around. 'Begin!' he commanded, and his men put down their pots carefully and began hacking away at every second wooden prop. Grant turned back to Gregoras. 'Haven't you business of your own?' He pointed ahead, then pulled out his silver whistle. 'But listen for my call, ye ken? It will not be long in coming.'

Gregoras had only paused for a few seconds, and there had been silence ahead. Now, as he again ran along the passage, sounds came, and soon sight – his men, in a crowd, striking with their daggers and axes at Turks who had rallied before them. The tunnel was wide enough for five to fight five, and the front rank grappled as others pressed from behind. There were some cries of fear, of fury, of sudden agony. Some calls to God too, however He was seen. But mostly Gregoras was aware of the lack of noise, as if each side was aware of the fragility of the earth that pressed in upon them and did not want to disturb it with a shout.

It was hard to see anything distinct in the flicker of torches and blades. Then Gregoras did, as two of his men fell at the same time, including his young lieutenant, face smashed with a mace. The man wielding it was a huge Turk, who should not have been there, making the space look small, and Gregoras could sense that point in battle fast coming when one side quailed and the other drove them back. Yet no whistle called him and he knew that the Greeks must stand. 'For the emperor and for Christ Risen,' he cried, and moved between his men. They had begun to turn away, were a moment from flight, so he passed through easily enough, crouching low, shifting left to dodge the falling mace, brought down with a force that would have stoved his brain. He did not try to take the blow on his buckler; his arm would have been snapped. Instead he let it fall, felt the wind of its passing even as he lunged up and punched the dagger into the flesh beneath the Turk's bearded chin.

The man fell away, landing with a thump that shook the ground. It was enough to rally Gregoras's troops, for the enemy to quail in his turn. Gregoras stepped back, as his men, with a cry of 'Christ Risen!', pushed past him, driving the Turks back. He heard a moan, looked down, saw the young lieutenant's smashed lips move in plea. 'Help me,' he whispered. Gregoras hesitated . . . and then they came, clear, shrill. Three blasts of a silver whistle.

'Come,' said Gregoras, dragging the fallen officer up. His men knew the signal too. As a body they turned and charged towards their safety. 'Here!' he yelled, and one of the soldiers slipped his shoulder under the arm of the young lieutenant that Gregoras held out. Together, with the young man's toes scraping the ground, they ran.

The Turks had turned back under the ferocity of the last assault. But fresh men, who had been kept always in readiness, had arrived and were now running down a passage they knew led straight into the city they had struggled so hard to take. It was a foot race, Gregoras and his helper just winning it. There was a slight bend to the Serb tunnel; they rounded it . . .

'Down!' came a guttural Scottish cry. Gregoras obeyed, bearing himself and his burden swiftly to the ground, sliding along mud that blood had made slick. He twisted as he fell, ready to leap up again on command. So he saw Grant above him lean back, then hurl his arm forward. Saw the flame that flew like a comet's tail through a night sky. Gregoras was rising to his knees as he saw the projectile smash – one of the clay pots shattering on the ground before the charging Turks. There was a moment when liquid splashed over mud and onto trailing clothes. Then, with a sharp fizz, the burning fuse ignited the liquid and the tunnel went up in flame.

'Come,' Grant cried, bending to help Gregoras rise, the Greek in turn aiding his moaning lieutenant. Together the three stumbled back, away from the screaming Turks, those who burned, those who sought to pass the flames and charge on. But more of Grant's men were against the tunnel's walls, and as they passed, each miner lifted a clay pot and threw it – not at the Turks, some of whom had come through the fire, but straight at the base of the wooden props that held up the roof.

Grant had a grin greater than ever before. Passing his burden to two soldiers who reached out their hands, Gregoras turned to the Scot as they ran. 'Won't they put out the flames?'

'Nay. Greek Fire cannot be stamped out and it's the devil's job to smother, because it just spreads and burns anything. Same with water, it'll burn atop it. About the only thing that would work is piss.' He laughed. 'And have you ever tried pissing when a roof's about to fall in?'

'Greek Fire?'

'Aye,' Grant nodded. 'Seems that I have rediscovered its secret after all.'

They'd reached the entrance to their tunnel, the last men back. There was a little bunching there as the soldiers pushed through, so Gregoras turned, hands before him, weaponless but ready to leap for the throat of a pursuer. None came through the smoke and the dancing light, but as he watched, what did come was sound, a deep rumble, a dozen screams suddenly choked off. A wall of dust hurtled towards him.

'Come now,' said Grant, seizing his collar, dragging him through the stone lintel of the archway, slamming the door shut, shooting its bolt. They both fell up the steps, lay there staring at the wood. Something hard hit it on the other side, but the lock and the solid oak held; while as they watched, through the edges of the doorframe a fine burst of dust blew out, like a man's last sigh.

TWENTY-SEVEN

The Tower

17 May: forty-first day of the siege

'Will I live?'

Behind her veil, Leilah rolled her eyes. If she had a ducat for every time she'd been asked that question recently, she could forget the fortune Geber's manuscript would bring her and retire for life. It came with setting up her tent in a war camp. Soldiers had few other concerns.

She tried again to seek his answer in the cards spread before her. Yet again, as it had been for days now, their symbols revealed nothing save her own confusion. She glanced up from them to the youth squatting on the other side of the kilim. Not yet twenty, she suspected by his wisp of beard, by his accent, a Vlach from beyond the Danube. Though she'd heard that Christians only formed one-quarter of the sultan's army, they were three-quarters of her clientele, those of the true faith more content to leave their destiny in Allah's hands.

'*Inshallah,*' she murmured, and bent over again. Still she saw nothing. She was not as gifted in the cards' use as she was with palms and mirrors. Her lover, the Kabbalist Isaac, had only just begun her instruction in his people's ancient technique when he'd . . . died. But the pretty pictures pleased her clients.

She frowned. Truly what did the querent need? Not for her to wrench up her soul. He only needed hope. That she'd always been able to fake.

She reached for a card's blank back, hesitated. For she needed hope too. Her vision had grown cloudy, her certainty compromised. Near seven weeks of siege, a never-ending bombardment, ceaseless assaults, a fleet in the Horn – and still the city stood. She knew from the women of this outer camp, mainly whores whose cooking fires she shared, and from some of the men who sat before her carpet begging for a sign, that doubt had overtaken most minds. The Red Apple had never fallen. Why should it now? Only yesterday, one of their greatest hopes had been crushed. The Greeks had discovered the tunnel that would have brought a great bastion crashing down and allowed the faithful to storm in. They had destroyed it, massacred the men who'd dug it, while those few who had escaped had been horribly burned, their death screams filling the camp.

Her hand hovered. The youth leaned in, transfixed. Still she did not reach.

She was thinking of Mehmet. She had not seen him, except from afar, since that night in Edirne when she'd prophesied his great victory. Should she go to him now? He was as prey to doubts as great as any of his soldiers'. Greater, as were his ambitions. Should she soothe him with portents? Rouse him with prophesies? Hope could be faked for sultans as well as soldiers.

A voice jolted her out of her trance. 'You do see something,' the young man whispered. 'What is it?'

Leilah looked up into blue eyes wide with apprehension, then down again to her hand suspended over the deck. Now she let it fall, touched the card, turned it . . . crying out as her vision cleared fast, like a veil ripped back.

'What?' the youth gasped. 'What do you see?'

She'd been concentrating, but not on his question. On her own. And the answer was clear.

Ayin. So it was called in the Hebrew. To some it was the temple of God in Jerusalem, long destroyed. To others a stone pyramid. To others . . . a tower.

Lightning struck the structure, the first spark in its destruction.

She turned it back over swiftly, melding it in with the other cards, rising as soon as it was lost among them. The youth did not move. 'What did you see?' he repeated, his voice becoming shrill. 'Am I to die?'

She looked down at him. What had cleared her vision kept it clear. Death was stamped on his unwrinkled brow. His fate, and there was nothing she could do about it. 'You are in God's hands, as are we all,' she said, stooping for his coin, throwing it back between his knees. '*Inshallah.*'

Carelessly and swiftly, she stuffed the cards into her satchel. Grabbed her cloak, looked back. The youth had not moved. 'Take back your money. Come another day.'

Still he did not bend for his silver coin. 'You did see, didn't you?' he mumbled.

'Go!' She bent, snatched up the coin, shoved it into the same hand she jerked him up with. She pushed him through the tent flaps and he stumbled off. Leilah went the opposite way.

Sometimes the meaning of a card was obscure and she had to go deep within herself to find it. Sometimes it was as unambiguous as the symbol itself. That was true of this young man, marked for death. And unless she reached Mehmet, perhaps it meant something else too – the death of her dream.

'Ayin. The tower,' she muttered as she ran, weaving between the cooking fires. 'It must not fall.'

'The tower,' the sultan shrieked. 'It must attack. Not in a week. Not tomorrow. Now! Now! Now!'

Hamza stood at the back of the group of men that Mehmet was screaming at. He had not yet been seen and for that he was grateful. The sultan's fury was a wild fire that could switch direction in a moment. When he was first summoned, Hamza had thought that Mehmet wanted to chastise his new admiral for yet another failure to capture the boom across the Horn and unite the two Turkish fleets. Like the unfortunate Baltaoglu, he feared he would soon be feeling the strokes of the *bastinado* across his back. But he'd been met at the entrance to the sultan's *otak* by Zaganos Pasha, who revealed that *he* was the one who'd sent for him.

'We need you, old friend,' he'd said, greeting him. 'Perhaps he'll heed you as he will not me.'

Hamza had stared at the man, wondering if the siege had carved such fresh lines upon his own face. He recalled the apple-cheeked youth from their time together in the old sultan's household. Zaganos had been part of the levy, the *devsirme*, that took the strongest and brightest – and the prettiest – from the Turk's vassal lands. A Christian from Albania, but such a Muslim now that he put those born in the faith to shame. He was also a 'coming man', completely dedicated to Mehmet and so at odds, like Hamza the tanner's son, with the old nobility. Both knew their own star rose and fell with Mehmet's.

Taking his arm, the Albanian had led Hamza aside and spoken to him in urgent whispers. 'The Greeks blew up his mine this morning,' he'd said, 'and the long-bearded bastards somehow keep patching every piece of wall he knocks down. It is making him, as you hear, crazy.' He jerked his thumb over his shoulder, to the almost unintelligible noises of rage within the tent. 'Now he wants to send in the tower, which is only half finished. Now, this hour, in broad daylight, right up against the section that that immovable goatfucker Giustiniani defends. I think Mehmet means to fling himself from the tower top, sword in hand, and take him on in single combat.' A man had come out of the tent and stared at them, so Zaganos pulled him further away. 'For the love of Allah, most revered, you have to stop him. I don't know how many more setbacks the army can take. That shitfaced Anatolian is already sowing doubt: "Oh, most exalted, I feared this would be the outcome. Perhaps it is time to reconsider."' Zaganos turned and spat onto the *otak*'s silk-draped side.

Another time Hamza would have smiled. It was an almost

perfect impersonation of the high-pitched Iznikian accent of the grand vizier, Candarli Halil. 'What do you think I can do that you have failed to do?' he said. 'He is hard to move once he is decided. That's why we are here, after all.'

'Think I don't know? I do not ask you to stop the storm. Just deflect it. Get me a night at least. If we can finish the tower and move it into position so the Greeks wake up and see it there at dawn, we might have a chance.' He'd taken Hamza's arm, half squeezed, half shoved. 'Go, before it is too late.'

So Hamza stood at the back of the crowd of apprehensive men, watching the sultan rage. Zaganos's likening of it to a storm was accurate. Mehmet's arms whirled as if in a high wind; his breath came in great gasps and was expelled with gobs of spittle like fat raindrops. Accusations, of treachery, of incompetence, of cowardice exploded like thunderclaps.

Like any storm, though, it needed force to sustain it, and Hamza could see that Mehmet lacked the stamina. It had only been three weeks since he'd last seen the sultan, on the day he'd been appointed *kapudan pasha*. But Mehmet had thinned, his big wrestler's body diminished, his vibrant thick red hair hanging lank around his temples. His eyes were sunken, sockets bruised by lack of sleep. He looked younger because of it, younger even than his twenty-one years. And it was the youth who, lacking the breath to continue, suddenly subsided, leaned on his knees in tiredness, raising his face with a look that was more appeal than fury.

It was his time. 'Balm of the world,' Hamza shouted, pushing through the startled men, who turned at the noise. 'I beg you to let me be the one to lead this attack. To die, if Allah so wills it, a martyr for Him and for you.'

He'd reached the front rank now, and Mehmet could see him. He knew he had the advantage of not being tainted with this recent failure. He had his own, true. But the past could be lost, for a time, in the present.

Mehmet looked up. 'Hamza. My *cakircibas*. Have you a hawk for me to fly?'

'Fly me, master,' Hamza said, prostrating himself on the ground, kissing Mehmet's curling slipper, 'at any game you desire.'

The sultan stared down for a long moment, then quietly said, 'Leave us alone.'

Hamza did not move, did not look up. Didn't need to, to hear a familiar high-pitched whine: 'But, lord, let your most trusted stay and speak more on this. Perhaps it is time to reconsider . . .'

'Go!' Mehmet roared. 'You dare to dispute with me, Candarli Halil?'

The tent cleared, swiftly. Hamza heard the fall of cloth at the entrance, then Mehmet's voice, a single word. 'Rise.'

Hamza rose. Mehmet had flung himself back onto the divan at the centre of the room and covered his face with his hands. He spoke through clenched fingers. 'The cowards try to thwart me, falconer. I cannot bid them to my fist.'

Hamza stepped closer, spoke softly, as he would to a bird that was straining to the limit of its jesses. 'So bid others, lord. You cannot fly a heron against a hare.'

After a moment, Mehmet gave a sharp, muffled laugh, then dropped his hands. 'He is a proper heron, that smug Anatolian. And he wants to see me fail. He tries to make me fail.'

'Yes, lord,' Hamza continued, as softly. 'But there is a goshawk outside, awaiting your command.'

'Who?'

'Zaganos. May I call him in?'

After a moment of staring, Mehmet nodded. Walking slowly to the entrance – you didn't make sudden moves with a nervous bird – Hamza pulled up the cloth, sought Zaganos, beckoned him with his eyes. The Albanian came swiftly, his own eyes wide in query. At Hamza's nod, he sighed and followed him into the tent.

'Well, Zaganos?' Mehmet said. 'Are you willing to obey my orders?'

'Every one, star of the sky. And to hurl myself with your other good servant from the tower. We will be the first to die for your glory.'

The younger man was rising during these words, but he stopped halfway, like a wrestler ready to counter a move. 'Eh? Are you both so ready to die?'

'As you command, lord. I admit I would rather take my chance in the half-light of the dawn tomorrow, with the tower fully finished,' Zaganos replied, then snapped his fingers. 'No! As it is, and in the blazing sun of this afternoon, so all will witness the loyalty that surpasses death.'

Mehmet straightened now, looking between the two men. Both could see, for the first time, some uncertainty in his eyes. 'You truly think the dawn a better time?'

Zaganos tipped his head to the side, considering. 'Well, it would mean that we would have time to not just once but triple-ward the front of the tower with soaked ox hides. They would better resist their fire arrows.'

Mehmet looked at Hamza. 'What think you?'

Hamza also took a long moment to consider. 'I can see another advantage, lord. Imagine if the Greeks wake up to see a mighty tower standing flush to their wall where no tower existed before. They would think it magical. They would gaze upon it with the same awe . . .' he paused, 'as the Trojans did upon the horse that brought their city low.'

It was the best arrow in his quiver, for he knew the young man's obsessions. And he saw it strike home. 'Yes,' said Mehmet, smiling too. 'Yes! Let it be so. It will give me time to supervise the last parts of its construction. And choose the men who will fight from it. The ablest that I have. Come . . .' he gestured to the back of the tent, his table there, filled with rosters and maps, 'advise me.'

The young sultan led Zaganos back. Servants appeared, bringing flagons, sweetmeats. Hamza, breathing deep and about to follow, stopped when he heard a hiss. He turned. An officer stood at the entrance, beckoning. Hamza moved to him. 'What is it?'

'A message for the sultan, *kapudan pasha*. A woman brings it.'

'A woman?' Hamza sighed. Mehmet had forbidden all his officers their wives. But he had brought a few concubines from his own *saray*. 'It is not the time,' he said, turning away.

'Forgive me, pasha, but it is not that . . . that sort of woman.' The officer's voice dropped to a whisper. 'It is a sorceress. She has a prophecy for the sultan.'

Hamza sucked in air, then stepped past the officer out before the tent. A dozen paces away, at the gap in the silk rope that surrounded the *otak* like a thin crimson wall, stood a woman in a veil and cloak. Hamza shivered, although the sun was hot upon him. She could have been any woman. But she was not. She was the witch from Edirne, who'd predicted the Red Apple's fall, and sealed the decision in the blood of an importuning Jew.

He crossed to the unmoving figure. 'Do you know me?' he said, more sharply than he meant.

The voice came muffled through indigo-dyed cloth. 'I know you, master.'

'You cannot see the sultan now.'

'I must. I have a prophecy for him.'

'I tell you that you cannot. You can tell your prophecy to me.'

'It is not for you.'

Hamza hesitated. He knew his lord set much store by portents. Too much, many said. And though Hamza himself did not altogether discount them, he preferred to trust in what he could see rather than in the stars or in the guts of a freshly slaughtered goat. Like a hunting bird, he had just recalled Mehmet to the fist. He would not have him jostled again. 'You cannot see him, woman,' he said harshly. 'Be gone.'

He'd taken a step back to the tent when her words came. He did not turn, but he heard them clearly enough.

'I do have a prophecy that is yours, Hamza Pasha,' Leilah said softly. The man was a blur through her veil. But her vision of him was clear. 'Enjoy your glory. All the success you could desire will be yours. Until a forest grows where no forest has been. And a dragon makes you climb upon a tree.'

He turned then, fast, but she was gone. He thought he glimpsed a flash of indigo, thought to chase it, catch her, ask what she had meant. But Zaganos was behind him, calling. So he went.

'Up, peasants. Up, lazy sons of the devils. It is our turn.'

Achmed opened his eyes, squinting against the late afternoon sun. Farouk, their *bolukbasi*, was moving among his company of men. The lieutenant, they said, had one eye that saw all, one ear that heard all, one cock that fucked all and one thumb . . . Well, he used the other hand to grip the *bastinado* that he wielded now, poking and striking his men to their feet.

Achmed sighed. The sun was hot and he would have been content to lie in it and sleep some more, maybe dull the throbbing in his head, maybe find some more *boza* to dull it with. He saw a few of his comrades hiding a bottle of the fermented barley from Farouk's single, eagle eye – not because he would have objected, but because he would have demanded the lion's share of it.

It had been the same with the hundred gold coins that Achmed had won raising the Prophet's standard upon the walls. Half seemed to have gone into the lieutenant's bottomless war chest, the rest to drink and better food for the company. There was nothing he could do about it. When he complained, he got his answer. 'You wouldn't have got to the wall without us, giant,' Farouk had said, when Achmed had woken from the three-day delirium caused by the Greek stone that had opened his head. 'So we will drink to the martyrs now

331

in paradise who died for you, and we will reward those who survived your immense stupidity.'

Achmed didn't want to drink. Hadn't, in the long march from his home to the walls of Constantinople. It was forbidden by the Qur'an and there were many, like him, who kept faithful to the law. There were also many who did not. His little companion Raschid, with his twisted right leg and endless dreams of women, was one such. And he had fed Achmed *boza* when he was helpless in the darkness of his wound. It had reduced the pain, kept reducing it as the weeks passed. It had reduced the fear, when they were called again and again to the attack. For a while it had given him dreams – of home, of his beautiful wife, of his sons. And of his dead daughter, his wild rose, little Abal, alive again and running through his fields of golden wheat.

It was surprising how fast a hundred gold coins went – on *boza*, on sheep bought for feasts held in memory of the dead, in payments that his lieutenant and some of the company made to certain women who lived in a tent village on the shores of the Marmara sea. Achmed did not go, though Raschid always did. But when the hundred coins were gone, the company found rougher liquor that brought pain almost as soon as it brought oblivion. Achmed had tried to drink less, pray more. But the cannon that boomed above him day and night needed quieting, as did his fear.

'Up, hell hounds,' bellowed Farouk, nearing him and Raschid. 'The sultan would unleash you.' He stopped in front of them, struck Achmed's bare toe. 'Up, *gazi*! Allah, most glorious, calls you to Him.'

'Is it another general attack, lieutenant?' Raschid pulled himself up to standing, using Achmed's shoulders.

Farouk smiled, something that Achmed always hated. It was not just the ugliness of the face, the near-toothless mouth stretching under the puckered eye socket to the missing ear. He'd smiled like that each time he ordered them to the walls – twice since the first attack when the standard had been raised.

Each time many comrades had not returned. Yet the company was full again the next day, for the largely unschooled *bashibazouks* sought out an officer like Farouk, his experience written on his face, while his reputation for seeking the best plunder once a city fell was unmatched.

Now he smiled, spoke loudly, addressing all. 'A general attack? Not now. But perhaps later, and perhaps it will be the last of them, the one that sweeps the Greeks from their walls and opens their coffer lids and their wives' legs to us.' His few teeth gleamed. 'For our glorious sultan, praised of heaven, has found a new way to do that. He has enlisted the services of a great djinn, a powerful wizard who has, overnight, created a marvellous tower that reaches to the skies and overlooks the Greeks' puny walls.' Gasps came at this, many men reaching within their clothes for talismans and protective objects. Farouk's smile broadened. 'So come, devil spawn, and see what magic has wrought for the destruction of our enemies.'

Achmed had been lying bare-chested because some fool had vomited on his shirt. Now he dug into his satchel and pulled out the vest he'd purchased from a gypsy with one of the few coins he'd managed to keep for himself. The girl had merged four letters of his name – ACMD – with one of the ninety-nine names of Allah, al-Qarib. He could not read, but he knew it meant 'near', and when he chanted the names, he did feel near to Him, the garment and the conjoined names protecting him.

He needed to void the *boza* he'd drunk. But Farouk was already organising them into their files and he could not move. At their *bolukbasi*'s command, they left the lee of the hill, went up and over it. He expected the sight to be the same as ever – the walls sweeping to the sea, the flapping standards, the crumbling stone bastions, the stockade the Greeks would have thrown up in the night to close each breach the mighty cannon had opened. But this time he could see nothing but what magic had wrought.

The tower. It was so large it must indeed have been made by

a powerful djinn and his thousand helpers, only the most potent of spells raising something so vast, so swiftly, where there had been nothing before. Set up in the fosse, flush against the low outermost wall, it loomed over that, dwarfing even the second wall, the one the Greeks defended. It faced one of their bastions, one so battered by cannon that only a single stone crenel still stood, like a solitary tooth in Farouk's mouth. And Achmed, who had begun to learn a little of the way of the siege, could see what the djinn's tower had achieved: archers on top of it, sheltered on a roofed platform, could shoot directly down on the infidels, keeping them from their repairs, keeping them from harassing the swarms of the faithful who attacked the stockade with axes and poles.

He watched flaming arrows shot from the third, last and largest wall behind and saw them bury themselves in the thick hide that covered the structure. But the material did not dissolve in flames; the hides had to have been soaked, and even as he watched, he saw one small fire doused with water thrown from that sheltered platform.

They had reached their own wooden stockade. 'Line up! You too, whoreson dog.' A blow accompanied Farouk's words. 'Only swords! Leave the rest here.' There was a clatter as axes, spears and the few shields were stacked against the stockade. 'Now, each man grab as much wood as he can carry.' There were stacks of logs, each about half the height of a big man. Achmed bent with the others, lifted. 'Come on, giant.' Farouk prodded him with his *bastinado*. 'You can manage more than that.' As Achmed bent and lifted three more logs to add to the three he had, Farouk continued, 'Good. Good. Now . . . forward!'

Achmed took his gaze from one miracle . . . to another! From the base of the hill, a wooden tunnel ran the hundred paces to the tower. They would be sheltered the entire way from the arrows and quarrels and flung stones that usually fell hard upon them. Men were filing out six abreast, so wide was its entrance. Then Farouk peered into the tunnel and yelled, 'Forward!'

They marched into the darkness. Yet it was not pitch; Achmed could see men ahead of him, though he was near the front, and there were openings every dozen paces that admitted the sun. It got darker as they got closer to the noise. It wasn't just the ever-present screaming of men in combat. As they neared the tunnel's end, he also heard the distinct sound of digging.

The tunnel splayed wide, and Achmed realised that it gave directly onto the tower. The front of it, which was in the fosse and pressed against the Greeks' lesser wall, was open, and bare chested men stood there, hacking into the earth and stone, yelling and cursing in a foreign language. They had already carved out a cave, and other men were erecting props to hold up its roof.

He looked up . . . and gasped. The tower rose above him, hollow save for the stairs that went up inside it, and the three platforms the flights linked that rose to the very top. Raschid stood beside him, also looking up, the same awe on his face. 'Man could not have made this,' he whispered. 'The djinns of the earth and the heavens fight for us.'

Achmed saw that their *bolukbasi* was listening to a senior officer, in a rich wool *gomlek* and purple turban, who was talking rapidly and gesturing all around. Farouk nodded, then turned back to his waiting men. 'Everyone behind Iqbal stack their wood to the side. Carry these sacks of earth back down the tunnel and fetch more logs. You at the front, you dozen . . .' he gestured to Achmed and the men around him, 'bring yours up the stairs.'

He led the way. Achmed, strong though he was, felt the pressure in his knees as he bore his double load up the stairs. Felt the pressure in his bladder too, still unrelieved, but he knew that was not just his burden. The noise of battle inside the tower was muffled, by ox hides and thick wood, but the screams of men, killing, dying, still came through along with the thump of arrows, the drum of flung stones, the steam hiss of flames suddenly engulfed in water. More faintly, he could hear the never-ceasing call of the pipe and the drumming of the *kos*. And the tower, like all the earth around it, shook when the big cannon roared. He was hot too, and not just from the exercise, as he struggled up the second flight. Hell, he thought quite clearly, would be like this.

To his relief, Farouk halted him at the first platform. 'Here, giant. Set it down, but keep hold.' He turned to a man, another officer, who was peering through slits in the tower's front wall. 'We are here, master,' he said.

The man turned. 'Good,' he said simply, then gestured to a soldier beside him, who immediately pulled hard upon a rope that ran to a hoist above. A section of the front wall swung up . . . and Achmed was looking at Greek stonework twenty paces away.

'Throw!' the officer commanded, and Achmed was the first to lift his logs again, step to the open doorway and fling his wood into the evening air. He heard them clatter below, stepped back and heard more of the same as his comrades threw their burdens. When the last had done so, the officer peered swiftly out, down. 'Water!' he called, a bucket was handed to him and he tipped the contents down the front of the tower. All heard the fizz as flames died. 'Good,' he said, putting the bucket down beside five others, then turning back to Farouk. 'More wood,' he commanded.

He was not quite sure what they did – raising the level of the land, he supposed, up to the Greek battlements – but it was better than fighting. It reminded Achmed of the work he did upon his own land, the clearing of stones from the fields he needed to sow. The constant bending, lifting, carrying, throwing. His back, legs, arms all soon ached but, just as at home, he did not stop. It was comforting, the rhythm, even the pain, the memories that brought. And no one was running at him with a sword, no one was flinging a stone at his head or an arrow at his chest.

336

He carried, more than other men, up and down the stairs. It got dark, outside and within, but still they laboured. Soon another pain, one that had never really left him, became too strong finally to bear. 'Master,' he said, turning to Farouk after he'd dropped his latest logs, 'I have to piss.'

'Can't you wait?' his lieutenant replied irritably. He was as exhausted as any of them. 'We are about to be relieved.'

The officer brought his head back in from looking down the front of the tower, empty bucket in hand. As the door lowered, he held out the bucket and said, 'Piss in that. Save us bringing up more water. Giant like you will probably fill it.'

Gratefully, Achmed dug within his robes. He was so desperate now that he couldn't start under Farouk's impatient gaze; also the Christians were screaming even louder, as if begging him to stop. Finally he trickled, trickle became flood and he sighed in joy. He did near fill the bucket, to the wonder of his watchers. 'Now, man, one more load,' said Farouk, 'and then we can fill you up again with *boza*.'

They descended to the ground. Achmed could see by torchlight that the tunnel under the wall had progressed, was a few paces in. In the edge of the flame flicker crouched Raschid. He had complained that his twisted leg could not stand so much climbing up and down and had sought to avoid it whenever he could. But Farouk knew him and his lazy ways of old. 'Up, dog,' he cried, striking at him with his *bastinado*. 'Why should we carry for you?'

Whining, Raschid picked up two small logs, Achmed two more than his usual six. Now it was near the end of the work, now his inner pain had ended too, he was content. He needed to eat, drink, pray, sleep, dream. The djinn had come and helped the children of the Prophet. They were filling in the land of the Greeks for the forces of Mehmet to run across. Soon, maybe as soon as tomorrow, they would storm the city, and then, if Allah let him live and did not claim him as a martyr, he would be rich and go home.

One more load. He climbed the stairs, grunting on each one,

Raschid complaining on each one behind him. When they reached the platform, even Achmed's legs wobbled, and he moved to the side to set down his load against the wooden wall. Raschid, unwilling to move a step further, just set his down in the middle, closest to the rising shutter, closest to the ending of his task.

Achmed watched the officer step to the gap, one hand raised behind him to signal them forward, saw him lean a little way out, to check that the hides were still unburned . . . and saw a huge tongue of fire flash through the gap. It consumed the man, almost on the instant; one moment leaning carefully out, the next a swirling mass of flame. He whirled, staggered, flesh whining as he burned, his scream snatched away by instant white heat.

'Dragon!' Achmed tried to cry the word, tried to warn, but it stuck in his throat. Tales in the camp had told of beasts that fought on the infidels' side. The dragon had come to fight the work of the djinn.

The officer fell at last, shooting sparks. The roaring flame leapt past him, as the beast sought another victim.

And found Raschid.

Perhaps the ferocity had slackened a little. Or perhaps the other men standing in its path distracted it, because the monster did not instantly destroy Raschid as it had the officer. Like the other, the little man caught fire, shaking a flaming arm that burned beyond the consuming of his clothes. 'Allah!' he screamed, one of scores crying the name, on their platform, above it, for the dragon ranged afar, seeking more victims.

Achmed looked up in time to see the top archer's platform dissolve. A man fell shrieking from it and on through to the ground, flames increasing with his speed, a human comet. The giant was stunned, staring, unable to move – unlike Farouk, the veteran, who had also not caught fire and leapt now, snatching up a bucket of water, turning, throwing it onto the nearest of his men. But the water did not douse the flames. Instead, it seemed to spread them, carrying them to every part of the platform not already burning. Achmed jumped over a tongue that lapped at him, stumbled towards the buckets. He did not know what else to use, though the first had had no effect.

He hoisted one by its rope handle, swung it round. Just before he flung it, he was aware of its sharp, sour tang, knew it for his own excreta. But that did not stop him as he hurled the contents over Raschid.

Instantly, the flames died. The soaked little man looked at him in astonishment . . . and then his eyes rolled up in his head and he fell. Achmed, moving fast now, caught him before he reached the floor, flung him over his shoulder. Dodging trails of fire borne on swinging tarred ropes and the sparks from imploding wood, he leapt down stairs that dissolved as he stepped off them and then out into the tunnel. Men staggered ahead of him, some yelling piteously and beating at flames that would not go out. Eventually, up ahead, Achmed saw stars and ran to them.

The defenders lay draped on the crumbled ramparts, or spread on the open ground of the Peribolos. Genoan, Venetian and Greek, unable to move, while screams reduced to moans and flames dissolved into the embers of the vanished tower.

Perhaps because to breathe he had to shove aside the body of a Turk who'd fallen over him even as he killed him, Gregoras moved first, slipping down the tumbled stones, between the rock-filled barrels. Some men started and reached for weapons, though they looked too tired to lift them. Gregoras knew it was hard to tell friend from enemy, for all were smeared in soot, earth and blood. 'Peace,' he said in Greek, staggering past men falling back again. He wished he could have lain down too. But first he had to check that the man who had saved the city twice in two days had survived.

He climbed to the bastion, keeping his head low, for there was some fireglow still. At first he thought that the Scot must be dead, so still was he, one hand yet clamped to the bronze pump. Then he heard him, the whisper in his own language, the one that seemed stuck in his throat and made every man, to his annoyance, consider him a German. Gregoras did not speak it, and did not think any could. But he had heard Grant cry out his clan's war cry often enough to recognise it now.

'Craigelachie,' came the murmur. 'Craigelachie.'

'Come,' Gregoras whispered.

Grant looked up, his eyes the only light in his blackened face. 'Did it burn?' he rasped.

'To the ground,' Gregoras replied. 'Come.' Crouching, still keeping in the lee of the last ruined crenel, he pulled his friend away till he could tuck his shoulder under his arm.

Other people were stirring in the Peribolos now. Some he recognised, though all seemed much changed by the day and night of fighting. Even the Commander looked smaller, as if shrunk by exhaustion, hands resting on knees as he spoke. 'I'll see to the stockade,' Giustiniani said. 'The Turk might have lost his tower, but he will come again with the dawn.'

'I will see to it.' The familiar voice came from beside them, though there was nothing familiar about the face caked in mud and blood.

'Sire,' said Giustiniani, 'you must rest.'

'I am younger than you,' said Constantine, 'and it is *my* stockade, after all.' He looked at the Scot whom Gregoras held up, both men swaying like drunkards. 'We owe you a great debt, *kyr*. You have, beyond doubt, and with the aid of God on highest, saved the city this night.' A smile split the soot. 'To your beds, all of you.'

He turned away, to other men rising, began to issue orders. 'Well,' yawned Giustiniani, 'when an emperor commands . . .'

The three of them turned toward the gate. Enzo, the Sicilian, offered a shoulder, which Giustiniani took, gratefully. Grant murmured something else, looking to the bastion, and Gregoras said, 'Do not fear. We'll bring the pump down later.'

The Scotsman's next words were clear – and sad. 'No point,'

he said, 'for I used up the last of the fuel for my Greek Fire. I hope it was worth it.'

'It was,' Gregoras replied, 'for you have slain the Heleopolis. It will take no city.' He sighed. 'And we will just have to find other ways to save Constantinople now.'

— PART THREE —
Omega

TWENTY-EIGHT

Messages

23 May: forty-seventh day of the siege

The Man with Long Sight was still at his post atop the Golden Gate.

It had been over a month since he was the first in the city to spy the four Christian ships and cry out their coming, to the pealing of bells and universal joy. A month of less and less sleep, as the Turkish guns fired through the night and the enemy launched attack after attack against the walls. A month when the bread ration was halved, then halved again, and the bread came ever thicker with sawdust. He'd been sick, too. A rat had bitten him in a tussle over a fallen crust, and though he had killed the rat and roasted it for his supper – the last meat he'd had, two weeks since – the nip it had given him had festered and brought a fever. He'd only just returned to his post and his eyesight was not what it was. Half the time he was squinting at the horizon, he forgot what he was meant to be looking for.

So it took him a while, to turn the sails into something other than birds or dust motes. It was a dull early evening, with thunderclouds building to the west, so the sun was not glinting on the Sea of Marmara and for once he was able to stare with eyes near full open. He assumed that it was just another enemy vessel, since they ruled the waters. Until the ship tacked and swung side on to him and he was able to note that it had not one mast but two, the smaller foremast square-set, the larger main mast rigged fore and aft.

'Brigantine,' he whispered, but only to himself. He had

made mistakes before in his delirium, laid himself open to ridicule. Besides, there was one particular brigantine he was watching for, the one that the emperor had dispatched to search for the relieving fleet. It would fly the enemy's red crescent, as it had when it set out, to try and deceive the watchful Turks. But it would unfurl a white sheet over its gunwales when it came in sight of the city, as a signal to the defenders to prepare to admit it.

The man waited, watched, prayed. He could see it quite clearly now, his eyesight improving with his hope. See the men on deck in the turban and robe of the Turk. See the barefoot sailors in the rigging, adding more sail to catch the *lodos* wind that had blown them from the Dardanelles. See, finally, the white sheet lowered on the larboard side, thrown out casually as if shaking it clear of crumbs. 'Lieutenant,' he called, and had to call again, his voice a dry whisper.

The officer came slowly up the stair, ducking into the shelter of a crenel – there were Turks who would shoot an arrow as soon as they caught the glint of armour. 'Well?' he rasped.

'It is the one, *kyr*.'

'You are sure?'

The sentinel nodded. 'See for yourself.'

The lieutenant bent, peered, rubbed his eyes, peered again. His sight was not as keen, but the vessel was moving closer fast and he could make out the details. 'Alone,' he muttered, rubbing his untrimmed beard. 'Where's the fleet it's supposed to bring?' He pointed his finger at the other man. 'Not a word,' he said, and went back down the stair.

Slumping into the stonework, the Man with Long Sight closed his eyes. He could do with some sleep, now his job was done. No bells would disturb it; this discovery would not be greeted in joyful carillons as before. For the moment, only two men knew that the ship had returned. The other, whose footsteps were still upon the stair, would ride straight to the emperor and tell him in person. A few more would then be told, but only those needed to raise the boom for the messengers. Then, depending on the message, the bells would ring of approaching salvation and many more Christian ships to come. Or they would remain untolled, and Constantinople would face its fate silently, and alone.

Gregoras rubbed his eyes and looked around the table again. The faces of the men at it, awake or asleep, had become a little clearer. He knew this could have nothing to do with his senses, as dulled by the night's debates as any there. Glancing up to the windows, he saw them etched now in light, and then, as if in confirmation of the hour, he heard the bells of the monastery of Manuel, the nearest of the religious houses, summoning the monks to dawn prayer.

He looked back. The sleepers were mainly elderly and had dropped off in order of age – the Castilian Don Francisco had been the first, rapidly followed by the emperor's older advisers – George Sphrantzes, John of Dalmata, Loukas Notaras. The clerics had followed, Leonard and Isidore, then Minotto, the Venetian baillie. Last was the Commander himself, Giovanni Giustiniani Longo, whose vehemence had kept him awake even though he was as old as most there. It was hard to tell he slept, as his head rested on one enormous hand and one eye was half open. But Gregoras had seen him sleep thus on their many campaigns together, snatching moments to fuel the next bout of fighting. He would be awake the moment he was called, sword in his hand a moment later.

Sleep was a dream, the temptation to rest his head almost overpowering. Gregoras did not, for two reasons: the only other men still awake. His emperor. And his own brother.

Constantine had perhaps slept less than any man in the city for weeks now . . . because it was *his* city. It was he who had led the debates that raged through the night, ever since the captain of the brigantine had been brought before the Council at midnight to tell his sad tale. He who had maintained, with all his quiet dignity, that whatever choices were made, surrendering Constantinople to the Turk was not, could not, be one of them. How it was to be saved, what options military, religious, logistical, all those he would listen to. And somehow he had kept his temper while others repeatedly lost theirs and accused their fellows of lack of true faith, of true courage, of true loyalty; while Papist denounced Orthodox, Venetian insulted Genoan, most despised the Greeks. Gregoras had, in his heart, always thought that Constantine was competent and no more. But he had seen the man grow with his mission. Not puffed with arrogance. Filled with his inheritance. He had been placed there at this time of crisis to do all that he could. And he would do it.

More than his emperor, the other man awake was the real reason Gregoras could not sleep – for how could he close his eyes before his brother? Theon sat opposite him, barely glanced at him, never spoke to him. Indeed neither of the Lascaris said much. They were not leaders in the defence – but they would put the decisions made by the leaders into effect. Yet as the night slipped towards dawn, Gregoras found that he was staring more and more at his twin, almost daring him to look up, to meet his gaze, to see the questions in his eyes, perhaps to read the truth there. Exhaustion, and the realisation that the siege was approaching its climax, that all their fates would be decided in the next few days, was making Gregoras reckless. He wanted to reach across the table, snap his fingers beneath his brother's eyes, force them to meet his and say, 'Your son is mine. Your wife still loves me. And I am going to take them back.' Amidst all the long night's talk of the crisis that approached, of no rescue fleet on the horizon and the failure of Pope and kings to come to the city's aid, of a defence stretched to breaking point and an enemy that would not stop, this had become the most important thing: to claim what was his again. To defeat not the Turk, but his own brother.

Perhaps he would have done it, in the silence that followed Constantine's last, quiet vow to continue when all around him stopped, if it hadn't been broken instead by the opening of the hall's door once more, and the entrance of the steward, who stared in some surprise at a table of largely sleeping men before approaching the emperor, bowing, whispering in his ear, handing him a scroll. Constantine broke the seal, rubbed his eyes, read. 'You were right, Theon Lascaris,' he said. 'If the sultan did not already know by his own intelligence that Christendom has forsaken us, he has learned of it through ours. But I marvel. Was it ten hours ago that the brigantine docked? Can rumours truly spread so fast?'

'They can, *basileus*.' Theon shook his head. 'Though the sailors were commanded to silence, yet they are men. They will have told their families, who would have told their neighbours, who would have told the shopkeepers, who would have told the Genoan merchants from Galata who supply them . . . who supply the Turks as readily as they do us. More readily, since the Turks have more gold.' He sighed. 'And may I ask how you know that Mehmet knows already, sire?'

Constantine raised the cone of paper. 'Because he says so here. As a brother sovereign, he is sorry for my disappointment. But to cheer me he has sent me an emissary – a Greek, no less, a vassal of his, one Ismail of Sinope, son of the prince of that province. This Ismail brings another offer for peace, one that will gladden my heart it seems. And he asks that emissaries be sent to negotiate.' A faint smile came, dispelled immediately by a yawn. 'Well,' he continued, 'shall we rouse these sleepers and hear what terms Mehmet now offers for our capitulation?'

Gregoras leaned forward. 'Lord,' he said, 'let them sleep. Or rather, wake them and send them to more comfortable beds. And let us go to ours as well. We know what Mehmet wants, however generously he gilds his offer. He wants our city. So let us answer his emissary, not unshaven and unwashed, and with a just rage that exhaustion might bring, but considered, rested and refreshed. Then let this Ismail take back the message that we are strong and united.' He smiled. 'And the longer it takes the better. Perhaps the guns will play less upon our walls while

Mehmet awaits our response. We can repair the breaches, amass our arms, and let our soldiers rest.'

Theon nodded. 'I agree with . . . I agree, lord. Rest and the full ceremony that an emissary requires might gain us some respite – and show us unwavering. Perhaps other forces are on their way – the Serbians. Hunyadi's Hungarians. Rumours can be spread that they are anyway. And as for emissaries . . .' he licked his lips, 'send me, lord.'

Constantine smiled. 'Ah, my loyal brothers Lascaris. Perhaps I should send you both?'

Theon stiffened, but it was Gregoras who spoke. '*Basileus*, my brother is versed in the subtleties of diplomacy. He is highly skilled in deception.' He felt Theon's eyes come onto him at last, held his gaze for a moment, then continued, 'Whereas I am a soldier. I can go where he cannot, see what he cannot. Not the nuances of leaders trying to convey an impression, but what the ordinary soldier is feeling. If they have heard tales of us, we have heard of them also. Of men who have sat in a wet field for seven weeks and watched the greatest army ever assembled stumble against our walls, die in their scores, again and again.' He smiled. 'Genoan traders work both sides of the walls and I am, at least in part, a Genoan now. Send me, lord, where I can be of most help: discovering just how disaffected many of Mehmet's army are. Finding where he is weak as well as strong.'

Constantine stared at him for a moment, then nodded. 'Let it be so. Rest, then go, both of you to your tasks. I will wake these others and try to sleep too.' He yawned, leaned on the table, closed his eyes. The brothers began to move to the door . . . but the emperor stopped them there. 'Not all the rumours I hear are of war,' he called. 'I have heard another: that though you were born almost at the same instant, from the same womb, there is no love between you. That you do not speak. Is it true?'

The two men froze in the doorway, half turned back. Neither answered.

'So, it is true.' Constantine moved round the table, came to them at the door. 'I know what it is to have brothers. I have three . . . had, since our late emperor, my brother John, is dead. Of the other two, Thomas loves me and Demetrius . . .' he sighed, 'Demetrius claimed the crown. Many a time I have wished he had it now. That he was standing here and I was in the Morea, raising an army to come to this city's aid. But is he? He hates me, so I doubt it. Would I have done? I would like to believe so, but . . .' A half-smile came, fading fast. 'But if he does come, if he was standing here, I would say to him what I say to you, what I have said to the squabbling Italians, the sundered Christians. There is a time for strife between brothers. But this is not that time. This is the time only to trust in God and defend His city. To ask forgiveness for any harm each has done to the other, for both will have harmed. And to go into the righteous fight with anger only for God's enemies.' He stepped closer, put an arm around each of them. 'Do I not speak the truth?'

They were trapped, between an emperor and an oaken door. There was little either could do. It was Theon who reached a hand, Gregoras who took it. Brother touched brother for the first time in an age, and Constantine gave a cry of joy and pressed them closer. Yet he could not see their eyes, the gaze that met, held, parted.

'Go now,' said the emperor, 'in brotherly amity and about God's work.'

He turned back, calling loudly. Their hands sliding away as if from contagion, Theon and Gregoras left the room. In the narrow hallway beyond, servants scurried to Constantine's call and the two men had to wait for them to pass. 'Well, brother,' Theon said, 'do you heed our sovereign's words? Will you part from me in peace?'

Gregoras turned. The servants had passed and they were alone in the lightless antechamber. 'I heed a portion of them, Theon,' he replied, as softly. 'There is only one enemy to be fought – for now. But know this: whether the city stands or falls, if both of us are spared what is to come, I will find you, and there will be a reckoning.' He leaned closer, took his brother's arm in a very different grip. 'For you have what is mine.'

Strangely, Theon felt no fear. When they were infants, he had learned that he could never better his brother in strength. But he had also learned that there were many ways to defeat a man. 'Then come, Gregoras. Come at the beginning or the ending of the world. And discover, yet again, that there are bonds not even the strongest man can break.'

With that, he was gone, through the door a servant left ajar. Gregoras let him go, listening to the sounds of the room stirring behind him, of voices he knew, grown men woken suddenly and so as querulous as children. Beyond them, he heard another sound, a rumbling that he took at first to be cannon fire but realised was a low peal of thunder. Storm's coming, he thought. Shrugging, he moved towards it.

TWENTY-NINE

Thunder

24 May: forty-eighth day of the siege

'Does the storm come to fall on us, my friend, or will it pass us by?'

At first, Hamza did not turn at Mehmet's question. Standing at the entrance to his lord's great *otak*, he shifted his gaze from the departing Council – from Candarli Halil and Ishak Pasha, conspiring still as they walked away, all smiles – to the west. 'Lightning plays there yet, noble one. But it does not seem to have moved any closer.' He dropped the tent flap as another roll of thunder came. 'Yet I wish it would. The air craves it. It feels like the whole world is about to explode.'

'You want more rain?' Mehmet shook his head. 'Did you not hear that ten of my janissaries died when their sodden trench collapsed on them? Drowned.' He shivered. 'A bad sign, when men drown on the land.'

Hamza came back to the table, looked at the two men sitting at it. Zaganos Pasha, most loyal of the sultan's commanders, most fervent for the war, gave an almost imperceptible shake of the head. Do not let him read the signs, the shake said. Do not let him plunge further into this gloom.

Hamza looked from one man to the other. To Mehmet. He had changed in the seven weeks of the siege. The strain showed in a face made lean by struggle and doubt. But it was in his actions, his reactions, that the change showed the most. If the two councillors who had just left had spoken to him then as they had just done now, urging an immediate cessation of the siege, a return to Edirne, a dispersal of his army, Mehmet would have driven them from his pavilion with shrieks, perhaps even with blows from his *bastinado*. All had seen how he had treated the disgraced Baltaoglu. Instead he had dismissed Halil Pasha, Ishak Pasha – cautious men he loathed, his father's men – with a shrug, an *inshallah*, murmuring how he would consider their good advice.

Hamza knew as well as Zaganos that they must not let the sultan dwell on signs like the drowning of janissaries. Like any man, his mood could be shifted with thought, with a focus on what had been accomplished, not what had failed. And in this too, Mehmet had surprised his chief falconer who was also now his admiral. Hamza had believed him to be naïve in the ways of war, book-taught, lacking the practicality of experience, dreaming of the great heroes of the past, of Alexander and Caesar, with no understanding of how to become like them. Yet in seven weeks, in some ways he had shown himself their rival. It was Mehmet who dispersed the forces to pressure all sides of the city, Mehmet who commanded that ships be taken across land to infiltrate the Horn and turn the Greeks' flank, Mehmet who studied the working of guns and calculated the angles and trajectories needed to fire over the walls of neutral Galata and still hit the ships that guarded the boom. He took advice from experts – another sign of good generalship and of his maturing – but the drive, the impetus, the commands came from him.

He had become a soldier. Grown into a man. And yet, like many who shed the heat of youth for cooler considerations, he was more prone to doubts. Seven weeks, and all his drive and innovation had not led to success. The boom still held his biggest ships from the Horn. The walls his cannons knocked down were patched with a wooden stockade that the Greeks defended as vigorously as any stonework. His tunnels were discovered and blown up, his tower consumed in flame. Wave after wave of Allah's warriors had hurled themselves forward, and only once had the Prophet's standard been raised on a bastion . . . and then but for a moment.

Hamza studied the sultan, wondering how to begin, how to counter the doubts that the two old pashas had left behind them like a sack of ordure upon the table. He hesitated, seeking words . . . and then, in the camp, two muezzins began to call almost simultaneously. Both had fine voices, one with the fire of youth, a dramatic passion in the rising notes, commanding the faithful to prayer; the other older, his voice like silk, his call almost a seduction. Each had their adherents. And it seemed to Hamza, as the three men removed their slippers, knelt, touched their foreheads to the floor and began their whispered prayer – 'God is great. God is great. No God but Allah. Muhammad is His messenger' – that a blend of both their calling was what Mehmet needed now. Fire tempered by consideration. Steel swathed in silk.

When the prayers ended, Hamza was ready. He laughed. 'Old goats!' he said. 'How they can turn good news into bad to suit their purposes!'

'Good news, Hamza?'

'The brigantine, lord of the horizon. It skulks back into Constantinople, bearing its tale of woe – no Christian fleet is coming, popes and kings have deserted them, the starving Greeks are on their own – and Candarli Halil the castrated ram and Ishak Pasha his ewe bleat that just because they were not found does not mean they are not on the way. They prefer what is not to what is.'

Zaganos leaned in, his face as eager. 'Bleats indeed! But it was always so with that pair. Baaing "nay" to everything you propose, lord. "N-a-y-ay-ay ay."' The Albanian pulled back his lips, stuck out his tongue, in a near-perfect imitation of the animal.

Both men laughed. 'It is true. All I have achieved they put down to God's will. All that has gone wrong is my fault,' Mehmet said.

'Is it not so?' Hamza nodded, continued, 'So why should we pay them any heed now? And even if they do come – though there is no sign of them – what do we care if another thousand

Christians show up? What care we for another ten? You slaughtered three times that at Kossovo Pol, lord, to the glory of Allah. Let them come, I say.'

'And I.' Zaganos thumped the table.

Mehmet flushed. 'Kossovo. Yes. We soaked the Field of Blackbirds in infidel blood that day.'

'Did you not, magnificence?' Hamza leaned in. 'And we can soak the stones before us too. Zaganos and I have been talking. We agree with you, lord. You urged the goats to one last effort, one huge attack. One that will make all others so far seem gnat bites to the savaging of a lion.' His voice dropped. 'One more, with all your forces, from all sides. One night attack, and the city falls.'

Both men stared at their sultan. They could see the conflict playing on his face. Desire, ardour, doubt came and went in succession. At last, he spoke. 'To do it, those forces would need to believe it could be done. They would have to forget seven weeks of failure and hurl themselves forward again and again, climb over the bodies of their comrades, die in their turn, on and on . . .' He faltered, and both men could see the horror come into his eyes. 'Only men who believe could do this. And I have heard rumours that the army has lost heart . . .'

'More bleatings from goats!' Zaganos stood to shout it, banging on the table. He had not risen from slavery to the command of a division to be frightened, even of a sultan.

But Hamza leaned closer, his voice silk, contrast to the other's fire. 'My friend, your loyal subject, speaks truth, lord. But let he and I go amongst your forces, and bring you news of them. Of the strength of their hearts. And remember, lord, that men fight for many beliefs. For Allah, most merciful, and the paradise that awaits should martyrdom call. For the glory of their people, the finest soldiers on earth. And for what the city promises – for they have not sat before these walls and fought as well as they have to return to their villages poorer than when they set out. Let us go amongst them, lord, and confirm this for you. And let us then pay no more heed to the bleatings of goats and listen only to what our hearts tell us.' He reached then, took the younger man by the arm. 'One more attack, lord. One more.'

Mehmet stared back, then laid his other hand atop of Hamza's and squeezed before releasing it and rising. 'Go amongst them, both of you. Tell me their hearts. And if we discover to be true what we all believe . . .' he smiled, the first time in a while, 'then I will lead them myself to the walls and beyond them.'

Both of the other men knelt, each reaching for one of Mehmet's hands, touching them to their foreheads. 'As you command.'

A noise from the tent's entrance. At first Hamza thought it might be distant thunder again. But then he realised that a man stood there, clearing his throat, the sultan's steward. 'Lord,' he said, when beckoned to speak, 'your emissary Ismail has returned from the city. He brings a Greek with him, one Theon Lascaris.'

'I know him, lord,' Hamza said. 'He is as twisted as the roots of a cedar from Lebanon. And, if I read him right, he has little stomach for the fight. If you were to make of him and his emperor impossible demands . . .' he smiled, 'then let me work on him again; we may have an ally when we need one. Not all goats are on one side of the walls.'

Mehmet nodded. 'Leave him to me.' He snapped his fingers. 'Bring me my armour, my sword. Let my household guard surround me.' Men began rushing to obey his commands. 'You two go – and find me out my army's heart.'

They left by the rear of the tent. When they were a safe distance from any ears, they crouched, raised their hoods against a spatter of raindrops. 'Do you think we will find what we seek, Zaganos? Will the army fight in the way we need them to?'

The Albanian nodded. 'They will. As you said, offer them God, glory and gold, and most men will fight for one of them.'

Hamza nodded. He looked to the west, where thunder

rolled and lightning jabbed at the earth. Then he looked to the east. He could just glimpse the top of the tower at the St Romanus gate. Even at this distance it looked huge. He shivered, though the air was close. 'But can we triumph?' he asked in a whisper.

'We can. We will.' Zaganos rose with a creak of joints, then turned and marched away. 'Don't you turn into a goat now, Hamza Be-ey-ey.'

The bleat was perfect. Hamza laughed. 'Go with God,' he called after him, then went the opposite way.

Gregoras felt the first of the rain and looked sharply up, glad that the storm was upon him at last, and that the terrible waiting – air growing so thick it began to choke him, lightning jabbing down in vivid spear thrusts, thunder crashing ever nearer like a titan's approaching footsteps – was over. Yet when he saw clouds that were not grey but a rusty-brown, and that they filled the sky in flat waves from the distant waters of Marmara to the Golden Horn, driving now towards the city, he looked swiftly to the earth again. He was not a man who set much store by signs and portents. But above all the battlefields he'd fought, he'd never seen a sky so full of blood, fat drops of it now thudding into his hood, as if bodies were dangling above him, with throats freshly slit.

He pulled his cloak tighter around him, hot though he was. He wanted air, and lifted his mask to get some, sucking in deep draughts, tasting its foulness, spitting out the iron. He thought of taking it off, didn't, for the same reason he wore one in most places in the world – his false nose attracted looks, some insults, attention.

He did not need it as a disguise. Not when he was among so many fellow Christians. The first of these he'd accompanied from Galata, joining a party of Genoan merchants of that city, off to trade with the Turk, riding one of their pack horses the long land route around the Horn, abandoning ride and traders before the towering walls of the Blachernae palace, from which he'd set out only eight hours before. And then he was with more Christians, for a good part of the sultan's army worshipped the Cross. As he'd begun to walk up the hill, unchallenged along the siege lines that paralleled the city walls, he heard Vlach cavalrymen from Wallachia, Hungarian gunners, Serb miners, the guttural bark of Bulgarian *azaps*. At last, when he'd forded the stream called the Lycus, where one hill descended and another began to climb, the languages shifted too, eastwards. To a variety of oriental tongues, most of which were unintelligible to him. But mainly to Osmanlica, which he spoke well. The river marked a boundary, that between the European levies of the sultan's army and its Anatolian heart.

It marked another boundary too. And Gregoras knew that his one long glance at the city there was as responsible for his shortness of breath as the foul sky above him. The vast numbers of the enemy was one thing. Their mighty cannon, the mightiest of which drowned out the thunder even as his feet got wet at the ford, was another.

But the wall . . .

He took more breaths, finding enough sweet amidst the foul to steady himself. He could not succumb to despair. He was there to spy, to report. So he looked again . . .

. . . at the outer wall, middle of the three, the one the generals had chosen to defend, because the higher, inner one was in such a state of disrepair and the one over the fosse too low. And here, where two hills climbed away from each other and a river ran, here Mehmet had moved his biggest cannon and increasingly concentrated his attacks. Gregoras knew because he had stood there upon the battlements, three hundred paces from where he stood now, could clearly see his comrades, many Greeks with the soldiers of Genoa, under the red cross. He had fought with them, helped drive each assault back.

'How?' he muttered to himself. 'Holy Father, how?'

Because there were no battlements. The middle wall was no longer there.

He knew that already, in his heart. He had seen the damage that the enemy's huge cannons had wrought. He had helped to repair it. But only standing here, behind their lines, could he see the extent of that damage, those repairs. The wall had been replaced, for a good four hundred paces, by a *stauroma*. This stockade was made from the slabs of broken stone of the former battlements, of timbers from pulled-down buildings and destroyed boats, of the trunks and branches of trees. Crates had been filled with straw and vine cuttings. Earth had been scooped from behind and bound the structure tight, and together with the skins of animals formed a softer surface for the cannon balls to sink into, absorbing some of their ferocity in a way the walls had not. Surmounting it all, barrels filled with earth and stone took the place of the former crenellations.

Gregoras knew all this. He had scooped, filled, levered, stacked. And yet seeing it now from the enemy's viewpoint, it looked so fragile, a toy built by a child for play. He could not understand how the vast forces arrayed against it and concentrated in this spot did not just walk up to it and, with one soft breath, blow it away.

The rain was a deluge now, the stockade shifting before his eyes, vanishing as he expected it to vanish. He turned from it. He had a full reckoning of his country's weakness. Now he had to do his job and gauge its enemy's strength.

Yet it was near impossible to see, let alone make any sort of tally. Hard too to keep his feet, in tracks transformed to mud streams in moments. A lightning bolt snatched his vision, forking down onto one of the few trees left standing on the plain. Fire shot from it, flaming branches tumbled onto shapes that screamed, leapt from the little shelter it had provided. And in a heartbeat, less, before the light was gone from the searing of his eyeballs, thunder came to assault his ears, right above him, Gregoras now the centre of the storm, dropping to his knees with the force of it.

He could not stay there, in the open. He knew that atop the hill facing the St Romanus gate, Mehmet had pitched his pavilion at the centre of the fight and a canvas city had grown up around him, and spread far behind. Somewhere, surely, in those winding alleys, there was someone who would give him shelter?

Head bent, he drove himself against the rain and up the slick slopes. Gaining the summit at last, at the same time he felt a slight lessening of the water's force, heard the thunder peal behind him, realised that the main body of the storm was moving past to engulf the city. He could see ahead now, Mehmet's tug to his right, its horsetails lying lank and sodden beneath bells too waterlogged to chime. He moved away from that, from the guards who would challenge any who got close, heading instead into a narrow path that nonetheless ran straight between the tents, one of many conduits in his camps that the Turk scrupulously left clear to speed his messengers. Men crowded beneath every eave, water cascading before them, others already shoving ahead of him to be admitted. Gregoras walked on, seeking a sign, some gap he could squeeze into.

He came to a crossroads of sorts, hesitated. To the right, to the north-east, were the European levies, more Christians amongst them. Perhaps they would give one of their faith, howsoever lapsed, some charity? But then he remembered who these men were, who they fought for, who against, and stepped forward.

Another crossroads, another choice. He looked to the left, and saw it. Before a small tent, a pole. At its apex, a scroll of vellum, sodden now, ink running from its folds like black blood. It was peculiar, and so he went to it, poked in a finger, peeled back the parchment enough to see the remains of a zodiac, his own symbol of the Gemini, just where his finger touched, dissolving as he did.

'A magus,' he muttered. The sign was an invitation to consult. He had three gold *hyperpyra* in his purse. They were meant to be used as bribes, if he needed them. One was far too much for even the most gifted of seers. Yet for shelter, a chance to get out of this rain?

He bent to the flap. 'Are you there?' he called. 'May I come in?'

It took a while for the reply. When it came, it was a woman who answered, her words clear. 'I have been expecting you.'

As Gregoras pulled open the flap, he was smiling. What sorceress worth a gold *hyperpyron* wouldn't have seen that I was coming? he thought.

He stepped inside . . . and his smile vanished.

Sitting on a carpet, in the centre of the tent, was Leilah.

THIRTY

Signs and Portents

Three horoscopes, inked on large vellum sheets, lay before her. Her own and those of her two men of destiny. Twins, in a way, for Gemini ruled the heavens now and both Mehmet and Gregoras.

Leilah stared down. There was a day five days hence, one of such power that she had never seen its like before. Mercury and the Sun were in conjunction, so huge achievements were possible. But Mars, god of war, was almost touching Uranus. So the risks that must be taken for such achievements were enormous.

It was a day when one world could end and another begin. When one man's triumph was another's disaster. With her between them, needing them both for her own triumph.

Yet the stars, as ever, spoke of opportunities, not certainties. They impelled. They did not compel. And for all her calculations, Gregoras's part was still dark to her; she could not bring him into the light. She could not simply trust to fate, not with so much strife in the heavens.

She needed to see him. She needed to compel him. Perhaps she needed to go and seek him, before the world exploded.

She'd thought all this — and then there he was. Standing in her tent, eyes so wide above his mask that she could only laugh. Laughter of joy, of doubts banished, of hope and prophecy both fulfilled in a moment. 'What . . . ?' he was saying. 'How . . . ?'

Delight bore her up, flowing from the ground, to stand before him, look up into those wide eyes, as green as she remembered them. Her tent was hot, for she kept a brazier ever alight to burn her incense upon, to heat liquids, to turn to smoke certain words she wrote down. She could see wisps of steam already rising from his soaked cloak. 'Come, Gregoras,' she said, as calmly as she could, reaching up to the clasp at his neck. 'Surely you will be more comfortable if you are not wet?'

His hand folded over hers. He was shocked, he who did not shock easily, and for a long moment he could not think beyond the surprise, could only hold her hand, feel the heat in it, in the tent, in her eyes. Then something in them shifted something in him. He could not remember the last time he'd laughed. With her, probably. So it seemed right to laugh with her again.

He did, letting go of her hand. 'What kind of sorcery is this?' he said.

'My kind,' she replied, flicking the clasp at his neck now, heaving the sodden wool off his shoulders. She reached with her fingers, pushing them up into his sweat-damp hair.

'Leilah,' he murmured. She was dressed for the heat and for privacy, dressed in little, a silken shift, held in straps from her shoulders. The brazier-light flickered from below, casting shadows, showing a deeper darkness at the tip of her breasts, at the joining of her legs. 'Leilah,' he said again, more thickly.

'Talk, talk,' she replied, slipping her hand around the back of his head.

They kissed, her mouth opening, tongues meeting, she sucking hard upon his as if to draw him down, her weight adding to the tug. He fell to his knees, her before him, and she swung onto hers so she could grab the buttons on his doublet, open them one by one. When the last one popped, he shrugged out of the garment, then out of the *shalvari* that swathed his legs. 'Better.' She reached again, pulling his mask aside. 'Best.'

He groaned, reached to the silk at her shoulder. It was her hand that closed over his now, her delay. 'Tell me . . . and I will know the truth . . .' she breathed. 'Am I the first you have had since Ragusa?'

He had no need to lie. 'Yes,' he whispered, his eyes in hers.

She saw her again, the aristocratic bitch he had followed in Constantinople. He loved her, she knew, she had seen, in his face then, in her dreams since. But he had not lain with her. Could not, perhaps. And that was good.

She cupped his face in one hand. 'And I have had no one. Wanted no one. Want no one . . . but you.'

She released his hand. He tore the silken shift from her then, followed where she led him. She was swollen thick with her desire. But here, now, at last, he had no need to rush, and it took a time before he reached her limit, with her huge dark eyes a hand's breadth away. Life is strange, he thought, before thought became impossible, just one more impossible thing.

The storm returned, or another one came, burst upon them, thunder rolling them up in its roar, rain clattering onto the hide roof so loud it drowned all their sounds. For this she was glad, for she never liked to restrain the joy she took in lovemaking, and giving vent to it in a war camp, even so close to the whores, would have drawn attention or worse. The storm was at its height for a long while, as long as they were joined, and only when it began to pass did their cries subside. Not fade entirely, for one bout of lovemaking bled into another, less wild, more like a dream. At the end she was above him, barely moving, staring down into eyes that stared into hers. Till he rose up, clasped her tightly, burying his last cry in her breasts as the rain finally ceased.

They lay there, naked in each other's arms, as heartbeats slowly returned to normal. Gregoras would have been content to lie there for a day and a night, to sleep as he had not slept in weeks. He tried for a little while, let his eyes follow the shadow play of lamplight on the tent walls, where pinned parchment scraps bore zodiacal signs, Arabic script, that moved as if speaking. But he could not last long. Time pressed him, his city called. And questions crowded.

He sat up, stared down. 'How . . . ?' he said.

She was up in a moment too, a finger to his lips. 'How is lost. It was written and it has come to pass. Ask, rather, why.'

He smiled. 'Why?'

Instead of answering, she reached, pulled the silken shift over herself, then moved to a corner, returning with two beakers. He took one, sipped, and cool sherbet delighted his tongue. Draining it, he put the vessel down, looked at her again, asked again, 'Why?'

It was time for truth, simple and direct. 'Because I need you to get something for me. From Constantinople. When the city falls.'

'*If* it falls.'

'When. It is written. It is seen. It is destiny.'

He looked up, at the sigils on the walls. The strangeness of it all, of their reunion. It made him suddenly angry. 'I do not believe in any destiny I do not see and write for myself,' he said brusquely.

'Then see this, Gregoras.' She leaned closer. 'Believe or not, a wise man prepares for what may be. Even you must think that the city may fall.'

He shrugged. 'It is possible. Yes. So?'

'So prepare for the possible.' She took a breath. 'There is a monastery, just within your crumbling walls. The monastery of Manuel.'

He frowned. Only that morning he had listened to its bells. It was not anything he'd expected her to say. 'I . . . I know it.'

'A library is part of it.'

'It is a place of learning. For certain schools of study.'

'Certain schools? One especially.' She nodded. 'The monks there study the alchemical arts, do they not?' He did not respond, so she continued. 'They have collected many manuscripts, books and documents. Unique. Beyond price. There is one especially, written by Jabir ibn Hayyan, whom the Latins call Geber. His works have been translated. But the original manuscript, in his own hand, with *his* notes in the margins, the monks of Manuel possess. It is, possibly, the most important book in the world.'

'How do you know this?'

'Another how. Another unimportant how. Again, only the why matters.' She reached, took his hand. 'I need you to steal it for me.' Gregoras gave a little gasp, tried to withdraw his hand. She held him tight, leaned still closer. 'When the forces of Allah storm in, the monastery will be one of the first places they sack, for it is close to the walls. They will steal what they can and burn what they cannot carry away. I will come, with a troop of soldiers that the sultan will give me, and secure the place. But if I come too late . . .' She sighed. 'So you must go there, steal it, protect it, till I come . . .'

'And why would I do that?' He smiled faintly. 'It would be hard – but you notice I do not ask you how.'

She smiled back. 'From the moment I met you, when you rescued me from those thugs in Ragusa, I knew you were the chosen one, the man of destiny who would do what I needed done. And as for why?' She lifted his hand, licked the length of one finger, teeth closing briefly over its tip. 'Will you not do it for love, my lover? For the rewards I can offer?'

He freed his hand, ran the finger down her face, withdrew it, turned away. 'I cannot. Not . . . not just for love. There are people in the city . . .' he hesitated, 'people I . . . care for. If it does fall, I must protect them. And if you have some way of doing that, then . . .' he shrugged, turned back, 'then we may have a deal.'

Care for? she thought. He was going to say 'love'. A flash of the aristocratic beauty's face flung red into Leilah's eyes but she swallowed the jealousy down. 'The troops that Mehmet gives me I can lead anywhere. To a house, perhaps? They will protect any inside it if I order them to.'

Gregoras shook his head. 'And how do you have such power over a sultan?'

'He owes me a boon.'

'For what?'

She did not answer straightaway. Instead she stood, reached to the tent's ceiling, plucked a parchment from it. Then she bent to the brazier, held the papyrus above it. Immediately it began to crisp, then burn. Holding it till flames seemed to swallow her fingers, when the paper was ash, she dropped it into a copper tray. 'For his victory,' she whispered, not looking at him.

Gregoras stood too, turning away from her, needing to bend under the roof as she did not. He was suddenly chilled, despite the warmth in the tent, and he began to hastily pull on his clothes. He was a soldier, an educated man. He did not set much store by the seeing of witches. And yet . . . ? This reunion. The way they were bound together. And there he was – about to do a witch's bidding.

He knew he would do it, though there was a part of him that burned to even contemplate his city's fall. Yet she was right – a wise man prepared for the possible. A soldier scouted a line of retreat. A thought came, and quadrupled. 'I have a better idea,' he said, turning, starting on the buttons of his doublet. 'A better place than a house.'

'Name it.'

'It is a church, a small one: St Maria of the Mongols. It is half a league from the Blachernae palace, less. About the same distance from the monastery. It does not look much like a church from the outside, and a high wall surrounds it. A few determined men could hold it for a short time . . . until protection arrives.' He hesitated. 'I may not be one of those men. I may be delayed – or dead upon the walls. If so . . .' he leaned closer to her, 'in exchange for this text, all within the walls must be protected. All.'

She studied him. He was speaking of this lady now, perhaps her children. Well, she thought, if he is dead and the woman gives me my great desire, I will protect her and hers. But if he lives . . . I will win him from anyone.

Reaching down, she rubbed her hand between her legs before raising it to his brow. He felt the slickness upon them as she slid her fingers down, making his eyelids sticky, passing over his ivory nose. 'So,' she said, as she did, 'I believe a bargain has been made. And sealed,' she added, pressing her fingers onto his mouth.

He could taste the two of them, conjoined. It excited, as much as it disturbed. 'Leilah,' he murmured, reaching up his own hand to hers.

But she slipped away, bent to a box, opened it. There were inks within, a stylus, scraps of paper. 'Draw me a map to your church. Draw it from the gate of Charisius.'

He wiped his mouth, bent, sketched. It did not need much, so close to the walls was the place he'd named. When he finished, she took the paper from him, and replaced it with another. 'This is a copy of the front piece of the book you seek.'

He studied the cursive script. He spoke very little Arabic, read less. But he could see the name in a signature: Jabir ibn Hayyan.

'Will you be able to find it?'

He looked up. It was the first time he'd heard anything other than complete certainty in her voice. He nodded. 'I was not always an ugly soldier. There was a time when I knew my way around the libraries of Constantinople.' Besides, he thought, but did not say, I know an alchemist. 'I will find it for you.'

She took his hand, kissed it. 'I know you will. For . . .'

' . . . it is written,' he said, as she did. And they both laughed. 'Leilah . . .' he whispered then, 'there is something . . .'

There had been a murmuring under their talk, a building background they had ignored. But they could not ignore the rising clamour that ended in a huge shout. 'Come,' she said, pulling on a dress, a headscarf, a veil.

He finished dressing too, slipped into his boots, wound his sword belt round his waist. When they were both ready, they stepped out of the tent.

369

No one noticed them, though there were plenty of men about. All of them were facing east. Not in preparation for prayer, though some had dropped to their knees. Her tent was on top of a hill, and they could see down over the canvas city to the stone one beyond. To Constantinople, where man's weapons had been succeeded by God's, as lightning bolts fell.

She took his arm. She whispered, 'Signs and portents.'

— THIRTY-ONE —

The Cursed City

24 May: forty-eighth day of the siege: later

Those who were not on the walls – defending them, repairing them – were in the streets. For the longest time Sofia, shuddering as she remembered the other crowd she'd been caught in three weeks before, could not make herself step from the portico on the edge of the Forum of Constantine. But though this crowd was large, it was quiet as it shuffled slowly forward, the eyes of the people lifted to the heavens from which lightning had only just ceased to fall, their arms falling rhythmically onto their chests, their mouths moving in prayer. They were not there for bread. They were there for the Virgin. And when the statue was borne past, when Sofia glimpsed her husband among the courtiers who attended the emperor as he walked, head bared, just behind the bier, she grasped each of her children firmly by the hand and plunged into the procession.

The crowd was thick, yet all took care for their neighbour and her fears soon calmed. Not so Thakos, her sensitive son, still with the slight limp that was the bread riot's legacy, the tic that came every little while, as if he was always startled. So many of the children of the city jerked thus, and looked like him. Thinned by lack of food, shadowed around the eyes from too little sleep, and that little disturbed by the ceaseless play of guns. He never stopped looking about him as if seeking someone, and held her hand tight to the point of pain.

It was different with her other child. She had to be held, for Minerva would happily have slipped away to run among the mob. Her dauntless daughter, five and unafraid. Sometimes

371

Sofia wondered at what children took from their parents. Thakos was bold Gregoras's son, and Minerva the child of cool Theon, yet both could have sprung from the other's seed. And both from her, of course, and maybe that was what made them. Her ardour in the one, her reserve in the other.

Holding tight, held tight, she looked ahead. First to her husband, a few paces back from the emperor, behind the priests but many places closer than he would have been before the siege began. He had made himself valuable. It was he whom Constantine had just sent to reject the latest demand to surrender. It meant she seldom saw him, which she did not truly mind. It also meant that, on occasion, their children were better fed than those of her neighbours, with scraps from the imperial table.

She looked beyond Theon, above Constantine, to the moving platform that preceded them. At what – who – was upon it. And then her voice joined with those around her and she forgot that *she* was a mother and focused instead on another. The statue was life-sized, the face so exquisitely rendered that it did not seem to be plaster and paint but living flesh. Holy Maria was among them, above them yet connected to them, leading them, not carried by them, alive in every one of them. Christ's mother, the protector of them all, and her city was Constantinople, as it had always been, as it would be for ever, she the mother of it and every single soul within it.

And this her day of days. It was always important. Yet all knew how much more in need of her protection the city was this day. All knew that the final crisis was upon them, that the Turk was making preparations for one great assault. So the journey she took yearly, from her home at the Church of the Holy Apostles, along the Meze and through the great forums to the cathedral of the Hagia Sophia, had a special meaning today. That was why all who could be spared from the walls followed her now. It no longer mattered who professed the Roman creed and who the Greek. They were all her children, as Christ was, brothers and sister under the Cross, however it was shaped.

'Holy Maria. Holy Mother. Listen to our prayers. Stay by our sides. Deliver us from all evil. Save us sinners. Save us. Save us. Save us.'

As she intoned the words, Sofia felt her limbs ease. It was ever thus for her, but usually the release came when she was where another Maria was reverenced, at St Maria of the Mongols. Often alone there, tending the holy place, she could surrender to the mystery, yield herself, lie before the altar screen, stare up at the ikons, pray and weep. She was less open when others gathered there, less comfortable in a crowd. The Holy Maria was her mother, and alone Sofia heard her speak in her heart.

And yet? Here she was, in a vast crowd, and she felt the feeling come over her. Never had she needed it more. Not for herself. For her city, which she loved. For her children, who she would see live free there. For all her family who had lived there for a thousand years, she believed, and would, by Christ's good grace, for another thousand and more. She looked up to the Virgin's face, as it turned towards her when they rounded the corner. She saw the Virgin's tears, felt them as that and not as the raindrops that had begun to tumble again from a tormented sky. Saw her sad smile, saw in it her compassion for all.

'Holy Maria. Holy Mother. Listen to our prayers. Stay by our sides. Deliver us from all evil. Save us sinners. Save us. Save us. Save us.'

And then she saw it. The fear in the Virgin's painted eyes. As if she was looking straight at Sofia, appealing to her alone, in unspoken words that passed straight into her heart. 'Save *me*,' the Virgin cried, as she began to fall.

It was such a little misstep. Theon saw it because he happened to be looking at him, the oldest of the bier bearers, marvelling at the pure whiteness of his long beard. Ten men bore the

Virgin up, priests all, the handles of the platform distributing the weight amongst them. They were not all as old as the one Theon looked at; most were younger and as vigorous as any man, black beards flowing over their robes. It made him angry again – how could a city where priests and monks outnumbered soldiers four to one be defended? Yet he knew they had their function too. Monks watched the walls while warriors slept, and were the main movers of materials for repair. Priests? They did what they were doing now. Kept the eyes of the people focused ever upwards, to God and His protection. To the Virgin, whose special care the city was. The mass of people truly believed that between them – Holy Father, Holy Mother – Constantinople was safe. That any invader, even if he breached the walls, would be smitten with divine fire on the very threshold of Santa Sophia, the archangels leading a counterattack that would drive the infidels to hell.

Theon was not so sure. It was not that he did not believe, did not pray. But only that day he had been beyond the walls to the enemy's camp. He had counted till the numbers were beyond even his counting, had seen how strong that innumerable horde was, how well fed and armed. Had seen the monstrous guns close to, looked back at what ruins those guns had made of the city's vaunted defences, and the pathetic melding of mud and timber thrown up in their place. It was the first time he had truly feared, even as, on behalf of his emperor, he rejected the offer the sultan had made, noting by the ill-disguised relief on Mehmet's face that it was one never meant to be accepted. Even as Theon made an unacceptable counter-offer in his turn. Both sides knew they had gone past the point of compromise, if such a point had ever existed. Then he had looked beyond the gloating sultan to his shadow, the man he had met twice before – Hamza, a pasha now, wearing the arms and insignia of the admiral he'd become.

They had not spoken. The Turk obviously saw no need. His comradely smile was enough, his knowing eyes. We will be in your city in days, the look said. Taking care of our friends.

And, to his shame, the first thing Theon did on his return to Constantinople was to check that no one in his household had disturbed, in its hiding place, the gift Hamza had given him. The banner with the Turk's *tugra* upon it was safe. And if valiant defence and ceaseless prayer yielded to incredible odds . . .

It was while brooding on this, even as his lips moved in prayer for salvation, that Theon's eyes fixed on the oldest of the bier bearers, on the cumulus whiteness of his beard. Saw the stumble, a slip of foot on stones slickened by ceaseless rain. Saw the next man ahead try to adjust to the sudden shift of weight, fail, the man ahead adjust more, fail. Saw the Virgin's eyes, till then fixed on heaven and the mercy she was seeking for them all, swivel to the earth.

She fell. Slipped off the side of the platform, her base pivoting off the bearer to her left, who tried to halt her and could not, succeeding only in accelerating her spin, so that her hooded head was pointing down and she plunged like a jab of lightning towards the earth. Enough hands reached in panic to slow her, so that she did not shatter her plaster face on the ground. But she landed hard, stood for a moment as if balancing, then toppled over.

Prayers fractured into screams, into howls of horror, terror, despair. 'Holy Maria! Virgin Mother! No! No! No!' It was all their mothers lying in the filth, as the sky, which had darkened as they advanced, began to spew wind-whipped rain.

The emperor came out of his horror first. 'Up! Up!' he cried, striding round the bier. 'Cardinal! Patriarch! All of you. Join me. Raise her!'

Ten paces back, Sofia tried to push forward. But the crowd was as united in horror as that other had been in hunger and formed as impenetrable a wall before her. So instead she stepped to the side, pulled her children, did what she could do. Fell onto her knees, heedless of filth. Prayed. 'Holy Maria. Holy Mother. Rise. Rise and save us.'

She was one of scores, lamentations poured into the louring

sky. But prayers will not do this, thought Theon, who had pressed forward with his emperor and saw that desperation was making people pull and push in opposite ways, too many leaders there, of Church and State, trying to command. 'Leave her,' bellowed Constantine finally, and men at last stepped back. 'Only you, my guard,' he yelled, and his own soldiers stepped forward, bent, and at his command and with his aid, lifted. The virgin came up, wobbled, was held firm. The platform was raised again, onto guards' shoulders now, and the statue, its face besmirched, placed upon it.

'Forward!' commanded Constantine, at the head of the bier, Theon at his side. All knew the impression that the people would have taken. It was a ghastly omen at the very moment when all needed the very best. The emperor had to counter it, to proceed to St Sophia and the ceremony there. Despite the horror, most people would not have seen the fall. Maybe something could be saved.

And then the storm, the latest, the mightiest, fell fully upon the city. The wind had changed, drove from the east now, filled with the water it had lifted from the Black Sea. Theon smelled the salt tang of it, even as it smashed into him and all there, drenching them in moments. Constantine exhorted, cardinal and patriarch shouted, prayers were snatched away by the wind. To no avail. It was as if the Virgin, having fallen in that spot, refused to leave it. They had progressed not ten paces before the statue began to wobble.

'Lord,' cried Theon, shouting to be heard, 'she must not fall again. We must take her back. Try later!'

Constantine stared at him for a long moment, then looked up to where Maria swayed. 'You are right,' he yelled back, then reached to the captain of his guards and bellowed in his ear. The command was passed, the bier was lowered, the Virgin steadied then lifted from her place. Sofia, who had followed despite the rain and two complaining children, had pushed her way close through a crowd that the sudden violence of the storm had thinned. She was a few paces away when the Holy

Mother was brought to the ground. She saw the guard take off his sodden cloak and throw it over the statue. Saw the Virgin's muddied face just before it was covered. The rain had battered it, unfixed its paint, and from her dissolving eyes Maria shed black tears.

Sofia sobbed. Then she took a deep breath and pulled her children away from the sight, through the wailing mob. I know where she still stands, she thought. And I will seek her there.

With the wind now at her back and the rain pushing her forward, Sofia began the long walk to St Maria of the Mongols.

25 May: forty-ninth day of the siege

'Could you kindly explain to me, Greek, why we are groping around here like the blind?'

The Scotsman's voice came from no more than an arm's length away. Yet the Scotsman himself could not be seen. 'Shh!' said Gregoras.

'Shh?' queried John Grant. 'Shh because you think there's more than you and me here, or—'

'I am trying to find our way, man.'

'Are you another Greek like Theseus, with Ariadne's thread in your mitt? That may be the only way through this pig's ordure of a fog. Or are you sniffing our route out? No, sorry, forgot. Sniffing's not your strongest ability, is it?'

'For the love of Christ, will you stop talking?'

'Oh, and is it Christ's work we do here? When you dragged me from my important tasks with whispers and nods, I thought it might be the other fella's work we were about. Certainly this fog could only be the devil's own creation.'

Gregoras was about to snap again, to bid silence. But he knew it would do little good. If sight had been taken away from them, it seemed that sound had too. There was no noise in the city, apart from Scottish prattling. Even the Turkish guns were silent, as if the enemy also thought that the Horned

One had the world beneath his cape and should not be disturbed. 'Not you too, Grant,' sighed Gregoras, pressing his back into the wall of what he still hoped was their destination. 'Do you believe this is another curse upon our city?'

'Well, I am more a man of science, ye ken. But this cannot be good, can it? Has the city ever had a fog this late in May before?'

'Not in a thousand years, that I heard. And together with the fall of the Virgin yesterday, the lunar eclipse and the strange light that played on St Sophia . . .' He shivered. 'It would be hard not to believe in ill omens.'

'Well, let people believe what they will. You and I are soldiers and we know that, omens or no omens, there are things we can be doing for the defence. Things I should be doing now, if it weren't for this mole's game.' Gregoras heard the sound of a beard being scratched hard. 'Or are you telling me that this secrecy we are about is *for* that defence?'

'Yes. It is,' Gregoras lied, feeling bad, but for a moment. He needed the alchemist here, not the engineer. Besides, Grant owed him. The Scotchman would not be here, defending, if it weren't for him. Despite the mist around them, Gregoras's knowledge of the city had got them from the walls the few hundred paces to what he hoped was their destination. But he couldn't be sure until . . .

'Shh!' he said again, not because he was listening for his desire again but because he thought he'd heard it. And there it was . . . plainsong, a score of voices raised in prayer. Close by, if the grey muffling did not deceive him. 'Come,' he said, groping for an arm, finding it. 'We are here. Come!'

Grant rose with him. 'Where?' he asked.

'The monastery of Manuel.'

'Bugger a virgin!' the Scotsman exclaimed, jerking his arm free. 'Why have you brought me back here?'

Gregoras halted. 'Back? You know it.'

'It has one of the finest libraries of alchemical texts in God's wide world,' Grant replied. 'Not to mention some interesting treatises on explosives . . . which of course is linked to alchemy. You think I would not consult them?'

'So you know your way around the library?' Gregoras's heart was beating a little faster as he once more reached and pulled the other man forward.

'Aye. Is that what we are here to visit?'

'It is.' Gregoras was running his free hand along the stonework. As it hit wood, the chanting grew a little clearer. 'And this is the gate.'

'Shall I knock upon it?' grunted the Scot.

'Better not.' Gregoras was feeling the wall beside the gate. He seemed to remember . . . 'Yes,' he said, feeling vegetation, the thickness of vine. He guided the other's hand to it. 'Better to climb.'

'Indeed,' Grant said, not moving. 'To enter unannounced, like . . . thieves, perhaps? Are you planning on stealing something?'

'Borrowing it. Borrowing to protect it. Just in case the omens are correct.'

'Indeed,' the Scotsman said again, and there was a long pause during which Gregoras's heart beat all the faster. He did not know what he would do if the other man baulked. 'Rightho,' Grant suddenly said, pulling away, beginning to climb.

Gregoras peered into the mist. 'You'll help me?'

'I will. Anything for a comrade. Besides,' he called down, 'since I am here, there are a few texts I intend to *protect* too, ye ken.'

Gregoras reached for holds, hoisted himself up, soon encountered a hand that grasped his and tugged. Both men straddled the wall, though further reaching found no more vines. 'Ach, come, it can't be a long drop,' whispered the Scot, and launched himself into the mist.

It wasn't, though both men stumbled. Then they were up, Grant leading, long arm waving ahead, finally scraping on another wall. 'I think the door is this way,' he hissed, 'but might there not be fellows about?'

'With fortune they will all be at their prayers for a while yet.' Gregoras turned his ear to listen to the swell of plainsong. 'A little while. Make haste.'

The Scot groped up the stairs, turned the latch, opened the door . . . and though it only had a few oil lamps in it, the light in the hall dazzled them. 'This way,' Grant whispered, striding away from the now much louder sound of chanting that came through a chapel door, half ajar. They moved down a corridor, to another oaken door at its far end. This had a symbol on it, a strange arrow with a circle in place of flights. Grant paused. 'And what knowledge is it that you seek within, adept?' he said, his tone suddenly deep.

In answer, Gregoras reached in his pouch and pulled out the copy that Leilah had given him of the front piece. He held it up, and Grant squinted, then whistled. 'Geber?' he said. 'They have that here?'

'So I am told.'

'By the one you are *protecting* it for?' The Greek nodded. 'Aye, well, I'll find it for ye, if I can. But if I do, you may have to give me a wee look at it myself. For the knowledge it contains is beyond price.'

And with that, the Scot pushed open the door.

The library was well lit. It revealed to Gregoras a large room, a scriptorium filled with the writing lecterns of the monks, lined in shelves that reached from the floor to a high ceiling, and these filled with wooden boxes, great vellum-bound tomes, leather canisters. Seeing them, Gregoras groaned, aware of the plainsong in the distance. It had been a while since he had heard a liturgy through. But the notes seemed to be heading towards a climax.

'Don't concern yourself, lad,' Grant said, heading to the south wall. 'It is a library, and there is an order to such places.'

'Can I also look?'

'Aye, ye can,' Grant called. 'On the west wall there is where the alchemical texts are found. I believe they are stacked according to country. Spain, France, the German states. The

Byzantines. Seek the ones with Arab sigils on the spine. Do so while I delve in chemicals . . . Ah, here!'

Gregoras stood before the walls, stared. At first the symbols all bled together, but, focusing, he soon began to sort the familiar from the strange. The majority of the texts were in ancient Greek and Latin, both of which he could read. Soon, on a lower shelf, he spied first the cursive script of the Persians, then the Arabs. But there were so many, he began to chew his lip, repeatedly looking down at the symbol on the paper he'd been given, looking up and losing it in the variety before him.

Despairing, he turned to call . . . and Grant was at his elbow, rolling several sheets of paper into a cone. 'There . . .' he gestured to the lower shelf, 'that is all Jabir ibn Hayyan. Do you not see his *tugra*?'

Gregoras did not . . . and then he did, the same one that was on his paper. He crouched, stared at several tubes before him. Grant knelt beside him. 'Let me see, it could be . . .' he peered, 'any one of these.'

Gregoras looked back, to the door. Only silence came through it now. 'Swiftly,' he said. 'The monks have finished chanting.'

'Aye, so they have,' Grant replied distractedly, scratching his beard. Then he shook his head. 'You know, it is not here.'

'What?' Gregoras exclaimed, rising with the Scot. 'It must be.'

'It's not . . .' Grant looked around the room. 'It's not, because it's . . . there.'

He pointed, then crossed the room to one of the lecterns. As they got near, Gregoras saw a wax seal hanging down, dangling at the end of a blue ribbon. It spun slightly as they approached, and he saw the same symbol that was on his paper. 'Aye,' said Grant, stepping close. 'Geber for sure.' He peered closer, then whistled. 'Man, you never told me it was an original. Mind that . . .' he hissed, as Gregoras moved round and reached. 'That paper will be fragile.'

'It cannot be helped.' Gregoras rolled the crackling pages as swiftly and as carefully as time allowed. Which was none. Not with footsteps in the corridor, voices getting nearer.

'I am a scholar,' said the Scot, stepping forward. 'Let me talk our way out.'

'I am a soldier,' replied the Greek, cramming the papers into a leather canister before yelling, 'Retreat!'

There were five men in the corridor. But the two thieves were tall and burly and the suddenness of their bursting out of the door did not leave the monks much time to react. By the time they had, screaming to their brothers to bar the gate, Grant and Gregoras were already through it and the mist that had shrouded their arrival swallowed them again, hiding them swiftly from all pursuit.

They halted after a time, crouched in the portico of a church. The fog appeared to be lifting a little, for faces had come clearer. Grant looked into Gregoras's. 'And where might you be taking that now?' He pointed at the canister under the Greek's arm. 'I doubt there's the gold left to buy it in all Constantinople.'

'Somewhere safe.' Gregoras hesitated, unused to confidences. He did not know the value of the scroll he held. A fortune, Leilah had said and the Scot had just confirmed. All he did know was that in the days to come, death could take him in a hundred ways. It would be a shame if the location of something so precious should die with him. 'There's . . . there's a church,' he said softly. 'St Maria of the Mongols. A last refuge perhaps, and . . .' He hesitated. He hadn't thought much beyond the taking of the text. He'd supposed that he'd find a place to hide it there. But where?

A memory came, something he'd loved as a child, and seen again when he'd followed Sofia. 'There's an ikon of St Demetrios. There is a small gap behind, between the painting and the altar screen . . .'

Grant studied him for a moment, then stood. In the time they'd talked, the mist had cleared considerably. Wisps clung to stone eaves, but they could see across the small square. 'You are thinking you might not live to reclaim it?' He shook the papers he held. 'Well, this will be in my cave, with all the rest of them. It might not fetch as much as yours, but it's still worth a bag or two of gold. Enough to build you that house you're always talking about, anyway.'

The fog was lifting elsewhere too, judging by the sound that came then – the crack and smash of a large cannon. 'Come then,' said Gregoras, rising too. 'There are Turks to fight.'

'Aye. Hordes of the bastards. And by their recent preparations, I think they'll be coming all at once.' He nodded. 'Where do you face them?'

'I do not know. I am an imperial archer again. But Giustiniani likes me near, so . . .' He shrugged. 'And you?'

'The palace. Turks are still burrowing near it.'

A silence came. They looked at each other. Each knew that he had bequeathed the other the little he had.

After a moment, Gregoras nodded. 'Well then . . .'

'Aye.'

And then they were moving opposite ways. Gregoras was at the edge of the square when the soft call came. 'I've something else in that cave – a batch of aqua vitae on the go. I think it could be my finest brew yet. We could taste it . . . och, in about five days, if you're interested.'

'Then I will come and judge it . . . in five days.' Gregoras turned the corner, kept moving. Five days, he thought. What will this world look like then?

THIRTY-TWO

'It Is Written'

26 May: fiftieth day of the siege

It was time.

Carefully lifting the paper, Leilah blew the fine golden sand across its surface, most falling in a shimmer through the air, what remained glinting in the etched black lines, at the conjunction of virgin and lion, in the bowls of the scales, in the stingers of the scorpion.

She turned the paper into the shaft of sunlight from the open flap of her tent, studied the horoscope. She was pleased to see how little it differed from the one she'd cast for Mehmet a year and a few weeks before at Edirne. The timing was a little different, a moon not waxing but waning. The Greeks and their allies had fought better than anyone could have predicted, soldier or seer. But the result was the same: in three days' time, if Mehmet was resolute, Constantinople should fall.

She frowned, staring at that 'if' in gilded black lines on her chart. One man was there, one who would dictate the outcome. His rise and fall. She'd assumed it was Mehmet, since it was for him the chart was drawn. Yet she saw now that the person came from the tenth house, the house of ambition. Controlled by Pisces. Ruled by Neptune. Someone else, someone who would influence the outcome as greatly as the sultan himself.

She bit her lip, suddenly not as certain as she'd been. Tasted blood, leaned forward, waited, until a drop fell upon the paper. It slid down the lines of black and glimmering gold, pooled in that tenth house. Mehmet and someone else then, at a moment of crisis. A decision made, changing everything.

But which way? She shivered. It was unlike her to be so uncertain. And then she heard it, the called command to clear a path, the rhythmic steps, the clink of sword harness. They were coming to bring her to Mehmet. Certainty would once again have to be faked.

She knelt, rolled the paper, slipped a ribbon over it. Then she rose, drew the scarlet cloak over her shoulders, donned the headdress, letting the veil fall over her face. As the marching stopped on a command, and a man's shadow, made long by the evening sun, spilled onto her carpet, she reached up under the silk to rub the blood into her lips. It reminded her of other tastes there, of her and Gregoras conjoined like planets, and what they had planned. It reminded her too that there were always things in the stars that were unknowable, however skilled the sorceress. And that all she could do was concentrate on her will, her desire, which was Mehmet's desire too. To achieve it, the city must be stormed. If wielding her crossbow would accomplish that, she would happily take her place in the siege lines. However, it was her other skills she needed now. Skills of enchantment. Skills of persuasion.

'Are you ready?'

She recognised the voice. Hamza, the sultan's shadow. The new *kapudan pasha*. The risen man. She knew he was wary of her, wary perhaps of the influence she had, that he could not control. He had prevented her reaching Mehmet before. But now he was there to take her to him. 'I am ready,' she said, picking up the horoscope, stepping into the sunlight.

Hamza had bent to call. Now he straightened to study. She was more hidden than she had ever been before, except behind the screen in Edirne, the first time he'd encountered her, in her robe now and a headdress of so many layers her face was only visible by its features pressing the silk out. It made him uneasy, the unreadable face. He wanted to see her, to be able to gauge if what she would say to Mehmet was what they both wanted to hear. The lord of lords wanted to be told that the stars still foretold his victory. Hamza wanted to be told it too. But there were many in the army, especially those of the highest rank like Candarli Halil, who did not. Who would delight in hearing that the sultan's favourite sorceress was doubtful of success. Mehmet, for all his growing skills, was still a young man. And when greybeards carped . . . Hamza could not see her. He could not gauge by her look. But he would find a way to ask, and tell it in her voice, in the short walk back to the sultan's *otak*.

He bowed, gestured with his arm. She stepped forward, and he followed, into the gap between two bodies of the household guard, their halberds at port across their chests. 'Forward,' he called.

They fell into step. Despite the urgency, he did not know how to begin. 'Does Allah, most mighty, show His blessings to you?' he asked, formally.

'He does.'

She smiled beneath her veil at the silence that followed his first words. She could sense the energy in the man, the questions that filled him. She would answer if she chose, or not. The only man that truly concerned her waited ahead. Through layers of silk she looked to either side, saw what she had been hearing for some time now in her tent. Men celebrating. And it brought a question of her own, though she hid it in a statement. 'The army is happy.'

Hamza, who had been about to speak, nodded. '*Irade* has been commanded. Two days of feast and one of fasting. To prepare.'

'For what, lord?'

'For a great attack. The greatest yet. If . . . if the sultan commands it.'

'If?' She let the word hang a moment, continued. 'The final one?'

'Perhaps. *Inshallah.*'

'*Does* God will it?'

'The imam, Aksemseddin, most revered, believes he does. Most in the army do, though . . .' he hesitated, went on, 'though many do not.' Hamza sucked in a deep breath. 'Do the stars?'

She smiled. It was the question of questions for him, she who was skilled in guessing men's desires could tell. But she had learned that words were most powerful when uttered for the first time. So she did not answer him. 'I do not see many here who doubt of its success,' she said.

'No. The doubters are elsewhere. Waiting for the sultan's command. To advance to God's glory or . . . or to strike their tents. Return to their farms. Some are close to him.'

'You, Hamza Pasha?'

'Not I,' he said, too firmly, then looked about him, at the soldiers gathered around fires where whole sheep were revolving on spits, goatskin sacks being passed from hand to hand, squirted into mouths. And he, who never drank al-kohl, suddenly craved it, for his dry throat, for his doubting mind.

She sensed his doubt. It reminded her of her own, back in the tent. Yet she knew their doubt would not be resolved anywhere but in the very heart of the breached walls . . . and perhaps at one moment of destiny. And she found there were words she could give only to him. 'I see you, master, with great wealth, with many wives, many children, one of the most eminent men in the land. Will that happen if Constantinople does not fall?'

Hamza thought of the doubters ahead, Candarli Halil, Ishak Pasha and the rest, the old Anatolian nobility. Their grip on the throne would be hugely strengthened by failure here, failure they'd always foreseen. The throne itself would have a new occupant soon after that failure, he was certain; and the new, ignoble men that Mehmet had raised would disappear like him, the mark of a silken bowstring on their necks. He shook his head. 'It will not.'

'Then . . .' she smiled beneath her veil, 'trust in Allah . . . and in the stars.'

It brightened him for a moment, until he thought of the other thing she'd said to him, when he'd prevented her reaching Mehmet before. 'You saw something else for me. Not my . . . eminence.' He swallowed. 'My death.'

She saw it again, a sudden flash of it, as clearly as she had before. The risen man rising differently, into the sky, in terrible agony. A dragon watched, and a gloved hand plucked out a pasha's heart. She swayed with the vision, stumbled into him. He steadied her, till she could speak. 'Every man must die, master,' she said. 'Surely all that matters is how he lives?'

He wanted to ask her more, but they had reached their destination: the rear entrance of Mehmet's great pavilion. The guard ahead of them moved to the side, the tent flap parted . . . and revealed the sultan. He was standing among a group of officers and clerks, clad as she had last seen him when he had tested the great cannon before the walls of Edirne, in a crimson coat, unbuttoned now so she could see the chain mail sewn into it, glistening in the last light of the sun. His face, though, under the silver helmet with its ostrich feather, was changed from the youth she'd first met. Thinner, older. There were dark crescents under eyes that brightened when he saw her, then filled again with fear. 'Come,' he hissed, beckoning her in, 'and quickly.'

He led her into a small antechamber. A canvas wall faced her. Beyond it, she could hear the murmuring of men – his council, ready to hear his words. He showed her no courtesy, made no offer of sherbet, nor of gold. Only the blunt question in his look from a man who needed to know, beyond his doubts. And seeing his, she put her own aside. 'King of kings,' she declaimed, her voice strong, 'possessor of men's necks. Allah's deputy on earth. These and many more names are you called. Now, I say, prepare for more titles to be heaped upon you. In three days, all will hail you as "majestic Caesar".' She paused, as Mehmet sucked in his breath. 'And you will for evermore be known by the title you covet most – "Fatih". For in three days' time you will be the Conqueror.'

'Ah!'

His face cleared in a smile as she unfolded the scroll and turned it towards him. 'See what is in the stars.'

Mehmet barely glanced at it. He looked back, to the murmuring behind him. 'I have not time to read it now. Later, perhaps. Later, when all is set in motion. But if you tell me that all . . . *all* is well . . .'

'Lord of lords of this world, all is as I have told you,' she said simply, firmly, gesturing down. 'It is written.'

Mehmet was not a small man, but he grew taller in that moment, till the ostrich plume on his feather almost scraped the tent's roof. 'Then I can do nothing but read and follow.' He turned to Hamza. 'Pay her. You know the jewel saved for this, an emerald beyond price for the prize she has given me.' He turned to face the entrance to the other, larger room. 'And let me give my commands.'

Adjusting his sword belt, he nodded to the guards either side, who moved to place their hands upon the split in the canvas. But all movement halted at Leilah's cry, as she threw back her cloak and flung herself down upon the ground. 'Most potent,' she cried, 'I ask for the boon you promised me.'

Mehmet's attention had been all forward. But beneath the cloak Leilah had put on only the silken shift she'd worn for Gregoras, and every man in the room could not help but stare. Even the sultan, who turned back. 'What boon?' he murmured.

She peeled back her headdress, so he could look into eyes rimmed in kohl that made their darkness deeper. 'I crave no jewel, lord, however priceless. I ask only this for my services.' Her voice was deep, and as silken as the little she wore. 'There is a church in the city. I want it kept safe from destruction, by your order.'

Hamza stepped forward. She had surprised him before, but never so much as now. 'I did not think you were of the Christian faith?'

'I am not.'

'Then why do you ask such a thing?'

She had not turned to Hamza, kept her eyes on Mehmet, took a deep breath. 'For my own reasons. May I keep them hidden, O Conqueror, as many things are hidden?'

Her breath had raised her breasts within the silk. She watched his eyes follow them, saw his face tinge near as red as his beard. 'I asked you another thing that day,' he said, his voice rougher. 'Do you remember it?'

'Indeed, lord.' She lowered her eyes, allowed a blush to take her face. 'You asked that I . . . I offer you what I need to preserve, to keep my visions clear.'

He stepped a little closer. 'And now you have had the vision of visions, is there any need to hold out longer?'

She raised her eyes, dropped her voice to a whisper. 'Once you are Fatih, how could any of your subjects refuse you anything?'

Mehmet smiled, doubts swept from his face. He turned to his scribes. 'See that such an order is written. Stamp it with my *tugra* and give it to her. And you . . .' He gestured to an officer. 'Assign a body of my guard – for her gifts I will spare her twenty men – to escort her to whatever place she wants protecting, once we are inside the walls. Let no man touch it, or feel my wrath. You are under her command.' He bent, ran a finger down from her forehead to her lips, and she did not pull away. 'And mine – to bring her to me once the city, and everything in it, is in my power.' For another moment he stared, then withdrew his hand, turning again to face the entranceway. 'And now . . .'

He nodded. The tent flaps were lifted aside and the noise of murmuring doubled, then ceased as Mehmet swept through. Hamza, with one more glance at the kneeling woman and one shake of his head, followed, and the canvas closed behind them.

The officer, the scribe assigned, came to her, eyebrows raised in question. Leilah, who'd stood swiftly as the sultan left and gathered her cloak again around her, held up her hand to command their silence so she could listen.

The young sultan's voice came clear through the canvas. 'Children of Allah,' he said. 'Followers of Muhammad. Sons of Osman. The time has come to put aside all doubts, all divisions. To unite under the green banner of the Prophet, peace be upon him. What he foretold is come to pass. In three days' time, the richest fruit of all, the Red Apple, will fall into our outstretched hands.'

A great shout came. 'God is great! God is great! God is great!' When it passed, as suddenly as it started, his voice came again. 'Each shall have his place. All shall join in the last great attack, for we shall attack in every place at once. Thus all shall partake in the glory, either as martyrs sent to an eternal paradise, or to share equally in the fabulous wealth of the city of the Caesars. What was heard in the prayers of all believers, dreamed for a thousand years, is now upon us. It is written in the stars and in the hearts of all God's chosen people.' His voice soared in the same cry as before. '*Allahu akbar!*'

The voices of all within the tent repeated his words.

'God is great! God is great! God is great!'

The canvas swayed with air and passion. Smiling, Leilah turned and beckoned the scribe, who dipped his quill, looked up at her as she spoke. 'Let it be known that Mehmet, lord of lords, Conqueror of Constantinople, takes under his protection this church . . .'

— THIRTY-THREE —

Forgiveness

28 May: fifty-second day of the siege: 10 p.m.

Like all the women, Sofia could not see the main body of the great church. It was filled with men, crowded for the first time since the union with Rome was declared and most of the Orthodox shunned their former temple as they would anything unclean.

No one shunned it today. Those who could, and could be spared from the walls, squeezed in, whatever their faith. Those who could not – mainly the poor of the city, for it was the leaders who claimed precedence – were packed into the churchyard to hear the liturgy sung, to add their voices to those swelling within.

She had loved the Hagia Sophia before she'd even seen it, as a child thinking it was called, of course, after her; loved it when she found out it was not, that it was named for divine wisdom. And she did not mind that she could not see, that her sex restricted her to the side. She would not have had it any different, for she was in the place she loved most in the old building. In the north-west corner of the north aisle, flush against the column of St Gregory. The Miracle Worker, as he was known, had worked a miracle for her, once. Pilgrims had sought his aid for centuries, pressing themselves against the marble, rubbing a cavity in it in which moisture gathered. That precious liquid, used to anoint, could cure ailments, could bring birth. It had brought her a second child, her Minerva.

Now, as the very last sung note rose from the thousands of voices there and seemed to echo forever inside the great dome,

Sofia reached and touched the cavity, seeking another miracle, one sought by every single person around her, everyone inside and outside the great church, everyone in the city, in that moment. 'Holy saint. Holy Gregory. Bring us salvation this night. Let your shining light guide us to triumph over our foes. Help us. Bless us. Save us.'

Though so many had reached before this night that the fullest well should have been dry, she still felt a touch of moisture on her fingertips. Perhaps it was only the transferred tears of those who had been there before her, for nearly everyone present wept. But she took it as a sign of grace and brought it to her lips.

The last note clung still, sustained by yearning. Everyone who heard it knew that when it ended, it could – could! – be the last Christian song ever heard in the great cathedral. If their prayers went unanswered. If God had chosen to punish them. If the infidel stormed the city this night, as he had vowed to do.

Then it was gone, and with its going, people began to move, swiftly leaving. God and the saints had been called upon, and now men had to make their earthly dispositions. She let the other women jostle past her. She would have a last moment with her saint and then she would follow, for there was also much she needed to accomplish this night.

'Wife.'

The familiar voice. She turned. Theon had been kneeling with the emperor, right before the altar screen. He had partaken of the holy mystery, been shriven and blessed. In the flickering light of a thousand candles she thought she still saw the wine upon his lips. 'Husband,' she answered.

They looked at each other. There had been a formality in their greeting, as if they were acquaintances. Indeed, she had seen little of him in the recent weeks of the siege. He slept near the emperor, ready for any command. The times he returned to the house, she was often gone. Lately she had led a party of women, daughters of the city like herself, to carry materials to the walls for the stockade that needed constant repair. With her son at her side, she worked as much as she could, slept little, ate less and less.

'You look tired,' he said, continuing the formality, echoing her thoughts.

'As do you,' she replied.

He did. The armour he was forced to wear had never suited him, and he looked small within it, as if he'd borrowed it from a much bigger man. He saw her stare, and perhaps something of what she felt showed on her face, because he came to her more briskly, took her arm. 'Come,' he said, 'I will see you home.'

'I do not go home.' She moved with him, as they both headed towards the doors.

'And where do you go, if not there?'

'The same place as you. I go to the walls.'

He stopped, stared at her in shock. 'The walls? Do you not know that the Turks will attack them this very night? Not as before. Again and again and again till they have stormed them or all died trying.'

'I know this. But until the moment that they do attack, there are stones to lift. It is my duty.'

'Your duty is to your family.'

She slipped his grip, kept moving, threading her way through the crowds, seeking. 'Thakos will be with me, for boys work beside the women. Minerva is with Athene, at the house.'

He followed, caught her arm again, halting her. 'And you must join her there. With our son. You must obey me.' Anger coloured his voice now. 'Obey me!'

She stared at him for a long moment. 'I hear you. At any other time I would seek to please you as I always have,' she said softly. 'But there are others I must obey before you now, Theon. The emperor who has ordered that monks, women and boys do the work that soldiers cannot be spared for. The

394

Blessed Virgin, who protects us and urges that we protect ourselves. And . . .' she hesitated. 'Myself. My will.'

'Your . . . will?' He looked incredulous. 'When have you ever had a will?'

'Since the Turk first came to take everything that I love,' she replied, gently pulling her arm from his grasp.

He let her get a few paces, followed, grabbed her yet again. She turned, and there was fury in her eyes. Just like her damned cat, he thought, ever ready with its claws. He thought of striking her. He'd done it before. But they had come to the front of the building, Constantine was close, men who knew him. Wives had to be struck in private. Besides, he did not need her to be humbled here. Time enough for that pleasure later. He only needed her to obey him. 'Listen to me,' he said softly, releasing her arm. 'No, I do not command, as is my right. I ask you to hear of something that, if the worst happens, may save the lives of our children.' He saw he had her and he continued, emphasising each word hard. 'If the Turks triumph, they will be thinking only of pillage. Of rape. Then, after both, of enslavement. But certain places, certain people, will be spared. So when you have done your duty at the walls, you must return to our home—'

'How do you know this?' she interrupted him, something she would never have done before.

He swallowed his anger. Sphrantzes was beckoning him and he did not have time for it. 'I know. I know how they will do it, too – with the marks of important men placed upon doors. With flags. You will find one such flag under our mattress. If the Turks break through . . .' He bent, to catch once more the gaze that left him at his words. 'Yes, I say "if". I will try to come. But if I do not – or cannot – do you hang this flag from the upper windows. And then do you lock our doors, shutter our windows, and seal yourself and our children with you on the roof.'

She looked at him for a long moment. 'What have you done,

Theon,' she whispered, 'to earn such a favour from our enemies?'

He felt the itch come again, his rising hands moving into fists. He breathed, let them fall. 'I have done only what a father should do. A husband. I have prepared for the worst that may come.'

She stared at him a moment and then was moving again, darting between horses that prevented him following. By the time he could, she'd reached a cart, two asses in the traces. Other women were crammed on it, two helping her up, all as haggard and determined as she. He pressed up to the edge, as one of the women took the reins. 'Did you hear all I said, wife?'

She looked down at him. At the restrained fury in his eyes. But for all his politician's guile, he was also a husband. A father. Trying to care for his own. And though she had prayed, though she believed in miracles given by saints, though she would do all she could of her duty, she was a mother and there was a part of her that needed some other hope too. Some plan if God and man failed. Perhaps a flag beneath a mattress, however it had got there.

'I did. And I will . . . obey,' she said, as the woman at the reins shouted, 'Huh!' and the cart lurched off. Standing, she looked back at him, suddenly wondering if she would ever see him again. 'I will. Go with God, husband. May the Virgin and all the saints protect you this night.'

Ignoring the calling of his name, which had become more insistent, he watched the cart recede into the crowd. His hands were still balled in fists and he lifted them, looked at them. That was how we parted, he thought, my last touch of her an angry grip upon her arm. Was there not a kiss for me, Sofia? I would have preferred that a thousand times more to Christ's blood upon my lips.

Then another thought came, and he looked sharply up. But the cart was lost in the swirl of men and women scattering about their tasks, the city's, their own. As he turned away to the insistent call, he wondered this: if the kiss she'd spared him was saved for another. A man whose armour fitted him well. And whether it was *duty* that took her to the walls at all.

Gregoras had tried to keep Thakos close, and his head down. Though it was night, enemy archers still had an eye for a target, and arrows constantly fell to harass those who were ceaselessly filling and repairing the gaps in the stockade. But the boy was ever curious and would rise up to look at the Turkish lines and the wonders there.

'Why are they burning so many fires, Uncle?'

'Two reasons. They feast – can you not smell that succulent lamb?' Gregoras's mouth flooded with saliva at the thought. 'Because they have fasted this day to prepare their souls for the assault and now need to feed their bodies for it. And they do it to show us their numbers, to make us afraid.'

'But we are not afraid, are we, Uncle?' Thakos said, looking frightened.

'We are. We should be. Only the lunatic is not afraid. But a man controls his fear, uses it.'

'I see.' The boy nodded. 'And do they play that music to fright us too?'

Gregoras listened. The drums, the trumpets, the *ney* and *sevre* and all manner of stringed and piped instruments had been sounding the day long so that he had almost forgotten them, a constant clamour against every thought. 'They do. And to fill themselves with courage.'

'We have trumpets too. I can play one. I wish I had brought mine and not . . .' He lifted the slingshot from the ground beside him. 'Is it time to practise again, Uncle?' he asked, a quaver in his voice.

And in his hands. He had never truly mastered the weapon, despite his desire. He was not a warrior; Gregoras could tell that it was not his nature. That he was too gentle. And he was only seven years old. Gregoras shook his head. A city that needed seven-year-olds to fight for it was a place in its last agony. 'No. Save your stones for later.'

The boy swallowed. 'When will they attack?'

It was no secret. The Turks had been proclaiming the hour in their camp all the long day. 'Soon after midnight,' he replied.

'And where?'

He looked down the length of the valley, along the long line of flame. 'Everywhere,' he murmured.

Somewhere this side of that line was his emperor. Constantine, on his return from mass at the Hagia Sophia, had ridden out immediately to visit each bastion, to inspire his troops, to show that he was undaunted and so should they be by the enemy's fire and noise. But he would return here ere long, for all knew that even if the attack was to be general and encompass all the walls of both land and sea, it would, as ever, be most concentrated here. It was why the imperial tent was pitched right there, just behind the walls – a long bowshot from Mehmet's tent, set up on the brow of the hill opposite, above his great guns. Here, at the Fifth Military gate, known by most as the St Romanus for the civil gate of that name it was near, where the Turks had destroyed the outer wall and where the Greeks had built a stockade to replace it. Here, where the great Giustiniani stood with his Genoans. Here would be the crisis, all knew. So Constantine would return here, and soon.

The only order he'd given before he departed was that the Commander must cease his unending supervision of the defence and rest. Giustiniani had reluctantly agreed to sleep for a couple of hours, but only if his two deputies – Enzo the Sicilian and Gregoras, formerly Zoran Rhinometus – saw that all that could be done was. And it had been. Enzo was down at the *stauroma* still, shoving last barrows of mud between the timber and the stones. But Gregoras had retired to the inner wall, to the crumbling bastion where he had placed his armour and from which he would shoot his great bow.

The music directly opposite them slackened, so that a single voice could be heard above it, crying out. 'Another call to prayers, Uncle?' Thakos asked.

Gregoras listened, shook his head. 'Another reminder of what their sultan has promised them. A swift journey to a martyr's paradise or three days of pillage once the city falls.'

'What's pillage?'

Gregoras opened his mouth to answer, only to close it again. What could he say to a boy about the horrors he'd witnessed? That he'd taken part in, for Christian nations pillaged cities of the Turk and of other Christian nations too. It was what a mercenary lived for, the opportunity for booty. He'd looted enough to buy that piece of land in Ragusa. And if he had not taken part in other aspects of pillage . . . well, he still knew what would befall Constantinople's people if that fragile stockade was toppled. Slaughter for the men who resisted, rape for their women, enslavement for all. The boy might be seeing it all too soon. He did not need to see it in Gregoras's words now.

He thought of him as 'the boy'. He found it hard to call him his son, despite what Sofia had revealed. Yet they were soon to part – despite his fear, his gentleness, Thakos was determined to fight, and Gregoras was equally determined to get him away from the battle. Should they leave one another, and Thakos never truly know the man he called uncle and who, more than likely, had died in the final battle for the city? Should Gregoras not be remembered as something more than a noseless curiosity?

'Why are you looking at me like that, Uncle?'

'Thakos—' Gregoras began.

And then the boy interrupted him by leaping up. 'Look! It's Mother. Mother!' he called.

Gregoras pulled the youth down, as an arrow flew over. Then he peered between the crenels, to the outer wall. A party of women were just dropping earth and timber onto it. One was looking up, bucket in hand.

Sofia.

Gregoras leaned into the gap. 'Behind this bastion,' he

called. Then, stooping to pick up his bow and quiver, he dragged Thakos to the archway, crouching low.

She met them at the bottom of the stair. 'My son,' she cried, and he rushed into her arms, stayed there, until he remembered he was meant to be a soldier and a man and pulled away.

'Here,' Gregoras said, holding out the slingshot he'd also picked up, 'take this and find some more good stones. Practise. I need to speak to your mother.'

Thakos nodded, snatched the rope weapon, ran off. 'Not far,' they both called, and laughed when they realised they had. A silence came then, as each looked at the other.

Sofia broke it. 'I have not . . . not seen you,' she said at last.

'No. I have been . . . busy.'

'As have I.'

Silence again, more awkward than the first. Then both spoke at once.

'I was looking for—'

'I found him wandering—'

They stopped, laughed again. Gregoras raised a hand. 'He was lurking by the wall. I thought it was safer to have him near me.'

'We had arranged a meeting point nearby. But the Turkish fires must have lured him.' She looked up. The flames cast a weird, flickering glow onto the low clouds that pressed down on the land, turning them reddish brown; moved too over the white sides of Constantine's command tent a hundred paces away. 'The world burns,' she added on a whisper.

'It does.' He looked at her, most of her face in shadow, what he could see shifting in the strange light. There was a little pulse in her neck that he had not noticed in all their recent meetings, since his return. But he remembered it now from their time before, when they and the world had still been young. He did not think. He just did, bending into her, kissing that pulse. 'Sofia,' he whispered.

Her arms fell around him and she was stumbling back. His head lowered, her face rose, they kissed. Kissed until she pulled away, held out a hand to stop him coming closer. 'Look,' she said. 'Our son.'

Thakos was standing perhaps fifty paces away, looking around nervously because they'd disappeared into the shadows. She pushed herself off the wall, into the light-spill. 'Here, love,' she called, waving.

He waved too, then resumed his scouring of the ground. 'Don't come close,' she whispered, keeping her back to Gregoras, 'and say what you need to say.'

Need? he thought. Which one shall I speak of? But then he saw, beyond Thakos, the blur of approaching horsemen, heard the jingle of their harness a moment later. The emperor was returning, time was about to end or begin, and there was only one need now. 'Listen to me,' he said, his voice low and urgent. 'If the Turks break us here this night, if they storm this city, you know what will happen.'

'I have heard . . .'

'I have a place that might be safe. Might, if valour, stars and saints and all your prayers unite in our cause. It is a chance anyway, if doom befalls us.'

Her voice came faintly, still turned away from him. 'What place?'

'One you love. St Maria of the Mongols.' He heard her gasp, rode over it. 'Go there now. Take those you love and seek shelter behind its strong walls. I have arranged . . .' He hesitated. 'I have arranged for the storm to pass it by.'

'How?'

He remembered then what the other had said, the one he'd loved, did love in some strange way he only just realised at that moment, yet loved so differently from the one before him. He repeated that other's words. 'The how is unimportant.'

'But it is important.' Her voice came stronger now, anger in it. 'Are you telling me that you have "arranged" this safety with the enemy? Are you a traitor too?'

'No! I . . .' He stepped forward then, so he could see at least the side of her face. 'I am a soldier. A soldier always keeps open a line of retreat. I will fight as hard as I can for our victory. But if we fail, and I somehow live . . .' he reached out, took her arm, turned her, 'I want to live with those I love.'

She looked down at his hand. 'Another held me thus, not two hours since, telling me what a man must do. Arranging something with an enemy. Not a soldier, but a politician.'

He dropped her arm. 'Theon.'

'Yes.' She stared at him, hurt clear in her eyes. 'Perhaps the twins are not so different after all.'

She stepped out further into the fractured light, opened her mouth to call. Beyond her, reining up at his tent, was Constantine.

Gregoras did not reach, did not grab. 'Sofia, if you ever, ever loved me,' he whispered, 'listen before you go.' She froze, and he went on, 'Whatever happens tonight, whether this city stands or falls, the world has changed, changed utterly. And whoever is the victor this night, if I live through it, know this: I will come for you. For you and our son.'

She did not move. He watched her staring at Thakos, then watched that pulse again in her neck. 'And for my daughter?' she said at last, the harshness gone. 'Another man's daughter?'

He felt the relief, did not let it come into his voice. 'For her too. For the only people I love.'

She turned to him, stepped closer. 'Then come,' she said, and kissed him, swiftly, fleetingly, achingly, before stepping away. 'But Thakos will try to stay here,' she said.

'I will not let him.' He looked to the tent, men dismounting there, others already being dispatched. 'Call him.'

'Thakos!'

He stepped up beside her, as the boy ran towards them. 'A last thing,' he said. 'If I do not come . . . if . . . In St Maria's, wedged behind the ikon of St Demetrios, you will find a leather case. It contains what will keep you safe. Give it to . . . to the woman who will come and ask for it.'

'The woman?' She stared at him a moment, questions in her

eyes. Yet she knew she had no time for them. So she simply nodded, as the boy ran up. 'Thakos, come. We leave.'

'Leave?' He looked at the man he thought of as his uncle. 'No. I stay. I fight.'

'Listen to me, lad,' Gregoras said, stepping closer, putting an arm around the boy. 'You have become good with the sling-shot. Very good. But slingers are no use in this bastion, the wall before it too far to hit with any accuracy. Only archers can do that.' Thakos made to interrupt, but Gregoras continued, 'But if the Turks break through, then, then you will have your time. Running across the rooftops. Raining down your stones.' He nodded. 'The emperor has appointed the younger sons of our city as the second line of defence. If we fail here, at the wall, it will be your duty, you and the other young men, to drive the infidel from the city. And you will be the one protecting the women of our family.'

Thakos's eyes contained different things – pride at the words, doubt too. Finally a look of pure relief, swiftly sup-pressed. 'Then I will go . . . and do my duty,' he said, trying to make his voice deeper. 'Come, Mother.'

As he tried to step away, Gregoras held him. Stooping, he put the other arm around him, pulled him close, felt the small heart racing, as he had felt his mother's pulse. 'My boy,' he said softly.

'Uncle.' Embarrassed, Thakos pulled away, took Sofia's hand. With one last look, she turned and they began to walk away.

Gregoras took a step after them. 'Pray for me this night. Pray for us all,' he called.

They stopped, turned, their faces lit by flickering Turkish light. His breath caught as he saw her, whom he'd always loved. Saw them both in the boy beside her.

'Come for us,' she said.

And then they were gone, threading through the troops of soldiers assembling for the fight. He watched them till they

403

were lost among the spears and shields, then picked up his bow. Hefting it, he headed towards Constantine's tent.

'You have done everything that Christian knights could be asked to do. More, for never did any knight face the adversity that you have faced and none have borne it so bravely. I know that there have been divisions amongst us, between Genoan and Venetian, between Roman and Orthodox, between the Greeks who call this city theirs and those from other lands who have come here for profit. But that is all forgotten now. This night all divisions are put aside. This night unites us in a brotherhood of arms . . . and gives us an opportunity few Christian gentlemen have ever had – to defeat a monstrous and infidel enemy, more numerous than daisies in a spring meadow. If the odds against us seem great, how much greater then shall our victory taste? Remember our history! How many times have our generals and emperors triumphed over numberless foes? Think of Belisarius and his tiny army driving the Vandals from Africa. Of Narses retaking Rome, then the whole of Italy, from the all-conquering Goths. Of Basil crushing the vast forces of the Bulgars. These heroes' blood is in our veins. Whatever happens, whatever fortune comes to us this night, the least we shall do is write our names under theirs in the book of legend.'

Constantine paused, looking down from the low platform on which he stood, at the upturned faces of every man of rank, of Church and trade and State, of every nation. A hundred men crammed before him into his command tent, with only his closest companions behind – Sphrantzes, the aged Don Francisco of Toledo, John of Dalmata. Theodore of Karystenos, the captain of his guard. And Gregoras, for the old archer had beckoned him up and they stood there, either side of the emperor, just as a sultan's guards would stand, bows in hand, arrows notched.

'And yet, are the odds truly so great?' Constantine continued. 'They have many men, yes. But we have seen how they

404

attack, screaming like animals, without skill or true courage. We have repelled them again and again, in every place they have assaulted us. They have laid our walls low with their cannon and still have they failed to breach them. They will fail so again this night.' His voice lowered. 'We know that this is their final attack. We know that so many of the enemy, most perhaps, despair. They know our city has never fallen to siege, that slave armies have broken themselves on our walls for a thousand years. Twenty years ago I saw an army greater than this one, led by a greater leader, Murad Han, fail in his repeated attacks. His callow son will fail this night.' He raised his voice, his eyes, looking all about him. 'For see who he sends his slaves to fight. The flower of Christian nobility from all the lands of the world. Greek gentlemen, with names that have resounded in this city since its foundation. Notaras, Cantacuzenus, Lascaris, countless others. Dauntless Minotto, *baillie* of Venice, who along with the three intrepid Bocciardi brothers of his state defends my palace; while his countrymen – Diedo, Contarini and the rest – stand deep at every other rampart. Men of many other nations – Catalonia, Crete. Even, as I have learned,' a slight smile came, 'my loyal engineer, John Grant of Scotland.' He paused. 'And though I do not exalt him and his countrymen above any other, perhaps no one will grudge that I mention this name last. The lion of our defence, the bulwark over which no single Turk has managed to sweep, the foremost warrior of great Genoa – Giovanni Giustiniani Longo.' He stepped to the edge of the platform, bent to lay his hand on the Genoan's shoulder. 'Shall we triumph this night, my friend?'

'Beyond doubt, lord,' the Commander growled. 'By the morning your Turkish daisies will lie scythed beneath our blades. For the honour of God and for all Christendom.'

'Yes.' Constantine straightened. 'For the honour of God. Let us not forget the last, the greatest of those who fight for us this day. Christ and all the archangels raise their swords beside us. The Holy Mother shines her light on us. Almighty God breathes in us.'

Amens were being called all over the tent now, the sign of the cross made, each according to his faith – the crossbar left to right for the Catholics, right to left for the Orthodox, the dividing difference at last unnoticed by all. Except perhaps by the emperor, who stepped off the platform now, the crowd hushing with his descent. 'And let me go into this night with all your blessings. If there is any man I have offended here, I ask his pardon.' He turned to Giustiniani, embraced him. 'Forgive me.'

'I do,' replied the tall Genoan, 'and ask to be forgiven in my turn. Of you, *basileus* . . .' he came out of the embrace and turned, 'and of you, Minotto of Venice. Our countries are often in conflict, and you and I have crossed blades more than once. Perhaps we will again. But this night you are my brother in arms. I will die for you if God calls me to. And I ask your forgiveness for any wrong I have done you.'

The Venetian's face flushed red with emotion. 'Mother of God,' he cried, 'and I will die for you, General, and for any gentleman of Genoa.'

He fell into the Commander's huge arms. They hugged, breastplate clanking on breastplate, which sound spread rapidly throughout the tent. Genoan and Venetian, Catalan and Cretan, priest of either faith, Greeks of every stripe, embraced, asked forgiveness. Tears fell on steel, smiles split beards.

'And have you a hug for me, brother?'

Gregoras turned sharply. 'Do you want one, Theon?' he replied, easing his finger's grip on his bowstring.

'I do not know.' The politician looked long at the soldier. 'I wonder what it would settle.'

Gregoras shrugged. 'Nothing, for the future. You and I still must have a reckoning one day. For this.' He reached up, tapped his ivory nose. 'For many things.' He looked back at the still embracing crowd. 'But if a Venetian can hug a Genoan, if a Notaras can embrace a Palaiologos, then perhaps the Lascaris can put aside their enmity for this one night. It might help us to do all we can for that which we love.'

Theon smiled. ' "That"?' he said. 'Are you speaking of our city now?'

'Our city, and some of those within it. Those we love.'

'To do all we can for those we love,' echoed Theon. 'Well, for that I can put aside enmity. For this one night.'

Gregoras took the arrow from the bowstring, lowered the weapon. The two brothers embraced, held for a moment, parted. 'Well,' was all they both said, before turning swiftly away.

A soldier had come in the back of the tent. He was looking around and Gregoras saw him spot Theodore, move to him, whisper. The old archer nodded, and moved straight to Constantine, whispering in his turn. Immediately the emperor climbed back upon the dais, raising his arms for a silence that swiftly came. 'Listen,' he said, pointing through canvas walls to the stone ones beyond.

A moment, before Minotto of Venice spoke. 'I hear nothing, *basileus*.'

'No,' replied Constantine. 'The Turks have stopped their music.' A murmur spread through the tent. All there knew what the silence foretold. 'Yes,' the emperor said. 'You know your positions. To your posts, with God at your shoulder and courage in your hearts. Those who are to die, be sure your names will live for ever, wreathed in glory. Those who are marked to live, let us meet tomorrow at the Church of the Holy Wisdom, at sacred Sophia, and celebrate a glorious victory.' Constantine raised his arms above his head and roared, 'To your posts – for God, for Christendom . . . and for Constantinople!'

'Constantinople!' The name was shouted back, then each man departed at speed. Gregoras turned, but Theon was gone, off to his own position. Gregoras knew his, and made for it. 'Commander,' he said, as he appeared at Giustiniani's elbow.

'Ah, Rhinometus! Or Zoran, or . . . Gregoras. Whatever you

call yourself now, you're still a noseless bastard.' He squinted at his bow. 'Are you become Constantine's pampered guardsman, or do you come to fight where the action will be hottest?'

'The emperor has spared me for you. Though I do not think he will be far from the heat himself.'

'Good. So let us to it.' He clapped his great hands onto Gregoras on one side, and the Sicilian on the other. 'Let us to it, boys,' he cried, driving them toward the entrance.

'You are merry, my lord,' Gregoras said, coughing.

'Of course,' Giustiniani bellowed. 'I am about to kill Turks.'

Through squadrons of soldiers mustering to trumpet calls, they crossed the short patch of ground to the bastion, mounted it. Constantine joined them, Theodore as ever by his side. All looked to the Turkish lines, the fires still raging there, silhouetted men crowding before them. Below them, fifteen paces away, men were still cramming timber and mud onto the stockade that, in this spot and for hundreds of paces in either direction, had replaced the outer wall. 'Enzo,' Giustiniani called, 'admit the chosen men of Constantinople and of Genoa into the Peribolos.' He gestured to the space between the inner and outer walls. 'When they are all in, and we with them, lock the gate. Then let the key be placed here, in this tower.'

The Sicilian nodded and left. 'Lock them in?' Constantine queried. 'Might you not want to bring more men in and the wounded out?'

'More men?' Giustiniani laughed. 'What men would they be, *basileus*?' He shook his head. 'No. All my men will be here, fighting beside the elites of your city, and the wounded and the dead will lie where they fall. Nothing focuses the mind of a fighting man better than knowing there is no retreat. Do you do the same, lord, further up at the Charisius gate. And give the key into the charge of some steady fellow who is not going to succumb to the weeping of men.' He nodded towards Gregoras. 'The man of many names will guard ours here.'

Gregoras frowned. 'You are certain you do not want me beside you, lord, down there?'

'No. I need you for the task I have just stated – and for your prowess with the bow. From here you will see more clearly if some sheep-fucking Turk is trying to stick me in the arse. Before he does, you will kindly put an arrow through his throat.'

Gregoras nodded. Though he was good with falchion and mace, he was better with the bow. He looked down, as the gate on the inner wall swung open and the Genoan mercenaries, the light from reed torches glinting off their black armour, marched four by four into the Peribolos. Following them, less ordered but almost equally well armed, came the chosen Greeks.

'I will away,' said Constantine briskly, 'and go wherever I am most needed.' He looked down at the *stauroma*, frowned. 'Most probably close to here.'

'Most probably, *basileus*,' Giustiniani grinned. 'And bring a few hundred Venetians with you if you return. Otherwise the bastards will sit on their arses for the entire battle and still claim all the glory.'

Constantine half turned, hesitated, turned back. 'Commander,' he said, his face a frown, 'I wish I could . . .'

He broke off. Giustiniani nodded, spoke softer now. 'Go with God, lord. And let us kneel together tomorrow and praise Him in the Hagia Sophia.'

The emperor descended the stair. Theodore briefly ran his fingers up Gregoras's bow arm, muttered, 'Better,' then followed. Giustiniani and Gregoras peered down again into the Peribolos. All who were to enter it had come.

'When you have the gate key, put it in that alcove there. Tell another archer, in case you fall. Tell him too that nobody gets the key but on my command, or if I am dead . . .' he paused. 'Well, if I am dead, a plague on it, do what you want.' He smiled, gripped the younger man's arm. 'Go with God, my friend.'

'Go to the devil, lord,' Gregoras replied, putting a hand behind his ear. 'Can't you hear him calling his son?'

A smile, a wave and the Commander descended, reappearing a moment later in the Peribolos. Enzo locked the gate behind him. 'Zoran!' he called, and threw something up. A glitter reflected torchlight as it spun up through the night air. Then the key was in Gregoras's hand. He held it a moment, before laying it carefully in the alcove.

Other men joined him – archers, crossbowmen, Greeks, Genoans. All placed their quivers beneath a crenellation, then peered over them. A short distance away, figures moved before the flames, trumpets calling them to assembly, voices crying both to Allah and to man. Silhouettes, it was hard to tell much more about them, what type of warrior the sultan would fling at them first. It does not much matter, thought Gregoras, trying to conjure some moisture into his mouth. Come, whoever you are.

And then, as if God had thrown a blanket over his sight, all the fires ahead of him went out. The darkness spread rapidly along the Turkish line, flames extinguished down the ramparts toward the distant Sea of Marmara, up the hill towards the Charisius gate and no doubt all the way to the Horn beyond it. Maybe the odd fire spluttered before it died. But darkness came swiftly, everywhere. It was masterfully done.

Gregoras had fought them perhaps a dozen times and knew that, whatever Constantine had said to raise his officers' hopes, the enemy were mainly not slaves and certainly not cowards. They were some of the finest fighters in the world.

But so are we, he thought, looking down at the silent, black ranks. Sucking in a breath, he reached for his bow. 'Come, Turk,' he repeated, to no one in particular, and notched an arrow.

TWENTY-FOUR

A Place Called Armageddon

29 May: fifty-third day of the siege: 1 a.m.

As soon as the fires went out, the chanting began, a single word exhaled, followed by a sharp inhalation.

'Ismicelal.' Breath. 'Ismicelal.' Breath. 'Ismicelal.' Breath.

Achmed did not join in. He had before, on other attacks, had felt the heat rise in him till sweat broke from his skin. Chanted again and again, the short breath fuelling it, exploding it out. Filling the faithful with hate, making them stronger, more vicious, determined to slaughter all the infidels or offer themselves as martyrs in the attempt, one of God's ninety-nine names on their lips, the rest in their hearts.

Achmed did not hate the men he would try to kill. He assumed they were men much like him, fighting for what they believed in. He had never needed anger to accomplish what he must. As for God, he had appeased and appealed to Him in three days of fasting while others took one, only breaking bread, eating meat at each sunset, as at Ramazan. And he wore beneath his robe the only armour he had aside from his shield – his name and Allah's, merged in eight squares, stitched into the centre of his undershirt.

So, as Raschid and one-eyed Farouk and such men of their troop who had survived till this moment chanted themselves into a killing rage, Achmed murmured his name, conjoined with one of Allah's. Then, as an officer with a plumed headdress walked along their lines, urging them off their knees and their weapons into their hands, as the men around him grew louder, he changed to a different chant.

'*Ya daim. Ya daim. Ya daim.*'

It was what he would chant in the fields, grasping the stalks of wheat, scything them down, again and again, the rhythm helping him keep going, long past exhaustion, till all the work was done, the fields clear, his family's future waiting to be collected, threshed, milled, made into life-sustaining bread. What lay ahead of him now was the same. The sultan had promised three days of pillage. Raschid had told him again and again of the fortunes that were theirs if the city fell. The gold to be stripped from infidel churches, from the very street stones. The slaves to be sold.

Achmed did not desire a fortune. He did not want, like the others, to return to his village and be the lord of it. He only wanted to be sure that his family would never lose another child to hunger. For that, and for Allah, and for the sultan, he would kill as much as he must. With his scimitar he would scythe the Greeks who stood between him and that hope.

They were on their feet, then they were moving forward, down the slope of the valley, across the stream, up the other slope. They were swung round, jabbed and prodded into rough lines. Only when he settled did Achmed allow himself to look up, over the heads of archers and slingers and the wheeled barricades they sheltered behind to what lay beyond them. It was there, what remained of the wall, chipped crenellations scattered like teeth in an old man's mouth, the gaps between filled with wood, and barrels, and earth. He could see it by the torches the Greeks had placed, for their own army was still shrouded in darkness.

The tremulous whisper came from beside him.

'Ismicelal.' Breath. 'Ismicelal.' Breath. 'Ismicelal.' Breath.

He looked down at Raschid. He was attempting fury but his eyes darted everywhere in fear. His arm, which had been scorched by the dragon in the tower, twitched repeatedly, a mass of scars and livid flesh. The dragon's hot breath had taken what scant courage the little man had had.

Farouk walked before them, tapping every second man with

his *bastinado*, his one eye fixing on theirs. 'Each of you touched, pick up a ladder as you pass forward. You will throw them against the Greek stockade and the man next to you will climb up.' The wooden stick jabbed into Achmed's chest, rested there. 'But you, giant, and every man from here down, have a different task.' He stepped back, bent, lifted something from the ground. 'Here,' he said, offering a long pole with an iron hook at its end. 'You men are to try and destroy the Greek's barrier. Grab the timbers that stick out. Pull them down. Dislodge the barrels. Understand?'

Achmed took the pole, hefted it, nodded. Glanced at Rashid, who had stopped chanting and looked ever more terrified – he was next to a ladder man and so designated as one to climb and fight. As Farouk moved off down the line, assigning tasks and tools, the big man whispered, 'Stay behind me. No one will see.'

Raschid nodded, swallowed, lips moving again, no noise emerging. Then they both started as sudden, violent sound came in a great crash of drums, in the smash of cymbals, in a wild fanfare of trumpets. Farouk was before them again, right in the middle of the troop. Drawing his sword, he thrust it high into the air, shouting to be heard above the musical din.

'*Allahu akbar!*' he cried.

The shout joined thousands more, rippling down the lines, reverberating over the hills, from the waters of the Golden Horn to the Sea of Marmara, drowning out even the *mehter* bands. Then, as one, ten thousand *bashibazouks* charged the walls of Constantinople.

There were men ahead of them, fighting first, firing culverin and *kolibrina*, the hollow sticks exploding in flames, shooting bullets that buried themselves in earth, ricocheted off barrels, sank into wood, sometimes into flesh. Scores of archers drew and shot, drew and shot, walking slowly forward behind the wheeled barricades till these stopped just before the fosse. Slingers, twirling their ropes, stepped from shelter to fling and dart back. But many were caught, as were many archers,

413

by scores of bullets, bone arrowheads, flung stones hurled from the stockade and from the towers behind it.

They had halted, as the barriers halted. Now, with their missile men shooting when they dared ahead of them, and the music growing ever louder behind them, with the chanting of God's name and the declaration of His greatness resounding from thousands of mouths, the order came.

'Forward!'

Achmed had charged the walls a half-dozen times now, by day, by night. Night was better, the Greeks found it harder to see and so to kill. Night was worse, for death came unseen and sudden from the darkness. All he could do, he did now. Made sure his scimitar was safe in the sling across his back. Lifted high the large round shield strapped to his left forearm, covering as much of his body as he could, leaving his name conjoined with God's to protect the uncovered rest. Beyond the shield, his left hand held the great pole an arm's span below its hook, his right near the butt.

By day and night, during scores of assaults, the fosse had been filled in to almost a height with the low, outermost wall. Running up the slight slope, Achmed vaulted the crumbling stonework. A short drop, a crouch, scores of men ducking and flinching into a torrent of metal and stone. 'On!' yelled Farouk, up and moving, shield raised, projectiles falling on it like hail onto a roof. All around him men ran forward, with ladders, with hooked poles, many dying in the running, their burdens snatched up and taken forward again. Over their heads their own archers shot, flighted death snatching men above who screamed and fell away. Achmed saw a gap between two barrels, suddenly vacated, ran towards it, jabbing the great pole up, hooking the end of a tree branch wedged there; dropped his full weight backwards, jerking the pole down hard. The branch sagged then shot out, and suddenly he was dodging heavy falling wood, and earth that filled his mouth, choking the roar he had not realised he was giving.

Spitting, he fell back, kicking away the branch. He looked to the side, where Raschid was trying to seem busy, prising a ladder from dying fingers. Farouk was shouting, but his words were lost in so many others, in so many languages – Greek and Italian from the defenders, Turk dialects from many of the assailants, but by no means all, for there were as many Christians attacking the stockade as defending it. Achmed could heard the Hungarian's yell, the guttural grunt of the Bulgar, the mercenary's shout and the vassal's. He heard a man beside him crying out in Osmanlica, 'I will braid your beard into a dog leash, Greek!' Heard the shouted reply in the same tongue, 'Come feel my bite!'

A babel of language, in curse, in prayer.

Again and again Achmed reached up, seeking to snag parts of the stockade, to pull it down, his shield rattling with flung stones, his magical undershirt warding off all arrows. Until one cry pierced them all, a universal one. 'For the love of Allah! Run! Run!' None stopped to consider if it was a command from any officer's throat. It was still obeyed; men turned as one and ran.

Dropping their tools, back they poured, pursued by jeers and bullets, over the low wall, slipping down the mud and bracken of the filled-in fosse. Thousands of men fleeing, laughing as one, laughing to be alive and out of hell, Raschid laughing louder than any – until a sharp crack changed his laugh into a shriek of pain. Men were ahead of them in a loose line, wielding lead-tipped whips or heavy wooden clubs. 'Back, dogs!' they screamed, lashing, jabbing. 'Back!'

Achmed crouched to pick up Raschid, who was clutching his face, a purple welt clear between his fingers. With a shout, he rose, and three men before him gave back. 'You dare . . .' he roared, stepping forward, arms outstretched. And then he was struck from behind, hard across the back.

He turned . . . and it was his own officer, Farouk, his scimitar raised for another blow with its flat side. 'Did you think we were done there, giant?' he yelled. 'Back, hound of the sultan. Back until your master calls you to the leash. Or would you rather run past these and meet . . . them!' He pointed with his sword, past the whip-bearing *chaouses* to where torches had been lit and flames glittered on ranks of men. Men in tall white turbans, row on row. 'Janissaries!' spat Farouk. 'While these will merely beat you, those will kill you if you seek to flee before your task is done.'

More *bashibazouks*, fresh men, had filed through gaps in the janissary ranks and were charging now, past them, running towards the enemy. Farouk swivelled with them. 'Now come! Come all of you!' He turned, laughing, pointing back the way they had fled. 'Follow me to paradise!'

Fury filled the large man, fury he had not managed to raise against his enemy – until now. Now it was guided, directed by his officer, who turned him, shoved him, stooped to lift and fling the whimpering Raschid after him. Both men stumbled forward, picking up speed on the slight slope, urged by the men charging just ahead of those who had already fought, the universal cry in their throats.

'*Allahu akbar!*'

Once more the filled fosse was climbed, the lowermost outer rampart straddled, the body-strewn stretch of ground the Greeks called the Parateichion run across. They were at the stockade again, but this time Achmed had no barbed pole in his hand. This time he leapt, wrapped huge arms around a thrust-out beam, kicked hard against the remains of stone beneath it, and shot from the wall, still clutching the wood, showered by the earth that came with it. He landed hard on his back, the air knocked from him, looking up at the hole he'd made, an enemy tottering in it, a Greek judging by the length of his beard, looming over the sudden gap then falling through it. His enemy landed two paces before him, struggled up, terror in his eyes, turning back to the stockade, sword dropped, fingers scrabbling at the mud-faced wall. A spear passed Achmed's face, thrust hard, piercing the Greek, who screamed, did not turn, still tried to climb. Then men were rushing at him, Raschid among them, swords slashing. The

Greek squealed, thrashed, could not avoid them, still trying to crawl upwards to his safety. Somehow he managed to get halfway, before Raschid dropped his sword, grabbed the man's legs, pulled him down. And then Achmed lost him, in the sprayed blood that misted his eyes.

Air returned to his lungs along with his rage. Rolling onto his feet, sidestepping the writhing mass on the ground, he drew the scimitar, ran again at the stockade and the gap he'd made in it. He got purchase on the debris there, his shield hand reaching up to grab another piece of wood. Hauling on this, digging his sword elbow into the earth, he swung his legs up and over. And suddenly he was sitting on the lip of the rampart, in the gap between two barrels.

He did not know if he was more startled than the men who faced him. Perhaps they were, their shock expanding as he rose to his full height. He had stood here once before, weeks earlier, had earned gold for his feat that his brothers, in arms and in Allah, had drunk and pissed away. He saw the faces before him, mouths wide in shrieks of rage and fear. But all he could hear was the music of the *mehter* band, the drum beating like his heart, the *sevre* singing like the blood in his ears.

'Allah . . .' he began, then stopped, as something sliced across his chest, opening his shirt, passing through the place where his name and God's were joined, straight through his shield arm, pinning the flesh to the wood. It spun him, the force of it, his feet slipping on the uneven edge of mud and timber. He grabbed for the barrel before him to stop his fall, wrapping arms around it. And then he was plunging back down the slope, ripping the barrel from its mount, just managing to tip it to the side as he fell.

His landing was softer this time, for he landed on a body, his head jerking down and slapping the ground hard. Stunned, he lay there a moment, until his eyes cleared and he was staring into other eyes, ones he'd seen filled with horror before, filled with death now. The fallen Greek stared at him through blood-sheen, and Achmed looked past him, to his own splayed-out shield arm. Still held in leather straps, it did not look the same. It took him a while to understand that there was an arrow in it.

He lay there, while his arm streamed blood, while air slowly returned and brought back other senses. Men were rushing past him, screaming, falling. Stones were thumping into the earth near him, jagged pieces of masonry from destroyed walls. One hit him in the side, the sharp pain finally clearing the mist from his eyes. Words came, a tugging at his chest.

Raschid was there. 'You are wounded. Come!'

They didn't go far. Crawling and slithering over mud and bodies, they slid over the outermost low wall, sheltered in its lee. More men ran past them to attack, yelling to God in all His different names, to Christ Risen, to saints, mothers, lovers. One officer tried to raise them, drive them forward again, but Raschid lifted Achmed's shield arm, displayed the arrow driven through it. So the officer ran on to harry other men.

'Rest easy,' Raschid whispered, tearing cloth from a body to staunch the flow of blood. 'We have done enough.'

Men passed into the attack, again and again. Some came back, some only as far as the wall they sheltered behind, to cough out their lives beside them. Many fled and were whipped and beaten back yet again. Later, much later, within the music and the screams, a different sound, piercing all, a single clear trumpet. Something familiar in it, Achmed had heard it often enough, been taught to recognise it, and eventually he did, words shouted in his ear confirming it.

'They recall us. Our task is done. Come. Come!'

They rose, as men ran or staggered or crawled past them. Crouching low, for shot and arrow still came from behind and before them, they stumbled back up the slight slope to the siege lines and through them. The *chaouses* with their whips and clubs were gone and other men were there to greet them, water bearers with jugs, surgeons in purple turbans and grey robes, their assistants moving among the men who now fell gasping to the ground.

'How fares the giant?'

Achmed looked up. Farouk stood over them. Raschid eagerly thrust his companion's arm out, to a groan. 'He is wounded, as you see. He cannot fight again.'

Farouk stooped, bringing his own blood-splattered face close. Light came into the single eye, a smile twisting the maimed face. 'Good enough to let you lie here, giant. But call that a wound? After you stood again upon their ramparts and took all they could give you, that is all you have for it?' He pointed to his puckered eye socket. 'This is a wound!' He pulled his half-ear. 'This is a wound!' He laughed, straightened, called to a turbaned man nearby, 'Master, I have a wounded hero here.'

The surgeon came over, knelt, carefully lifted the arm and shield together, felt. 'Hmm!' he said, examining. 'You are blessed by Allah, most merciful. It has passed through the flesh under the upper arm, but I do not think . . .' He tilted the arm. 'Yes,' he said, tapping the shield. 'Hold this.' His assistant did. 'And now . . .'

He pulled a pair of sharpened tongs from a bag and snapped the arrow beneath its bone head, drew the shield off. Then, as Achmed sank back, the surgeon gripped near the feathers and slid the shaft from the wound. He gestured, and his assistant poured water from a jug over and over, the surgeon squeezing as he did. Then he pulled a long strip of clean cloth from his bag, wound it tight, tied it off. Rising, he nodded. 'Rest it. Keep it bound. Wash it every day. With fortune you will have no more than a memory and a scar to frighten your grandchildren with. *Inshallah.*'

He was gone, to another man groaning nearby. Raschid pointed after him. 'You heard what he said, master. My recruit must rest.'

'Your recruit? And the recruiter with him, I suppose?' Farouk shook his head. 'Well, I don't think you will be called upon to display your courage again, Raschid. I think our time of fighting is done. It will be up to others now.' He looked up, as the music that had halted since the retreat began again.

'Others who come now. You can get our wounded hero to your tent.'

He moved away. Raschid leaned in. 'Does he think we will sit in our tents and wait while the walls are taken and others get the plunder? No.' He stuck his hand under Achmed's good arm, bidding him rise. 'Come.'

The ground seemed a good place to be. 'Where?' sighed Achmed.

'Away from this place of flying arrows.' Raschid grinned. 'I heard Farouk say that the walls by the Horn are the weakest, and the palaces and richest churches close behind them. When they fall, that is where he'll be, and we with him. Come.'

Achmed rose, groaned. He seemed to hurt everywhere and in his arm the least.

'That's right, hero.' Raschid was smiling now, though his body and voice still shook. 'Let us go and find our share of plunder.'

29 May: 3 a.m.

While his fellow bowmen jeered the fleeing enemy, Gregoras threw a knotted rope over the tower's wall. Making sure it was secured to a crenellation, he climbed over and lowered himself swiftly, knot by knot, into the Peribolos below. He was the first but the others would follow, intent, as he was, on refilling their quivers, all but emptied by the sustained attack. He pushed through the throng, through men praising God, the Virgin, each other for their victory. Praising themselves too, for feats of combat and courage. For the miracle of survival.

Gregoras made for the stockade, crouching when he neared it, though only the occasional arrow still flew from the enemy lines. There were bodies dangling off the timber there, and before the Greeks cleared them away he wanted his share of their bounty. Turkish arrows or his own, he didn't much care as long as he was armed for whoever was to come next.

He gleaned his harvest, sometimes using his knife to prise free any deeply lodged barb. When he came to the point of the stockade where a barrel was missing, he risked a quick look outside, down, but he did not see the huge Turk's body below. He could have been buried beneath others, there were plenty there. But somehow Gregoras felt he'd missed, or at least not killed. He'd seen the giant fall, that was all. He'd have liked that arrow back, to make surer of his target the next time.

His quiver was nearly full, he was crouched over a last body, when someone tapped his back. 'You live, Ragusan.'

He looked up. 'I do, Sicilian. And it is Constantinopolitan. Especially today.'

'Too many syllables. Like Greg-or-as.' Enzo grinned. 'I prefer Zoran.' He extended a hand, pulled the other up. 'The Commander wants you.'

Giustiniani was in a small huddle of officers, near the back of the Peribolos, just before the ditch that had been dug out to provide earth for the rampart. It was being refilled – with bodies, men clearing them from underfoot and dropping them in, friend or foe, at peace in death. He nodded at Gregoras, was about to speak, when another's arrival distracted him.

'Have we triumphed?' the emperor called as he moved through bowing men whom he gestured off their knees.

'Your majesty is hurt?'

Giustiniani stepped closer to study the stained breastplate, but Constantine waved him away. 'Not my blood,' he said briskly. 'A mix of many, for they kept coming and coming.' He glanced down into the ditch as another body was tumbled in to join the mass. 'As here, I suspect. As all down the lines, for I have had reports from the palaces and the fight was as hot there, the enemy as unsuccessful. Some seamen did try to land at different points along the Horn walls but all have been repelled. Have you heard from further down?'

Giustiniani gestured to a begrimed officer, who saluted. 'Your cousin, Theophilus Palaiologos, greets you, majesty, and says the Pege gate holds. He sends word too that venerable Cantacuzenus has driven off an assault on the Golden Gate.'

A cheer went up from those near enough to hear. 'Have we won, then, Commander?' said Constantine. 'Was that an attempt to take the city by surprise and, having failed, will they draw off?'

Giustiniani pointed at Gregoras. 'Tell your emperor, Rhinometus. Let it come to him in Greek, so he will not think it is only Italian crows who croak the bad news.'

Gregoras turned to the emperor. 'Majesty, if you look at the bodies, you will see that none are men of the first rank. *Yayas.* Foreign fighters. All *bashibazouks.*'

Giustiniani interrupted. 'They were sent first to weaken us, for what is yet to come. Peasants from Anatolia. Scum from Balkan slums.' He spat. 'Expendable.'

Constantine grimaced, swallowed. 'I feared as much. And what *is* to come, think you?'

The Commander gestured Gregoras to continue. He hesitated. And as he paused, sound came. A great blast of trumpets, the smashing of cymbals, the hammering of deep-voiced *kos* drums. 'That is, *basileus,*' Gregoras said.

The group moved to the stockade, peered. It was still too dark to see anything clearly. But then a darker mass flowed over a ridgeline marked again in fire and there was another sound this time beneath the war music, one that had not been there before – the rhythmic pounding of shod feet on the earth. A more regular chanting came then too, the inevitable appeal to anger and to Allah.

'Give me fire,' commanded Giustiniani, the order passed back in shouts to the looming bastion and beyond. In moments, a huge ball of flame shot over the walls in a high arc. There were a few mangonels, siege slings that had come to seem almost redundant with the bringing of the great guns. And though there was little naphtha left for fuel, most having gone to the Scotsman and his Greek Fire, there was enough for this ball. It passed in flame across the sky, then dropped, to plunge into the advancing black mass. Fire briefly lit the sweeping ranks of armoured men – and, in their midst, one yellow *oriflamme*.

'The Anatolian division,' declared Giustiniani grimly. 'Back to your position, lord. The real battle is about to begin.'

Constantine sighed, saluted, turned and was gone, his guard following at a run. The Commander looked at Gregoras. 'And to yours, Noseless One. I need your arrows.' As he turned away, Giustiniani called after him, 'Did you see that huge fucking Turk that danced atop the stockade?'

'Yes.'

'Why didn't you kill him?'

'I tried, master.'

'Well . . . try better next time, will you?' Giustiniani grinned. 'Kill them by the score!'

There were other men lined up at the knotted rope and Gregoras had to wait his turn to climb. While he did, arrows began to fall thicker over the stockade, *kolibrinas* cracked and their bullets whined off walls. The music drew closer, the *mehter* band of the Anatolians accompanying their men right up to the fosse, the music a ferocious blare. But the Christians had music of their own. Every bell in the city pealed the alarm, recalling its citizens to the fray, beseeching God. Somewhere nearby, a water organ groaned with the approximation of a hymn.

When his turn came, Gregoras climbed swiftly, slid over the battlements, grabbed his bow, slipped the finger ring he'd had fitted into place, notched an arrow. With one eye only showing past the crenel, he watched the stockade jerk and dance as if alive as the enemy poled and hooked it. A ladder drew his eye, the first of scores slapping down. 'Come on,' he whispered, and when a helmeted head appeared, he put his first arrow through it.

It was harder to shoot after that. The Anatolians in their black armour, the Genoans in theirs merged into one long, seething, striving mass along the ill-lit rampart, friends and targets near as close as lovers. And in their bastion, he and his bowmen were targets too, for the mass of Turkish archers, slingers and culverin men clustered a bare sixty paces away, just the other side of the fosse. Arrows careened off the crumbling mortar of the crenels; bullets struck, sending splinters of stone near as fast as lead. To lean out, to take that hard shot, was to lean into a death-bearing storm. Yet the bowmen did it, again and again, and many paid death's price for it, reeling back with a shaft jabbing through a limb, scoring fire across a skull, buried in a chest; with a ball lodged in lungs fast filling with blood, coughed out with a last plea for forgiveness. Gregoras felt death pass him on each side, above, below. Once he felt a sting at his temple like some biting insect, reached up to wetness, rubbed blood between his fingers then off onto his jerkin. And still he leaned out more than any other, defiant, a wild thirst taking him as he sought another victim for the next arrow, one less Turk to stab at his friends, to push his way into his city, to threaten what he loved. He sought, shot, missed, sought, shot, killed, and then his quiver was empty and he was reaching for what belonged to the dead and the dying beside him. When those arrows were gone too, he looked about him, spied a falling crossbowman with a bunch of quarrels, snatched the weapon up even as the man went down. It was big, heavy, did not have a stirrup; but a crannequin leaned against the wall to hook and pull up its string. He placed the metal hooks, wound up the cord, loaded a bolt, stepped forward again, glanced through projectiles to the scene below.

There was enough fire to see by. The Greeks had poured burning pitch down at spaces along the rampart. Ladders, stacked wood and men all burned. The Turks were shooting fire arrows from their lines, and Gregoras watched the flaming arc of one, its exquisite parabola ending as it thumped into a barrel and spread flame over wood. The black mass of men at the line heaved as the disciplined Anatolians threw themselves again and again up the ladders, and many straddled the walls. For the moment there was not a distinguishable target to be had there, so Gregoras looked again to where the enemy archers had to be in the darkness, and when an arrowhead of flame appeared there and started to slowly rise, he aimed two hand spans to its left and squeezed his trigger. The arrow jerked up in its place, then fell to splutter in the mud.

A sharper, higher-pitched trumpet cry in the night. The indistinguishable line at the stockade separated into two, the Anatolians stumbling away, the Greeks hurling insults and a few last stones at the black-armoured backs. Gregoras didn't even look for another quarrel, to take a last man as he fled. He wasn't sure he had the strength to draw his string up, crannequin or no.

The music had stopped with that one clarion call, all the noise was being made on his side of the rampart, the arrows and metal ball had ceased to fly his way and Gregoras could look down safely and for longer at the men below, many on their knees from exhaustion, many weeping. He looked for his close comrades – and found them together, Enzo helping to lift the Commander's great helmet off. The Sicilian looked for him too and he put a thumb up. Both men returned the gesture and then Gregoras sank back, reaching to the stone jug beside him, drinking deep of the water it contained. He looked at the dead and the exhausted around him. More alive than dead he was glad to see, and the wounded already being helped.

He raised the jug again . . . then stopped without pouring. Put it down, struggled up, leaned again into a gap in the front crenels to stare out into a darkness that moved beyond the rampart. 'What is wrong, brother?' A voice came from beside him and he lifted a hand to silence it, kept peering out, trying to hear beyond the noise of his own soldiers into the silence of the enemy.

Something *was* wrong. The Anatolians, the heart of the enemy, proud warriors with a legacy of triumph and a belief in Allah, had drawn off quickly or been allowed to withdraw, far faster than the wild, undisciplined troops who had preceded them. It did not make sense. Unless one of their main commanders had been killed. Or unless . . .

He did not want to think of another reason. Tried to avoid thinking of it with unaccustomed prayers. He only prayed in battle, when everyone else did.

'Holy Maria, bless us. Protect us, your servants. Shield us with your light. Hold us . . .'

He ceased murmuring, to strain his ears for what he did not want to hear . . . and did. The roll of something heavy, like a stone down a metal slope. The squeak of too much cloth pushed into a space too narrow for it. The sudden splash of water, a bucket thrown.

And then in the darkness close to where he'd sent his last bolt, he saw flame. Not a fire arrow raised and shot, a light that rose steadily as if someone was climbing with it. It halted, hovered.

He was at a side gap in an instant. 'Commander!' he screamed, trying to be heard above the drone of prayer, the moaning, the bells. 'Enzo! It's . . .'

He saw Enzo hear him, raise his hands in question, his shoulders a shrug. And Gregoras shouted the word, but it was lost in the action of the word he screamed.

'Cannon!'

He turned to the roar, saw the giant flash of flame spat out from a huge, round mouth. Not even a second passed before what the great gunshot smashed into the stockade, sweeping away a huge section of it, and the men behind it, vanishing them, a dozen or more, just gone. Gregoras saw the gap, the gaping hugeness of it, a moment before a vast bank of thick black smoke rolled over it, swallowing sight.

There was silence then, for a long moment, before the screaming began, of agony, of terror. Then of something else, as thousands of voices gave out the same deep-throated cry.

'*Allahu akbar!*'

The Anatolians were coming again.

From the cloud the great gun had created, into the gap it

had made, over the destruction it had caused, Turks were charging, twenty abreast, infinitely deep. All the defenders who had stood at that point of the stockade were gone, as if snatched away by God's own hand. There was no one there to stop the rush, and those survivors nearby were deafened, blinded, stunned. Gregoras could see that the first Turks over the wall were already spreading out, widening their front, allowing more and more of their own to join them.

And then he heard another trumpet, one he recognised: Constantine's. He peered beyond the spreading Turks, but smoke and darkness obscured all. Yet another trumpet he knew answered – Giustiniani's. Emperor and Commander called to him. His city. His comrades. Swiftly, Gregoras strode to the rear wall, pulling off the thick quilted jerkin of the archer. Beneath, he had already put on his arming doublet against this eventuality. He bent to his armour. 'You!' he called to a young archer nearby. 'Help me.'

The youth came up, his mouth working, no sounds emerging. Still, his fumbling fingers did the work Gregoras directed him to. He got the breastplate around him, ordered the youth to tie the front plate to the back while he slipped the twin vambrace over his upper and lower arms. Judging from the screams and steel clatter coming from below, there was time for little else. His legs, shoulders, neck would have to be exposed. He bent for his metalled gloves, thrust them on. 'Helmet,' he commanded, and the young man lifted it, and pushed it on. Unlike the borrowed helm he'd worn in the sea fight, this was a barbuta, open at the face. In a night fight, he was happy to trade the protection of a visor for keener sight.

He considered what was left, reluctantly disdained his shield in favour of two weapons – a fluted mace and the falchion he'd acquired to replace the one he'd lost at sea. Shoving each into loops at his side, just as the youth tied his last knot, Gregoras flung the rope over the battlements.

He took a breath, bent to his study. It showed him a fight that had progressed. Not a rout, for the Anatolians had only spread a little further, their front perhaps a hundred men across, all that could force themselves into the gap their cannon and their initial rush had made. But Gregoras could see that they were slowly pushing forward against the still rallying Genoans and Greeks, allowing more of their men in, with still more forming behind.

He bit his lip. What little could he do? Then he heard again, from the far side of the melee, that distinct cry of the emperor's bugle. And this time he glimpsed something flying there in the torch flare: the double-headed eagle of Constantinople. Saw the part of the enemy's line it soared above bulge inwards.

He looked to the base of his tower. On the fringe of the fight, men milled. Directly below him was an open patch of ground. Climbing onto the rope, he slid down to it, faster than he had the previous time, the heavier for the metal on his back.

He landed in a group of about ten men, of his country he could tell by their longer beards and ragtag armour; pushed to the fringes of the fight by the heavily armed, better-trained Genoans. They turned to him, startled at his sudden appearance, several lifting their swords. 'I am Greek!' he yelled, then pointed with the mace he drew to where the bugle sounded again. 'And that's our emperor coming.' Now he drew his falchion, raised both weapons high and crying, 'For Christ and country!' ran into the fight.

He aimed at an angle, just behind the enemy's rough front line. He could not heed if he'd been obeyed, if men followed. Not when his trumpets called him. Could only strike at the Turk half turned away from him, turning back to raise his shield too late to stop the falling mace. Gregoras did not have time to prise the weapon from the crushed turban helmet before another Anatolian had turned on him, more prepared, striking before he was struck, sweeping his scimitar in a great arc over his raised shield, down, aiming for Gregoras's unarmoured shoulder. The Greek had no time to lament his own missing shield, could only twist round, jerking his mace free,

428

lifting his falchion as if punching its pommel up, reversed across his head and angled down. The weapon's wide blade was short but strong, the scimitar smashed against it and slid down with a steel scream. It pulled the Turk into a slight stumble forward, lowering his shield, let Gregoras jab the blunt end of his freed mace into the face revealed, knocking the head up. Not a blow to kill, only to shock, which it did, enough for death to follow, the falchion pulled back, turned, swept forward, pitted blade slashed deep into the exposed throat.

Men *had* followed him into the small gap he'd opened. One lost his sword hand to a scimitar's cut, but a second drove his spear point through a shield and pinned the man behind it. This Greek was huge, not all the giants were on the other side, and finding he could not jerk free his spear, he just bent, grunted, lifted, charged. The wailing Turk was a human battering ram, men were buffeted aside, the side rank of the enemy driven in.

'On!' Gregoras yelled, and followed. The big man was roaring, swinging his awful, living burden from side to side. Finally, a spear thrust in from the side, slicing across his leg behind the knee. He stumbled, still roaring, but his own spear lowered before him and blades swung over it. Gregoras had gained enough ground to knock two aside, one with each weapon he held. But another spear snapped the man's head back and he disappeared from Gregoras's vision, full now with enemies of his own.

He saw a man, an officer by the elaborate *kalafat* of peacock feathers on his helm, trying to close the gap the huge Greek's charge had opened. Gregoras ran straight at him, smashing his mace into the shield that rose, dropping to his knees and scything parallel to the ground with his falchion. The officer's boots were armoured but the blade was heavy and smashed the metal in. The man staggered, yelping in sudden pain, and Gregoras was up, driving his shoulder hard into the man's huge square shield, sheltering behind it as he pushed the officer into his men.

And then he felt it, the sudden giving. Not just the man leaping backwards, though he did, and it made Gregoras fall himself to his knees. A space opened before him, widening in moments as the enemy began to run. He had seen the same thing in birds, flocks of them turning in the air in an instant, as if one will governed all. Perhaps they were birds here, the sudden looming of a double-headed eagle turning them to prey, and so to flight.

'Constantine!' came one roar above so many. And Gregoras looked up to see his emperor beneath his standard, leading his own guard of men, right in the centre of his enemies who were there and then were gone, flinging themselves over what remained of the stockade, sliding down slopes of bodies and mud.

There was no need to pursue, no strength to do so. It wasn't a silence, there were too many moans, but the music had stopped and men did not have the breath left to jeer.

Gregoras knelt, gasping, as did most around him. Constantine, though, leading his guard, surged on, up to what remained of the stockade. There for a moment the eagle flew above the heads of the defenders, before a volley of arrows and culverin shot made them stoop, give back.

'There! There!' came a familiar voice, and Giustiniani was striding forward, directing a dozen men who rolled barrels and bore wood to the gap the Anatolians had just swept through. 'Do not fear!' the Commander cried, when he saw the men hesitating to approach the expanse. 'The great cannon can only fire every two hours. Stack it up, boys. And, Enzo, bring up a squad.'

Gregoras watched the Sicilian run forward with twenty armoured men, who crouched behind the barrels rolled into position. More came forward with barrows full of earth, with tree limbs, with nets filled with vine cuttings. In moments, the gap the cannon had blasted was loosely filled.

Constantine, raising his visor, joined the Genoan. 'Is that your blood or your enemy's?' he said, pointing.

Giustiniani took off a gauntlet and wiped his face. 'Mine, curse it. A rock splinter, I think. Enzo!' he bellowed. 'Some cloth here.'

'Do you . . .' Constantine hesitated. 'Do you need to withdraw to have it tended?'

Gregoras noted the hesitation. The emperor knew – all knew – what effect Giustiniani's leaving would have. He was the heart of the defence. Men would lose theirs and fast.

The Genoan knew it too and shook his head. 'No. I do not leave this place unless I am carried out.' Cloth came, and beneath his dabbing he glared at Gregoras. 'You are meant to be up there,' he said, as if the breakthrough was his fault.

Gregoras smiled. 'And miss the glory? Besides, you needed help.'

'That we did,' Giustiniani muttered, wincing as Enzo dabbed, 'and will again.'

Constantine, who'd been drinking from a water jar, looked sharply at him. 'Surely . . . surely the Turk is beaten now?'

'Beaten? No.' Giustiniani looked at the cloth. 'There is more blood to be shed yet.'

'More? But—' Constantine began, and then was interrupted by a shout.

'Where is the emperor?'

'Here he stands!'

The shouting man was pushing through the armoured Genoans, as begrimed and bloodied as any of them. He knelt, as much from exhaustion as respect. 'Liege,' he gasped, 'the enemy fly their flags on the palace of Porphyrogenitus.'

Though he was hissed to silence, a murmur spread rapidly through the mob of soldiers. All men turned to the north, straining into the darkness, though even had there been light, no one could have seen beyond the hillcrest topped by the gate of Charisius. 'I must . . . must go there,' said Constantine.

'No!' Giustiniani shouted, then lowered his voice. 'We discussed this, *basileus*. We cannot rush to every alarm. Each leader must hold his position, retake it if necessary. Ours is here. Here!' He thumped his breastplate, making the armour clang. 'For they will come here again, believe me.'

Constantine closed his eyes, swallowed, nodded. 'You are right. And we have good men there, resolute men. Minotto the *baillie*. The incomparable Bocciardi brothers.' He glanced down, spotted Gregoras where he still knelt, smiled. 'And your brother, Theon Lascaris.'

'My . . . brother?' Something Sofia had said of him, of his politician's arrangement with the enemy, came back to Gregoras now. His brow flushed cold, chilling the sweat. He rose. 'My liege,' he said, his dry voice cracking, 'Theon is—'

'To arms! To arms! They come! They come again!'

Shouts drowned out his cautions. All around him, men were lifting weapons.

'Back to your place, lord, and we to ours,' Giustiniani commanded, dabbing a last time at the still flowing blood. 'And you to yours, Zoran.'

It was true. Each man had his position. And he could no more run through crowds of warriors to the old palace and hope to find Theon than Constantine could rush there to defend it. Each man had his destiny that day, for good or ill. Gregoras straightened. 'I am out of arrows, Commander. So I may as well stand beside you here.'

Giustiniani smiled. 'Good. Then take your place.' He looked Gregoras up and down. 'But for Christ's sweet sake, put on the rest of your armour. You look like a *bashibazouk*.'

As drums beat, as bells and trumpets sounded, Gregoras turned to the bastion and sighed. The rope looked unclimbable now; it was hard enough to raise his weapons above his head. 'You! You! Nico!' he called. The young man who'd helped him before peered down. 'Tie the rest of my armour to this rope. Lower it to me.'

He turned as he waited, looking north. There was the faintest lightening in the sky. Dawn was coming. But even with it, he wouldn't be able to see to the palace of Porphyrogenitus, and the green flag of the Prophet flying over it. 'Theon?' he murmured. 'Brother?'

The palace of Porphyrogenitus
One hour earlier

'Megas Primikerios! The men hear movement below. Perhaps they come again.'

'Good. I am tired of waiting.' Theon pushed himself slowly off the ground, groaning, careful not to use the left arm in its sling. He had spent much time giving the impression of great pain; he did not wish to dispel it now before his sharp-eyed junior officer. He also did not raise his head. A tic had started near his left eye and distorted his whole face. 'Go ahead,' he said. 'I will follow.'

But he didn't. Instead he stepped up to the bastion's front arrow slit and peered through it. The Turks had put out their torches again, which usually boded ill. And the music had stopped, which would be a blessing if it was not also a bad sign. It would start again, after the cannon's blast and fire arrows lit the night; just before they stormed up the rubble- and body-strewn slope created by the tumbled bastion beside the one he stood in.

They had charged five times. Each time they'd been repulsed. But each time more of the few defenders died. He'd avoided the front line of the fight so far, an already hurt officer standing aloof but in command. He wouldn't be able to do that much longer, sling or not. Soon, perhaps, only hurt officers would be left.

He looked at his father's sword, leaning in the corner of the stone room. Cursed thing, he thought, bequeathed to him from a cursed man because he was the elder of the twins by a mere few moments. He had hated his father, though he had known him but little. A soldier, always away defending the empire's shrinking boundaries. A rough man, given to

433

boisterous jokes, ones he shared with the younger brother, for plain reasons. When only his sword returned from war, it was also plain which of the brothers should have the fine weapon. So Theon had insisted on his birthright, and enjoyed Gregoras's impotent fury.

He could barely draw the thing. He was not the son his dead father would ever have been proud of. Though he possessed many other skills, greater weapons by far than any rusting blade. Skills of diplomacy. Skills of intellect.

Skills of survival. He had raised himself to the point where an emperor called him *oikeios*. And were all those skills to die with him because he was a failure at others? With a sword, the bluntest of all tools? It was unfair, as well as foolish.

It was obvious what was about to happen. Possibly here, in this next attack the Turks were preparing. Probably elsewhere, down the Lycus valley, where the feeble stockade stood.

Beyond obvious. Certain. Even to a man who was not a soldier. Theon thought back to his meeting with Hamza Bey, in the avenue of Judas trees. The Turk had asked a question. 'What do reasonable men do, when certainty is reached?' And he had replied, 'They consider their options.'

Now he twitched and considered those options. To go out now and wield a sword he could barely lift? To die in a breach that was going to be stormed anyway, defending a city that was doomed to fall? Or to . . .

He thought about Hamza's banner. Hung from his house, it would protect his property, his family, himself from the ravagers, the pillagers, the slaughterers and enslavers. But only if he had done something to earn protection. For only then would that protection be maintained. His family, the very name of Lascaris, made safe.

What was it the Turk had said at their first meeting in Genoa? That they had more in common with each other than the Greeks did with the Romans. That they were men of the East. 'You of the city will stay on and see it great again . . .

434

Help us restore its greatness, the centre of an empire it once was and can be again.'

It was true. Theon gave a little laugh, reached up to rub at his jumping face. He was about to lose his life for a corpse that would not lie down. And yet Mehmet promised a renewal, and toleration too, no forced conversion to Islam . . . or to Catholicism. Orthodox Greeks at the heart of that renewal. Men with skills, with intellect.

Reasonable men like himself.

Theon pushed himself away from the arrow slit and the sounds of impending assault. It was beyond obvious. It was inevitable. More than that, it was his duty. To his family. To his faith. To his city. And he could not trust Sofia to do what must be done. A frightened woman cowering with her children? No, he had to take care of it. He had to go home.

But first, he had something to do. To prove his value.

He was at the door to the bastion, just about to step out onto the battlements, when the young Greek officer almost barged into him, such was the haste of his return. 'Excuse me, Megas—' he began.

Theon interrupted him briskly. 'I have assessed the situation. I go to Minotto. We need more troops here. To your post.'

He turned the opposite way to the fight, headed for a descending stair. The young man called after him, 'Megas Primikerios . . .'

'Do what I command,' Theon roared, taking steps swiftly.

'But, *kyr* . . . you have forgotten your sword.'

Theon stopped. He looked up – at the young man above him, the cursed weapon in his hand. He reached up, snatched it, continued down the stair. 'To your post,' he called. 'Hold the breach till I return.'

Any further reply was lost in the cannon's blast. Their own trumpets blared the summons. Men passed him, armour jangling as they ran up.

He reached level ground, swiftly walked fifty paces further, seeking. To his left was the avenue of Judas trees, long since stripped of their pink bloom. To his right, a deeper darkness. Grabbing a flaring torch from its sconce, he descended the stair. Just then he heard the sharp bark of cannon fire, felt, a moment later, the shudder as great stone balls slammed into the wall close by him. His torch crackled and sparked as dislodged roof dust fell into it. He steadied himself against the wall.

It was as he remembered it from when he'd escorted Hamza after his last embassy – a bare room, scarce four paces across. A plain, thick oak door, the Kerkoporta itself, criss-crossed with bolts and iron bindings before which tall barrels were set as further barrier. He looked around, placed his torch in a sconce, leaned his sword against the wall, then stepped to the nearest barrel.

'And what might you be doing here?'

The voice was soft enough, but it made Theon gasp and reel back. His hand made three attempts at his sheath before he pulled out his dagger. 'Who . . . who is there?' he called, his voice quavering.

A shadow moved out of the gloom of the stair. 'I am,' the voice came again . . . Then a man leaned into the flickering light.

And Theon recognised him. 'Johannes Grant,' he hissed, his voice still high.

'Plain John will do,' replied the Scotsman, stepping off the last stair.

Theon had had dealings with the fellow before. As few as possible, for he was always demanding this rare chemical or that precious commodity. Demanding them in execrable if fluent Greek, heavily larded with blasphemous obscenity. No gentleman, though he had been useful to the State, above and below the ground. While he wondered at the Scot's sudden appearance, Grant spoke. 'Are you here for the same reason I am?'

For a wild moment, Theon thought it might be true. If one

reasonable man would betray the city, why not two? But before he could consider a way to voice this, Grant continued, 'I was fighting alongside those mad Venetians, the Bocciardi brothers. Christ on the cross, they delight in slaughter, those shitters. We'd just driven back yet another attack, and were all excited about how those bastard Turks kept failing, when a vision of this place popped into my head. Just came like that.' He snapped his fingers. 'I always had it marked as a weakness, ye ken, even though it canna be seen from the front, being as it lies in the dog-leg of the wall. Still . . .' he leaned over and spat on the floor, 'I couldn't shake the vision so I thought I'd best check. You?'

Theon was breathing a little more easily now. 'Much the same.' He gestured to the arm he'd slipped back into the sling. 'I took a wound and was sent to a surgeon. Returning to my post, the idea came to me . . .'

Another ball struck, even closer this time, making both men reach to steady themselves. Funnelled down the stair came the sudden roar of music, and the loud glorying of Allah.

Grant turned to the sound. 'That's them donkey-loving sodomites coming again. I'd best away back so's I no miss the fun.' He turned. 'You with me, Lascaris?'

Theon nodded. 'Once I have done what I came for. Checked the bolts, the hinges of the door.'

'Aye. Do that. And give my salutations to your brother, if ye see that madman.'

He went, and Theon leaned back against a barrel, cursing softly. By what evil chance had he been witnessed here? But there was little he could do about it, save run after the other man and stab him. And the foul-mouthed Scot looked more than capable of defending himself. Besides, the man had given him a reason for being there. Checking a weakness. No one was to say what happened after they both left.

Slipping off the sling, Theon bent and grasped the nearest barrel. They were filled with bits of broken stone and sand; heavier, certainly, than his father's sword. But he found that, using his weight to tip it onto its metal-hooped edge, he could shift the barrel. And two more after that, clearing a path to the door. The bolts had been used recently and so slipped open easily. The hinges squealed as he opened the door, though their sound was swiftly lost in the noise of battle, the shrieks and curses, the music and the blows. He pulled it fully open, leaned out. The Scot was right; the sally port was in a dog-leg of the wall, not visible directly from the enemy siege lines. But he assumed that since Hamza had asked him to open it, he would have told someone that it might be opened.

A rising shriek came from closer by, someone crying out in sudden agony. Then, soft but distinct, he heard whispers beyond the door. In Osmanlica. They were coming.

Theon drew back inside, snatched up his sword, stumbled across to the stairs, up them, his legs barely taking him so much did they shake. The Kerkoporta was a cold place to die and the Turks about to come through the door would kill him in a moment. But his horse was near, and warmth a short ride away.

5 a.m.

The cry to arms had been unnecessary. The Turks had not come through the dark again . . . yet. Gregoras had had time to don the rest of his armour so that he was accoutred like the Genoan mercenary he had been, swathed in sleek black metal from barbuta to sabaton. Then time to remove his helm and lean his head on a stoved-in barrel. All around him warriors slumped in equally uncomfortable positions and tried to rest while keen-eyed men stared into the night – a task that got easier as the world grew lighter.

But though the Turk did not come, there was no ceasing of his activity. Cannon still blasted, knocking chunks of masonry from the crumbling inner wall, sweeping away swathes of hastily raised stockade, which were just as hastily rebuilt.

Arrows still flew at any who dared show their head. The *mehter* bands still played, bass drums and cymbals keeping the beat for the seven-note shriek of the *sevre*, the cry of the flute, the wailing of pipes. Though he had slept through many a bombardment, sleep, so desired this time, could not come, and after a while Gregoras rose, stretched to ease the cramp that had taken every limb, looked about. He saw Giustiniani twenty paces away, neatly severing the flesh from a mackerel's spine, picked up his helm, and went to join him.

The Commander sat on a small wooden camp stool. 'Help yourself,' he said, pointing into a bucket beside him, where a dozen or so of the blue-dappled creatures lay. It was one foodstuff that consistently made it into the city, for not even the Turk could cut off the swimming of fish, and any soldier not manning the land walls stood at the sea ones and cast lines and nets into the water. Though Gregoras rarely broke his fast before noon, he reached and ate. He did not know if he would see another noon, nor when he might eat again.

The Genoan waved the skeleton at him. 'What do you think? Are they done?'

Gregoras, knowing he was not being asked about what they chewed, answered simply, 'No. They will come again. And soon.'

Giustiniani nodded, throwing the bones over his shoulder and into the ditch behind him, under the inner wall, where it fell amidst the bodies of Greek and Turk. 'I agree. Mehmet must sense how hard pressed we are. He will try again, one more time. And he will try here.' He leaned over, spat beside him. 'While you were lost in dreams of naked *houris*, messengers came reporting the Turk's failures elsewhere. Those flags said to fly on the palace bastions? Torn down. Some of the enemy had got in, no one knows how, and it looked bad for a while. But then those mad bastard Bocciardi brothers – who almost give Venetians a good name – drove them out, and hoisted again the eagle of the city and the banner of St Mark.' With a groan and a clink of linked armour, Giustiniani rose.

'No. He will make his final attempt here. Hold here, and we will have won. Certainly this day's fight. Perhaps . . . all. Pray God I am right.'

'Amen.' Gregoras rose too, looked up into the Commander's eyes, near as black as his armour. 'And who, think you, will make this last assault?'

The eyes narrowed. 'I am sure you know.'

'Aye.' Gregoras nodded, crossing himself. 'May God protect us.'

It was Giustiniani's turn to say amen. And just as he did, the ceaseless music ceased. It had been building to a climax with a shrieking of *sevre*, with a smashing of cymbals, with simultaneous strikes on fifty *kos* drums, exploding like the cannon shot that had rarely stopped their pounding on the walls. Men flinched, many ducked, as if anticipating some blow, as a complete silence, as terrifying as any of the sounds that had come before, took over the enemy lines. Joined by Enzo, Gregoras and the Commander moved forward and cautiously raised their heads above the parapet.

No arrows flew at them, where twenty would have flown before. And of all the strange sights he had seen, Gregoras knew this for one of the strangest.

The enemy's advanced line, as close as the filled-in fosse, was almost deserted. Behind the wheeled screens that usually sheltered hundreds of archers and gunmen, within the always bustling wood-lined trenches, nothing moved. And no one did on their side either. Like Gregoras, all simply stared at a barren landscape, which stretched from the ditch to the ridge two hundred paces away, ground usually crowded, thrumming with life. Stared and wondered what the silence and the emptiness foretold.

Until one man nearby gave words to everyone's hope. 'They have gone!' he cried, his young voice soaring. 'Gone! We have won!'

Acclamation could have come then, relieved men filling the

horrid silence. But Giustiniani cut it off with his bull's roar. 'Quiet, you dogs. Hold your barking!'

The silence returned. Held but for a moment. Ended with the stillness as a single figure stepped over the ridge line. He was tall, almost unnaturally so; a monster perhaps, for he was wide as well. Then he turned slightly into profile, and all could see that it wasn't a vast and swollen belly but the father of all *kos* drums that he bore. See him raise twin sticks high into the air. See him let them fall. Hear the strike of wood on stretched skin.

It was the only clear sound for a while, for the men barely made any, the thousands that marched now over the hill's lip. They were not in formation but they came slowly, with disciplined stride, the sun that rose behind the defenders, over the city, glinting off what they carried – scaling ladders, poles with hooks, the barrels of culverins and *kolibrinas*. Mostly, everywhere, arrowheads.

'*Solaks*, in their white turbans,' whispered Gregoras. 'The archers of the household guard.'

'*Peyk*, with theirs of yellow,' said Enzo. 'Guards too, Mehmet's near companions. Some with their halberds, many with ladders.'

'And see.' Gregoras raised an arm, pointed. 'See the men wearing the leopardskin cloaks. The *serdengecti*. If all will die for Allah, these crave death, joyfully.'

'Enough,' grunted Giustiniani. 'Let these come and no more and we will eat them. Men who seek death so are wild with their lives. It is the calm soldier who wins battles. The others, well . . .' he shrugged, 'the sultan's guards are no prouder, nor any more martial than the Anatolians we drove off.' His eyes narrowed, as he peered at the hill's crest. 'It is who follows them that I would see.'

'And I,' muttered Enzo and Gregoras together.

Then they did, for even as the rough crowd of men reached and halted at the lip of the fosse, that monstrous drum was struck once again and one voice called a single word.

'Forward.'

At which command, in perfect order and with measured tread, the janissaries marched over the hill. Rank on silent rank they came, four hundred in each one, their first reaching the men already drawn up at the fosse before their last had crested the ridgeline.

'Holy Mother of God, protect us.'

No one said amen now to Enzo's whispered prayer. No one could speak; they could only stare as the last rank halted. There had to be close to ten thousand men drawn up silently before them. The elite of the Turkish army, the best trained, best fed, best led and most experienced soldiers of all. They had been used sparingly so far, taking part in few assaults. They had been saved – for this moment.

Something rippled in the very middle of the first silent rank. From behind two tall warriors bearing huge shields a man stepped out. It was hard to see him completely, with men surrounding him. But Gregoras glimpsed a scarlet surcoat, saw sunlight flash over gold links that joined the breastplate, noted the silver turban helmet, trimmed with more gold. Yet even without the richness, even if he was dressed only in the armour of the janissaries he had led to the fosse, Gregoras would still have recognised him by the *solak* archers beside him, one with bow in his left hand, one with it in his right. And so he breathed the name.

'Mehmet.'

He had brought them as far as he could. He would have led them further, as ready to die for his cause as they were for him, and all for Allah. But those closest to him had dissuaded him – Hamza Pasha, out there now upon the waters of the Marmara, attacking the sea walls. Zaganos Pasha, as vigorously assaulting the palaces to the north. Lastly, tellingly, his spiritual adviser, Aksemseddin, cautioning against the vanity of such an action. Though both knew he could wield a scimitar with as much skill as any of his janissaries, that his wrestler's lithe body was as primed as any for the fight, that he was as young and fast as any of his guardsmen, the imam had reminded him of the general's holy duty to command, to make the decisions still needed to be made beyond the parry and the thrust.

Yet Mehmet knew one certainty among all his doubts – that before this sun had reached its zenith he might still choose to run at the walls of the city he so desired and set his life at the hazard of the sword. For if this ultimate attack failed, it would be the last he could command. All those who had cautioned against this war, and carped while it progressed, would have been proven right. *Inshallah*, they would say. It was not written for us to succeed this time. Candarli Halil and the old men who surrounded him would quietly rejoice in the retreat to follow, the disbandment of the army, the slinking back to Edirne. And soon enough they would find a way to rid themselves of the young and troublesome sultan.

Instead of that, Mehmet thought, I will borrow the leopard-skin of one of my *serdengecti* and offer my life to Allah, most merciful. Rather a Greek steel blade through my throat this dawn than a Turkish silken bowstring round my neck one night.

In the silence that lingered he looked again at the men before him, in their gleaming armour, at their bows, turban helms, spears, swords. The fiercest warriors in the world. Yet he knew that all their fierceness, all their skills, might not be enough this day. The Greeks and their Latin allies had fought them off for seven weeks. Driven back every brave and brilliant assault, survived every trick and chance that war threw up. Not two hundred paces away another monarch stood, as convinced, however mistakenly, that the God he worshipped stood also at his shoulder. Closer still, the lion Giustiniani still roared. What land, what fortune, would he have given to have had the Genoan fighting beneath the crescent and not the cross? He had held the centre throughout the siege, even up to this night's work. Driven back thousands of *bashibazouks*, broken the proud nobility of Anatolia. He stood there still, awaiting this last roll of the bones upon this *tavli* board.

Mehmet peered, hoping to see, if only for a moment, this leader, this esteemed warrior. Yet if he did, he knew he would snatch a bow from one of his *solaks* and try a shot. Kill the Commander, he thought, and I cut the throat of their defence.

Disappointed, he looked away from the dark ramparts and the dark men manning them to the lightening sky. It ended now, he knew, within these next few hours, before the sun had reached its high point in the sky.

His mind was drifting. He saw that the *agha* of the janissaries was staring back at him, waiting. This silent advance, this pause, had been Mehmet's idea. But you could only hold a greyhound on the leash, or a goshawk by its jesses, for so long.

Mehmet focused. First on his commander; next on the banners: the green of the Prophet, the red and yellow of the corps itself, the cleft sword of Ali emblazoned in its middle. Lastly on his own sword, which he drew now. He took a breath, hummed to make certain his voice would not crack. Ready, he thrust the scimitar high into the air, the writings on it – his name, the *basmala* and other prayers for victory in exquisite calligraphy vanishing in the flash of morning sun that transformed it into one shaft of pure white light. Cried what he always cried, what they all cried. Breaking the silence with the universal declaration of their faith.

'*Allahu akbar!*'

The roar of ten thousand janissaries drowned out the roar of the great cannon, which fired again. One last time.

5.30 a.m.

It was sight that told Gregoras just before the sound, the perfect ranks splitting in one place; the little flame, almost lost in the sunlight, stabbed down.

'Cannon!' he screamed, even as he leapt sideways, throwing

his whole weight into it so that he could take down the armoured bulk of Giustiniani. As they tumbled, many men around him reacted to the call, fell as they did. Those who did not were swept away as the great ball smashed into the stockade.

The Commander was up in a moment, Enzo and Gregoras with him. There was no time for thanks, as foul-smelling smoke engulfed them, the enemy's cries within it as if devils rode it. Those cries had to be answered, those devils fought. 'For the emperor. For the city. For Christ,' roared the Commander, and hundreds of men took up the cry, doing as they had always done – rolling barrels to replace the ones the cannon had torn away, timbers and branches borne in to fill the gap. And then, as the smoke shredded, more sounds came from within it and men were screaming, 'Down!'

There had been few moments when arrows and bullets had not fallen onto them. But what passed before had been a spring shower to this storm, for the great mob of men who'd preceded the janissaries – archers and other men of the sultan's guard, gunners from every part of the army – now charged forward, shooting bows and crossbows, firing the smaller *kolibrina*, the longer-barrelled culverin. Projectiles fell, many glancing off fluted breastplate or hastily snapped-down visor, their sheer number meaning that some found their way into the gaps between pieces of steel or punctured what was less well forged. Men fell back, silently or with screams, blood pouring from a wound suddenly opened or feebly plucking at a shaft as if to remove it quickly was to deny its entry.

Crouching, face bent toward the ground, Gregoras listened to the whistle, the ricochet, the strike, his body tensed for intrusion . . . that didn't come. After an age, the metal falling ceased as suddenly as the halting of a hailstorm. Silence followed – and lasted for the eternity of ten heartbeats. He knew it in the thumps against his breastplate, saw it pass in the eyes of the man crouched next to him. They had been there before, he and Giustiniani, alone in the waiting silence. Yet as his heart counted down the moment, Gregoras knew something else: he had never been in a fight like this one, the stakes never as high as the ending of the world.

Then with the tenth heartbeat came an end to the silence in a different thump – the strike of one huge drum.

And the janissaries came.

Gregoras was up in a moment. 'To arms,' he cried, one of hundreds. He looked both ways along the lines of the stockade, that narrow, fragile gap between the points where the outer wall still stood – after a fashion, for at no place were the stones undamaged. Saw the surge all along it as scores of men rushed forward to its defence. To his right, perhaps a hundred paces along, he saw the banner of Constantine and of the city, the double-headed eagle swooping to the forefront of the fight. Turning forward again, he peered over the lip of his shield.

The janissaries marched, as much in step with their martial music as the shattered ground, a carnage of discarded weapons and broken bodies, allowed. Their standards waved and Gregoras, who had fought them enough, from the Hexamilion and afterwards, saw the symbols upon them and remembered some. Each *orta*, the cohorts of the force, had its mark. Against red and yellow backgrounds, camels walked, elephants trumpeted, lions roared. He looked for but did not see the red and gold of the household janissaries, elite of the elite. They would be further back, held till the very last. Yet Gregoras knew, as he drew his mace from the sling at his side, that he would be seeing them soon enough. If he lived.

A ladder slapped into the gap beside the barrel he sheltered behind, and into every gap. He could hear few single sounds within a din comprised of so many – the roar of men on each side calling upon God; the shouts of defiance meeting defiance; the ring of blade on blade, blade on helm, blade on breastplate and shield; the scream of death defied, accepted. If the *mehter* band sent the Turks' challenge in drum and trumpet, the Greek trumpets answered them, while their water organs wheezed and their bells tolled, deep or shrill, from every holy place.

The ladder top cut into the earth with the weight of the men climbing it. Several, for one would come hard upon the other's heels. He waited for the first, clenching the leather grip of the mace, and then, when the janissary appeared, his bearded face beneath his turban helmet split by his yelled challenge, Gregoras stepped into the gap and smashed his shield into that yell. The man tottered, somehow did not fall, struck back, his scimitar rising in a great arc behind him, falling with all the weight of the weapon's folded perfection. Gregoras jumped close, halting the fall with his thrust-out shield before it became unstoppable, swinging his mace sideways into the space above the Turk's own shield that the man just failed to close. The fluted weapon bit, the man fell. Another man rose.

His blow had taken him close to the edge. Drawing back, readying to strike again, Gregoras heard a cry. 'Aside,' Enzo yelled, shoving forward a man, a Greek by his long beard, who held a great slab of stone in his hand. The man raised it high, threw it straight down over the wall, along the ladder. He ducked aside as the Sicilian ordered two other men forward. They held a short, stout ash pole between them, tipped in a forked iron hook. Slamming it into the ladder's top rung, they heaved. The rung snapped, so they hooked the ladder's edge and, with Enzo joining them, shoved the ladder, slowly at first then faster as it reached its equilibrium, up and over.

The janissaries came and they came again and there was no pause in their coming, despite the fury unleashed upon them, the terrible toll of their dying. They came like the lions they were, over the piles of their dead, in the presence of their sultan and in the ever-presence of their God, twin names on their lips, shouted even as they died. And Gregoras wondered at them, that relentless courage, even as he killed them, stepping into breaches when another did not, striking at helmet, at turban, at snarling face. All the noises, of trumpet, bell and bullet, of steel on steel, of roars, challenge, defiance, prayer, all resolved for him into one continuous shriek. Within it, his arm rose and fell and murdered, until he could no longer feel it, his arm and the weapon at the end of it one solid club, which he managed to lift and let fall, lift again, let fall again. Somehow the weapon in it changed, he had no memory of how, the mace gone, his wide-bladed falchion in its place, used in its different way, to the same effect. Turks died, he had no idea how many, some on the ladders as they climbed, others who crested the rampart or were pulled behind it to be slaughtered on ground churned by feet, slickened by blood.

He did it, he saw it done. Saw comrades die because they were too tired to lift a shield or sword, lowering their heads like oxen under a butcher's maul.

There was no time. There was only the killing, and it went on and on.

And then he felt it, even as he ducked beneath a scimitar swept sideways at his head, as he punched the point of his sword into another neck, just between the mail shirt and the chin. Felt it as he had before with the Anatolians, the slight giving, the slightest hesitation, the thought manifesting in one mind perhaps, spreading to many. Men, instinctive as birds, suddenly doubting as one.

His throat would not let him express it, his voice lost to smoke, shouting and blood. Crouching, he turned each way along the ramparts, saw the *ortas'* banners thrown back, ladders toppling, the eagle still aloft. And he wondered, allowed himself to think the unthinkable.

Have we won? Despite it all . . . have we saved the city?

He turned to the stockade. Another wave was sweeping in. Was it only his hope, or did they yell with less fervour?

He raised his shield, peered over its lip. A few more to kill and then . . . a vow never to kill again.

This would be enough. Merciful father in heaven, let this be enough.

He had only lately mastered the art, for art it partly was. Selected for his accuracy with the crossbow, the young janissary had been thought to have an eye suitable for a different weapon. Not to load it, that was another man's skill, his partner in the two-man team. Till the other had done, the janissary could only wait, lying flat in the shelter of the shallow trench over which Greek arrows still sometimes passed.

The powder had been crammed down within its leaf pouch. More had been applied to the breech. Now was the time. The little stone ball was placed at the barrel's end, released, and even though he could not hear it above the terrible noise, the young man still thought he did, like a trickle of water, the roll of smoothed stone down metal. The wadding was poked down after, the padded stick plied and withdrawn.

It was his time. Rising over the lip of the trench, his partner drove the short forked stick into the earth there. The young janissary took a deep breath then lifted the culverin, a feat of strength in itself, for the metal barrel was long and thick. He did it swiftly, wanted to join his companion now sprawled face down in the mud. He sighted above the heads of his charging comrades, into a gap that suddenly opened. An arm rose there. It held a sword. Sighting just below and to the side of it, he brought the glowing end of rope down into the pan, breathed out as he did, closed his eyes, lowered his head . . .

. . . and sent the ball that changed history into the body of Giovanni Giustiniani Longo.

'They weaken! They fail! Once more for God. Once more for Constantine. Once more for Genoa!'

In the tumult, only those nearest him could hear. But Gregoras was one, watching the Commander raise his sword above his head. It gave him the strength to raise his. Giustiniani had sensed what he had – the attack was weakening.

'Once more,' Gregoras cried, stepping towards the Genoan, to be at his right shoulder, just as Enzo stepped to his left, the ghost of Amir in his saffron cloak completing the trinity to guard his leader's back.

Then everything changed. Giustiniani's sword slipped from his hands. His fierce smile vanished, the battle light passed from his eyes, his whole face contracting into puzzlement, into a question, his huge body folding in on itself, knees crumpling. Only because they were so close did Gregoras and Enzo prevent the Commander crashing to the ground. With huge effort they held him up, slipping shoulders under the man's arms. The sudden weight pulled them close, their heads conjoined like conspirators, whispering some treason.

Which Giustiniani did. 'Holy Mother,' he croaked, 'but I am hit.' Then he hissed, 'Bear me up. Do not let them see me fall.'

Men were already turning. Gregoras and Enzo, their shoulders under Giustiniani's arms, lifted him onto his feet – and the Genoan let out a terrible groan. 'Ah, Christ! Back! Bear me back.'

They bore him away, the short distance to the little patch of clear ground before the ditch, under the inner wall, lowered him there. Behind them, the next wave of Turks smashed against the ramparts, up and down its line. Enzo ran into the crowd, seeking, while Gregoras knelt and tried to untie the laces that bound the front and back breastplates together. But they were slick with blood, livid and bright, so he used his dagger, slashed them. By the time he was done and was lifting the armour off, to Giustiniani's constant groans, Enzo was back, dragging a long-bearded Greek, who knelt too, cut away the arming doublet and shirt beneath, reached to seek by touch, for sight was lost to the red flood that pooled in the Commander's armpit.

'I . . . I cannot find . . .' The surgeon probed, then raised his voice above the moans. 'A bullet, I think, still within.'

A silence amongst them within the uproar, as each looked at the other, helplessly. Then one voice broke it. It did not sound like him, the voice high, the tone piteous. 'Fetch the key. Open the gate,' Giustiniani cried. 'I must go.'

A gasp from all there. Gregoras looked at Enzo, who shook his head. Both knew, all knew, what it would mean. One of the reasons the defenders fought as hard as they did was that there was no other choice, no avenue for escape. The gate was locked. They would triumph or die. But if it was opened . . . more, if the man who in so many ways *was* the defence fled through it . . . 'Master,' said Gregoras, leaning close, 'if we do that . . .'

And then he did not have to make the argument, for someone else arrived who would. 'What is happening? What?'

Men parted and the emperor came through them, stopping dead when he saw who was sprawled on the ground, kneeling by him a moment later. 'My friend! What is wrong?'

'I am hit, *basileus*. It is bad. I . , ,' His voice rose as a vibration of agony shook him. 'I must go. To my own surgeon. The other side of this gate.'

Constantine's eyes went wide. 'My friend . . . do not do this.'

Giustiniani reached up, grabbing Constantine by the gorget at his throat, tugging him down. Two of the imperial guard stepped rapidly forward, but the emperor waved them off. 'I will leave you my men,' the Genoan hissed, 'but I will go. I will return when my wounds are dressed.'

'Brother, do not!' Constantine wrapped his own mailed hand around the other's bloodied one, spoke as softly as the battle noise allowed. 'The crisis is upon us. You are the rock to which our ship is moored. If you leave, men will know and weaken, here at the last when we need them to be their strongest. Here, in the very heart of it.' He leaned closer, his lips beside the other's ear. 'Stay. Stand. Men will bear you up. Let all see the lion lives. For one more attack. Just one more!'

Giustiniani opened his eyes. There was terror in them, in eyes that had never held it, and all who saw took terror in their turn. 'No,' he spluttered, through the blood on his lips. 'I cannot. I have done enough. Ah, Christ save me, the pain!' He groaned, and as his gaze and grip moved to Enzo and Gregoras, his voice hardened. 'I order you to bear me away. Bring the key.'

The Sicilian looked across at Gregoras . . . who shrugged, rose, turned towards the bastion. A hand grabbed his arm, jerked him round. 'Where do you go?' Constantine said. 'Do not . . .'

'Majesty, I cannot disobey my leader's command.' He glanced back, shuddered. 'His last, perhaps.'

'But what of your city?' Constantine pleaded.

'I will stay. I will give my life for it. But I cannot ask him to do so. He who has already done so much.' He looked down at the hand on his arm. '*Basileus*, please. If I do not fetch the key, someone else will.'

The emperor held him a moment longer then released him with a sigh. Gregoras ran to the base of the bastion. Men were craning over the crenels, staring at the huddle below, and he spotted the young archer to whom he'd passed on the task he'd been given. 'Throw down the key,' he called. The man gasped, then obeyed. A moment later, a glitter fell from the tower and Gregoras caught it. 'Now, keep shooting,' he yelled before turning back.

Enzo and two other black-armoured Genoans had raised the Commander, who sagged between them. Constantine stepped between him and the gate, his face under his raised visor blanched. 'Brother, where do you go?' he cried.

Giustiniani raised his head. His voice suddenly was calm, almost normal. 'Where God and the Turk would send me,' he replied.

The gate was opened. Enzo helped him through it, but returned immediately. 'Others will see to him,' he said, picking up his sword and shield. 'I stay and fight with you.'

Constantine was staring at the gate. Men had tried to reclose it but a stream of others slipping through prevented them. Now he turned back. 'For God and Constantinople,' he cried, dropping his visor, hefting his sword, charging back to the stockade.

Mchmet despaired.

Was now the time? To take off his sumptuous robes, his

gold and silver helm, all marks that distinguished him as sultan? To strip to his *jelabi*, leave his father's sword for his infant son, pick up a battered shield and a pitted scimitar and charge into the battle, a simple *gazi* offering himself to Allah, most merciful? Across the bridge of Al-Sirat, paradise awaited the martyr. If he could not have what he most wanted on earth, he could have what was beyond it.

He had failed. Here, at the last, with every man in his army who could bear a weapon attacking every part of the walls, still they held. Each wave he'd sent in had been repulsed. Even the very best of his army, his janissaries, fighting like the heroes they were, even they had not forced the breach. The double-headed eagle still flew over the stockade. The banner with its red cross marked where the lion of Genoa yet roared.

He looked at the men around him. Most avoided his eyes. Only one, Aksemseddin, his spiritual guide, returned his gaze, spoke. One word.

'*Inshallah.*'

Mehmet turned back. Yes, it *was* God's will. It was time to go and greet Him.

And then he started, peering harder at the rough line of the stockade. To many it was only a seething mob; but Mehmet had stared at it for seven weeks, and his gaze had barely left it in the hour since sunrise. Like a fisherman who knows the different surges of a sea, and what its shades betoken, he knew its infinite variety. And it was . . . different. There was a giving, there, right in the centre where his cannon had pounded most, where the fight had always been the fiercest. A few less defenders. His men lasting moments longer atop the rampart before they were felled.

He sensed it as much as saw it. Leaping onto his white horse, he drew his scimitar. He would not strip off his splendour, not yet. Not when he had the three *ortas* of the household janissaries as yet unblooded beside him. He would lead them himself, the very elite of the elite, right to the fosse. Only if they failed would he climb over their bodies and cross the bridge of Al-Sirat.

'They falter,' he cried, his voice strong. 'A thousand gold pieces to the man who plants our standard in their hearts.'

And with that, the *mehter* band, whose playing had slackened in ardour, struck up vigorously again. The cry came, '*Allahu akbar!*' as the household *orta*, following their red and gold standard and their sultan, swept down the slope and charged the stockade.

He took blows upon his breastplate, on helmet, vambrace and greave. Flesh opened but he lived. And while he lived, he would kill.

Enzo was beside him, killing too. And the Sicilian would know the same as he. The band of Genoans was diminishing with every assault. More Turks were atop the stockade, or through it, each taking longer to kill, their lives, sold slowly, allowing still more of their fellows to step up.

Yet, along the bloody way, the double-headed eagle still flew. While it did, Gregoras would not slacken. He had been on a wall that collapsed, seven years before, at the Hexamilion in the Morea. He had seen the rout that followed. Been blamed for it, lost his nose for that mistaken blame. He had turned away from his city then, his emperor, everything he'd ever loved. But he was here now, and he would not turn again.

He watched it rise, in the jerky steps of a man climbing a wall of bodies. It was a banner, different from those before, this one red and gold. He knew it, had seen it before, from a distance.

The household *orta* of the janissaries had arrived to try their untried strength.

He was enormous, the man who bore it, holding it within the same vast fist that grasped his shield grips. His other held a huge scimitar and he used that to brush away the first Greek who ran at him, dashing the spear from the man's hands, slashing him across his neck. He fell away; another defender tried, died. The banner was raised high, driven down into the earth, shield and sword now spread wide as the Turk yelled his battle cry and dared any arrow, any stone, any blade.

Enzo was closer and moving fast towards him. He fought with a bastard sword, light and well-tempered enough to be used in one hand, near unstoppable with two. Yet the Turk stopped it, bending to take it on his shield and swat the blow away. And perhaps the Sicilian was surprised, or perhaps just too tired, for he stumbled, and Gregoras, still two paces away, could do nothing to halt the scimitar's swooping arc.

He was close enough to catch his friend's body and lower it to the ground, near enough to hear the words he whispered as he died. 'Tell the Commander . . .' was all he said.

The giant was kneeling now, shaking his head as if puzzled. Something had hit him in the forehead, a flung stone perhaps, and blood was streaming. But he wiped it away, smiled, began to rise. Gregoras's falchion blade was short but Enzo's bastard sword lay where it had fallen. Snatching it up, Gregoras drove it straight between the man's knees, up under the mail skirt. The force knocked the giant over, back. He twisted, disappeared, the sword lodged in him and snatched from Gregoras's weakened fingers. But the planted banner still flew, and Gregoras could not reach it, not with so many janissaries leaping past it over the stockade.

The Muslims had turned like birds in flight, one mind governing the mass. Now the Christians did the same. Where there had been two of the enemy, ten stood. Then fifty. And Gregoras, the falchion he'd dropped lost, gave back as did all there. He did not run to the gate, immediately jammed and blocked by screaming men. Only slaughter awaited there. Besides, over the surge that eagle still flew, perhaps thirty paces away. Somehow he made it, shoving aside men who died beside him, slipping under blows struck or taking them on his hastily raised shield.

Only thirty paces to a different world. Constantine stood amidst the solidity of five armoured guards and his closest companions – John of Dalmata, the aged Castilian Don Francisco, Theophilus Palaiologos, who had come up from the Golden Gate; Theodore of Karystenos, Gregoras's old mentor, his bow as ever to hand, though his quiver was empty. The stockade before them was still being held. 'Liege!' Gregoras knelt, as much from tiredness as respect. 'It is time to go.'

'Where, Lascaris?' Constantine looked about him.

'Into the city, lord. To a ship. There may still be time.' He looked at the men about the emperor. 'Cut our way through . . .'

Constantine raised his hand, commanding silence. His voice was loud, to rise above the noise, but he did not shout. 'No. If God decides that the city has fallen, then He has decided that I will fall with it. It is my fate and His will.' He looked around at his servants. 'Begin,' he commanded, 'for I will not have them desecrate my body.' They did so, swiftly stripping him of all imperial marks – the gauntlets that bore the double-headed eagle, his cloak where it also flew, the thin circlet of gold round his helm that was his battle crown. As they worked, and his guards held off any who would come near, Constantine looked around. 'I do not ask that anyone else accompany me. I release you from your allegiance. Save yourselves if you can.'

John of Dalmata stepped closer. 'I am with you, sire.'

'Cousin,' said Theophilus Palaiologos, 'so am I!'

'And I.' The Castilian Don Francisco hobbled forward. His breath came in a wheeze but he spoke clearly enough and with a smile. 'What unexpected fortune, at my age, to die with a sword in my hand.' He raised and kissed his bloodied Toledo blade. 'What better day could I hope to live for than this?'

Constantine was soon stripped of the last of what marked him as emperor. As the eagle flag lowered, he kissed it once, then pushed it away. A plain knight stood there now and his gaze moved to Gregoras. 'And you, Lascaris? Have you something – someone – to live for?'

Gregoras hesitated. He saw Sofia, Thakos, at the place where they might be safe. But they would need him, to make sure they were. He nodded. 'I do, *basileus*.'

Constantine smiled. 'Then go. You have given enough to your city.' His gaze rested for a moment on the ivory nose, then was drawn away by a sudden increase in shouting. All turned, to more janissary banners on the walls. 'Go. Each man to his destiny. And all of us into God's hands.'

And with that, the last emperor of Constantinople lifted his sword and, with his closest companions around him, charged into the thickest press of the Turks.

A voice sounded in Gregoras's ear. 'I am with you,' said Theodore of Karystenos. 'For I have a great-grandchild just born who I would see before I die.'

Gregoras gripped his old mentor's arm. 'Come then,' he said, raising his head above the throng. Everywhere men fought or fled. But the emperor's last charge had sucked many of the enemy towards it – and away from the bastion from which Gregoras had shot his arrows an eternity ago. From one of its crenels, a knotted rope still hung. 'Stay close, and follow fast,' he said, stooping to snatch up a fallen dagger, shifting his shield to his right arm to cover that side.

There was a channel of sorts between him and his goal. And for the Turk, filled with the madness of the conqueror who at last had his enemy by the throat, there were many easier victims than two determined warriors running hard. Gregoras used his strength to shove men aside with his shield, used the dagger only once to open the hand of a man whose own slash he'd just ducked. Used it again to cut the laces between his backplate and breastplate as he had cut Giustiniani's. 'Can you climb this, old man?' he yelled at Theodore.

'Watch me,' the old man replied, slipping his bow over his head and then, with the strength in his arms of the archer he'd always been, hauling himself up fast.

Dropping what armour he could, Gregoras steadied the rope and turned each way, dagger before him, warding. But most of the mob was concentrated near the gate, Greeks and

Genoans trying to flee through it, Turks striking at their exposed backs, at men who were bunched and could not move. Yet not all fled. Knots of Christians still fought, and the Turks were hampered now by so many men packed into the Peribolos. Many of the living tumbled into the ditch of the dead.

A shout. Theodore had scrambled over the top. Gregoras dropped his shield, put the knife between his teeth, and leapt. As he did, he was aware of a man running at him. He swung to the wall, kicked away from it, kicked the man in the face. The Turk staggered back, came on again – and then an arrow entered his neck. He fell, and Gregoras went hand over hand and fast up the rope as above him Theodore notched a second arrow.

Scrambling over into the bastion, Gregoras lay gasping for a moment. Behind Theodore, the few surviving bowmen stared back, terror on their young faces. The other half were dead. Breath recovered, Gregoras looked to the inner wall, to which the bastion was attached. Some Turks had already swung up onto what their great cannon had all but destroyed. They seemed to be in a race to raise the green banner of the Prophet on the next bastion along, and having to kill the Greeks who were still trying to prevent them.

Gregoras turned back to the survivors. 'Notch an arrow, if you have one,' he said, picking up the bow he'd left. There were still two arrows left in the quiver he slipped over his head. 'And follow me close.'

They descended the stair to the level of the wall. Throwing the bolts on the door, he stepped out. There were Turks along the battlements, and more climbing up the wider stairs below, who yelled when they saw them. But none so far had climbed up the other way. 'Shoot!' Gregoras commanded. Of the dozen arrows, three struck home, the others skittering off hastily raised shields or flying wide. The Turks scattered. Gregoras turned and led his men fast the other way.

Soon another stair descended. From its summit, he could

see men running into the city. Greeks and their allies now, but Turks would be following soon enough. He had a view both ways along the walls. In some bastions, the defenders' banners, of the city, of Venice, of Genoa, still flew. In others, the green banner of the Prophet, or of some *orta*, had been raised. News of the collapse had spread fast and men were fleeing or standing according to will or chance.

A voice beside him echoed his thoughts. 'Each man for himself now,' Theodore of Karystenos said. 'Go with God, son.'

With a last squeeze of his arm, the old man was gone. So too the other bowmen, joining those now fleeing the walls for the city. But Gregoras lingered, peering into the Peribolos. It seethed. He knew the sultan had brought a massive army. He had walked among it for a while. But the horde below! It was immeasurable, with every man in it bent on getting into the city; the mass preventing, for the moment, the entrance of the many.

It was over. Constantinople had fallen. Though its death agony would continue for a time, as the conquerors ravaged, a shroud would soon be laid over its corpse and a thousand years of history, of Rome of the East, of Byzantium, interred in its sacred, storied ground.

Gregoras reached up – to moisture on his face. If it was pink-laced with blood, it was still mostly water. Well then, he thought, shrugging. One tear for my parents. One for my ancestors. And the last for my mother the city, the greatest there has ever been.

He glanced back along the walls for a last time, to the place where a double-headed eagle once flew and did no more. Then he turned north, and wiped his eyes. 'Let me have no more cause to weep,' he said out loud, prayer and determination both.

His way lay there, at a rendezvous in a church. *Two* rendezvouses, he remembered, if both women kept their word. He did not know how he would explain each to the other. But if both were safe, and he could keep them safe, it would be enough, for now.

Shouldering his bow, he ran down the stairs.

THIRTY-FIVE

Aftermath

One by one, the bells fell silent, as the Turks swept into the city and took the places of worship. They did not only come from the breached land walls but from the Golden Horn and the Marmara shore as well, for once the news had spread with all the velocity of terror, the defenders along the sea walls abandoned their positions too and made for their homes or sought the ships of their nations.

Theon watched them, from the vantage of the hilltop above his house. Twin surges – the *azaps* abandoning their vessels to pour through the opened sea gates, bent on looting before the land army arrived; Venetians and Genoans going in the opposite direction, cutting their way to their carracks, hastily placing masts that had been taken down and stored, like a locked inner gate, to prevent flight; raising canvas, seeking wind, dipping oars. He could see the ships were packed with people, see the hordes who jostled on the docks and sought to join them. Mainly Greeks, he suspected, begging passage that the Latins would be unlikely to give. Each would look after their own now. Biting his lip, Theon turned to his.

The narrow alley he took was quiet, the screams from the wharves muffled by the houses on either side, and his boots sounded loud on the cobbles. He heard shutters slamming ahead of him, was aware of eyes upon him, glimpsed between the slats. It was an affluent area, members of the government, merchants, their families living in single dwellings. All knew that the looters would come, seeking booty – and worse. All hoped that perhaps their house would be somehow spared, passed over, like the Jews had been passed over in Egypt. But no sheep blood marked their doorways to turn desecration away. Men bolted doors, slammed shutters, offered prayers that it would be enough. That it would be a neighbour, a friend who was murdered, his wife raped, his children taken for slaves. Someone else.

Theon stopped before his own front door. Round a corner he heard something shatter, a burst of laughter, wondered if the enemy had already come. Then he heard a voice cry out in Greek, slurringly, 'More, bastards, more!' Not every citizen was awaiting the doom in prayer, it seemed.

He tapped with his knuckles on the door. ''Tis I,' he called softly, and immediately bolts were drawn, a heavy key turned. He pushed rapidly in, Sofia giving back.

'Do they come?'

'Soon enough.' He leaned against the door for a moment. He had not realised his heart was beating so fast. With a breath, he rebolted the door, then moved past her, mounted the stairs, entered the living area. Three sets of eyes were on him, fear in them – Minerva, Athene the maid and Thakos, twisting the rope of his slingshot between his fingers. Something pressed against his legs. He looked down, saw the cat, kicked it away.

Sofia came up the stair behind him. 'What are those?' he asked her, pointing.

'Bags,' she replied.

'I can see that,' he snapped. 'What is in them?'

'Some food. Some clothes. In case we have to . . .' She shrugged.

'You still question me?' he said, his voice choking on sudden fury. 'I told you. We are not going anywhere. We are staying here. We will be safe.'

'I know.' Sofia came to him, laid a hand on his arm. 'But . . . if anything goes wrong, Gregoras says we will be safe at the chur—'

'Gregoras.' He threw her hand off. 'Gregoras lies dead on

462

the ramparts. His noseless head cut off. So put no more hope in him.' The sudden sadness in her eyes made him laugh, harshly. 'Yes. Weep for him. But know your only hope lies in me.'

Her eyes narrowed. Her voice, when it came, was calm. 'My hope lies in God, husband. For Gregoras. For us all.'

He'd opened his mouth to sneer a reply when a sudden burst of shouting came from the street. 'Bring me the banner,' he hissed, 'and swiftly.'

'The Turks?' she asked, turned, not moving.

Theon listened, to drunken cursing. 'Greeks,' he said. 'Sewer scum. But the Turks will not be far behind.' He shoved her. 'Fetch me the banner.'

She did. He took it, crossed to the window that faced the street. As he reached it, someone began kicking the front door. He listened. It was his own language still being shouted. He pushed open the shutters, looked down. Three figures stood there, two men and a woman, shabbily dressed, swaying. One clutched a large glass jar.

He'd been right. Scum from the streets. The same people he'd taught a lesson when they rioted for bread. He leaned out. 'Be gone,' he shouted down. 'The Turks are coming. Seek shelter and pray for forgiveness.'

'Ooh, "The Turks are coming! The Turks are coming."' The larger of the men, his belly thrust out before him, did a little jig while singing the words. Then he stopped, looked up again. 'Well, we live here. Why should they take everything?' He jabbed the jar upwards. 'Give us silver and we'll guard your door.'

'Give us silver,' the other two called, as one.

'Give me mine.' That was the nonsense phrase the mob had chanted, demanding bread. Well, he had silenced them. He would these. 'Go,' he shouted. 'I warn you . . .'

'He warns us. Warns us!' the larger man shouted, and kicked the door again before shouting, 'Silver. Give us silver!'

The woman joined him in kicking, while the other man ran

across the way and returned with a piece of timber, which he began to hammer into the door.

Sofia joined Theon at the window. 'Come away. Leave them. They will not break the door in. Leave them.'

Theon looked down the street. He thought he'd heard something, shouting, not far away. The enemy was coming. It was time to hang Hamza's banner. But he could not do that with the rabble below. Besides, the larger man had handed his wine jar to the woman and both men had the timber now, driving it again and again like a ram into the door. It might not hold. These scum were attacking his house. His!

He tucked the banner into the front of his doublet, returned to the main room. His father's sword was in the corner. His rage made it seem less heavy as he lifted it, unclasping the scabbard, shaking it off.

'Husband, do not—'

'Do not tell me what to do, wife,' he snarled, and pushed past her to the head of the stairs. 'These are peasants, filth. I will drive them off and then we can hang the banner and be safe.'

She called after him as he walked down the stairs, but he could not hear her words over the thumping on the oaken door. He threw the bolts, jerked back the door. The two men stumbled forward at the sudden opening, then fell back.

Theon stepped out, the sword resting on his shoulder, gleaming in the morning sunlight. 'I say be gone, you curs, now!' He hefted the sword in two hands. It still felt light and he felt strong. An enemy was before him, more ancient even than the Turk. The mob of Constantinople, who had deprived more than one emperor of his throne, and assaulted their betters in the ruling classes. 'Rats,' he said, smiling now, 'crawl back to your holes.'

He lifted the sword high, feeling what his father must have felt, what his brother felt each day. Delighting as the two men cowered back, turned and began to slink away.

'Who are you calling rats?' the woman shrieked and, leaning

back, threw the jar. It smashed into the side of Theon's head, exploding there, covering him in shards of glass, and wine, knocking him sideways. The sword was heavy again and its tip plunged to dash against the cobbles.

Then they were on him, the timber smashed down like a club, striking his shoulder. He tried to raise the sword, could not. He fell to one knee, looked up, his eyes burning with sour wine, near blinding him. He saw a glimmer rising, light refracted through glass, a rainbow on his face. Then the man drove the top of the jar, with its jagged edge, into Theon's neck.

Now he was looking at a cobblestone. Liquid, darker than wine, was flowing around it, on all four sides, turning it into an island. The rainbow was gone. But Theon wouldn't have been able to see it anyway.

The men and the woman stepped back, breathing hard. 'Pig,' spat the large man, throwing the jar neck down onto Theon's dead body. Then he looked at the open door. 'Let's take what's ours,' he grunted.

He made the third step before a heavy clay pot took him in the chest, knocking him backwards. The woman, managing to avoid his fall, looked up and saw another woman at the top of the stairs, another pot raised above her head. 'Go!' she cried, before hurling. This jar smashed above them, on the lintel, showering them in thick, pungent olive oil.

The big man lay on the ground next to the body, rubbing at his chest, moaning. The other was staring down the street. 'I think . . . I think I hear them.'

The woman listened to the sounds – wails, smashing – getting closer. She bent to the groaning man, started to help him rise. Bent over, she could see up the stairs, see Sofia there, another pot above her head. 'I'll be back for you,' she shouted. 'I'll gut you, bitch.'

The three staggered down the road, away from the approaching noise.

Sofia slowly lowered the pot, then set it carefully down

beside her. Through the doorway, she could see a pair of leather soles. One was splitting. If it wasn't mended soon, her husband's shoe would be ruined. She would take it to the cobbler. She would . . .

'Mama?'

Minerva was beside her, trying to peer past her. 'Stay here,' Sofia said, as calmly as she could. She walked down the stairs, pausing in the doorway as she saw the whole of Theon's body. She knew he was dead, by the amount of blood that surrounded his head like the aura of a frescoed saint. But she stooped anyway, looked into his dead eyes. Reaching, she closed them, closed her own. 'Merciful Mother,' she said softly, 'forgive him his sins.'

'What's wrong with Papa?'

She turned. Of course her indomitable daughter would not stay when there were excitements to see. Minerva was wide-eyed, staring at her father's head, its bloody halo. Sofia grabbed her, turned her away. 'He's . . . sleeping, sweetness. Sleeping. Come.'

A shriek turned her. At the bottom of the stair was Thakos, his mouth wide. 'Papa! Papa!' he screamed, falling down beside the body, reaching, weeping. Sofia knew the same lie would not serve with him. He had seen his share of death already, at the walls.

Shouts over the crest of the hill. A drum suddenly beaten, then wood being struck repeatedly. Men yelling, rhythmically, as if heaving on a rope. Not in Greek. 'Thakos. Thakos!' she snapped, drawing his terrified eyes onto her. 'Quickly! We must fetch our bags and go.' He looked down again. 'Thakos!' she cried, shaking him. 'We go or we die!'

She wasn't sure he could even see her through his tears. But he understood, rose, ran back up the stairs. Sofia followed, carrying her daughter, who tried to crane her head round her mother's neck to see the body. In the room, Athene had gathered the leather bags, clutched two herself. 'Is the master . . . ?' she said.

'Gone,' Sofia replied, stooping for a bag, still clutching Minerva. 'Listen,' she continued, addressing them all. 'Stay close to me. Whatever happens, never leave my sight. Whatever you see . . .' she swallowed, 'do not stay to regard it. And if fortune separates us . . .' she blinked back sudden tears, 'you find me again at the church you know. At St Maria of the Mongols. Yes?'

Thakos, the maid both nodded. Sofia led them down to the street. She paused in the doorway. The shouts had diminished. Perhaps the Turks had found another route, though theirs led straight to the heart of the city. Then a man ran down the centre of the roadway. He kept looking back over his shoulder, stumbling when he did, his face white. He disappeared round a corner.

'Silly Ulvikul! Don't wake Papa up!'

Sofia looked down. The cat had stepped out, and was licking the pool of blood right by Theon's chin. Just below it, Sofia saw a flap of indigo banner poking out of his doublet. She stooped, but not for it. An enemy's flag would protect her and hers no more than it had her husband. Only faith could save her now. 'Holy Mother!' she murmured. 'Protect my children's lives. Save theirs and I will dedicate mine to you.' Then she dragged the cat from its feast, handed him to her son. 'Bring him if you can,' she said.

She looked up the street. The shouts, the screams – lamentation, exultation – all were nearer now. There were major thoroughfares she assumed the Turks would come down. But there were alleys that they might not, not yet. There was one almost opposite the house, and she led her charges into it, just as a squad of yelling *azaps* ran over the crest of the hill.

THIRTY-SIX

The Sack of Constantinople

Leilah needed a Greek.

It shouldn't have been hard, with so many about. Fleeing, hiding, dragged from their cellars and holes. Many were dead, of course, especially the old or very young and so with no value, joining anyone who showed the slightest will to resist. There were not many of those, not now, not when the walls had been so fully breached and the sultan's army was pouring in through every opening.

Leilah, at the head of twenty of Mehmet's elite guard, the *peyk*, with their halberds, their breastplates, yellow turbans and bronzed shields, had been waiting by the Charisius gate, the nearest point for her destination, and had entered early on. The throngs gave before the march of armoured men. But many had preceded her, and many had come over the sea walls and got ahead of the landward army. In the frenzy of killing and looting that followed, all was chaos; and though she had the map Gregoras had given her, the twisting streets, filled with shrieking, confused her straightaway.

She needed a guide – and sought one in the square before a church, where scores of citizens were squatting, heads lowered on knees, eyes averted from the sights around them, many praying loudly to block out the sounds, until beaten to silence by their guards. Some attempt had been made to tie them together, but it was evident that rope and chains had run out fast. Lengths of silk, of sliced blankets and torn sheets loosely held them prisoner. Most could have broken their bonds in a moment. But there was nowhere to flee. Death waited beyond their huddle, and not a swift one either, judging by the screams nearby. In the slavery that was to come, there was life. Of a sort, at least.

Leilah looked beyond the dazed crowd. The doors of the church had been torn half off their hinges and dangled before an entrance from which smoke issued. Someone had been careless with fire, or over enthusiastic for Allah. Others, less fervent perhaps, were engaged in saving anything of value from the growing flames. She saw ikons, angels and apostles in wooden frames, tossed down the steps. Others, which had silver or gilt inlaid, were attacked with knives, their metals gouged out, the painted faces slashed and thrown aside. As she watched, some men rushed forth with a casket, joyfully hacked off its iron clasp, jerked open its lid to reveal the fortune in treasure within . . . to discover nothing but bones, wrapped in cloth that bore inked Greek letters and the symbol of the cross. Furious, the *azaps* destroyed the box, seeking what had to be a hidden compartment, and, finding none, scattered the femurs, pelvises and jaw bones of the city's sacred saints over the bloodstained cobbles.

She looked again at the prisoners. 'Wait here,' she said to the *peyk* captain, and began to walk among them. Few met her gaze, pressing their faces into their knees, shoulders braced for a blow. One young man watched her come. He was better dressed than others around him, though his clothes were as filthy and stained. He had a bloody bandage across his forehead, and under it his eyes moved away, then found hers again when she drew near. 'You,' she asked softly in Greek, kneeling. 'Can you read?'

He stared at her for a long moment, perhaps surprised that a woman's voice came from beneath the cloth mask she wore, for she was dressed otherwise as a man, with a doublet and flowing *shalvari*, both black. She had a turban helmet on, her only armour, and a crossbow slung across her back. 'Can you read?' she repeated.

A slight nod. She pulled the map from the pouch, held it up

to him so he could see the writing. 'Do you know this place? Can you take me to it?'

He peered, read. After a moment, he nodded. 'And can you speak?' she asked.

He tried, producing only a gurgle. Then he cleared his throat, tried again. 'I can,' he said in a soft, educated voice. 'I live near that . . . that place. I can lead you there.'

Leilah nodded. She took out her dagger, sliced through the cords that bound his wrists. 'Stand up,' she said. 'Follow me.'

She turned as the man rose. But another was standing in front of her, larger, his face almost lost in a beard. 'And what, by my great hairy balls, do you think you're doing?' His voice was guttural, his accent harsh. Vlach or Bulgar, she thought.

'This slave is wanted. On the sultan's business.'

'Fuck his business. This slave is my business. Oi!' He reached out, grabbed Leilah's shoulder as she tried to step by him. 'You are not going—'

It was as far as he got before Leilah reached up, grabbed his wrist, twisted it against its inclination so he had to bend suddenly to stop the pain. 'Listen,' she said, in Vlach, putting her mouth near his ear, 'I am willing to pay. See?'

The hand she held suddenly had a silver coin in it. Her father had taught her to conjure from the time she could walk. It was a useful addition to her trade.

The man seemed more aggrieved than impressed. And she'd guessed his race correctly. 'He's worth three times this,' he spat, in the same language, rubbing his wrist.

'By noon, there will be so many slaves in Constantinople you couldn't sell him for half,' she said. 'So you will take this and let me pass.'

He looked like he was going to reach for her again, thought better of it, looked around. 'Why don't I call a few of my friends over to discuss it?' he said, more loudly.

'I agree,' she replied. 'You call your friends and I . . .' she pointed past him, 'will call mine.'

He turned, went white under the beard. 'Sultan's guards,' he said. 'Sultan's business. Of course.' He stepped aside, trying to smile. 'Anything to oblige our glorious leader, praise his magnificence.'

Without another word, she threaded through the prisoners till she reached the *peyk*. 'This man will lead us there,' she said to the captain. She turned back to the Greek. 'Fast now. And do not try to run.'

'Run . . . where?' The youth swivelled and led them to the right of the church and up the steeply climbing street beside it.

Had she made a dreadful mistake? Had her dead husband been right to try and stay at the house, behind the indigo banner?

There were just so many of them, every lane and avenue filled with them, and the throng grew thicker the further they progressed. Sofia led her brood through gardens to avoid the thoroughfares, and every second house was filled with the sounds of smashing, with screams of rage, terror, worse. She'd given up trying to shield her children from the dreadful sights, there were just too many. Thakos, for his part, stared largely ahead, white of face, mumbling prayers, of which the only word she could clearly hear was 'father'. Minerva looked at everything and showed nothing on her face.

'Shh!' Sofia hissed, commanding them with a raised hand to stop while she slowly approached the last building on the alley. Peering around, she recognised with relief the marketplace before her. Across it, opposite the alley's entrance, a narrow lane led up. She'd brought them close. St Maria, and the sanctuary she'd prayed for, lay about two hundred paces away.

She hesitated. Crouched in the lee of the building, they were hidden. Yet for once the screams and smashing seemed a little further away. Shops and houses around the forum looked as if they'd already been looted, doorways kicked in, shutters torn off. There were three bodies, unmoving. All that did were feral cats and a few dogs, sniffing and licking among the blood pools; and ravens too, come for the bounty, tearing, gouging. Only a few of the huge black birds, and silent for once, not squabbling. What was the need when the whole city was laid out before them like a banquet?

She shivered. There was this open ground to cross, and now was as good a time as any. She turned. Her charges gazed up at her with huge dark eyes. 'We are close,' she said, 'and there does not seem to be any danger here. Walk swiftly when I say; do not stop for anything. Come!' She leaned out again, raised a hand. Nothing moved but feeding animals. She dropped her hand.

They were halfway across, halfway to safety, when they passed a wall-eyed dog tugging at a corpse. It must have been deaf, or too focused on its gorge, for it only seemed to hear them when they were upon it. It reared back, torn ears flattened, teeth bared, snarling. Thakos had a stick, raised it now above his head, shouting. But to do so he had to let go of the cat he'd held till then inside his doublet. It jumped to the ground and the dog, seeing it, lunged, snarling again. The cat ran away, in the arch-backed scamper of the panicked.

'Cat! Cat!' yelled Minerva, slipping her maid's grip, running in pursuit.

'Minerva! No!' Sofia shouted, taking a step. But her son's cry turned her back. The dog had attacked, had sunk its teeth into Thakos's left boot. He hit it again and again with his stick, but it would not release him, tugged till he overbalanced, fell. 'Get her!' Sofia screamed at Athene, then turned and kicked the dog hard in its side. It gave a whimper, ran limping off.

Thakos rose. 'I am well,' he said, brushing filth from his cloak.

Sofia turned. Athene had caught up with Minerva, but the girl was dodging among the upturned market stalls, seeking. 'Come!' her mother called. 'Come swiftly.'

And then, from a roadway halfway between them, a group of soldiers emerged. They were concentrating on what they were dragging between them – iron-bound boxes. They flung them down onto the cobbles. Then one of the soldiers looked up . . . straight at Sofia. 'There's one,' he yelled. 'She's for me!' He pointed at her. 'Stay there, you Greek slut.'

Three of the men began walking towards her. Beyond them, unnoticed, Sofia saw Athene snatch up Minerva, reaching still for the cat. One hand went over the girl's mouth as the maid ran silently up the alley before her.

Maria protect them, Sofia thought, as the men advanced. Forty paces away now, jeering as they came. Strangely, she felt calm. She thought only of her daughter. Perhaps if she distracted these men enough, Minerva would escape.

But she'd forgotten about her son. Only remembered him when she heard a sound she'd heard before. A drone, as of a beehive. She turned.

Above Thakos's head, his slingshot whirled. His face was caught between terror and determination.

The approaching soldiers stopped. One shouted, 'Put that down, boy!'

'Thakos! No!' Sofia pleaded. He was young, he would survive; as a slave perhaps, but in life there was hope. If he resisted, he would die.

'Yes!' he said, his boy's voice even higher. 'Run, Mother. Run.'

She had no choice now – and this chance. Ducking under the swinging rope, she ran fast for the alley that led to sanctuary. She saw the soldiers start forward, shouting, saw her son fling the knotted end of rope, as Gregoras had taught him. Saw one of the soldiers' legs sweep out from under him, hands reaching to his face. Then she heard her son running, and she was running too, up the alley, with the soldiers in pursuit. Only Thakos's need kept her from turning back to seek her daughter, despite the Turks. But Athene had been to St Maria near as often as her mistress. With the saint's blessing, all could yet find protection there.

Thakos stumbled. She reached a hand, dragged him up and on, as the shouts behind them doubled.

*

'Come, giant. If you want your share, do your share of the work!'

Farouk poked him sharply again with his *bastinado* and Achmed winced, looked down, to his comrades' labours. The church had been half stripped before they arrived in it. But the lure of easier booty had taken the first ravagers on, and, according to Farouk, experienced in such matters, they had missed a lot. He had led the search and swiftly found a store of ikons that the Christians had hidden in an alcove behind a layer of freshly laid plaster. The dust and paint they'd used to try to age it had not fooled him. It was not his one eye he'd used, but his one ear. 'There,' he'd tapped, getting the hollow sound. His squad had broken the hiding place in, pulled out the framed portraits, the boxes inlaid with precious stones. Now the half-dozen men were squatting on the floor, prising out anything that glittered. Silvered saints were stripped of their armour, Madonnas robbed of their necklaces.

But Achmed could not look down for long. Only up, at the wonders above him. He knew this was a place for infidels, that the God they worshipped was false, that holy men and angels should never be portrayed. Yet he looked into the painted eyes upon the walls, upon the ceiling, in curving archways and fluted porticos, and they took his breath. In his village, the mosque was the largest building – and could have fitted five times into the place where he stood now. It was but a single storey, while this . . . this reached up into infinity. Or at least to a dark sky where gilded stars twinkled. And though he knew He could not be there, yet he knew Allah was everywhere, and especially in places of beauty. Even here then, perhaps, in this holy place of the infidel.

'Gulyabani!' Farouk cursed him with the name of the monstrous. 'We need your strength. Break this . . .'

He stopped. Munsif, another member of the squad, had just come through the broken doors. He had someone gripped roughly in each hand – a woman, who squirmed and moaned, and a little girl, no more than five, who stared, terrified, from huge dark eyes.

'What's this?' Farouk said. All work stopped as the men looked up.

'I found them outside.' Munsif flung them both forward and they fell onto their knees. 'Thought they might give us some fun. This one, anyway.' He kicked the woman, who whimpered.

'Fun?' laughed Farouk. 'By the Prophet's beard, haven't you had enough? We must have had five each since we stormed the walls. Except for the giant here, who must be saving himself for his beloved goats.' He rubbed at his one ear. 'There's gold to be made here, you fools. You can buy five gorgeous slaves with that later and fuck them every night till Ramazan.'

'I haven't,' whined Raschid. 'I haven't had one. You all go first, just because I am small, and wounded for Allah . . .' he held up his burned arm, 'and then we move on before I have my share.' He stepped forward. 'I'll have her.'

'Wait,' said another man, Abdul-Matin, laying down his hammer, rising. 'I want her.'

'And I.'

'And I.'

The whole squad were dropping their tools, standing. Farouk laughed again, shrugging. 'Ah, youth!' he said. 'Well, be quick. There's other bastards out there who will be rich men ere nightfall and I would be one of them.'

As a pack, they fell on Athene. She screamed, tried to kick out, was engulfed and dragged down the nave to the only bit of furniture still standing in the wreckage, the altar behind its thrown-down screen. Raschid followed, still whining. 'No! Not again! Let me go first. Hold her for me!'

He was ignored, shoved back. He stopped, turned. Saw. 'I'll have her.'

He pointed at Minerva.

'Her?' Farouk shook his head. 'She's a child, you animal.

475

Too young even to sell as a slave. We should just slit her infidel throat.'

'No,' said Raschid, limping forward. 'Or later. Let me have her first.'

Farouk scratched his beard, then shrugged. 'Well, you've been talking about nothing else for the entire siege.' He stepped aside, waved his arm. 'Take her.'

Raschid took another step. And then Achmed was in his path. 'No,' he said.

Farouk, who had stepped towards the altar, where his other men were laughing and pushing the woman between them, ripping off her clothes, halted, turned back. 'Let him pass, giant. Pity the little runt.'

'No,' Achmed said again, placing his hand on Raschid's chest. 'She is a child. I have . . . had a daughter as young as she.'

'But she's a Christian. A Greek. Our enemy.' Raschid's whine rose still higher. 'Let me.' He tried to squirm past.

'No.' Achmed shoved him back, his voice dropping lower. 'She is a child.'

'Look, you!' Farouk came forward, anger glimmering in his one eye. 'I am in command here and I say he can. Look to the roof if you don't like it. Or go out there and keep watch. Just get out of his way.' Achmed did not move. Farouk raised his stick. 'Now,' he shouted, bringing the stick hard down.

It never struck. Achmed caught it, took it, snapped it, threw it aside. Farouk looked like he was the one struck, so shocked was he. Then he reached for the dagger at his side. 'Disobey me, will you?' he yelled.

The dagger never cleared the sheath. Placing his hand in the middle of his officer's chest, Achmed bent and pushed. The *bolukbasi* went flying back, thumping onto a pile of ikons. 'Men!' he screamed, scrambling up. 'To me. Kill this traitorous dog.'

At the altar, the five men froze, the near-naked woman weeping in their midst. Then they reacted as they had been trained. They dropped her, and ran down the nave of the church.

He did not think then, Achmed. Just bent and picked up the broken half of a heavy oak frame. After that, it was like the times at the stockade – once when he'd climbed it and held a banner high for a moment; once only that morning when he'd seen Turks whip fellow Turks and goad them to the fight. There were men before him now who wanted to kill him. He would have to kill them first.

The first to die was Raschid, who thought that if he came from the side when Achmed was facing the front, he could stick his knife in him unseen. But he mistimed his thrust, came too soon, and it was the matter of a moment to grab his throat in one spread hand, lift, crush his windpipe, drop. Then the rest were upon him, Farouk snarling at their head. All had stacked their swords to the side, came at him with daggers. He had only the timber, in one hand, the other still weakened by the arrow he'd taken in it. But he also had his own name and Allah's entwined in letters at his chest as a ward against their blades.

The frame fell like the adze he'd use to split wood for the winter. They came and they fell away, clutching at their stoved heads, screaming at their blood, falling silent. Farouk died last, his one eye leading him to misjudge and lunge just a little short, his other eye failing to see the wood that rose and fell as if from the painted starry sky.

It was over. Achmed was alone, looking down, and no one moved for a moment. Until the woman at the altar did, snatching up her clothes, covering her nakedness. There was a doorway behind the altar and she disappeared through it.

He turned. The girl was standing behind him. She had not moved. Her eyes were just as wide open, and yet she seemed to be looking at nothing beyond her, only something within.

He went to her, crouched. Her eyes closed and she began to shake. He lifted her, stood, pulled her close, felt her heart fluttering like a laughing dove against his chest, against the entwined names, his and Allah's. 'Abal,' he said, adding another.

He did not stop to pick up his scimitar. He had killed enough and never would again. Besides, he had got what he'd come for. All the booty he could ever desire.

— THIRTY-SEVEN —

Inshallah

Sofia ran, Thakos at her side. It was hard, ever upwards, but desperation drove them, their pursuers' voices getting closer with every bend.

And then there it was, the small building behind its high walls. It did not burn. No enemies looted it. Gasping, they crossed the little square before it, and fell against its oaken door. Summoning her scant breath, Sofia cried out, 'Open! 'Tis I, Sofia Lascaris. Open, for the saint's sake!'

A muttering came, then a louder voice speaking in a tongue she did not know, guttural and harsh. Finally, a different voice, louder still, speaking Greek. 'No! I have told you. We cannot. We are forbidden.' Something flew over the gateway, thumped into the wall beside them. 'Climb!'

Sofia pushed Thakos at the rope that now dangled. Then both froze, as men rushed into the square. 'Caught you!' came the cry, and they turned. Nine men had pursued them. They stood there, weapons unsheathed, each bent over their legs, breathing heavily. One, standing a little forward, pointed. 'Stay there or die.'

Thakos stepped away from the wall. He reached into his pouch, pulled out a stone, fitted it into the sling, had it whirling above his head a moment later. 'No,' Sofia cried as the men raised scimitars, some shields.

'Drop that or I'll cut off your balls,' cried the leader, then looked around at his men. 'Ah, maybe I'll just cut 'em off anyway.'

He took one step forward, then stumbled three. 'By the

beard . . .' he said, then fell face first onto the cobbles, an arrow sticking from his back.

He thought he'd be too late. On an ordinary day, it would have been the matter of an hour or less to walk from the St Romanus gate to St Maria of the Mongols. But the day was not ordinary, when every street was filled with men intent on slaughter. Yet the very number of them gave him some protection, for he'd stripped all his distinguishing armour off, wore only the long undershirt that reached to his knees. Just another running man seeking something. Only his bow revealed him for anyone other, his magnificent bow. But he would not part with that, his only protection since he had lost his falchion and mace. And he'd managed to find five more arrows in a quiver some other archer had thrown aside, to add to the one in his own.

Yet he was not too late, arriving a few moments after Sofia and their son, just as the rope fell between them. He'd have called out if he'd had the breath. Then it was just as well that he had not, for the enemy ran into the square.

The soldiers swirled now, shields and swords raised, seeking him. And he shot again, because he had to kill as many as he could before they moved, and his next arrow felled the nearest man, taking him through his neck. But it also revealed where he was, standing in the lee of a building. They would be on him in moments and he had no protection there, nothing save four arrows. He could flee, but perhaps no one would chase him, and he would be leaving his loved ones to their fate.

Truly, thought Gregoras, the only choice now is where and with whom I die.

So, stringing another arrow, he left his scant cover. The nearest Turk snarled and stepped towards him, and Gregoras put an arrow into his stomach as he ran. He reached the wall in moments.

'Sofia,' he said.

'Gregoras,' was all she could reply, before the Turks shouted and came and her son flung his stone and her lover notched and shot, and missed, notched and shot and killed. She drew her dagger, held it towards the five men still advancing.

'Craigelachie!'

The wild cry came from behind her, above, and no one there, Muslim or Christian, could help but look as a man in full and magnificent armour dropped from the wall, to land between them with a metallic crash. He had a sword in each hand. 'You'll be wanting this,' he said through his visor, thrusting one out, and in a voice Gregoras knew well.

'Scotsman!'

'Aye.' Hefting his own sword, Grant turned to the enemy, who'd stopped, as shocked as any. 'And now, ye sons of whores . . .'

His one step forward was enough. Four of their brothers lay bleeding on the stones, and an easier life, surely, lay elsewhere. As one, the Turks turned and ran.

Gregoras, still winded, bent to place his hands upon his knees. 'How . . . ?' was all he could wheeze.

'After our . . . visit to the monastery,' Grant said, raising his visor, 'you told me where you were going to be.'

'I did?'

'Aye, you did. Said it would be a refuge in the storm, or some such. When the palace fell, I thought: maybe I'll go there and see if that noseless bastard survived. I owe you, after all. For Korcula.' He grinned. 'Seemed as good a place as any in the madness. But they'll not open the gate again. I tried to get them to, for this fair lady.' He stared at her for a long moment before giving a slight bow and continuing. 'I offered them persuasion of a sort.' He lifted his sword. 'But they would nae fetch the key. Said they'd rather die, that the Virgin must be preserved.' He swatted at the rope. 'I suppose you could climb. But I cannot in this armour, and I'd be loath to doff it, seeing as it cost me three jars of aqua vitae from a Venetian knight.' He grinned. 'Besides, I've been fighting with those mad bastards the Bocciardi brothers. They offered me a place in their ship for the services I have rendered them. Said they'd have a boat for me at the gate of the Phanar. I was thinking I'd take them up on it. Perhaps now,' he added, as a further burst of shouting and smashing came from round a corner. 'You know, I'm sure I could persuade them to take a few more, if you'd like?'

Gregoras had turned also to the noise. Now he looked again at the wall. 'Are there only priests within?' he asked.

'Aye. Priests, monks, women and bairns.'

It was always a mad idea. A sorceress making her way through a dying city with a writ of safety for a church. One more mad idea. Others would be there soon, with a different plan in mind. He looked at Thakos first, then Sofia. 'Come then,' he said, reaching for her. 'Let us try to make the harbour.'

She was suddenly so tired, all she wanted to do was lie before the gate of the church she loved and sleep. Even unarmoured, she did not think she could climb the rope. But she could not rest. Nothing mattered except the one thing she had to do. So she stepped beyond his reaching hand. 'Minerva,' she said. 'She is lost out there. I must find her.'

She managed a step, before Gregoras seized her arm.

'You cannot.' She tried to slip his grip but he held tighter. 'You would be dead within minutes.' He saw her look. 'You and me and anyone who comes with you, Sofia. Listen . . .' All could hear the shouts, the triumph and the terror, the smashing, the wailing of many almost blending as if it came from one tortured mouth. While underneath it all, there now also came the rhythmic march of shod feet on cobblestones. Gregoras pointed. 'That's more of Mehmet's army, and they'll kill all of us. Sofia, they'll kill your son.' He watched her face as she looked at Thakos, slumped against the wall now, weeping in great shudders. 'Will you trust me?' he said, more gently.

Every instinct urged her to run back into the city. She bent with the pain of it, jabbing into her stomach like a dagger thrust. Because she knew she could not, must not. Not with her son beside her, who might – might! – be saved. 'Yes, I will trust you,' she whispered. 'For when have I ever not?'

'Then come.' He stretched out his hand again, took hers, just as a rank of men rounded the corner. Stopping only to snatch up his bow, never releasing her hand, Gregoras led his group along one wall of the church and sharply down another.

Leilah saw him the moment she turned into the square, through the swaying shoulders of her guardsmen. He was flat against the wall of the building crowned with a cross. She didn't know why she was surprised, for it was foretold; she had read it in dreams, in bloodstained water, tasted it on his lips. Yet the way had been hard and slow, despite her marching men, her guide, and she'd thought she might be too late.

I should trust more, she thought, smiling, and opened her mouth to call.

And then Gregoras ran, and the others followed. One of them was a woman. He held her hand. Even at that distance, she saw how he held it, knew who the woman was.

Her smile vanished. 'Them,' she screamed, slapping the armoured shoulder before her. 'I want them.'

'Forward!' yelled the *bolukbasi*. All the men lowered their grip on their halberds and began to run, their boots slamming onto the stones.

The gate of the Phanar was not far. Gregoras knew it well, from land and sea, for it was there he had fetched up when he'd nearly drowned after the failed night attack upon the Turkish fleet. And progress had become a little less hard. The sack had passed its initial stage of rapine and slaughter. Men who had waited a long time for their chance of plunder were now seeking it in its various forms. Troops' banners hung from the casements of houses and warehouses. Churches were being stripped. There were more men inside buildings than out upon the streets, and for a while their way was swift.

He brought them out on a hilltop overlooking the Golden

Horn. The waters were filled with vessels of every kind. Turkish biremes and *fustae* drifted, and even from this distance they could see that most were deserted, their crews ashore seeking their share of the plunder. Some higher-sided ships of Venice and Genoa were already at the mouth of the Horn; some were still at anchor, a stream of overloaded rowing boats making their way to these. Closer too, upon the docks right below them, lines of armed soldiers of each nation held back a yelling, beseeching throng of citizens as their countrymen boarded behind them.

'There!' gasped Grant, visor raised to take in great gulps of air. 'The Bocciardis.'

Gregoras followed his pointing arm. Two men sat on horseback beneath the lion of St Mark, behind a rank of their soldiers. 'Waiting for you?'

'Let us hope. Come,' Grant said, stepping then suddenly staggering forward. 'Heh!'

Gregoras had felt something pass his face. Saw it a moment later because it had glanced off the Scotsman's steel shoulder and lodged in the wooden wall of the house beside them. 'A quarrel,' he said, glancing at the feathered shaft, as he pushed his charges over the lip of the hill. 'Your armour was worth the wine,' he added.

Like the Greek, the Scot had kept moving. 'Aye. But I'd rather not give whoever shoots another chance to prove that.'

Gregoras turned to Sofia and Thakos. 'Ready?' he said. Breathless, they nodded their reply. 'Then let us run, before the Venetian ships are filled.'

They ran down a street without curve, leading straight to the harbour. It reminded him of somewhere else, some other time he'd done this . . . and then it came to him, in the grunting of the Scotsman beside him. They had fled the pirates of Omis together down an alley like this, on the island of Korcula. He'd chosen the straight one, not one that curved, and their pursuers had shot arrows at them . . .

It was that memory, and instinct too, from a thousand days

of combat, that made Gregoras suddenly dart to the side, and shove Sofia. She was running hard, downhill, and the shove knocked her off balance. She yelped in shock, and in pain, as she slipped, crashing into the tent poles that supported the awning outside a shop, bringing it down. 'Why?' she gasped, as the others slowed, turned.

'This is why,' he said, and snapped the shaft of a crossbow bolt embedded in one of the poles. He pulled her from the wreckage of cloth and timber. 'Are you well?' She nodded. 'Then run. And all of you – weave as you do so.'

They set off, obeying him. He was about to leave the shelter of the wrecked shop and follow when he looked at the quarrel in his hand. Saw how beautifully its flights were fashioned. Not with strips of leather or wood, but with feathers of heron, tipped in blue, with a helix to spin the bolt in flight. Realised he had seen others like it, before. One in Korcula, stuck into John Grant's leather satchel. One more when he woke up in the warehouse on the docks. Both fashioned by the same hand as the one he held now.

The same bowman was hunting him again. It was incredible, and it was certain, and realising that certainty, he unslung his own bow from his back, and reached for the last arrow in his quiver.

Leilah watched the others flee, saw that Gregoras did not. He was still there, concealed in the tumbled awning. As she shoved her foot into her weapon's stirrup, bent and smoothly pulled up her bowstring, she mouthed a curse. She had missed him . . . twice!

Him . . . or her? That was why – she had not been certain of her target. Fury had misted her sight. She'd wavered between killing the man who had betrayed her and the woman he'd betrayed her for.

Her man of destiny. Hers. She'd thought, as she led her guards through the burning streets, that her excitement was because she was about to achieve her greatest desire, the book of learning of Jabir ibn Hayyan that would make her rich. But when she'd seen Gregoras at their rendezvous, she'd realised: it was him she was excited about. Him. To be reunited with him, to go forward with him, their destinies entwined.

Until she saw the way he held another woman's hand.

Uncertainty was gone now. The woman was already a long shot, and a target that ducked and wove. Nearer, the man was about to emerge from the tangle of awnings. So Leilah drew out a quarrel, licked the heron's feathers smooth, dropped it into its groove. She was levelling when Gregoras stepped into the street. He did not run. He was facing her. She sighted on his chest.

He had one arrow left. The last he would shoot in the city. He stepped clear, saw the crossbowman on the hilltop, silhouetted against the open sky. He had already drawn to half-tension. Now he drew past his ear, sighted, and released.

He felt it the same moment he heard it, like the buzz and simultaneous bite of a mosquito at his ear, but he did not reach for the blood that would be there. At the crest of the hill, the black figure crumpled.

The world had gone quiet for him while two shafts flew. Now sounds returned in the hum of many voices, beseeching at the docks, wailing in the streets; closer too, ones he knew, calling him.

He looked back. Sofia, Grant and Thakos were standing before the final descent, beckoning.

He ran up the hill. He had to know if his last target was real, not some demon who would pursue him for ever. Nearing, he saw movement, a hand reaching. Slinging his bow over his head, he drew his dagger.

The man was small, dressed all in black, a turban helmet rolling beside him. A mask hid his face, or most of it. Some had been torn away by Gregoras's arrow, a jagged line across the forehead, gouting blood.

He reached and ripped the mask away. Then he stared for a long moment before he whispered her name.

Someone was calling her. She tried to blink away the blood. The voice – his voice, she now realised – came muffled through that red mist. She did not know if she was dead. She knew her head had hit the ground hard enough to crack her skull.

Metal on cobbles. Gregoras looked up to see bobbing yellow turbans, armoured men who'd run across a city struggling to run up a final steep ascent. From behind him came the summons of those he loved. Sheathing his dagger, he stooped, grabbed both of Leilah's arms and lifted her over his shoulder. Then he turned and stumbled down the hill.

THIRTY-EIGHT

Faith

Constantinople
29 May 1453: noon

Mehmet bent and touched his forehead to the carpet. Glory to my Lord the most high, he said silently. Allah is greater. He pressed his head there for a moment, knowing that when he raised it again his prayers would be almost over and thus so would his solitude. There was much to do, and he was excited about it: commands to give, men to muster again to his will. But for this moment, with his skin pressed into Izmiri weave, it was still just him and God, to whom everything was owed.

He uttered the short prayer for all Muslims, asked that his sins be forgiven. Finally, he lifted his head, looked to left and right, concluding with the salaam. 'Peace be with you,' he said softly, 'and the mercy of Allah.' Then he looked to the tent's entrance. 'Admit them,' he called, loudly and clearly. Canvas was lifted, men entered, knelt, bowed. His men.

'Well,' he said, smiling at Hamza and Zaganos, waving them to their feet. 'Is all prepared?'

'All, magnificence.' Zaganos gestured outside. 'The jackals gather at your horse's arse, seeing who can be close enough to lick it.'

Mehmet laughed. 'And Candarli Halil closest of all, no doubt. Now I have triumphed, he would lay a claim to my victory and pretend he has not spent these months trying to prevent it.' He shook his head. 'Well, my grand vizier must take his place, and may ride nearest to me this day. But he will feel the caress of the silken bowstring soon enough. Then you, my truly faithful, will come closer.' Both men bowed and he continued, 'What news from the water, *kapudan pasha*?'

Hamza studied Mehmet. He had seen the young man change during the course of the city's siege. Grow older. Now he saw another change in him, a maturing, a certainty. Coolness where before there had usually been flame. It is perhaps what happens, he thought, when one's life's desire is attained.

He spoke. 'The Latins have broken the boom, and many ships have fled into the Marmara. I think Giustiniani may be amongst them, for I saw his personal banner at the foremast of one carrack.'

'The lion,' Mehmet murmured. 'I would have liked to meet him. Offer him rich rewards for his services. What a warrior!' He sighed. 'And others?'

'Many other Christians have taken refuge in Galata. Still more have been captured and are even now being herded and counted, readied for the slave block.'

Mehmet nodded. 'And the ones I most seek?'

'Chosen men search for them, lord. Among the prisoners. Among the dead.' Hamza licked his lips. 'I know you most crave news of Constantine. There is none, beyond rumour. Some *azaps* say he fled to the sea walls and they claim to have killed him. But they cannot point to his body. Others say he lies yet at the breach, and men are searching in the piles of the dead. But it a long task, for the slaughter there is great.'

'Dead, you think?' Mehmet shook his head. 'Perhaps that is for the best. For what would I do with an emperor if he lived?' He looked beyond the canvas walls. As ever, as background to their every moment, there came the faint buzz of men, shouting. Tens of thousands of men. 'Do any still resist?'

'In a few places, lord. I have had reports of a company of Cretans who hold three towers and refuse to surrender them. They would rather die, they say, than live as slaves.'

Mehmet considered for a moment. 'There has been enough death – on both sides. Let them live . . . as free men,' he said. 'Order that they be accompanied to their ships and sent away with their weapons and flags.' Hamza nodded, and he continued, 'And the sack? It yet continues, I hear.'

'It does, lord.' Zaganos stepped forward. 'Three days was the *irade* you issued. But I have been in the city a little ways. From what I have seen, such wealth as remained was stripped from it in the first three hours.'

'But the places I ordered made safe? The libraries? The churches?'

Hamza frowned. 'Some, majesty. Your squads secured many. Perhaps not all.'

'It is to be expected, if pitied.' He sighed, then looked again beyond the *otak*'s walls. Musical notes were coming from there, musicians tuning their instruments. A drum was struck lightly, its voice deep. 'It is time,' Mehmet said.

Both men nodded, bowed. The sultan clapped his hands, and servants rushed in. He spread his arms wide and a cloak of deepest crimson, trimmed in ermine's fur, was passed over them. His sword was buckled on, and, lastly, his gilt-inlaid silver helmet was placed upon his head. 'How do I look?' he asked.

Both men knelt. 'Like a conqueror, lord,' Hamza replied.

Mehmet smiled. 'Then let us see what it is that I have conquered.'

He stepped from the tent. Immediately he was spotted a roar came, spreading from the troops of his guards, the *solaks* and the *peyk*, down through the massed ranks of the janissaries grouped before the gate, all crying the title of Conqueror in their own tongue.

'Fatih! Fatih! Fatih!'

He took the acclaim, arms raised. Then he strode to his white stallion, mounted it with an easy leap, gentled it swiftly with reins and soft words. When he was ready, he nodded. The *mehter* band struck up a march and, with *kos* drums sounding, trumpets blaring and banners dancing, Mehmet rode through what had been the gate of Charisius and now was to be called the Edirne *kapi*, into Constantinople.

It was the Meze, the widest road in, and so Hamza was able to ride close to the sultan but to his side, leaving the viziers and *belerbeys*, the most senior men of the court, to jostle for position at the white stallion's rump. Yet he was still close enough to see Mehmet's expression change, from the justifiable pride of the conqueror to something darker, angrier. He knew what that was. The city they rode through was not the magnificence of legend. Broken-down houses were surrounded by fields untended in years. Churches stood ruined that had not been despoiled by his army. Though indeed, as they got closer to the centre of the town, as they passed through the Forum of Theodosius and then beneath the great Column of Constantine, his army's work could be clearly seen. His stallion's hooves crunched the shattered remnants of ikon and offertory. Men had ropes on statues, and horses attached to them, tugging forgotten heroes down to where men fell on them with hammers.

Hamza watched his sultan's expression lighten, as they reined in before the building all had talked about, though few of their faith had seen. The greatest building in the world perhaps. When Hamza had first seen it, on an early embassy, he had had just such an expression on his face as Mehmet had now. The dome of the Hagia Sophia seemed to reach to the very heavens.

And then the look on Mehmet's face clouded again and he was off his horse and striding angrily through the great shattered doors. Men who had glanced up when the Conqueror arrived had returned to their task of gouging pieces of coloured stone from the mosaic floor. 'What do you do there, fool?' Mehmet roared at one man, who yelped, then prostrated himself on the ground.

'Lord,' he gasped, 'it is only the house of the infidel.'

'It is my house!' Mehmet shouted, drawing his great sword. The blade fell and all there winced, until they saw that it was the flat of the blade he brought down upon the man's shoulder and back. 'Mine! I gave you the contents of the city. But its buildings are mine!' The squealing man crabbed backwards and Mehmet did not pursue him, stood breathing heavily before turning to shout at the officers behind him. 'Give the order – the sack is to cease immediately. The army is to take such booty and slaves as it already has and withdraw to the camp. See it is done! If I witness one more man pillaging, it will not be the flat of my sword he feels!'

Men dashed away. Those who remained watched Mehmet as he sheathed his sword then turned to the interior of the building. His gaze rose to its heights, unparalleled anywhere in the world. Then he looked to its end, where the altar and altar screen had been thrown down. A man stood there in simple dark robes, a holy man who had been sent ahead for this purpose. Mehmet nodded at him and the man ascended the pulpit that only twelve hours before had been occupied by an archbishop.

'*Allahu akbar!*' Aksemseddin intoned, as soldiers poured into the space, into what was now a mosque, and, imitating the Conqueror, flung themselves to the ground.

'God is great! God is great! God is great!'

Hamza had lost Mehmet then, first to prayers of thanksgiving, then to crowds of acclaimers. He had himself gone straightaway to fulfil his sultan's orders. As *kapudan pasha*, the navy was his responsibility, and sailors were as much engaged in the sack as anyone else. It was midnight before exhaustion made him stop, and by then perhaps half his charges were back aboard. He would have to go out with more squads in the morning. He had not had any sleep for two days. He would have given half his considerable share of the city's plunder for an hour of it.

Yet it was to be denied him still. A *solak* came to summon him, and brought him to the long-abandoned palace of the old emperors, the Bucoleon. The archer left him at an entranceway where two other guards stood, its doors long since rotted away. Hamza stared into the darkness until flame drew his eyes, and a voice softly called, 'Come.'

The Conqueror was standing in the small pool of light his lantern cast. Beyond it, Hamza was aware of a vast hall. 'Can you feel their presence?' Mehmet murmured when he drew near.

'Who, lord?'

'The emperors.' The sultan lifted the lamp, causing the spill to shift. 'The great Constantine began this palace when he founded the city. Justinian stood here and planned the Hagia Sophia. Basil went forth with his armies from here to shatter the Bulgars. And where are they now, those great men?' He swept his foot across the floor. 'They are still here. But they are dust.' He turned to the other man. 'Do you remember what that witch said, in Edirne, a year ago?'

'She said many things.'

'And all have come to pass, have they not? But the first was that my sandals would stir up the dust in the old palace. And here I am, doing it.' He passed his foot across the floor again. 'And what became of her, my sorceress?'

Hamza shrugged. 'The captain of the *peyk* you assigned to her said she disappeared. She ran ahead of them and vanished. He returned to the church, secured it, as was his order.'

'Vanished, eh? That seems . . . appropriate. Well, I have no doubt she will appear again. Look!' Mehmet raised the lamp a little higher, moving away. 'Do you see the cobwebs? Do you remember what the Persian poet said?' His voice dropped as he softly spoke the lines.

'The spider has turned watchman in the palace of the Caesars,
And has woven his curtain before the door.
The owl makes the royal tombs of Efrasib
Echo with his mournful song.'

'It is a beautiful verse, lord,' Hamza murmured.

'Beautiful, yes. But what of their beauty? The women and

the men these emperors loved.' He stirred the ground again. 'Dust, too.' He turned. 'As we shall be. Before very long. Only dust.'

'It is true, master. Our bodies shall be. But our souls . . .' He smiled. 'They will be in paradise. For Allah, most beloved, will be pleased with us.'

Mehmet stared at him. 'Do you think so?'

'I am certain, Fatih. After this night's work? The Prophet's promise fulfilled? The holiest church in Christendom turned to a mosque? How could we not have earned our place there?'

'I hope you are right, my friend. An eternity in paradise.' The Conqueror nodded. 'But here? Such a short time before we join these Caesars in the dust.' He moved a few paces away, sweeping the ground before he turned. 'So what shall we do with our brief span before that, Hamza Pasha?'

Bey no longer, thought Hamza. A pasha. My father the tanner would be . . . pleased. He took a step nearer, used a title too. 'What would *you* do, Sultan of Rum?'

It was one many sultans had claimed. But only he who stood before him now had the right to own it.

'Sultan of Rum? I have taken the Rome of the East, it is true. The Hagia Sophia is the Aya Sophia *cami* now, a holy place for the true faithful to worship within.' A smile transformed Mehmet's sadness, a gleam came into the eyes that Hamza recognised. 'But why stop there? What say you that we turn St Peter's into a mosque as well? What say you if now we go and conquer the Rome of the West?'

Hamza smiled too. 'Of course, lord. I am your servant, as ever. A warrior for you and Allah most merciful. Let us go and conquer Rome.' Then a great yawn came that he could not help, so he added, 'But can we not do it in the morning?'

Laughter rang out then through the palace of the Caesars, and as they left, the two men's feet raised the dust of emperors, and broke the spider's curtain at the door.

EPILOGUS
'A Surer Possession than Virtue'

Ragusa
September 1460: seven years after the fall

He finished reading, then let the paper curl back into its cone. He thought of placing it beside him on the wall where he sat, but there was a breeze blowing off the sea this morning, a small but welcome respite in the summer heat. Perhaps he would want to read it again later. Perhaps she would. So he let it drop to the tiled floor behind him where it could roll on the terrace, safe.

For a moment, Gregoras watched the swallows swoop, soar and drop, hearing their sharp cries, then closed his eyes to the sunlight, enjoyed its heat upon his face. If he sat there longer, he would have to change his silver nose for the old one made of ivory. He should not sit; there were things he should be doing this day. Yet the breeze felt so good and the city markets would be hot and crowded. No. He would move back into the shade and watch the vessels busying past. Later, when the worst of the day's heat was done, he would slip down to the water and swim. He sighed, content with his decision.

'Sad news?' she said, coming as silently as ever, slipping her arms around him.

'You can read, if you would like.'

'I would prefer it if you tell me.'

'So.' He opened his eyes, squinted at the horizon, sails upon it. The breeze here was a wind out there, pushing the ships east. 'Another *irade* has been issued. All who once lived there are again asked to return. To repopulate the city. Help it rise.

This time Mehmet has promised a bounty – of money, tools for their trades, a home. And all are still free to worship as they please.' He tipped his head to the paper, caught in an eddy of air, drifting toward the entrance of the house. 'Though Thakos says that those who go to church or synagogue must pay an extra tax and that many are converting to Islam to avoid that. I think . . .' he shrugged, 'I think he is considering doing the same. He says he will rise higher, faster if he does. And he is ambitious, as most fifteen-year-olds are.'

'And does he consider what his mother will say?' She released him, moved away as she spoke, her tone light. Since he knew that often meant danger, he turned to look at her where she now leaned upon the wall.

'I am sure he knows well,' he said carefully. 'Since she is the recently appointed abbess of the nunnery of Santa Maria.'

Leilah reached up, smoothed fingers along the white scar that ran half the length of her forehead. Another warning sign. 'You could return,' she said bluntly, less coolly, turning to him. 'Take the sultan's offer. Find a house with a view there.'

He looked her up and down. Made his look obvious. She was wearing only the light silken robe she'd put on when they'd risen a short time before, and her body pushed through it at certain points. He smiled. 'A better view than here?'

She did not smile. 'Abbesses renounce their orders. Sons convert to Islam to rise. You could finally tell him that you are his father. You could tell him what you and his mother . . . are.'

'*Heya*,' he said, moving closer, though Leilah folded her arms against him like a barricade. He stopped, his voice lowering. 'What is the matter, my love?'

'I . . . do not know.' Her hand reached again, rubbing puckered skin. 'Yes, I do.' She pulled her arms beyond his grasping hands. 'I had the dream again last night. Of Jabir ibn Hayyan's book. It was in my hand at last. But I could not decode any of its symbols. I tried and they just blurred.' She dropped her hand, jerked her head to the horizon. 'Sometimes all this feels like the dream. I think I must wake up and it will end.'

'*Heya*,' he said again, gentling her with his voice, reaching slowly to uncross her arms and step between them. 'I have no desire to return there. Not one. That city is steeped in blood and memory. It took many things from me . . . and yet it also gave me so much.' He pulled her close, raising the chin that fell, looking into her dark eyes. 'It gave me you.'

He kissed her, gently. It took a moment before she responded. But then she did, in the way she always did, completely. They turned, pressed close, to stare out at the Adriatic Sea. 'I told you once what the old poet said,' he continued. 'Here, in the old shack when first we met. "A room with a good view is a surer possession than virtue." And in the whole of Constantinople I cannot think of a better view than this. Nor better company.' He heard a cry from within the dwelling, and smiled. 'Nor no other son.'

She stared at him a moment, deep in his eyes, then squeezed his arms and went inside.

He turned back to the water, relieved he was free of her shooter's gaze. For though the memories came as infrequently as her dreams, and lingered less when they did, still something could set them off. Some noblewoman's surprisingly coarse laugh. The way brown hair fell across a stranger's neck. A letter from a fallen, rising city.

Then she'd be there again, as he last saw her; he with her, drawing her out onto the terrace of the house he'd rented in Chios, with Genoan gold. For Giustiniani had not forgotten his comrade in the end, and had paid off Rhinometus's contract in his will.

'Out here,' Gregoras said, taking Sofia's arm. 'I do not want to wake her.'

He led her onto the terrace, glancing back once at Leilah on the bed. Her eyes were closed again under the bandage and she seemed to be breathing easier. Softly, he shut the door. Sofia had gone to the low wall, from which she could look down on to the harbour. She spoke over her shoulder as he came near.

'Has the fever broken?'

'I . . . I think so. The salve you brought helped.'

'As did my prayers.'

Her voice sounded different. Calmer than it had been for a while. 'Perhaps,' he said. 'She's less hot anyway and was able to eat a little more the last time she woke. She still sleeps near the whole clock round.'

'I think that is good. It is what she needs to heal.'

Gregoras stared at Sofia's neck. Her voice was still soft, its quality detached, as if she did not truly care. And yet she had cared, once Gregoras had told her . . . not all, but a little of what Leilah was to him. Brought broths and poultices. Spared a little time in her prayers. 'Sofia,' he murmured, reaching a hand towards her neck, half hidden in falls of dark hair.

She turned suddenly, took the hand he'd extended. When it came, her voice was no longer dreamy but filled with excitement. 'Do you see in the harbour, Gregor? Do you see the difference?'

He looked. It seemed unchanged. The Genoans still readying to depart. Now Giovanni Giustiniani Longo was buried in his simple tomb upon the island there was no reason for the mercenaries to remain. They had offered their comrade a berth, and a contract for their next war. But Gregoras was done with killing. And he would not leave Leilah – nor the woman who was pointing so excitedly now.

'There's the difference,' Sofia said. 'There, next to the Commander's carrack. That trireme? It arrived this morning.'

It was not unusual. Various vessels had straggled into the port in the weeks since the fall. 'What news?' he asked, everyone's first question, though the answer was always the same – rumours of disaster, of slaughter, of desecration.

He was surprised – first by her smile, then by her words. 'It is commanded by a Greek. Flatenelas.' Gregoras was about to say he knew the man, but Sofia raced on. 'But he does not escape from the city. He brings word, from my uncle amongst others. For he has been *sent* from it. By its new ruler. Mehmet has asked all Constantinople's citizens to return.'

He snorted. 'Has he not got enough slaves that he wants yet more?'

She frowned. 'No, Gregoras. The sultan has issued an *irade*. It says he only ever wanted the city to be great again. He wants all its people to help him in that.'

'Is that what he says?' He sighed. 'You know the Turk, Sofia. He will say anything to get what he desires.'

'Which is what? More slaves? You already said he does not need them.' Her voice was harder now. 'And why would Flatenelas, a nobleman of the city, do the enemy's bidding if he did not believe it? No . . .' she raised a hand against interruption, 'do not speak against it. For you obviously do not see what this means.' She dropped the hand she still held and spread her arms wide. 'It means I can go back. I can go back and look for my Minerva.'

'Oh, Sofia.' He paused, seeing the hope he thought she'd drowned in a thousand tears bright again in her eyes. In the escape from Constantinople, in the journey to Chios and their time there, he had held Sofia as she wept, gentled her as she raged, restrained her when she thought to steal a rowing boat and return. Finally convinced her of what he truly believed. For he *did* know the Turk. They did not take slaves as young as Minerva. They were too much trouble. So they killed them. And if by some miracle one took pity and enslaved her . . .

then the child would already be in a house in some far-off city, being trained to wash floors, cook meals – and await her turn on the slave block when she came of age. It had happened to the woman who lay behind him now and fought with death. It would happen to Minerva – if, by that miracle, she lived.

He thought he'd convinced her. 'Sofia,' he said gently, reaching for her.

'No!' She stepped away, till her legs touched the low parapet. 'Do not try . . . Do not say . . . what you have said before. I have seen Minerva in my dreams. I have held her in my prayers. I know she lives. And tomorrow, on Flatenelas's ship, Thakos and I will go and find her.' She lowered her arms, her voice. 'Will you come with us?'

And there it was, the choice he'd known he'd have to make. He'd avoided it, consumed with other priorities. But now that he believed at last that Leilah would live . . . here, looking into Sofia's dark eyes, he did not know what to do.

She saw his arms rise towards her, fall away. Saw the torment in the eyes above the ivory nose, the gaze that rose over her head. She saw it and knew what she had only glimpsed before through her agony: the whole that had been hers entirely was divided in half.

She was thankful that her knees rested against the parapet. She would not fall. And while she waited for her strength to return, while she saw the eyes she loved seek an answer among the clouds above them, she knew this: she could win him back. But she would not try. He had chosen another. Though the thought brought red heat to her brow, that receded swiftly enough. For she had chosen another too. And she still loved him enough to tell him who that was; to try to lessen his pain, of which he'd had excess.

'Gregor,' she said softly, taking his hand, 'you cannot come. I know that. And I do not . . .' She swallowed, recovered. 'I do not need you to come. My family is still there, and those that survived are already making their peace with their new ruler. No.' She raised a finger to his lips to hold in his words, and continued, 'And I have someone else, someone else I made *this* vow to: that if my children were spared, I would give her my life. She has. So I will.'

He studied her for a moment, then spoke. 'You are talking of the Virgin now, aren't you, Sofia? Giving her your life?'

She nodded. 'Yes. The Holy Mother. Who knows all about the saving of children.'

He hesitated on the thought, then said it anyway. 'You only have Thakos. Minerva . . . you cannot know that she lives.'

Her smile flooded her face in light. 'But of course she does,' she cried.

Another cry came like an echo from beyond the door. He turned to it . . . but Sofia held his hand and did not let it go. And when he turned again to her, she raised his hand and kissed his palm. 'Live in God's love, Gregoras,' she murmured. 'And in mine, for ever.'

Then she was walking away, down the steps of the house. Another moan from within pinned him on the porch, but he could not help his words. 'And Thakos?' he said. 'My . . . my . . .'

Sofia stopped, looking back up from the path. 'My son has not stopped weeping since that day. And he rarely sleeps. He is convinced now that his . . . his father died valiantly, fighting Turks. I do not think he would take the news well that he is not . . .' She shrugged. 'Perhaps later. When he is older. Not now.'

She turned, began walking again. He wanted to run after her, but he found he could not move. All he could do was call. 'I will come to the docks tomorrow. I will see you both safe aboard.'

But she did not stop this time, did not look back, did not reply. Only a hand rose and fell to show that she had heard him. 'Sofitra,' he murmured, watching until the twilight swallowed her.

He hadn't gone to the docks. Couldn't, when he was not sure what he would do there. And just as the tide was turning, Leilah had woken suddenly, and hungry. While she'd fed, he'd made some excuse, gone onto the terrace. But the ships bound for Constantinople were already small upon the sea and soon vanished entirely.

A noise brought him back to the present, footsteps. 'Momma left me!' the boy cried, tottering onto the terrace. His outrage had already been soothed away – but he wanted to inform his father.

'You were sleeping, Constantine,' Leilah said, following, bending to scoop him up. 'You were dreaming too.'

'Good dream.' The boy rubbed still sleep-laden eyes, then looked up. 'I shot your bow.'

'Did you?' Gregoras smiled. 'Would you like to shoot my bow now?'

'Yes! Yes!'

Gregoras kept it there on the terrace, as men of Ragusa who lived beside its walls must do, in case of sudden attack. Between him and it rolled the letter from Constantinople. Gregoras bent, picked it up. 'This is a message for the sirens, Constans. Shall we send it to them on an arrow?'

'Yes! Yes!' the boy cried again, struggling out of his mother's arms.

There was no danger of hitting one of the swooping birds that they'd told him were sirens, who tried to lure sailors onto the rocks below. Gregoras stood in the centre of the terrace, so he would clear his own low wall and the city one beyond it, Constantine within the circle of his arms, one hand round his father's bow ring, the other clutching halfway down the archer's forearm. Leilah wrapped the paper cone tight round an arrow shaft, bound it with a thread, handed it to him.

Gregoras notched it, pulled the string back, aimed high. 'Now?' he asked.

'Now,' the boy cried, and together they sent the arrow and its message arcing above the great stone wall. A swallow dived at it, then spun away with a flash of white belly, flying high, up into the bluest of all skies.

Strathspey, Scotland
The same day

'Ye infidel bastards! Will ye not give me some peace?'

It was extraordinary. In the twenty years since his leaving, his home glen had become a place akin to paradise, where the light was always honeyed, the air fragrant with heather and gorse droning with bees and grazed by magnificent red-chested deer, the clear streams filled with silvery trout who needed but a bend and a scoop to transform into a feast.

So how, by the bearded balls of a sultan, thought John Grant, had he remembered all that but forgotten the bloody midges?

He could admire neither scent nor sights while he was flailing his arms, trying to drive off great clouds of nipping evil. Not that flailing did much good. In fact the heat he generated by the activity, and the sweat that it produced, which ran from sopping head and on down to soak his fine cambric shirt, seemed only to encourage the beasts. So goaded was he that more than once he'd reached for his long sword – only to remember each time that it was holding down papers on the table in his rooms at the university of St Andrews.

He stumbled swatting on, up. Then either the height he'd reached or some change in the atmospherics drove the monsters away. He paused, took a breath. The summit of Craiggowrie was but a hundred paces further. He'd eaten the walk as the midges had eaten him.

He pushed on, crested the ridge . . . and stopped dead. In

his youth, he'd been up there in all weathers, when driven snow tried to blast him off, or mist sought to lure his foot into a fall. But he'd always liked it best like this, with a cooling breeze tempering the late summer heat, a wind he could open his eyes and look into.

He'd come here twenty years before, on a day like this, the one when he'd taken to the self-exile's road. And the view had not changed – perhaps a few less trees in the forests of Glenmore and Abernethy as man took timber for the town of Aviemore, which had swollen to either bank of the Spey. To the south the same mountains filled his sight – Craig Dhubh and Dhubh Mor and, taller than them all, Cairn Gorm itself. While to the north, small mountains the size of the one he stood upon rolled away, to a distant, unseen sea.

'Craigelachie.' He murmured the word that he used to shout, seeking among those peaks for it. He had never been. The Grants had given up that land, that hill where the beacon of war would be lit and around which the clan would rally, hundreds of years before. The name still inspired them, but they had mainly settled here, below his perch, spread along both banks of the Spey; thrived there. It was known that if you walked into Aviemore and threw a stick, you'd hit five Grants. It was not advisable, though, even for a long-lost cousin, for they were a quarrelsome clan.

He looked down, seeking. There, in a fold of forest beyond the town, something glittered. Sun striking Loch Mallachie, warming the walls of the house . . . there! He saw, or thought he did, a line of smoke. Too hot a day for the fire to be for warmth. His father would have one set beneath a cauldron – if he yet lived. If he did not, one of John's younger brothers would, certain.

His gaze went north again. 'Craigelachie,' he said, louder, though he did not seek it now. He'd cried it often to conjure his own fire, and never more than on – and beneath – the walls of Constantinople. He'd been thinking of that place more frequently since his recent return to his homeland, in a way he had not done in the seven years since the city fell, through all the places he'd travelled, and those he'd stayed – Basle, Milan, Paris. Maybe because what he'd found there had finally let him end his exile and come home.

He smiled as he recalled the expressions on the faces of all his old tutors at St Andrews when he'd fetched up earlier that summer. Their memories were as long as their grey beards, and the student Grant had blown up a valued barn before he'd precipitously left. Yet that was forgotten, or at least put aside, when they saw what he returned with. Not his diplomas from the finest schools of Europe, though they impressed. No. What he added to their library, his booty from Constantinople, would have built a hundred barns. It had certainly won him the title of Doctor Illuminatus and a place for study and experiment . . . a long arrow shot from the main buildings.

He'd forgiven himself for stealing the Geber almost immediately. His noseless friend had had little time for it before the town was sacked . . . and afterwards? He was otherwise concerned. Gregoras had seemed content with the treasure he'd collected. He had the golden bounty he'd been promised for the saving of John Grant's life. He had the girl – though he came by her in a most strange manner. Besides, Grant had returned the favour and saved his life, and the lives of those he loved, by getting them out of the city. They were even, and the work of Jabir ibn Hayyan, annotated in the Arab's own hand . . . well, that was *his* bounty. And his future too. One of unceasing study – and perhaps the odd explosion.

The midges had found him again – and it was time to be leaving anyway. The sun would be up for a while yet in this season of the year, but his family ate at the same time each day, sun or snow. After twenty years, he was looking forward to a meal by his own hearth.

Walking swiftly down a deer track through the gorse, he collected the large bag he'd left under a tree, and made his way around the base of the mountain. The path through the forest was still there, and brought him out to the edge of his family's fields, filled with ripening barley. Through feathery stalks he could clearly see the farm. He'd been right. The smoke came from a small barn beside the main house.

He saw her first, in the yard, feeding chickens; saw the twenty years in her grey hair and her stoop. But the face his mother raised at his call was unlined, and the smile exactly as he remembered. She had to sit for a time and have her weep, but when she was ready, she led him across the yard. 'Look who's come,' she said, pushing open the barn door.

The air was heavy with the savour of heating malt. His father sat before the cauldron, feeding wood to the fire, and John Grant was sure it was the fug and the flames, nothing else, that caused his father's eyes to fill with water. He rose from his stool, hovered a moment, a hand raised before him, then sat back down. 'Where have you been to?' he said, turning away to shove another log in.

'Here and there.'

'Aye? And for how long are you back?'

'A time.'

His father looked up again, studied his eldest son for a moment – his rich quilted cloak, his fine stitched shirt, the silver buckles on his boots. 'Good,' he said at last. 'Because it's about time you began to learn the trade. A man cannot make his way in this world without a trade, son. Do you know that?'

'I know that, Father.'

'Good.' The older man gestured to the pile of malted barley laid out on planks nearby. 'That is the alpha – the finest barley grown under God's good sun. And this,' he said, reaching beside him and lifting a large stoppered jug, 'this is the omega.'

He uncorked, took a sip, then passed the jug across. John Grant raised it to his lips. But before he drank, he inhaled deep. And he knew, even before he tasted it, that he was truly home at last.

There was not much left to do, so he would do it now, although the light was fading and his family would be impatient and scold him for delaying, once again, the evening meal. But the day had lost its smothering heat, and the last corner of his field could be finished in the little coolness that had come, in the whisper of wind stirring the grey poplar trees at the field's edge before passing over him, a hint of the season approaching in the one near ending.

'*Ya daim. Ya daim. Ya daim,*' Achmed chanted as he grabbed a hand's grasp of wheat stalks, brought his sickle cleanly through them, let them fall, grabbed and cut again. He moved steadily through this last patch, laying low the summer's gold, the gold he would rake up tomorrow, load upon his ox cart, take to the threshing floor, sort chaff from the wheat to be carried in bags to the miller – the only gold he would ever possess. The day of the milling would be a good day, with nothing to do but sit, wait his turn, talk with the other men. Or listen, at least, catch up with the doings of the villages nearby and a little of the world beyond them.

He chanted and reached . . . and realised there was nothing left to grab. So he stood, stretching out his back, and especially his grabbing arm, for it always got stiff in the place where an arrow had gone through it. And perhaps it was that, or the feeling of an ending in the gold at his feet, or perhaps the curving blade in his hand and the tiredness in his body, that made him do what he almost never did, at least when he was awake – think about Constantinople. Seeing men scythed, not wheat stalks, and, in the last flash of the setting sun, a man aflame, plunging like a comet through a wooden tower.

He closed his eyes to the sights, opened them again . . . and she was there, crossing from the trees. She had a stone jar on her shoulder and a frown on her face. 'My mother says you are to come,' she called while still a ways away. 'She says she is tired of eating cold meat when all the other wives have theirs hot.'

Achmed took the water jar from her, drank deep. 'I come, Abal. I come. I just needed to . . .'

His daughter grunted, bent and snatched up the sickle, took his hand, pulled. He was big, yet she moved him, and he wondered how that was, that the little girl was starting to turn into a woman.

When they reached the track, she slowed a little, as he hoped she would, and he could walk while resting his aching arm on her shoulder. She often came to fetch him, because she liked to have him to herself; in their home, with three sons and two other daughters, there was no time to talk. Though in truth, as ever, he talked little now, content to listen to the happenings of the day – which goat had not produced milk; which *gelin* had been caught crying again, unhappy in her new husband's house; which brother had been cruel, which kind. He loved to listen to her sweet voice, especially as there had been a time, when he'd brought her back from the war, when she had not talked at all. The silence lasted a year, until one day she just began, slowly at first, then faster and faster. Since that day, she had barely ever stopped.

Yet today as he walked he found he only half listened, the last memories he'd had in the field still clinging to him. And so he did again what he rarely did. Thought of his two Abals as separate, when usually he only thought of them as one. He knew they were two, and he knew that he loved them both the same. The one was with Allah in paradise. The other he had his arm around, while she made of his life a little paradise, right there.

HISTORICAL NOTE

The siege of Constantinople was one of the greatest battles ever fought, and its full history fills volumes. I have got as many of the details in as I felt I could, from towers to tunnels, from ship fights to close-quarter combat, from the divisions that nearly pulled the city apart to the love that bound all in the end. There are the large truths of that last all-night assault that I discovered I had to write in one chapter. There are smaller ones, such as the cry of Turks to braid their Greek enemies' long beards into dog leashes . . . to Mehmet's written order to preserve the tiny jewel of St Maria of the Mongols. As a novelist, in the end I weave a fiction into the facts. Though I believe I have covered a lot of ground, there are many, many other extraordinary stories of 1453 that, alas, I have had to leave out. Read the histories. You will be dazzled.

My fictional characters have gone on to live their various lives . . . yet my historical ones did as well.

Giovanni Giustiniani Longo *was* carried to his ship by his faithful soldiers. But his wound was indeed mortal and his great heart gave out within a few days, either on his ship or on the island of Chios.

John Grant – 'Johannes' as he was known in all the chronicles – disappeared back into history and perhaps to Craigelachie, happy at last to be with people who knew he wasn't a bloody German.

The body of Constantine, last emperor of Byzantium, was

never found. Some say he lies in a secret cave beneath the city, awaiting his chance to rise again and make it a Christian capital once more.

For the remaining twenty-eight years of his life, Mehmet Fatih, the Conqueror, was restlessly, constantly at war in both the East and the West. There were many further successes, though perhaps none matched in glory his taking of Constantinople at the age of twenty-one. He never conquered Rome, though he always planned to, and in 1480, an army of his held the seaport of Otranto, on the Italian mainland, for nearly a year. But there were defeats too. In 1456, the White Knight of Hungary, Janos Hunyadi, beat him at Belgrade and Mehmet nearly crossed the bridge of Al-Sirat and achieved the martyrdom he sought, charging into the city scimitar in hand, only just escaping with a serious wound to his thigh. He died, some say poisoned on the orders of his son, setting out for another campaign in 1481, at the age of fifty.

The tanner's son from Laz, Hamza Pasha, continued his rise as Mehmet's trusted servant. But in 1462, when sent to apprehend the rebel vassal Vlad Dracula of Wallachia, he was captured, imprisoned and later impaled on the Field of the Ravens before the gates of Targoviste. (See my novel *Vlad: The Last Confession.*) Dracula was known as 'the Dragon's Son', so the sorceress's prophecy was fulfilled: Hamza would die upon a tree, where a forest had never been, looking down upon a dragon.

Perhaps the character that has had the most extraordinary life after the conquest is the city itself. Though Gregoras wept for it, Constantinople was not dead. More, it thrived, even as its name changed. Mehmet made it his capital, repopulating it from all parts of his empire, bringing back its former inhabitants, allowing religious tolerance, encouraging trade. He also built, including his palace, the luxuriant *saray* Topkapi; while his successors added buildings that dazzle to this day, rivalling even the still brilliant Aya Sophia. The Blue Mosque and the Suleiman Mosque are just two. The city remains fabulous, and it is made so by the descendants of those who fought either side of that stockade. It is still a crossroads of the world where Asia and Europe meet, where all races mingle and trade. And if the scars of 1453 are yet clear upon Theodosius's still standing walls, so is the glory, the extraordinary courage shown by men and women of all races, fighting for what they believed in. Attackers and defenders blended now by the years and all citizens of fabled Istanbul.

GLOSSARY

NOTE ON LANGUAGE

'Osmanlica' was the language of the House of Osman, and spoken throughout the land. It was largely Turkish but with many borrowings from Arabic and Persian. For simplicity, I have rendered it without its many accents – cedillas, umlauts, etc.

'Greek' means men of Constantinople. They were not referred to as 'Byzantines' at this time.

agha – senior teacher
alem – signpost or standard
alembic – neck of glass vessel
al-iksir – elixir
al-kohl – liquor, alcohol
Al-Sirat – martyr's bridge to paradise
Allahu akbar – 'God is great'
anafor – choppy waters before the city
archon – high ranking officer of no fixed function
azap – turkish infantry, often on ships
baillie – chief Italian official in city
barbuta – type of helmet
basmala – inscribed prayers
basileus – older military title for war leader and emperor
bashibazouk – irregular warrior
bastard sword – also known as 'a hand and a half'

bastinado – stick

Bektashi – branch of dervish Muslims

belerbey – provincial governor

bey – lord

bevor – armoured neck guard

bireme – Turkish vessel with two rows of oars

bolukbasi – captain of guard

bostanci – gardener/janissary/executioner

boza – fermented barley

buckler – small round shield

bura – cold easterly wind

cakircibas – chief falconer

cami – mosque

chaouse – whip-bearing guard

crannequin – winding mechanism for large crossbow

dayi – godfathers

deli – madman

devsirme – levy of Christian youths

enderun kolej – inner school

effendi – gentleman, master

enkolpia – religious amulet

falchion – wide-bladed short sword

Fatih – the Conqueror

fosse – ditch

fusta(e) – smallest Turkish vessel

gazi – holy warrior

galliot – small galley

gelin – new bride

gomlek – wool tunic

Gulyabani – fierce Turkish giant

haditha – sayings of the Prophet

histodoke – central gangway of Turkish galley

houri – beautiful young woman in paradise

hyperpyron – gold coin

inshallah – 'as God wills it'

imam – Muslim priest and teacher

irade – sultan's order
janissary – elite soldier of Turkish army; former Christian slave
jelabi – long woollen shirt
jihad – holy war
Kabbalah – Jewish mystical study
kalafat – elaborate headdress
kapi – gate
kapudan pasha – Turkish high admiral
kavallarios – knight or high-ranking assistant to the emperor
kilim – small carpet
kolibrina – type of musket
kyr – title of respect, like 'sir'
kyra – lady
lodos – a south-westerly wind
megas archon – highest-ranking imperial servant
megas doux – grand duke
megas primikerios – high-ranking civil servant, originally
    master of ceremonies
megas stratopedarches – high-ranking military officer
mehter – Turkish military band
Musselman – other term for Muslim
muezzin – calls the faithful to prayer
ney – Turkish flute
oikeios – familiar, kin
orta – janissary company; school class
oriflamme – war standard
Osmanlica – language of Turks
otak – canvas pavilion
pasha – highest-ranking Turkish official
peyk – halberdier of the guard, with spleen removed
podesta – governor of Galata
ragazzo – rowdy youth
Rhinometus – Noseless One
sallet – helmet
sabaton – foot armour
saray(i) – palace

serdengecti – suicide warrior
sevre – musical instrument
shalvari – Turkish baggy trousers
sipahi – armoured cavalryman
solak – archer of the guard
stauroma – stockade
Switzer – Swiss soldier
tavla/tavli – backgammon
trireme – Turkish vessel with three rows of oars
tug – horsetail war standard
tugra – inscribed symbol, brand or seal
ulica – Korculan street
vizier – high official
xebec – ship of the eastern Mediterranean
yaya – peasant recruits

AUTHOR'S NOTE

For me to write, a sense of place is vital. Unless I have been, there exists a chasm that imagination, however much I prize it, cannot fill.

This has never been more true than in this book.

I was fortunate to go to Istanbul twice, in three years. The first time, in April 2007, I was in Romania, researching my novel *Vlad: The Last Confession*. Istanbul was a short plane hop across the edge of the Black Sea.

This novel was not even a nag in my brain then. Though I am always interested in battles, and I visited the Theodosian walls, it was the post-conquest and modern city that captivated me. I did the full tourist thing, was suitably awed by the Hagia Sophia, the luxuriant Topkapi and dazzled by the Blue Mosque. Took my boat across the Golden Horn and up the Bosphorus. Played backgammon in alleys in Pera. Bought a rug in the grand bazaar and smoked narghile filled with apple tobacco in a place just beside it. Ate it, drank it, smoked it. Loved it . . . and left.

Three years later I returned, this time for a purpose besides pleasure. I was there to research my novel about the fall of Constantinople in 1453. I knew the city much better by then – from books. But I needed questions answered about the place – and especially its people. I'd already decided to tell the tale from both sides of the walls, defenders and attackers, Greek and Turk. Now I had to meet their descendants.

I have always been a lucky traveller. I think it's because I expect good things to happen, so they usually do. In all my travels – and in some quite dodgy situations – I have always been fine . . . and had my knowledge expanded. It was serendipity that in this case, I'd gone to explore one of history's truly great battles – and kept meeting warriors.

Murad Sağlam was one of the editor-translators into Turkish of my last novel, *Vlad* – which, in another example of Humphreys' Luck, had just been published in Constantinople. (Signing copies of one of my novels in a bookshop there was one of the thrills of my life!) He very kindly took me around, to the walls, out onto the Bosphorus (I needed to feel the *anafor*, the famous chop where three waters meet, for myself). He generously shared his knowledge on all subjects, especially on Islam and his own faith and philosophy of Sufism. And he was the first of the warriors – a former member of Turkey's national judo team.

The second fighter was Suliman. Undoubtedly 'magnificent', he joined me over a narghile to practise his English. And he was a national karate champion, a huge man with a smile to match. The model for many I would write about.

I was there for warriors – and for places. I wrote in *Vlad* how there is a resonance in stone, a vibration that can be picked up if you allow it to come. It did, upon the still fantastic Theodosian walls. I stood on them, gazed up at them, walked along them, sat and time-travelled upon them and wondered at the will it took to both attack and defend them. And I found a different vibe at a place I'd read about that was not on the tourist's beaten path: the tiny church of St Maria of the Mongols. It was hard to locate, tucked away in the working-class neighbourhood and steep, narrow roads of Fener. Somehow my publishers found it. It was locked. But twenty bucks to the caretaker opened it and bought us some time in its whitewashed vaults, before its gilded ikons. It had survived the fall, was still a church, a living echo of Byzantine Constantinople. How it was spared the sacking that destroyed so many intrigued, and its beauty inspired. I knew I'd have to write about it, make it central to my characters' lives. So I did.

What I gained most from this second, targeted, still too brief visit was a sense of the people. I talked with citizens, from warriors to publishers to concierges. With a man I'd met over a pipe before, the gentle philosopher Akay, disciple of Omar Khayyam. I soon realised that my ambitions had shifted. If I'd ever conceived this as a story between good guys and bad, between gallant, outnumbered Christian defenders and hordes of fanatical Muslims, that attitude swiftly changed. The people I talked to had ancestors who had fought either side of the walls. And they were united now in their love of what they'd fought for. My attitude even changed towards Mehmet, 'the Conqueror', whom I'd depicted as so evil in *Vlad*. He was still prone to blinding rage, as the chronicles tell, but he grew in my story from selfish youth to a man who was fighting for something other than pure self-glory. For a cause. For a history. For a most fabulous place.

There is one man whom I have not yet mentioned, who had a huge effect on the writing of this book, and to whom it is dedicated – Mr Allan Eastman. Allan optioned my first novel, *The French Executioner*, and most generously invited me to write the screenplay of it with him in Dubrovnik in the summer of 2002. He still lives close to that (other) fabulous city, hence the part of the tale from there; and from Korcula, whose curving/straight alleys – and the choice they presented to a fleeing man – I was always determined to get into a novel!

Both times I went to Istanbul I was in his company and benefited hugely from his advice. Allan is a film-maker, a history buff, a time-traveller, a lover of life, a warrior too. We talked and talked the battle, standing in the very places where it happened, sharing the resonances that came from the stones. Over pipes, apple tea and bottles of raki, his director's visual eye pointed out details I wouldn't have noted, while his sense of story, of character, of driving narrative helped to shape mine.

And when we were attacked by Turks upon those walls, he helped me drive them off!

Kinda.

What happened was this. We were trying to walk a pretty deteriorated part of the walls, not far from the Golden Gate. There was waste ground behind, some run-down houses across the way. Suddenly, a pack of kids were running across, about ten of them, the eldest maybe twelve. They were in school uniform and they were demanding first cigarettes, then cash.

They were young, but we were seriously outnumbered, as the defenders had been in 1453. They blocked our way. With hands raised and smiling, we pushed through. They muttered but didn't lay hands on us – until I felt what could have been a shove in my back. I turned, glared, retreated. We made the road and safety. It was only later, back at the hotel, when I was emptying my backpack, that I realised what the 'shove' was – when a lump of jagged masonry fell out. The boy had thrown a rock at me. Not only that – it was a piece of the fabled wall. Had probably been created by his ancestors' cannon balls striking the stones in 1453. My backpack had been open and he'd lobbed it in.

I had taken Turkish fire upon the Theodosian walls!

The lump sits on my desk as I write this. It always makes me smile.

There are so many people to thank in the creation of a novel. Briefly, and in no order of importance . . . John Waller, my fight mentor at drama school years ago, retired Director of Interpretations at the Royal Armouries, Leeds, who knows more about medieval weaponry and life than probably any man on the planet and who kindly showed me how to *shoot* ('For Chrissake, don't say "Fire!" ') a crossbow one afternoon in his garden in North Yorkshire. My Turkish publisher, Tahir Malkoç, who took me to the walls when the conquest ceremony was on – for I'd timed my visit for 29 May, the anniversary of the fall. His assistant editor, Celen Çalik, and the aforementioned warrior Murad Sağlam, for their tour guiding, the book signing . . . and all that raki after it! Hasmet Konsiz, now living in Vancouver, a poet who shared his poetic visions of the city of his birth. My wife, Aletha, always acute with her advice and who let me wander off to be attacked by Turks! While my six-year-old son, Reith, helped me make a new slingshot when my old one fell apart and inspired so much of the father–son stuff in the novel. And also my tabby cat, Dickon, who has the 'M' on his forehead and so inspired Ulvikul.

There's my agent, Simon Trewin at United Agents who somehow keeps my career from careening! And my team at Orion is extraordinary. Rachel Leyshon, who always observes kindly and keenly; Jade Chandler, who has a sharp eye for the art of editing, for character, structure . . . and the odd excess (I think she may have kept me out of the Bad Sex Writing Awards!). And of course, and ultimately, the man who commissioned the book and guided it all the way with his shrewd notes and bolstering enthusiasm, my editor, Jon Wood. Behind these talents lies an array of others, in design, marketing, publicity and management, too numerous to name in an author's note. You know who you are and I thank you.

I have named the many great sources in the bibliography that follows. But if I had to single out one influence beyond words and people it would have to be, again, the city itself. If Gregoras is right – that 'a room with a good view is a surer possession than virtue' – then perhaps one day I'll trade in my few virtues and seek one there. To spend the hours watching the sun run down the line of the Bosphorus, gilding the pink-petalled Judas trees, shining on the domes and monuments, on the crumbled walls . . . and on the people, descendants of both Greek and Turk, as the laughing dove calls.

C.C. Humphreys
July 2011

BIBLIOGRAPHY

My bookshelves sag with books about the siege and fall of
Constantinople, and the peoples who fought it. My brain is
filled with images from so many great websites I cannot begin
to list them.

Perhaps the single biggest influence was the spectacularly
detailed *The Destruction of the Greek Empire and the Story of
the Capture of Constantinople by the Turks*. It was written by
Edwin Pears and published in 1908. This man spent years in
research, both at the city and in the libraries of England. He
compares and contrasts the various 'eyewitness' accounts to
reach likely conclusions, and he lays out the ground brilliantly
– completely exposing, for example, the misnaming of the
'civil' St Romanus gate, which the Turks still believe was the
one referred to and where the city finally fell! (He lays out why
this is not so in exhaustive detail, and you only have to walk
the walls and see the destruction to know that the military gate
of St Romanus is about half a mile over!) If he suffers a little
from the prejudices of the time against the 'infidel' (he was a
Knight of the Greek Order of the Saviour, after all!), he is still
generous as to their ingenuity and courage. His was my bible
and I could not have written my book without his.

I skimmed both Runciman and Crowley (see opposite), but
knew I could not refer back too deeply – their writing is so
good, I would have been tempted to borrow!

Here, then, is a by no-means-complete list:

THE SIEGE
*The Destruction of the Greek Empire and the Story of the
  Capture of Constantinople by the Turks*: Edwin Pears
Constantinople: Roger Crowley
The Fall of Constantinople: Steven Runciman
Constantinople 1453: David Nicolle

GENERAL HISTORY
Byzantium: John Julius Norwich
Forgotten Power – Byzantium: Roger Michael Keen
The Late Byzantine Army: Mark C. Bartusis
The Janissaries: Godfrey Goodwin
The Mirror of Alchemy: Gareth Roberts

ISTANBUL/CONSTANTINOPLE
Istanbul – Imperial City: John Freely
Istanbul – The Collected Traveler: edited by Barrie Kerper

WEAPONS
Medieval Combat: Hans Talhoffer
Medieval Arms and Armour: J.H. Hefner-Alteneck

FAITH
The Orthodox Bible
The Holy Qur'an
Eyewitness Islam: Philip Wilkinson